TIME TO MAKE A MOVE.

Moving forward, Justin backed her up against the door. Bracing both arms on either side of her head, he took a deep breath and began, "I want you, Em. More than anything in the world."

"No offense, Justin, but men say that all the time."

"Not me." At least he didn't think he'd said those words. If he had, he didn't mean them. He meant them now. "My bones turn to butter when I look at you, babe. My heart swells when you smile. I can scarcely breathe when you turn your head a certain way. I ache for you."

"Well, you've certainly developed a new repertoire of seduction lines."

"Such a cynic!" He shook his head at her. "Hear me out, Em. I'm not promising you forever. I can't, and I'm not sure you'd want me to."

He licked his lips and continued. "What I can promise you is pleasure. And maybe closure. Doesn't it feel to you as if we never really ended things?"

JOIN IN ON THE HIGH JINX!

PEARL JINX

"Some like it hot and hilarious, and Hill delivers both."
—*Publishers Weekly*

"A hysterical, fast-moving page-turner, and the sexy love story between Caleb and Clair make it an absolute must-read."
—RoundtableReviews.com

"4½ Stars! Hill's books [are] inventive and heart-tugging. They are guaranteed mood boosters!"
—*RT Book Reviews*

"Hilarious... The characters are colorful and vibrant, coming alive with every turn of the page... Packed full of humor and adventure, sizzling SEAL sex, and enough romance to touch even the coldest heart... A real pearl."
—ARomanceReview.com

"[Hill is] the queen of humorous contemporary romance... The laughs keep coming... The audience will appreciate this zany Keystone State caper."
—*Midwest Book Review*

PINK JINX

THE CAJUN COWBOY

"Hill will tickle readers' funny bones yet again as she writes in her trademark sexy style. A real crowd-pleaser, guar-an-teed."
—*Booklist* (starred review)

✦

"A pure delight. One terrific read!"
—*RT Book Reviews*

TALL, DARK, AND CAJUN

"If you like your romances hot and spicy and your men the same way, then you will like *Tall, Dark, and Cajun*...Eccentric characters, witty dialogue, humorous situations...and hot romance...[Hill] perfectly captures the bayou's mystique and makes it come to life."
—*RomRevToday.com*

Snow on the Bayou

ALSO BY SANDRA HILL

Snow on the Bayou

A Tante Lulu Adventure

Sandra Hill

FOREVER

NEW YORK   BOSTON

Copyright © 2014 by Sandra Hill

All rights reserved. In accordance with the U.S. Copyright Act of 1976, the scanning, uploading, and electronic sharing of any part of this book without the permission of the publisher is unlawful piracy and theft of the author's intellectual property. If you would like to use material from the book (other than for review purposes), prior written permission must be obtained by contacting the publisher at permissions@hbgusa.com. Thank you for your support of the author's rights.

Forever
Hachette Book Group
1290 Avenue of the Americas, New York, NY 10104
www.hachettebookgroup.com
www.twitter.com/foreverromance

Printed in the United States of America

OPM

First edition: August 2014

10 9 8 7 6 5 4 3 2

Forever is an imprint of Grand Central Publishing.
The Forever name and logo are trademarks of Hachette Book Group, Inc.

The publisher is not responsible for websites (or their content) that are not owned by the publisher.

The Hachette Speakers Bureau provides a wide range of authors for speaking events. To find out more, go to www.hachettespeakersbureau.com or call (866) 376-6591.

This book is dedicated with much love to my husband Robert who lay fighting for his life in the ICU, then grueling rehab, while I struggled to finish this book. I think this story is better for my having done so since it is a tale of both humor and poignancy. Robert taught me to have a sense of humor, and he insisted that I continue writing even in times of despair. Love you, Robert.

And this book is also dedicated to those many readers who have written, telling me how the humor in my books has helped them through sad times, whether it be illness of themselves or a loved one, death, divorce, or employment woes. Laughter does help.

Snow on the Bayou

Chapter One

Consider your tail feathers clipped, Soldier...

Justin LeBlanc sat on the treatment table in the medical center at the special forces center in Coronado, California, waiting for the stern-faced doctor to give him the test results.

"There's good news and there's bad news, Justin," Dr. Andrews said.

"Cage," he corrected automatically. Cage was his SEAL nickname, a play on his Cajun ethnicity. He'd been so accustomed to it over the years, he no longer thought of himself as Justin.

"The good news, *Cage*, is that you haven't blown your knees to smithereens. No fracture. No surgery. The bad news is that you have severe cartilage damage and some ligament inflammation."

The doctor placed x-rays on the wall lightboard and went into a long explanation in medical jargon, which translated to the knee being a hinge joint that can not only move backward and forward but can also rotate and twist, but his wasn't doing diddly in any direction without a lot of pain and further abuse.

"What's the bottom line, Doc?"

"You're going to have to wear a soft brace and engage in daily physical therapy for the next few months."

"But I can remain on duty, right?"

"Not active duty."

"Can't you just zap me with a shot of cortisone or a painkiller?"

The doctor shook his head. "Numbing the knee won't cure anything, and a painkiller might fool you into thinking the joint can take full weight. You've already done damage by walking and running after you first injured yourself."

"Hey, when you HALO jump into Afghanistan with a hard landing, you don't stop and think, 'Oops. Gotta slow down. Maybe the tangos will invite me to tea?' You run like hell if the bad guys are on your tail."

He wasn't telling the good doc anything he didn't already know. "Are you sure? I could continue therapy while on active duty."

"I can't in good conscience approve that. Why don't you take a vacation, boy? Go back home to Louisiana and relax."

Are you kidding? Relax...at home? Hah! When snow falls on the bayou, maybe, that's when I'll return to my painful roots. "Not an option, Doc."

The physician gave him a knowing stare. Lots of SEALs had backgrounds they didn't want to discuss. With a sigh of resignation, he said, "Okay, let's take another look." The physician removed the ice pack from his knee, which had ballooned to the size of a cantaloupe. "Let's remove the fluids first." With quick efficiency showing how often he'd done the procedure, he inserted a long-needled syringe into the knee.

"Hoooly shit!" That hurt like a bitch, and Cage was about to say so explicitly when his superior, Commander Ian MacLean, walked in. Without thinking, Cage automatically attempted to rise to attention.

"At ease, Lieutenant," the commander said, watching as the doctor sucked out about a liter of water and was drilling for more. Or at least it felt like drilling to Cage. The pain was on a par with, oh, say a root canal without Novocain.

The doctor noticed his white-fisted grasp on the edge of the table. "Does it hurt?"

Well, duh! Just then, a Navy nurse stepped into the room, putting some gauze and tape on a metal tray. Lieutenant Susan Adler smiled at him, making it impossible for him to howl like a baby...well, impossible if he wanted a shot at getting a date with her again. They'd been out together last month, and it was an experience worth repeating.

Once she left the room, hips swaying, to the amusement of everyone in the room, including his dour-faced commander, Cage answered the doctor, "No, it doesn't hurt. I bite my lip bloody for the fun of it."

"Watch the attitude, LeBlanc," the commander cautioned. "And lay off the nurses. You know the non-fraternization rules."

"Lay?" He grinned.

The commander frowned him down, a particular talent of his. Then the commander turned to the doctor. "How bad is it?"

"He'll live," the doctor said with dry humor.

Cage wasn't laughing and neither was the commander.

"He's gotta take it easy on that knee for a while. With a

soft brace and physical therapy, he should be good as new in three months."

"One month," Cage disagreed.

The doctor shrugged. "Maybe two months with diligence."

Tapping a forefinger against his closed lips, the commander seemed to be considering all the options. "Okay, here's the deal, Lieutenant. Take off a few days, then report for a new duty billet on Monday."

Cage didn't like the sound of that. "Exactly what assignment are you giving me, Commander, sir?"

"BUD/S instructor."

BUD/S was the name given to the SEAL training program—Basic Underwater Demolition/Seals. West Coast training was done here in Coronado at the Naval Special Warfare Center. All SEALs hated this particular rotation and would rather be out in the field. But to have to be drilling new swabbies for two freakin' months... well, he'd rather be HALO jumping into tango land again.

"Or WEALS instructor."

That was even worse. WEALS were female SEALs.

"Or maybe you ought to request a liberty and go home to Louisiana for a few weeks," the commander suggested.

His skin went clammy at just the suggestion that he go home. He'd come so far in the past seventeen years. He was a medaled SEAL, recognized for his bravery and service to his country, respected by his comrades-in-arms, a friend to many. Hell, he'd even gotten himself a college degree. But just the thought of returning to his bayou roots caused his self-esteem to tank. He was the no-good son of a convict father and drug addict mother. Bad seed, he'd been called, and would be still. People on Bayou Black had long memories.

And there was another reason for staying away. Emelie

Gaudet. Em. The girl he'd left behind. A girl who would be a woman now. A married woman, last he'd heard. How pitiful was that? Pining over a teenage crush, who probably had a passel of kids by now.

"Thanks, but no thanks, Commander, sir. I can't think of anything I'd enjoy more than wiping swabbie noses."

Everyone in the room laughed, except Cage.

ᴥ

Being a busybody ain't necessarily a bad thing...

Louise Rivard climbed the steep steps of the bayou stilt house, huffing for breath. The twinges in her hinges creaked like a rusty door.

But then she got her first look at Mary Mae LeBlanc. Forget about hinges. Her good friend looked like her hinges done broke and she fell flat on her face. "Holy Crawfish, MaeMae, you look lak the tail end of bad times, bless yer heart. What happened?"

"I doan lak ta complain. Ya know what they say, the more ya complain, the more God makes ya live. I admit, I bin ailin' a bit."

Ain't no bit about it, sweetie.

"Guess old age is catchin' up with me."

Or death. Louise gasped. *What a terrible thing to think. I should bite my tongue.*

MaeMae motioned for her to sit beside her on the porch swing. "Come, Tante Lulu, sit a spell."

Not for the first time, Louise realized that everyone called her Tante Lulu, even folks who weren't her kin, to the point that she thought of herself by that name now. And actually, she and MaeMae would have become real kin if she'd married MaeMae's older brother Phillipe Prudhomme before he died in the big war. *Ain't life funny?*

MaeMae had said she'd been ailin' a bit, but she'd lost at least twenty pounds since Tante Lulu had seen her last year, and gray wisps of curls framed her skull. Either she'd had her head shaved for brain surgery, or her hair was just growing back after cancer treatments. It couldn't be some hot new hairdo she'd never heard about because Tante Lulu kept up on all the latest styles, being the great-aunt of Charmaine LeDeux-Lanier, who owned a string of beauty spas.

And it wasn't age either. Tante Lulu had a good number of years on MaeMae, and she still looked good, if she did say so herself. Not every woman over the age of ninety could wear puce biking shorts with pink orthopedic shoes, she thought, glancing downward. Not to mention a T-shirt that proclaimed: GROWING OLD IS MANDATORY, ACTING OLD IS OPTIONAL. Besides, MaeMae always took good care of herself. No way was her friend's appearance caused by age.

Suddenly guilt struck Tante Lulu like a ten-ton barge...guilt that she'd neglected to keep in touch with her longtime friend. She kissed MaeMae on both cheeks before dropping down beside her. "Warm t'day, ain't it? 'Specially fer February. Heard on the radio this mornin' that it would be sixty-five degrees." It didn't help that she'd worked up a sweat climbing those steps.

MaeMae nodded. "Feels more like ninety with all this humidity. The weather seems all screwed up these days. Mus' be that globe warmin' stuff."

"Thass fer sure," Tante Lulu agreed, but it wasn't really hot, just unseasonably warm. Maybe MaeMae had a fever or somethin'. Tante Lulu pulled her Richard Simmons fan from her large tote bag and began to fan herself, more from nervousness than anything else.

MaeMae smiled. "Ya still hankerin' after that exercise guy?"

"Doan matter how old a lady is, that boy kin still get the juices goin', guar-an-teed."

MaeMae rolled her eyes, like most folks did. They just didn't understand her fascination. Richard was a hottie, no matter what anyone said.

"Help yerself ta some sweet tea." A low table held a pitcher of tea, several glasses, and a plate of beignets. "The home care worker left it there fer my easy reachin' before she left."

Home care worker. That raised some red flags. "Mebbe later. Zackly what's wrong, hon? And doan you be fibbin'."

"Lung cancer," MaeMae said, and quickly added, probably at Tante Lulu's gasp of horror, "but I'm in remission."

Tante Lulu tried not to show her dismay. The Big C was bad, but the Big C in the lungs was real bad. "That figgers, I s'pose. You were a smoker from way back."

"Since I was sixteen, and I turned eighty-four on my las' birthday. Lordy, Lordy, the time does go by. Remember the summer we went skinny-dippin' over on Lake Ponchartrain with them Dawson twins?" She started to chuckle, then burst into a coughing fit, ending with her wheezing heavily.

Remission, my patootie! "Shouldn't you be on oxygen? One of the gals at Our Lady of the Bayou Church walks around with one of them portable tanks."

"Mine is inside," MaeMae said with a grin, her eyes shifting toward an ashtray and package of Virginia Slims on the nearby windowsill.

Holy smokes! MaeMae was chugging down oxygen and still smoking. *"Tsk-tsk-tsk!"*

"Listen, smokin' is one of the few pleasures I got left, and besides, I cut back ta three a day now. And I doan ever do it near my tank."

"Are you okay here alone?"

MaeMae stiffened with affront. "'Course I am. I been sick, not dead."

Tante Lulu nodded, understanding only too well. Folks thought that because she was old, she had one foot in the grave. She had news for them. There was lots of life in this old gal yet. Being over the hill was a heap better than being under the hill.

With a sigh, she glanced around the long porch that fronted Bayou Black, about thirty feet away, across a yard where several cats, at least three dogs, and a bunch of chickens roamed freely. One of those little midget ponies was tied up in a lean-to. And she could hear animal noises from inside the house, too. "You still have all those critters you 'n' Rufus rescued after Hurrycane Katrina?"

MaeMae nodded. "And more keep comin'." She sighed. "Truth ta tell, dearie, they keep me company, 'specially since Rufus passed on. I miss the ol' buzzard more every day. Some days it's hard ta shake the blues."

That alarmed Tante Lulu because she knew for a fact that MaeMae's husband, Rufus LeBlanc, died almost six years ago, soon after the double disasters, Katrina and then Rita. The blue devils could cripple a soul, worse than any disease. "Animals kin be a lotta work."

"Not so much. 'Specially those inside and the ones what can come up to the porch fer food and water. I gotta admit those steps are gettin' hard, though." She raised her chin defiantly. "I'll get by, though. I allus do."

"Mebbe I could send one of Remy's boys over ta help."

"No! If I cain't get by on my own, well, let's jist say, life wouldn't be worth livin'."

Now Tante Lulu was really alarmed. "Dontcha got no family left?"

"Jist my grandson, Justin. And my younger brother, Samuel." MaeMae reached over and squeezed Tante Lulu's hand. "Do you ever think about Phillipe?"

"Only every day." Tante Lulu swiped at her suddenly wet eyes.

Phillipe, her onetime fiancé, had been MaeMae's oldest brother by ten years. Samuel was two years younger than MaeMae. Two other siblings in between had already passed.

"Sometimes I regret not gettin' hitched before Phillipe was sent overseas. He wanted to, y'know."

"Regrets are as useless as a sidesaddle on a hawg, sweetie."

MaeMae noticed her tears and squeezed her hand again. "Samuel lives in Florida," she said, trying to change the subject so Tante Lulu could get her emotions under control. After seventy-three years, you'd think she'd have gotten over the man. "His wife, Ethel, died las' year. We ain't kept in touch much, but I hear he's thinkin' of movin' back ta the bayou."

"Mebbe Samuel..." she started to say.

MaeMae put up a halting hand. "No! Samuel's long retired from the post office, and he nursed Ethel through years of Alzheimer's. No way am I imposin' on his twilight years."

Twilight years? Tante Lulu liked the sound of that. "I've been tip-toein' through the twilight a dozen years or more myself."

"Hah! Fergit tip-toein'. You been jitterbuggin', if all the stories I hear 'bout you are true."

They smiled fondly at each other.

"Back ta yer grandson."

"Did I tell you Justin is one of them Navy SEALs? He's got so many medals he jist about sparkles. And he got hisself a college ejacation, too." MaeMae's skinny chest plumped with pride.

"Cain't he come home and help?" As Tante Lulu recalled, MaeMae and Rufus had raised Justin after his father died in prison and his mother committed suicide when Justin was barely into his teens.

MaeMae shook her head vehemently, which caused her breathing to increase. "He has his own life in California. He lives in Coronado near the Navy base. I doan wanna be a bother ta him."

Tante Lulu narrowed her eyes at MaeMae. In her book, family was everything. "When was the las' time the boy came home?"

MaeMae's face flushed before she disclosed, "He ain't been home since he was seventeen."

Tante Lulu inhaled sharply with surprise, then exhaled whooshily with disgust. Sad, that's what it was. By her reckoning, Justin must be close to thirty-five, about the same age as her great-nephew Tee-John.

"I saw him las' year in N'awlins, though, jist before I got my cancer diagnosis. He was there on some kinda Navy biz-ness. He's a good boy. Allus was, even when he was runnin' wild as a teenager. He calls me every Sunday night, and he sends money from every paycheck. Not that I need money. I do jist fine with Rufus's pension and my social security."

There was no excuse for the boy's behavior. Family was the most important thing in the world. More important than careers, or money, or fancy medals, or any other blasted thing. To her mind, a boy who stayed away from home for seventeen years was lower'n a doodlebug. "The boy should be home."

"Now, Tante Lulu, get that look off yer face. I'm jist fine here. I doan want ya doin' nothin' ta interfere. 'Specially, I doan want Justin knowin' I been sick."

"Whatever you say, *chère*," Tante Lulu said, but what she thought was, *Coronado, here I come.*

I ain't missin' you at all...

Emelie Gaudet hot-glued another layer of feathers resembling scales onto King Neptune's mask and laid it carefully on a long table in her French Quarter studio. Beside it were two dozen other elaborate, very expensive, masks in various stages of production. Just before delivery, she would attach her signature silver tags, etched with her stylized name, Mardi Gras, and the year. They were in the shape of alligators in homage to her Cajun roots.

As expensive as her masks were new, the older creations had become highly collectible. One of her earliest from ten years ago had sold on eBay recently for ten thousand dollars.

Besides that, she'd begun experimenting with porcelain Mardi Gras masks, the kind hung on the wall for decoration. They weren't cheap either.

"Hey, Em, don't you have to leave soon?" her partner, Belle Pitot, asked as she entered Emelie's studio from the front showroom, where she'd been arranging some costumed mannequins.

Five years ago, Emelie had purchased this shotgun house in the French Quarter with a legacy from her grandmother, enabling her to go into business with her good friend. Emelie made the masks, while Belle made high-quality costumes. The bottom floor housed the retail shop for E & B Designs, studios for herself and Belle, and storage space. Upstairs, which could be accessed from an interior, closed-door stairway at the front of the shop, or from exterior back steps, was her spacious apartment, which opened on the back gallery from her bedroom to a lush, fountained courtyard, and from a salon/living room onto a balcony that overlooked the street in front.

In recent years, the pre-Lenten Mardi Gras balls had become even more popular than the traditional parades. In fact, New Orleans was now the number one market in the United States for formal wear, including floor-length evening gowns. And, of course, exclusive costumes and masks.

There were six weeks until Mardi Gras, and they both had lots of work to do yet, but glancing down at her wristwatch, she realized she had only two hours to get ready for her moonlighting job. Once a week, on Saturday night, she had a gig as a blues singer, something she did just for fun, certainly not for the money or fame. Besides, it was a favor to her grandmother's friend Ella Pisano, who owned the club named Ella's...what else? In these hard economic times, Emelie worked for cheap.

Luckily, her studio was only three blocks from the restaurant, which specialized in Italian food, a change from the usual Creole or Cajun dishes famous in New Orleans. Her stomach growled, a reminder that she hadn't eaten since breakfast. She would have a plate of Ella's crawfish gnocchi in red sauce after her performance, she promised herself. Her stomach growled again, this time in anticipation.

After a quick shower, an upswept hairdo, chandelier earrings, and a layer of makeup thicker than she usually wore, Emelie pulled on a pair of white linen slacks and a black T-shirt. She would dress at the club. No way was she walking the French Quarter streets in a strapless sheath and stiletto heels, especially with her late-night return. She'd be mistaken for a hooker with her figure, which had been likened to Marilyn Monroe's, except for her black hair and height of five foot nine. The resemblance had been a bane, rather than a blessing, over the years. Especially when she was a young girl, definitive curves were not the ideal.

Just before she opened the front door to leave, Belle called out to her, "I'll lock up in a half hour, but did you check the mail?"

Emelie stopped and walked back into the showroom, which was beginning to resemble a fantasy wonderland. Several mannequins were dressed head to toe in Mardi Gras regalia. Murals on the wall depicted a stereotypical Southern plantation house. There was even a fake live oak tree with hanging moss. On the counter, she saw a number of envelopes, including the one she'd been waiting for. Emelie's heart skipped a beat. The return address said: "Dr. Charles Benoit, Southern Reproductive Services."

"Chuck's Sperm Bank?" Belle inquired, her right eyebrow arched with disapproval.

Emelie ignored Belle's teasing nickname for the reputable, highly renowned clinic and nodded. Had she been approved for insemination by one of the candidates she'd chosen? Did the letter contain a specific appointment for the procedure? Was it possible she would be holding her very own baby a year from now? She held the envelope against her heart.

"Honey, you don't know what you're doing, taking on a child." This from the single parent of thirteen-year-old twin boys, Michael and Max; she had a placard on her desk that read, MOTHERS OF TEENAGERS KNOW WHY ANIMALS EAT THEIR YOUNG. At the same time, her desk was cluttered with many framed photos of her little darlings from birth to Little League.

Emelie just smiled.

"I still say you should do it the old-fashioned way."

"Belle," she sighed, "I'm almost thirty-four years old, I was married once, a long time ago—"

"So, ask Bernard."

"If I didn't want to remain married to Bernie, why would I want him in my life *forever* as the father of my child? Nope, I do not want the baggage of a man in my life permanently."

"He's not that bad." Having never been married, Belle had long been hopeful that someday a Prince Charming would come riding his Lexus down Bourbon Street to sweep her off her feet. Unfortunately, lately, Belle was willing to settle for a good man with a pickup truck and a job.

"Furthermore," Emelie went on, "I'm fulfilled by my mask-making career and singing sideline. I'm financially stable. I enjoy time out with a small circle of friends. I take the occasional lover."

"Occasional is right," Belle muttered. "You could be a nun, if you asked me."

Okay, so Emelie hadn't been in a relationship for two years. That was just another reason to seek alternative paternity, in her mind. "Hey, I've even made peace with my father for what he did seventeen years ago. There's only one thing missing from my life. A baby."

Belle just shook her head at her. "You've become obsessed with the idea."

"No wonder! My biological clock feels like Big Ben these days. Tick, tick, tick! People probably hear it when I pass by."

"I thought it was your stomach growling with hunger."

"Honestly, I notice every baby I see on the street or at the mall. I stop at displays of baby items in store windows."

"You even bought a baby name book," Belle pointed out with a grin. "That's understandable, but I still say you should have a baby the old-fashioned way."

"Too complicated!" For some reason, a picture popped in Emelie's mind of a long ago time when she'd thought differently. Of course, she'd only been sixteen to her boy-friend's seventeen, but the big plans they'd made seemed silly now. They were going to get married, move to Cali-fornia, and have four kids, two boys and two girls. What they had been going to do for a living had never mattered then. They'd thought they were in love.

She laughed at the memory. It had been years since she'd even thought about Justin LeBlanc, hadn't a clue where he was these days. Probably prison, which was the road he'd been headed on the last time she'd seen him, thanks to her dad, the longtime sheriff of Terrebonne Par-ish. When she'd refused to leave with him, thumbing his nose at her father and the entire justice system, Justin had the nerve to swear that there would be snow on the bayou before he ever returned. As if it had been her fault! Later, she'd heard that he joined the Navy, but by then her life had changed immeasurably.

With a shake of her head, Emelie placed the unopened envelope back on the counter. Time later to angst. Should she or shouldn't she?

After waving good-bye to Belle, she headed down Chartres Street, swinging her tote bag beside her. She had so much to be thankful for, even without a baby.

Life was good. Sometimes a little lonely, but good.

Chapter Two

A Cajun hurricane hits the California coast…

Holy moly! I ain't seen so many hard man-tushies since you and me went ta that Chippendale show at the Moose Club in Baton Rouge. Remember that guy with the mustache who pulled you up onta the stage ta dirty dance with him? Whoo-ee!"

"Tante Lulu! Shhhh!" Charmaine LeDeux-Lanier cautioned her great-aunt, peering right and left to make sure they weren't overheard. "And just for the record, that was fifteen years ago, long before I was married. I don't do things like that anymore."

Tante Lulu snorted her opinion. "Was that before or after you decided ta be a born-again virgin?"

Charmaine loved the old lady dearly, but after twelve hours in various airports, confined in an airplane, and then a taxi with her, she was pretty close to wringing a scrawny, ninety-something-year-old neck. It was hard to know the exact age of the dear old bat since she kept changing her birth date, and the original records had mysteriously disappeared from the parish courthouse. Really, Tante Lulu would tax the patience of a saint, no matter her age.

Biting her tongue, Charmaine gave a "Whatever!" toss of her long black hair over her shoulder; it was a trick she'd learned years ago when she was Miss Louisiana, more years ago than she cared to admit. A woman could do or say just about anything, especially to a man, if she learned the hair toss trick. Her husband, Raoul Lanier—Rusty—for example, was always susceptible. Unfortunately, it didn't faze Tante Lulu.

They were standing inside a big, black-tarp-covered, chain-link fence in Coronado, California, looking over an asphalt area that resembled a penitentiary yard surrounded by a quadrangle of low buildings, including the Navy SEALs special forces building, where they had a scheduled meeting with the big kahuna. In the old days, before 9/11, visitors to Coronado could walk up to the fence and watch the SEALs exercise or run on the beach. Not anymore. Security was way too tight. Terrorists would love to get a bead on one of these superheroes.

But she and Tante Lulu had been given clearance to enter the compound. On the concrete in front of them, scantily clad, sweating men were engaged in all kinds of tortuous exercises with logs, climbing nets, ropes, and tires. In the distance could be seen huge gray Navy warships in the waters near the Naval Amphibious Base at the other end of Coronado. In another direction was the red-tiled roof of the famous Hotel del Coronado, where movies had been filmed and the rich and famous dined; she'd promised Tante Lulu dinner there later.

On yet another side, beyond the buildings, was the icy

blue Pacific Ocean, which shimmered under a blistering sun, almost as pretty as the bayou on a summer morning. That was where their attention had been riveted for the past ten minutes, watching about four dozen men wearing nothing but shorts and boots running along the beach.

And yes, all of their tushies were fine.

With effort, Charmaine did her best to stop complaining for about the fiftieth time over playing shotgun to the Cajun loony bird. You could say it was another Tante Lulu Great Adventure, and really, her heart was in the right place, bizarre as her schemes often were. In this case, she was bound and determined to bring a lapsed Cajun back to the bosom of his family. Justin LeBlanc didn't stand a chance.

But why did I have to be the one to choose the unlucky straw when it came to picking who would accompany the old lady on this hare-brained trip? Charmaine suspected that one of her LeDeux half brothers had fixed the straws. They were devious that way.

"You're always shushin' me," Tante Lulu complained. Apparently she'd been blathering on while Charmaine had been woolgathering. "Are you 'shamed of me or sumpin'?"

"Of course not. It's just that we're here on the sufferance of Tee-John's contact, who had to pull a lot of strings to get us an appointment. We shouldn't call attention to ourselves."

"Number one, if we doan wanna call attention to ourselves, how come you're wearin' those skin-tight leopard pedal pushers with high heels?"

"You're criticizing *my* clothes? That's like the gator callin' the water wet!" Charmaine exclaimed with a laugh.

Tante Lulu wore her Dolly Parton blonde wig, wedgie sandals, and a sundress from the Walmart Little Girl

Bimbo collection that exposed about two thousand liver spots on her bare arms and shoulders.

"Are you saying I look like a bimbo?" Charmaine grinned.

"Darn tootin' you do, Charmaine. Bless yer heart. Not that I'm sayin' bimbo is a bad thing. Nosirree."

Charmaine couldn't help but smile. Everyone knew she relished being called a self-proclaimed bimbo, with class. Still, her great-aunt had the subtlety of a horny bull in a field of pretty cows.

"An' that shiny red lipstick yer wearin', Lordy, Lordy, thass what Tee-John calls screw-me-quick lipstick."

Charmaine sincerely doubted that her cop half brother used the word "screw." But that was beside the point. "It's a new line we just started carrying in my beauty salons. I'll give you some samples."

"Number two..." Tante Lulu started to say.

Charmaine forgot what number one had been. Following a conversation with Tante Lulu was like trying to catch popcorn over an unlidded popper.

"Any woman what's been married as many times as you have, bless yer heart, kin hardly talk about hidin' yerself under a bushel."

"Huh?" Charmaine said, then shook her head to clear it. "You really shouldn't be insulting my marriage, Auntie."

"What marriage are you referrin' to, sweetie? You been hitched and unhitched four or five times, as I recall."

"Two of them were to the same man," Charmaine protested. "Besides, it turns out I was never divorced from Rusty the first time around. So in a way, none of those other marriages and divorces counted."

Tante Lulu rolled her eyes.

"Anyhow, what do my clothing or my marriages have to do with anything?"

"You're the one what brought it up."

"I did?" *Popcorn, for sure.*

"What difference does it make when we went ta that show anyhow? Studs are studs, no matter what. And these Navy SEALs could make their own calendar, guar-an-teed. I'd buy one, fer sure." She pressed her nose up against the fence. "Wish I had a pair of binoculars."

"We'd probably be thrown in the brig as potential terrorists. You saw how hard it was just to get on this base."

"Ms. Rivard, Ms. Lanier, the commander will see you now."

She and Tante Lulu spun around to see a guy with one of those painfully short military hairdos in a khaki uniform addressing them. Painful to her, at least, as a hairstylist. His demeanor was serious, but his widened eyes took in her body, all in one sneaky sweep. Charmaine was used to that reaction from men and wasn't at all offended.

When they'd first arrived, the receptionist in the special forces building told them the commander was delayed and they could wait in a conference room or go out into the yard and watch the SEALs in training. The red-faced sailor now led them inside the building to an office fronting the quadrangle where the SEALs were training. The plaque on the door said: COMMANDER IAN MACLEAN, U.S. NAVY, SPECIAL FORCES, SEALS. Inside, an officer sat behind a desk. He was about forty with a receding hairline. Not unattractive, but too stern-faced for Charmaine's taste.

The room was bare-bones military utilitarian, except for a few photos on the wall and a bunch of framed motivational sayings, including the famous Navy SEAL one, THE ONLY EASY DAY WAS YESTERDAY. But there were others, like FEAR IS YOUR FRIEND, SEIZE THE DAY, or THE MORE SEALS SWEAT IN PEACETIME, THE LESS THEY BLEED IN WAR.

Immediately, the commander rose to his feet. "Ms. Rivard. Ms. Lanier. Have a seat, please."

"You kin call me Tante Lulu. Everyone does."

The commander nodded, though Charmaine just knew there was no way in the world he was ever going to break protocol like that. And she could practically see the wheels turning in his head as he took in all that was Tante Lulu, wondering what kind of lunatic he had in his office.

That impression was heightened when his eyes widened on taking in all that was Charmaine, as well.

He cleared his throat and asked, "What can I do for you?"

"I need ta talk with Justin LeBlanc," Tante Lulu said right off.

Charmaine could see the surprise in his eyes. "Cage?" he said before he could catch himself. "You know Lieutenant LeBlanc?"

"Yep. I came all the way from Loo-zee-anna, and I ain't leavin' 'til I've said my piece ta the boy."

"The boy?" he sputtered. "Are you family?"

"Not exactly."

The commander turned to Charmaine for help.

"My aunt is good friends with Justin's grandmother. We need to talk with him about...well, something personal."

"Does he know you're here?"

"No, it's a surprise," Tante Lulu said.

It would have been a lot easier if they'd had Justin's home address, but the only way they could have gotten that was to ask his grandmother, and Tante Lulu had been adamant that MaeMae not be alerted to their activities. Charmaine suspected that MaeMae had warned Tante Lulu not to interfere. Hah! That wouldn't stop her determined aunt.

"Is this a joke?" the commander asked. "I swear, if *Candid Camera* or *Funny Videos*, or *Punked!* jumps out, someone is going to pay big-time."

"It's not a joke. We just need to speak with Justin. It won't take long," Charmaine pleaded.

"This is highly irregular. Strangers can't just come here and ask to speak with one of my men."

"What? You think we're terrorists or sumpin'?" Tante Lulu asked, narrowing her eyes at the commander. "I doan even have my pistol on me t'day. They wouldn't let me take it on the plane."

The commander's jaw dropped.

Charmaine groaned. Time to intervene before they got kicked out. "Justin's grandmother is sick, and he needs to go home."

Straightening with alertness, the commander asked, "How sick?"

"Very," Tante Lulu said grimly.

"And Lieutenant LeBlanc is unaware of this family crisis?" he asked Tante Lulu.

"Clueless as a crawfish in a hurrycane."

"Why?"

"Why what? I swear, you mus' be thicker'n swamp mud, bless yer heart."

The commander's jaw dropped even lower. "I still say this is irregular, but..." He picked up the phone and spoke into the mouthpiece, "Petty Officer Farley? Would you come in here, please?"

When the same sailor as before came inside, the

commander ordered, "Escort these ladies out to the grinder. Tell Lieutenant LeBlanc to take a break for the rest of the afternoon. Lieutenant Mendozo will cover for him."

"Oh, my God!" Tante Lulu exclaimed suddenly and jumped to her feet, rushing over to a far wall, where she was staring at a framed photo. To everyone's dismay, tears streamed down her wrinkled cheeks.

"Ma'am?" the commander inquired with concern, going over to stand beside her. He must have been six foot two, at least. The top of Tante Lulu's head came only to his chest.

"Thass Phillipe there." She pointed to one of six men in bathing suits and flippers in a sepia-tone photograph. "My fiancé."

"Your fiancé was on Omaha Beach?" the commander asked.

Tante Lulu nodded. "Yep. Phillipe Prudhomme."

"This is remarkable." The commander was no longer regarding Tante Lulu as crazy, but as someone worthy of respect. "Those frogmen were the precursors of today's Navy SEALs."

"Really?" she and Tante Lulu both remarked. It had never occurred to Charmaine that there was a connection, but it made sense. Both groups were sort of webfoot warriors.

"And Phillipe Prudhomme is famous among those of us who have studied Navy history." He tapped a fingertip over one grinning sailor. "Prudhomme was awarded the Purple Heart and the Congressional Medal of Honor."

Tante Lulu nodded, wiping her eyes with an embroidered handkerchief she fished out of her bosom. "I have both of them in my hope chest."

A hope chest after all these years? Charmaine's heart was about breaking.

Tante Lulu straightened and shook her head as if to wipe away the memories. "God's will," she declared, then turned to the commander and said, "When you gonna end that war in Af-ghanny-stan?"

"Me?"

"If I was over there, *cher*, I'd be teachin' 'em how ta make gumbo, not war."

"Ahem," someone coughed behind them, and they realized that the sailor was still waiting to escort them to Justin.

Just before the door closed after them, Charmaine heard the commander mutter, "If the old bird was younger, she'd make a great Navy SEAL."

Then aliens invaded the Navy Seals training compound...

"Move it, move it, move it!" Cage yelled at the most pitiful group of SEAL wannabees. "You call that sugar cookies? More like sand tarts, if you ask me."

Sugar cookies was one of many SEAL "torture" exercises. It involved the men walking into the surf, fully clothed and booted. Then when they were wet from head to sole, they were ordered to roll in the sand, making them into—ta da!—sugar cookies. After that, with sand in every bodily orifice and crevice, turning their shorts and jock straps into sandpaper, they jogged for a mile or five.

This was Cage's second week of instructor duty, and he was ready to tear his hair out, what there was of it. Usually he let his hair grow shoulder length, an exception the

Navy granted to SEALs because they had to infiltrate foreign countries where they didn't want to stand out. Good thing he had black hair; blonds or redheads had to dye it, even their eyebrows and eyelashes...and other places. But right now he was sporting a high and tight. By the time it grew out, he would hopefully be back on active rotation.

Today was PI Friday, and that didn't stand for physical instruction. Nope, SEALs were notoriously politically incorrect, and once a month, on a Friday, the SEALs celebrated their political incorrectness. His T-shirt proclaimed: IT'S GOD'S JOB TO FORGIVE BIN LADEN, IT WAS OUR JOB TO ARRANGE A MEETING. Some of the other instructors' shirts said: STOP GLOBAL WHINING; DEATH SMILES AT EVERYONE, SEALS SMILE BACK; EXCEPT FOR ENDING SLAVERY, FASCISM, NAZISM, AND COMMUNISM, WAR HAS NEVER SOLVED ANYTHING; A DEAD ENEMY IS A PEACEFUL ENEMY; BLESSED BE THE PEACEMAKERS; and his favorite, PRAY TO GOD, BUT PASS THE AMMUNITION. Each month they tried to outdo each other with crudity or extreme PI-ness.

He glanced over toward the grinder, the asphalt exercise area by the special forces building. Then he did a double take.

There were three people standing there. Two women and Petty Officer Farley, whom he recognized by his bright red hair, even in its short military cut. Farley was motioning for him to come over.

He told his men to stand at ease until he returned. When he got closer, he noticed in more detail the tall woman with big Texas hair, the likes of which he hadn't seen since he'd been back in the Southland, tight leopard print pants, high heels, and an itty bitty T-shirt that announced,

CURL UP & DYE, and underneath that in smaller letters, www.charmainesbeautyshops.com. Beside her stood a little elderly woman with more wrinkles than an elephant's scrotum, wearing a lopsided wig. She was waving wildly. At him!

He recognized them, even after all these years. "Holy Sac-au-lait!" he muttered. It was Charmaine LeDeux and that batty Cajun folk healer, Tante Lulu Rivard. From freakin' Loo-zee-anna bayou country.

His second reaction was a puzzled frown. Why would they be here in California…and staring at him as if he were in the crosshairs of their lethal weapons?

The fine hairs stood out on his body. It must have something to do with his MawMaw, the Cajun name for grandmother.

JAM, Lieutenant Jacob Alvarez Mendozo, walked by, heading toward the beach. He indicated with a motion of his thumb toward himself and the swabbies that he was taking over. He also winked at Cage after giving Charmaine a quick once-over. As if Cage would ever be interested in the bayou bimbo! And he didn't mean that as an insult. Charmaine had always gone out of her way to celebrate her bimbo-ness.

No, it was because Charmaine was lots older than him…and married, last he'd heard. Of course, he'd known her only by reputation. But then, everyone in southern Louisiana knew Charmaine, and not just because she'd been Miss Louisiana when he was a freshman in high school. About forty years old, give or take, she still looked damn good. As for the old lady…who didn't know the outrageous Tante Lulu? She was a friend of his grandmother's, but everyone from one end of the bayou to the other had heard of her antics.

Once Cage reached the group, Petty Officer Farley saluted him and went back to the command center, leaving him with the two women.

"Hey, Charmaine," he greeted her first since she was in front.

"Hey, Justin."

"Tante Lulu," he acknowledged as he got closer. "It's great to see you." *I hope.*

Charmaine shook his extended hand, but Tante Lulu grabbed on to him and gave him a hug, which was kind of awkward since he was six foot two and she was about five foot zero. She actually hugged his abdomen, and he found himself patting her blond wig, even giving it a little nudge to center it more on her head.

But why was she hugging him so hard?

Holding her away from himself, he asked right off, "Is something wrong with MawMaw?"

Tante Lulu nodded.

He braced himself before asking, "Is it bad?"

She nodded again.

"Oh, God! She's not dead, is she?"

Tante Lulu smacked his arm. "No, she's not dead, you lunkhead."

"Thank God!"

"No thanks to you."

"I beg your pardon."

"Justin LeBlanc, when was the las' time you was home?"

He stiffened. "That's none of your business."

"It is when my good friend needs her only gran'chile."

"If she needed me, all she had to do was ask. And by the way, why isn't she asking?"

"Mebbe she dint wanna be a bother to *her only gran'chile.*"

Cage bit the inside of his cheek to keep the irritation out of his voice. "Did she send you?"

"No. St. Jude did."

"St. Jude?" he sputtered.

"Thass what I said. Did they nick yer ears when they shaved yer fool head? St. Jude tol' me ta go find that rascally Cajun boy and drag him home by the scruff of his neck, iffen he's too stubborn ta know what's good for him."

Cage briefly closed his eyes. *I wonder what the sentence would be for throttling a senior citizen? Better yet, we could probably use her as a secret weapon against the Taliban.* He returned his gaze to Tante Lulu. "What does St. Jude have to do with anything?"

"Don't ask," Charmaine warned.

But it was too late. Tante Lulu put her hands on her little hips and glared up at him. "St. Jude is the patron saint of hopeless cases, and I'm thinkin' yer as hopeless as a woodpecker in a petrified forest."

"Now settle down," Charmaine told her aunt. Then to Cage, she said, "Is there somewhere we can go talk?"

He hesitated, then conceded, "The officers' dining hall should be empty." He pointed to a building beyond the special forces center and began to walk away. Rude, yeah, but he was in a rude mood. Something serious was wrong with his grandmother, and he was having to deal with two crazy women...well, one crazy woman and another who could be an old-time calendar girl. They were like aliens from another planet. He'd forgotten how eccentric Southerners could be.

As they walked toward the dining hall, he remarked to Charmaine, "It's been a long time." He glanced down at her ring-clad finger. "So you're married?"

She nodded. "To Raoul Lanier. Do you remember him?"

"I heard he was in prison."

"Not anymore. Rusty was wrongfully convicted."

Cage smiled. That was what they all said.

"Really. His record was cleared."

"And you own some beauty salons?" he asked, looking at her breasts . . . well, at the logo over her breasts.

She smiled, apparently considering his perusal a compliment. "Yep. Five at last count. And a spa out at Rusty's ranch."

"Would you two stop flirtin' with each other?" Tante Lulu griped as she huffed along next to them. "Charmaine is married."

"I wasn't flirting," they both said at the same time.

"What's wrong with yer leg? You're limpin' like Stumpy Benoit, who lost his toes in Vietnam."

"I fell and injured my knee."

"You always were clumsy."

"I was not! And for your information, I got hurt during a HALO jump."

"Well, thass what you get fer trying ta jump over some-one's halo."

He blinked at her, feeling as if he'd fallen into some alternate universe.

"He means that he was hurt during a parachute jump," Charmaine explained.

"Well, why dint he say so? I hafta pee. Kin I go in that building over there?"

"No, it's the SEAL locker room."

"So?"

"So men are naked in there."

"So?"

He shook his head and continued walking.

When they were almost to the officers' building, he

noticed Sylvester Sims, or Sly, supervising about a dozen heavily perspiring men and women in gig squad, a SEALs punishment for some infraction or other. At the moment they were doing walking, quacking duck squats. Humiliation was part of Navy discipline. Sly, a big black dude from Harlem, who had once modeled tightie whities for *GQ*, wore a shirt that said, in small enough print that it all fit over his wide chest, THE ONLY EASY DAY WAS YESTERDAY. FU . . . SCREW THAT! THERE ARE NO EASY DAYS!

"Hey, Sly," he said.

"Hey, Cage," Sly said back, but he was staring at Charmaine, waiting for an introduction, Cage supposed.

Not a chance!

Walking by, Charmaine asked him, "Is he who I think he is?"

"Probably."

"We have an old underwear poster of him hung on the wall of my Houma spa."

"Hung" being the key word. "Sly will love hearing about that," he said, and it was the truth. His good buddy milked his long-ago cover boy career every which way he could, and it didn't matter that he was a married man now. In fact, he would be hooting about it to Donita when he went home tonight.

"I thought there were no female SEALs," Charmaine remarked, watching the group that Sly was supervising.

"There aren't. Those are WEALS. Women on Earth, Air, Land, and Sea." He shrugged. "You could say they're female SEALs, sort of."

Tante Lulu sighed. "Wish I was younger. I woulda made a good female SEAL."

Cage gave her an arched eyebrow look.

"What? You think jist 'cause I'm small, I ain't got what

it takes ta fight bad guys? Hah! I been fightin' bad guys all my life."

He didn't doubt that for a minute.

"I think you Navy bigwigs discriminate against us smaller folks."

"The Navy does not discriminate. And height is not a requirement for SEALs."

"Oh, yeah? How come I dint see no midgets back there?"

Charmaine groaned. "I told you, Auntie, 'midget' is a politically incorrect word."

Tante Lulu glanced meaningfully at Cage's politically incorrect T-shirt logo and grinned. The old bird was pulling his leg.

Once they'd arrived at the dining hall and sat down with pastries and coffee, both of which Tante Lulu deemed inferior to good Creole chicory and beignets, she looked him in the eye and said, "Your grandmother has lung cancer."

He inhaled sharply. "Oh, my God! When...how... will she..." He inhaled again to catch a breath. "Tell me everything. I saw her last summer in New Orleans, and she seemed fine then."

Tante Lulu took one of his big hands in two of her tiny, veined ones.

He tried, but couldn't pull free, not without making a fuss.

"She was diagnosed last fall. She's already been zapped with radiation and sez she's in remission, but I doan believe it. She needs oxygen jist ta walk around. And she's havin' trouble carin' fer all those animals."

"All what animals?"

"*Tsk-tsk-tsk!* If you came home once in a while, you'd know which animals."

He squared his shoulders and counted to ten so he wouldn't say something particularly offensive to the old biddy, although he suspected that insults would bounce off her wrinkled Teflon skin.

"I doan know why you're stayin' away, an' I doan care. You gotta come home now. Your grandma needs you."

"I could probably get a liberty, especially with this bum knee. Yeah, I could probably come for a week or so."

Tante Lulu frowned at his limit on the time he would stay, but she had the good sense to keep her opinion to herself this time.

When Tante Lulu went to the ladies' room, Charmaine smiled at him and shrugged.

"How do you stand her?"

"She can be nerve-racking, but she's got a heart of gold."

"More like a lead sinker, if you ask me."

"How many ninety-something-year-old women do you know who would travel all this way to reunite an ailing grandmother and her grandson?"

"I don't know any other ninety-something-year-old women. What's with the ninety-something crap anyhow? Why don't you know her exact age?"

"She lies," Charmaine said with a grin, as if that were a good thing. "Family is all important to Tante Lulu. Did you know her fiancé was your grandmother's older brother, Phillipe Prudhomme, and he was one of the original Navy SEALs, a frogman? He died in the Big War."

"The Civil War?" he asked, before thinking.

"Idjit!" she said, smacking his arm lightly. "World War Two."

Feeling like an idjit, he defended himself lamely. "Hey, everyone in the South still thinks the Civil War was the Big War, don't they?"

She just smiled. "Are you married, Cage? Engaged? Involved?"

When he answered negatively to each of her questions, she gave him a pitying look and asked the oddest thing, "Do you have a hope chest?"

Chapter Three

Doing the horizontal boogie without the boogie...

Emelie was a list maker, and whoo-boy, this was some list!

—Six foot tall, brown hair, hazel eyes, Caucasian, Italian, age 22, medical student at an Ivy League college, marathon runner, favorite music: Aerosmith.

—Five foot ten, blond hair, light brown eyes, Caucasian, Irish-German ancestry, age 30, artist, favorite music: Mozart.

—Five foot eleven, brown hair, dark brown eyes, Cuban, age 24, law school intern, hobby: mountain climbing.

—Six foot three, black hair, dark brown eyes, Cajun, age 20, commercial fisherman, favorite music: Zydeco.

She was sipping at a cup of *cafe au lait* and scanning her culled list of sperm donors. It felt almost like arranging a blind date without all the fuss of dressing up and awkward initial meetings, usually followed by disappointment.

Inside her office, she had a folder with additional info on each of the candidates. Blood type. Three generations of family medical history. Facial features. Complexion. Sperm count.

It was Sunday, and Emelie was sitting at a table on her back, upper gallery, facing the fountain courtyard in the back. Her 150-year-old home was not large, but it was two-storied. In the old days, the living quarters were on the second floor, its shuttered, floor-to-ceiling windows open to catch every little breeze, the family in one section and the slaves out back.

She was soothed by the sounds of the trickling fountain and the bells of St. Louis Cathedral several blocks away calling parishioners to mass. The scent of the bougainvillea vines climbing the ornate, black iron lattice filled the air, along with that of potted roses that lined the gallery. She loved Sundays in New Orleans.

"Miss Em-el-ie!" someone called from down below, coming through the side passageway from Chartres Street onto her courtyard.

Oh, no! It was Bernard Landry, her ex-husband.

"Bernie, what are you doing here?"

"I knocked on the front door, sug-ah, but there was no answer," he said in his deep Southern accent. He was already walking around up the outside staircase...without being invited. As many times as she'd told him he was not welcome to drop in without notice in the past sixteen or so years, since their divorce, he still showed up periodically without warning. Some men just didn't take a hint that the welcome mat wasn't out all the time. Sometimes not at all.

"What do you want, Bernie?" She sighed.

Already he was helping himself to a cup of black coffee from the carafe on the table. "What's this?" he asked, picking up the paper before she had a chance to grab it back.

"Give that to me. Right now," she demanded.

"Are you usin' one of those Internet datin' services?"

"Something like that," she said, grabbing her list back.

"Dar-lin'!" Bernie gave her his hangdog look. "You don't hafta go to no matchmaker. I'm right here."

"Thanks but no thanks." Their divorce had been amicable, but that didn't mean she wanted him back in her life. Not one bit.

He didn't look as wounded as he might have at one time.

"Why are you here, Bernie?"

"Is it wrong for me ta worry about you? You live alone in a city. Anything could happen ta you. Just because I check up on you doesn't make me a bad person." He batted his eyelashes at her in an exaggerated fashion.

"I can take care of myself, and I never said you were a bad person."

"Then why—"

She raised a hand, cutting him off. "We are not going to discuss our marriage and divorce again." Every time he showed up, their conversation degenerated into the same old subject. "How's business? Are you ready for Mardi Gras?"

Bernie owned a pyrotechnics factory, producing all kinds of fireworks for putting on light shows typical of the Fourth of July, and here in Louisiana, Mardi Gras. Everything from retail sparklers and Roman candles to elaborate choreographed sky events. His professionals traveled all over the world and were renowned for the spectacular shows they put on.

"Actually, *chère*, that's why I stopped by t'day."

Okay, here it comes. Every time he calls me chère, he wants something.

"Do you mind if I park a vehicle or two in yer drive under the porte cochere during Mardi Gras? Ya'll know what a bitch parking kin be."

And costly. Truth was, Bernie was a world-class skinflint. In fact, she'd once heard a friend say he could squeeze a quarter so tight the eagle would scream.

"How many vehicles?"

"Uh, four."

"No way! You'll be all the way back here to the court-yard, crushing my flowers."

"Three, then."

"No! Two, and they better not be trucks or huge vans with your commercial signs on the side. And one day only."

He flashed his hangdog look at her again. Did it ever work for him? "Okay." He smiled. It was probably all he'd ever expected to begin with. "You're the best!"

Yeah. More like sucker of the year. "Bernie, you need to find a girlfriend. Get married again." *And stay away from me.*

He wasn't a bad-looking man. He was what they would have called a nerd when she was in school. A computer geek now. If he'd get himself some contact lens, instead of those thick bifocals that never seemed to fit—he was always pushing the frame up his nose—he could pass for handsome. Maybe work out in the gym to get some better muscle definition. And have someone help him shop for something other than khakis and loafers.

Luckily she wouldn't be the one doing all that.

"Maybe I could join that same dating agency as you."

He pointed to the sheet of paper she'd slipped under the Sunday edition of the *Times-Picayune*.

Her lips twitched with suppressed laughter. "I don't think so."

He rose to his feet and was about to leave when he tossed a bomb at her...the nonexplosive but equally deadly kind.

"Hey, Em, have you heard the latest gossip?" he asked. "Guess who's coming back to the bayou?"

She did not like the glint in Bernie's eyes; nor did she like gossip about anyone on Bayou Black. Not knowing was the only way she'd been able to survive for a long time. "I can't imagine."

"My cousin. His grandma's sick, and he's come ta visit."

"Which cousin?" Bernie had at least a dozen in his big family.

"Justin Le-freakin'-Blanc."

Without realizing what she was doing, Emelie tugged her list out from under the newspaper and crushed it into a tight ball.

☞

You can go home again, but it's damn hard...

Cage drove his rental car onto the crushed shell driveway at the side of his grandmother's house, turned off the ignition, and just sat, taking it all in. Seventeen years, and everything looked the same!

The house was built in the quaint bayou stilt fashion. Being raised up high made sense when you considered the high water table in Southern Louisiana, where no homes could have basements lest they wanted rustic indoor swimming pools, not to mention the proximity to the water, which occasionally rose to almost the first floor. Every tornado or hurricane that hit the Gulf Coast managed to change the course of the bayous in one way or another, eliminating some altogether and other times creating new ones. In fact, this house, when it was originally built about a hundred years ago by his trapper ancestors, had perched on stilts *in* the swamp water, and could only be reached by pirogue, a type of Cajun boat.

He'd tried to explain the concept once to a SEAL buddy, who just couldn't fathom it. "Why not just build farther away from the stream on a higher incline?" JAM had asked. "Or build one of those flood-control-type houses that were put up in New Orleans after Hurricane Katrina?" In other words, a glorified box. For some reason, his explanation of, "Because that's the way it's always been," didn't cut it. But then, Yankees were sometimes so dumb they needed a cue card to say "Duh?"

In front of him in the driveway was his grandfather's old 1985 Pontiac Gran Prix, which he'd affectionately nicknamed Priscilla in honor of the "King," of whom he'd been a huge fan. He wondered if the old gal still worked. The car probably hadn't been driven since PawPaw died six years ago.

He had to smile when he recalled how proud Paw-Paw had been the day he brought Priscilla home, her red paint brighter than a hooker's cheeks at Sunday mass—his grandfather's exact words. Cage had been only six at the time, and one of his jobs had been to keep Priscilla sparkling clean. As a reward, PawPaw would pile him and MawMaw into Priscilla every Saturday night and head off to the Dairy Queen.

Later, his memories of Priscilla and Saturday nights were even sweeter. They involved the bench backseat and Emelie Gaudet. Lordy, Lordy! He could almost taste her strawberry lip gloss. And to this day he had an affection for day-of-the-week panties. Wednesday was especially memorable. For a long time, he hadn't been able to think about Em without wild bursts of anger and, yeah, hurt. Funny how he didn't feel even a twinge now. Okay, maybe a twinge, but that was all. Time really did heal, he supposed.

He sighed and resumed a scan of his surroundings. It was a SEAL habit. Always secure your perimeter, wherever you are.

No danger in that live oak tree down there by the bayou. He remembered when an old tire hung from one of its lower limbs. Many a hot summer day he'd cooled off by swinging out over the bayou waters, despite the threat of gators and snakes. Sometimes PawPaw would even take a dip with him. And later, MawMaw would have a pitcher of sweet tea and a plate of homemade beignets waiting to hold them off until dinner, which usually consisted of gumbo, or jambalaya, or red beans and rice.

If anyone had asked him yesterday, while he was still in Coronado, if he had any good memories of his bayou homeland, he would have said no. He would have been wrong.

When had everything started to go to hell? And why?

He shook his head like a shaggy dog. What-ifs were a waste of time and a road he didn't want to travel today... if ever. Getting out of his rented vehicle, he started to walk toward the back of the house, and that was when he began to notice the differences.

First of all, there were animals everywhere. A dog

the size of a small horse with pure white fur and two
different-colored eyes. A Great Pyrenees, he guessed.
The wildly barking animal came bounding toward him
like a hopped-up polar bear, then came to a skidding halt
at his feet, where it sat on its rump and gazed up at Cage
with its tongue lolling and a silly grin on its face that said,
Like me, like me, like me.

And speaking of small horses, there was a small horse
tied up in the lean-to where they used to store the lawn
mower, which was now out in the yard, rusting away. No
wonder the grass was about a foot high.

There were also two or three other dogs, a half-dozen
cats, and a pot-bellied pig lazing about the yard. Not to
mention about a zillion chickens, none of which were in
the old chicken coop, where he could see that the wire
fencing had long ago rotted away.

Two flamingos stood near the edge of the stream, and
they weren't artificial ones either.

In the midst of all this craziness, a three-foot-tall St.
Jude statue held court in a little grotto. Tante Lulu had
been in the building, so to speak. Apparently St. Jude was
the patron saint of hopeless cases, and a notorious favorite
of hers.

He had to watch where he walked as he began to make
his way to the steep steps, moving slowly to accommodate his bum knee. Announcing his arrival were a
cacophony of squawks, yips and yaps, meows, oinks, and
neighs. And from inside the house, it sounded like birds.
For chrissake, his grandmother had a regular zoo going
on here.

And then it happened.

He was almost to the top of the steps, where a remov-
able, expandable gate, like those used to protect small

kids, kept the yard animals from coming up onto the porch. After he opened and closed the gate, he glanced over and saw his grandmother, wearing a flowered house-dress, step through the wooden screen door, alerted by all the noise. At first, she just cocked her head to the side before whispering, loud enough for him to hear, "Justin?"

"Who else would it be, MawMaw?" he asked in a sud-denly raspy voice. He hadn't expected to be so touched. "Didn't you always say that bad pennies had a way of comin' back?" Being careful to school his features to hide his shock, he limped over and grabbed his grandmother into a big hug that lifted her slippered feet off the porch floor. She didn't weigh any more than a bag of Spanish moss.

And her hair! His grandmother had always been so proud of her thick, straight, black hair, which she'd never cut as far as he knew, even when it had turned gray. She'd worn it in a single braid down her back, or twisted into a knot atop her head with Great-Grandma Jeannette's ivory combs on special occasions.

Once when he was about ten years old, he recalled waking in the middle of the night to hear his grandfather and grandmother on the other side of his bedroom wall. His grandfather had been murmuring something soft and mushy about what his grandmother's hair did to him. At the time, he'd been mortified.

Now her hair was short. Very short. Pure white, not gray. And curly. The chemo, he realized immediately, and braced himself. He had thought he'd prepared himself, but apparently he hadn't.

As he held her, he could feel a wetness on the curve of his neck where her face was nestled. She was sobbing softly.

Deep shame overwhelmed him. Despite all his reasons for staying away, none of them were worth a hill of beans if he'd hurt this precious old lady like this.

He set her down and away from him to look her over. "Lookin' beautiful as ever, *chère*." And she was, to him.

"Oh, you!" she said and put her hands nervously to her head. He could tell she was embarrassed and, yes, still a little vain. Good for her!

"It'll grow out, MawMaw. It ain't worth frettin' over. Isn't that what you always say? Besides, my hair is short, too." He rubbed his white walls to demonstrate. "Everyone will think it's the latest fashion. Grandmother and grandson matching do's."

She smiled...at least she still had all her teeth...and linked her arm in his, tugging him toward the house. "I have gumbo on the stove. Mus' be my guardian angel was whisperin' in my ear that I would be gettin' company."

Cage had stopped believing in guardian angels a long time ago. Hard to accept the concept of God, or angels, when you've witnessed a kid strapped with explosives going up in a pink mist after a suicide bombing in Iraq. And not just once.

"I'm not company," he said. "I'm family."

"Thass jist what Tante Lulu said last week," she remarked as she seated him at the kitchen table and proceeded to put enough food for an army in front of him. "Do ya remember her?"

How could I forget? Walking through an airport with the geriatric firecracker, stopping every five minutes so she could pee, or more likely, check out the restrooms for cleanliness and then file a report, was a memory that Cage would keep for a lifetime. And the airline attendant! Had Tante Lulu really told the woman her butt was too big for the skirt she was wearing and she ought to consider two sizes larger? Or check out Charmaine's beauty spa? Then she gave half the people on the plane little St. Jude statues, scaring them half to death because they thought she had inside info on an impending crash.

But Cage didn't want his grandmother to know just yet that it had taken the bayou busybody to get his ass home. So all he said was, "Yeah, I remember her. Louise Rivard, right?"

"Yep, but everyone calls her Tante Lulu."

While they were eating—him three platefuls, her only picking at one small one—he asked, "What's with all the animals?" Aside from the menagerie outside, there were three birdcages in the living room, one holding canaries or parakeets, or whatever . . . small birds. Then the other two held brightly colored tropical birds . . . toucans or macaws or whatever you called those big-ass birds. They were all squawking or chirping at his unwelcome presence.

At least the ginormous lizard in a glass tank wasn't making any noise.

"Yer grandfather and me took in some animals after Hurricane Katrina. I thought I tol' you that in one of my letters."

"You did, but you never mentioned how many, or all the different kinds. I thought you meant a dog or two. Maybe a few cats."

She shrugged. "There weren't so many in the beginning, but then folks that didn't want their pets anymore started droppin' them off in the driveway in the middle of the night. What could we do?"

"Find them homes?"

"We tried, and we did get homes for lots of them, but more kept comin'."

"Isn't it hard for you to take care of all of them?"

"It dint usta be, but lately..." Her voice trailed off. But then she straightened and said, "Remy LeDeux's boy came over yestiddy to help out, but it was raining so hard, I tol' him ta go home."

That was just great. She was having to rely on one of Tante Lulu's relations, not wanting to bother her own irresponsible grandson.

Neither of them had yet mentioned the portable oxygen tank sitting on the floor next to her chair, not even when she'd matter-of-factly inserted the nasal cannula. Apparently, she didn't need it all the time.

"Mebbe you could help find them good homes, if you have the time while yer here," she suggested tentatively as if she didn't want to ask too much of him.

"I'll make time," he said and reached over to squeeze her bony hand. "But only if you eat everything on your plate." *Shit! I'm talking to her like she's a child. She's sick, not senile.*

"Oh, you!" his grandmother said, not at all offended, and she did eat everything in front of her, including the two beignets he forced on her. Afterward, he talked her into letting the dishes go 'til later, and they went out on the porch with their coffee, the thick, strong chicory kind you could only get in Louisiana. An Elvis song, "Love Me Tender," provided a soft background through an open window. Probably from the old stereo console his Paw-Paw had bought for MawMaw on one of her birthdays.

She sank down onto a musty-smelling couch—was it only Louisiana where folks put upholstered sofas on an open porch? It about killed him to see her wheel the oxygen tank with her. It didn't escape his notice that there was an ashtray and a package of cigarettes—coffin nails, for sure—on a TV tray beside her. If he weren't here, she'd probably be lighting up.

Meanwhile, about two dozen animals were lined up on the steps before the gate, waiting to be fed.

"Should I feed them?" he asked.

"If you don't mind, sweetie." She pointed toward a large wood chest at the other end of the porch that presumably held the various pet foods. Water and feed bowls were scattered all over the porch floor.

If I don't mind? he scoffed inwardly. No wonder she hadn't contacted him about her illness if she thought this little chore was a hardship.

When he was done, and a couple of the dogs, including the polar bear, lay on the floor surrounding his grandmother, he went down and scooped some oats into the pony's feed trough, or whatever the hell you called it. He didn't know what to give the flamingos, so he just scattered an extra amount of chicken feed. The pig got leftover crawfish étouffée. On the way back, he gathered a dozen eggs in his shirttails. The eggs were everywhere around the yard. He'd come back later with a basket. What the hell did MawMaw do with all these eggs? And the chickens, for that matter? He hoped he wouldn't be expected to kill and pluck one of them for Sunday dinner.

His coffee was lukewarm by the time he returned to the porch, but it was still good. He sat on the swing, taking in the ambience. Even with all the animals, there was nothing like dusk on the bayou. It was mid-January, but the temperature today had been in the high sixties. Balmy. In this humid, sub-tropical climate, the flowers grew profusely and they were almost too fragrant. In truth, all the senses seemed heightened here in the bayou. The colors, the scents, the sounds, the textures.

He hadn't realized until this moment how much he'd missed his bayou home. But all that was beside the point.

"How bad is it?" he blurted out.

To her credit, she didn't lie or attempt to softsoap things.

"Bad. 'Terminal' is the word the sawbones use."

No! I will not accept that. "When's your next doctor's appointment? I'll go with you. I'm gonna call the doctor back at the base. Maybe he can recommend the best specialist for your kind of…of…cancer. Hell, science is moving forward every day. There might be a treatment your doctor doesn't know about."

She put up a hand and shook her head. "No. I've put this old body through too much already."

"How about chemo?"

"I've done all the rounds."

"Radiation?"

She shook her head some more. "They want me to, but I doan wanna. All it would do is extend my life by a couple of months…an mebbe cause me to lose my hair again." She laughed. "I refuse to go ta my Maker with a bald head. And there ain't no way I'm gonna let Rufus lead me through the Pearly Gates lookin' like a doorknob."

"Oh, MawMaw!" He was down on his knees beside her chair, holding her. Or was she holding him?

He cried openly…he couldn't help himself. He hadn't cried at the carnage he viewed in his work, some of which he'd caused. He hadn't cried when the judge had ordered him at seventeen to enter the military or go off to prison. He hadn't cried when Em had turned her back on him. He hadn't cried when his grandfather died. But this! His helplessness gutted him. "I should have come sooner."

"Yer here now. Thass all that matters." She was patting

his back, as if he was the one who needed comforting, not her.

"I'll stay as long as you . . . as you have," he choked out, "and I pray to God it will be a long time." There was no way he accepted her pronouncement that nothing more could be done, but he'd save that argument for later, after he'd met with her doctors. He raised his head and blinked back the tears that continued to sting his eyes.

"My only regret is that I hoped ta hold one of yer babies in my arms one day."

Oh, fuck! "If you promise to stick around, I'll get me one in nine months give or take." His joke appeared lame, even to him. There would be snow on the bayou before a mini-me LeBlanc was born.

They both laughed at the ridiculous promise. Even if he'd been willing or able to find someone receptive to taking on his swimmers, it was hopeless. Time was critical.

He could swear he heard a voice in his head say, *Hopeless? Did someone say hopeless?*

Just then, he saw snow floating around that stupid St. Jude statue in the yard. It wasn't snow, of course. Just blossoms from a fig tree.

Still . . .

And why were there blossoms in January?

A full body shiver came over him. He shrugged it off and turned to his grandmother. "Whataya say we crank up Priscilla and head on down ta the Dairy Queen, darlin'?"

Chapter Four

Daddy Dearest was back…

Emelie was up at dawn, fully dressed, and in her workshop downing her second cup of thick chicory coffee by 6:30 a.m. It was five weeks until Mardi Gras, and she was swamped with orders to be filled. In fact, yesterday she'd had to turn away two lucrative, last-minute requests for specialty masks because there was no time to spare.

Among her clients this year were the governor and his wife, the proprietor of a well-known New Orleans eatery, and HBO actor John Reed, who was this year's celebrity monarch for the Krewe of Bacchus.

At seven, her phone rang. It was Belle.

"Em, do you mind if I work from home this morning? I can come in about noon."

"Is something wrong?"

"No more than usual. I need to use my Quattro on that blasted leopard gown that Simone Grant wants by Friday." The Quattro was a hugely expensive, high-tech sewing machine with every bell and whistle imaginable, including a built-in video camera. Belle often said it was like a Singer on steroids.

There just wasn't enough room here on the bottom floor of Emelie's house for all the equipment needed to produce Belle's voluminous costumes, along with Emelie's masks and other Mardi Gras decorations. Emelie's house was a traditional shotgun style, running one room into another from street to back courtyard. The pre–Civil War appellation came from the fact that a shotgun shot from the street could travel back straight through the three rooms.

The front room housed a typical French Quarter shop with counters and display cases and costumed mannequins. The walls were painted with traditional Mardi Gras colors…purple walls with green and gold trim, purple denoting justice; green, faith; gold, power…and they were adorned with Emelie's decorative masks and framed photographs of past Mardi Gras events. Shelves held quality costume jewelry, purses, and lacy shawls. Inside glass showcases were collections of historical Mardi Gras parade throws…doubloons, beads, medallions, stuffed animals…as well as Carnival ball favors.

The middle of the house was Belle's headquarters, where she had a dressing room for customers to try on her gowns, bolts of fabric and trimmings, dress forms, and tables for doing handwork on the exquisite gowns and waistcoats…embroidery, beading, and such. It wasn't just the parades Belle and Emelie designed for, but all the numerous krewe and debutante balls, some of which were aristocratic and extravagant. In fact, in the old days… Mardi Gras went back more than 150 years…invitations were die-cut and printed in Paris. Even today, the invitations were considered works of art…highly collectible.

In any case, there was no room for the Quattro or the many other intricate sewing machines that Belle needed for her work.

Then in the back was a studio with French doors leading onto the courtyard. This was Emelie's workshop. She needed all that light for her artistic endeavors.

"Are you there, Em?" Belle asked.

"Yes. Just thinking. My brain's in its usual pre–Mardi Gras fuzz."

Belle laughed. "Listen. I know you're super busy, too. How about if I send Mike and Max in to hold down the fort in the front shop until I get there? It'll only be about three hours."

"Belle! They're only thirteen."

"I know, but how hard can it be for them to answer the phone and wait on folks who walk in? It will save you getting up every time the bell rings on the door. They can come get you if something important comes up, or if there's a customer whose questions they can't answer."

Emelie feared the boys would be more trouble than she needed today, but she didn't want Belle to come in when she needed to work at home.

"Don't the boys have to be in school today?"

"Teacher in-service day."

Emelie was beginning to understand. Belle needed her kids out of her hair so that she could work.

"Sure. Send them in."

"They can take the bus. Expect them about eight thirty, and don't you be worryin', hon. I told them they would be grounded for life if they used one swear word, flirted with any young girls who happened to come in, wrestled with each other on the shop floor, made any personal phone calls, farted out loud, tried on your masks, had anything stuck in their ears—like iPods—told dirty jokes, mooned each other or, God forbid, a passerby, or wore that current favorite T-shirt of theirs. I'M NOT A GYNECOLOGIST, BUT I CAN TAKE A LOOK.

Emelie groaned.

"Hey, it will be good experience for you to know what it's like having a kid."

"I was thinking about dipping my toe in that particular water, not belly flopping into the deep end."

They both laughed and hung up.

Emelie worked diligently for a half hour hot-gluing aquamarine blue crystals in the form of scales on a mask that would complement a mermaid gown Belle was creating. All of her masks were demis, covering only the upper half of the face, but the sky was the limit when it came to their height, width, and various extensions. A CD of Billie Holiday blues classics played softly in the background. Peaceful.

But then, she heard a vehicle pull into her driveway. *At 7:30 a.m.?* she wondered, glancing at her watch. *Who would come so early?*

She soon found out. As she turned and peered through the glass doors, she saw her father emerge from his old Lincoln and walk toward the stone-flagged verandah. There was an expression of worry on his face before he glanced up and noticed her watching him. Immediately, he broke into a smile.

Emelie and her father had been estranged for more than a decade, and they'd reconciled only two years ago. Even then, it was a tenuous relationship. They spoke on the phone once a week, and occasionally she visited his home in Houma, but he rarely came into the city, and then only at her invitation.

She unlocked the door and held it open for him to enter. Once inside, she kissed him on the cheek. Her father was sixty-nine-plus, but he looked eighty-nine today. His gray hair appeared rumpled, and his face wrinkled with some worry or other.

"This is a surprise," she said, waiting for him to tell her what the problem was.

He nodded. "I have a meetin' at the Petrol offices and thought I'd stop by ta see mah little girl first." Ever since her dad took an early retirement as sheriff in Terrebonne Parish, he'd been working security part-time for one of the Gulf's oil companies. She couldn't imagine what reason he'd need to visit their main headquarters.

It must be an awfully early appointment, she almost said, but bit her tongue, not wanting to rock the already shaky boat of their relationship.

"Would you like a cup of coffee?" she asked.

He shook his head and walked around the room, examining her works in progress. "Yer busy, I see."

"Very. It's that time of the year."

"Yer mother, bless her soul, woulda been so proud of yer success."

Oh, boy! When he mentioned her mother, Emelie knew he must have big things on his mind. Mary Gaudet died of MS complications when Emelie had been five years old. Her only memories of her mother were in a wheelchair and then bedridden. Her father had raised her single-handedly. He should have remarried. Hell, he'd been "seeing" Francine Lagasse, like forever. Maybe then he wouldn't have been so overprotective, interfering in every aspect of his daughter's life. Maybe then, he wouldn't have... well, that was water over the dam now.

"Sit down, Dad. Tell me what's wrong." Oh, God!

Maybe he was ill. On the brighter side, maybe he was finally going to make an honest woman of Francine.

"LeBlanc! Thass what's wrong. That rat bastard is back in town. Lak a bad penny, he is. Allus showin' up."

Emelie inhaled sharply. Justin LeBlanc was a taboo subject between them. The only condition she'd demanded when they'd finally made up was that her father never discuss Justin LeBlanc again, not after what her father had done. "Dad! Don't even start."

"You already knew?" He jerked back, as if she'd struck him. "Holy crawfish! Has that lowlife been here already?"

"This is so not a subject we are going to discuss. Yes, I heard he was back, visiting his sick grandmother, I believe. And no, he hasn't visited me. Why would he?"

"That boy, he was always sniffin' after yer tail, girl, and you know it. Doan think he won't be wantin' more. Remember the condition he left you in before he skipped town. Talk about!"

She stood and braced both arms, palms down, on her worktable, glaring at her father. "That was crude and totally uncalled for. I think it's time for you to leave."

"I'm sorry, sweetheart, it's jus' that I worry 'bout you. All alone. You shoulda stayed with Bernard. I doan want you ta be hurt again. Please, promise you'll show LeBlanc the door if he comes here. Better yet, let me read him the riot act. He's a Navy SEAL. He won't want his superiors ta hear anything bad 'bout his shenanigans."

Shenanigans? Good Lord! What world does my father live in? "Don't. You. Dare!" Her hand was shaking as she pointed to the door. "Leave. Before I say something we'll both regret."

"Now, Emelie, I'm only thinkin' of yer well-bein'."

He was halfway through the now open door before he turned. "Doan be mad at me fer caring."

"Caring? That's not caring. It's smothering. And downright none of your business. I'm thirty-three, almost thirty-four years old. I can make my own decisions. Seriously, Dad, if you approach Justin...if you say anything at all to him, I swear, I won't speak to you again. And I mean it."

After he left, Emelie put her face in her hands and wept with sheer frustration. She did not need this stress today, not when she had so much work to do.

Her father's interference was pointless anyway. Justin had no reason to contact her. It was her father's fault he'd left seventeen years ago, having threatened to charge Justin, without her knowledge, with statutory rape. Her father and the judge between them came up with an alternative. Justin had to leave Louisiana immediately and join the Navy, with no notification to Emelie or even his grandparents. For months, none of them knew where he was, not even when she'd needed him most.

But Justin hadn't been blameless either. Why had he continued to break the law when he knew his bad acts just made her father, the sheriff, hate him even more? He was continually in trouble...at school, with the police, at home, everywhere. Why, after leaving, when he had already broken so many other rules, had Justin complied with her father and the judge, and cut himself off from her, the girl he'd sworn to love forever? Not one single letter or phone call.

She grabbed a tissue from the box and wiped her eyes, then blew her nose loudly. *Enough!* She had work to do, and no time to waste on childhood fantasies of love ever after.

The phone rang a short time later. When she saw on the

caller ID that it was her father, she let it go to voice mail. After a few minutes, she dialed in to listen to the message.

"Emelie, I'm sorry. I shouldn'ta interfered. Old habits die hard, I guess. I won't punch out LeBlanc's lights. Ha, ha, ha. Not that I'm in any shape ta fight a Navy SEAL these days. Just kiddin'. Seriously, I'll back off. Be careful, though, and forgive yer old man, okay? Love ya."

What could she say? Of course she would forgive him. *Unless* he interfered again.

Mike and Max arrived soon after that. She got up to open the shop door for them and turned the OPEN sign in the window. They carried cardboard containers the size of buckets holding soft drinks. No coffee for them. They also brought a carton of Krispy Kreme donuts they'd purchased the night before while shopping with their mother in Baton Rouge. Belle knew the sweet treats were Emelie's favorites. A bribe. Or guilt gift. She took two of the glazed ones for herself and, after giving the boys some instructions, went back to her workshop to resume her unfinished project.

It was only later that something her father had said registered with her. A Navy SEAL. She'd learned eventually that Justin had joined the Navy, but he was a Navy SEAL? She never knew that. Well, it was understandable that she wouldn't know. Once she'd married, and after everything that happened from then on, she'd let it be known that she never, ever wanted to hear anything about the boy who'd abandoned her.

But a Navy SEAL? The baddest boy of the bayou, the one her father was sure would end up at Angola, a member of that elite special forces group? She'd seen a History Channel documentary on Navy SEALs, and they were presumably the best of the best. What could have happened to change Justin so? Back seventeen years ago, even Justin wouldn't have described himself as the best of anything, always being conscious of his roots. A father who died in prison and a mother hooking for drugs, God only knew where since she seemed to move from city to city and state to state with her pusher boyfriends. Emelie hadn't judged him for that, but others had, especially her father, and Justin was hardest of all on himself. That was why he'd acted out.

It was probably a woman who had turned him around, she concluded. Something she hadn't been able to do.

A sudden clenching, like a fist, surrounded her heart. She bent over with pain, gasping for breath.

After all these years, how could it still hurt so badly? And why now, when she was finally moving on to a new chapter in her life?

ℐↄ

Some guys just limp along in life until…bam!…

"Give it to me straight, Doc. How long does my grandmother have?"

Cage's posture might have appeared casual—legs extended and crossed at the ankles to accommodate the brace under the denim of one knee—as he sat in front of Dr. Evan Posniak's desk at the Ochsner Cancer Center in New Orleans, but he was far from calm.

To give him credit, the busy oncologist, who was part of the team treating his grandmother, had spent more than a half hour with him so far. Showing him x-rays and MRIs. Telling him what courses of treatment had been tried so far, what further treatments his grandmother refused to pursue, her prognosis in everything except time.

The doctor combed his fingers through his thick white hair, disarmed by Cage's blunt question, then looked Cage directly in the eye. "Six months to a year from the time of diagnosis, that's what the textbooks tell us."

He'd thought he was prepared for bad news, but Cage felt as if he'd been sucker punched by a lethal g-force, his heart racing like a Thoroughbred thundering to the Preakness finish line. When SEALs went up in jets on tight maneuvers, they were taught to suck in their abdominal muscles in a procedure called "hooking" to fight the gravitational pull, or g-force. He'd forgotten to hook today, and the terminality of his grandmother's disease was just such an assault on his mind and body.

"No offense, but wouldn't it be smart for my grandmother to get a second opinion? Cancer Treatment Centers of America? Mayo Clinic? Johns Hopkins? Sloan-Kettering. Whatever? Maybe there are trial drugs, or something. Even outside the country. I don't know. Damn, damn, damn!" He put his face in his hands, then looked up. "I feel so helpless doing nothing."

"Your reaction isn't unusual, Justin, and I'm not offended by your suggestion. You should know, though, that Ochsner's reputation is outstanding, and I've been a practicing oncologist for more than forty years. Frankly, son, it would be a waste of time."

"Time! That's what it's all about now, isn't it?" Cage couldn't keep the anger out of his voice. Not so much anger at the physician, but anger at himself. "Maybe if I'd come home earlier, when MawMaw's cancer was in the early stages, there might have been something that could have cured her."

The elderly physician shook his head sadly. "Not at her age. Lung surgery and aggressive chemo and radiation would have killed her."

Cage winced at the blunt words. The word "kill" was so final. *What else is new, Cage, my boy? Cancer is final.*

"Keep in mind, those numbers, six months to a year, aren't set in stone. There *are* things that extend life for some people, or at least make the time they have left more bearable."

Hope sprang suddenly. "Like what?"

"Diet. Exercise, even walking. Pain meds. A positive outlook. Having family or friends around to avoid depression. Even prayer."

Hope sank suddenly. *Prayer? That's his lifeline to me? Has he been talking to Tante Lulu?*

At Cage's skeptical expression, the doctor shrugged his shoulders and laughed. "There's so much we don't know about cancer, Justin. I personally don't rule out anything."

Cage's brain was spinning with all the information he'd been given and all the questions he still had. "Will her condition deteriorate...I mean, I know it will, but MawMaw would hate having to go into the hospital."

The doctor nodded. "Most folks like to stay at home as long as possible, even to the end. We don't recommend that unless there are family or friends to stay twenty-four/seven. In the latter stages, I mean. And there's hospice, of course."

Well, that sealed it. Cage was going to stay, even if it meant leaving the teams. He was her only close family left, he wouldn't shirk his responsibility. And it was more than a responsibility. Not even as a payback for all the years she and PawPaw spent raising the difficult child he'd been. No, he would stay with MawMaw for love.

"You won't realize this now, but you're luckier than many people, having this time with a loved one," the doctor concluded.

They must teach that platitude in Bullshit 101.

"Just try to make your grandmother as comfortable and happy as possible. If she changes her mind about further radiation, give me a call."

"Are you sure the further chemo and radiation wouldn't extend her life significantly?"

"No guarantees, and the side effects can be brutal. Your grandmother is lucid and she knows what she wants. Bottom line, Justin. If it were my mother, or grandmother, I would respect her wishes." The doctor checked his wristwatch and stood.

Cage stood, too, carefully. His knee screamed with pain when he sat in one position too long. He laughed then and told the doctor, "I know the one thing that would make MawMaw happy. A baby."

The old man's harried face eased into a smile. It must be tough dealing with cancer patients all day long, year after year. "Oh. I didn't know you were married. When's the little one due?"

"I'm not married, and there is no baby."

The doctor's brow furrowed with confusion.

"My grandmother is trying to guilt me into rushing the blessed event."

"The wedding or the birth?"

"Both. Of course I'd have to find a woman first."

"Well, that would certainly give her something to hold on for."

Cage's eyes widened with shock. Was he actually suggesting—

The doctor laughed. "I was teasing."

As they were walking out to the reception area, the doctor said, "A Navy SEAL, huh? My grandson has been thinking about becoming a SEAL ever since the raid that killed Bin Laden. He's a premed student at Tulane. Any advice?"

"Tell him to go to med school."

The physician arched his unruly white eyebrows in question.

"Becoming a SEAL is ten times harder than becoming a doctor. And doctors have better chances for a long life."

After shaking hands and leaving the building, Cage roamed the streets of the French Quarter for a while, not an easy task with his gimpy leg. But exercise was good, within limits; otherwise the knee would lock up on him. He limped slowly down the narrow streets, avoiding busy Bourbon Street and other tourist traps. He paused occasionally to gaze into store windows with their ornate displays of antiques, jewelry, and New Orleans oddities, but the whole time his mind was on his grandmother and how he had to have a bright face on when he returned to the bayou this afternoon. A Hurricane or five, heavy on the bourbon, might do the trick, but he had a long drive ahead of him. Instead, he would stop for some oyster po-boys to bring for their supper.

Just then, he noticed a shop with colorful Mardi Gras costumes and masks. E & B Designs. Not that he was into that whole Fat Tuesday hoopla. Even as a teenager, he'd been a spectator, rather than a participant. Who was he kidding? The drunken Mardi Gras crowds had been a field day for an experienced pickpocket as he'd been, before moving up to harder crimes. And all the women exposing their boobs for a mere set of beads? What young boy didn't love that?

Things were different when he'd been with Emelie, his steady girlfriend in those days. He'd behaved to please her. And she'd loved everything about Mardi Gras, especially the parades. He smiled, remembering the one time he'd snuck Priscilla out of the garage after his grandparents had fallen asleep. He and Em had watched the parades and stayed out all night, ending up in the backseat of the big old car. They didn't make bench seats like that anymore. A pity!

He was still smiling as he prepared to walk on when his attention was caught by a framed newspaper article on a small easel inside of the window about E & B Designs from the *Times-Picayune*. What stopped him cold was the photograph that accompanied the article. There were two women smiling at the camera, and he knew both of them. Belle Pitot and Emelie Gaudet. Em! Apparently Belle designed the costumes and Emelie made the designer masks.

Holy shit! What were the chances of this kind of coincidence happening? For a blip of a second, he wondered if Tante Lulu might be lurking around the corner, having planned the whole thing.

Now that he thought about it, he could see Em designing Mardi Gras masks. Her two passions, aside from her passion for him, had been art and singing... the blues mostly. He'd even bought her a fancy wooden box filled with colored pencils for her sixteenth birthday, along with a boxed set of Bessie Smith CDs, and he hadn't even shoplifted them. Instead, he'd worked his butt off, dawn to dusk, on his grandfather's shrimp boat one whole weekend.

He stood frozen in place, wondering if he should go in or not. There was a lot of history between him and Emelie Gaudet, and some of it not very pleasant. He'd carried an angry chip on his shoulders for a lot of years, courtesy of Em. Did he want to stir up that old hornet's nest?

But then, he recalled that Em had married within months of his having left Louisiana seventeen years ago. To his cousin Bernie, the geek, no less. She was probably fat with a bunch of kids by now. Hell, her kids might even be as old as he and Em had been when they were screwing each other like Energizer bunnies.

With that thought in mind, he opened the door and stepped inside.

Big mistake!

Chapter Five

Tears of a clown, or was that a SEAL? . . .

Cage stepped into the colorful shop and stopped dead in his tracks at the double whammy standing before him. Twin boys. Just when he'd been wondering if Em had children, there stood before him not one, but two dark-haired, dark-eyed Cajun mini-Ems.

"Hey, man, what's up?" one of them asked.

The other twin elbowed the first and asked, "How may we help you, sir?"

The first twin elbowed the second right back, though harder, and muttered, "I was about to say that."

"Dweeb!"

"Dork!"

As one they turned to face him, realizing how inappropriate their bickering was. Their faces went comically blank. "Welcome to E & B Designs, where every day is Mardi Gras," they sing-songed.

Cage bit back a laugh.

They were identical twins...well, almost identical. Tall and lean. Gangly. Anywhere from thirteen to fifteen years old, he would guess. They both wore braces and St. Ambrose Football T-shirts tucked into well-worn, holey jeans. St. Ambrose was a Catholic boys' school in New Orleans.

"Um. Just lookin' around," Cage said. "That okay?"

"Sure. Our mother is part-owner of this shop."

"She must be very talented."

"She is."

"I'm Mike," offered the twin with a bruise on his cheekbone that was turning yellow. Probably a football injury.

"And I'm Max," the other twin said. He had an Alfalfa-type cowlick growing on the back of his head.

Cage reached across the counter to shake their hands. "Justin LeBlanc. People call me Cage."

"How come?" Mike asked. Never let it be said that teenagers had tact.

"Because I'm Cajun. Born and bred on the bayou, before I moved away."

"No shit!" Max exclaimed.

Mike elbowed his brother and said, "You know what Mom said."

"Sorry," Max said to Cage.

Cage grinned. "I've heard worse."

"Where do you live now?"

"California. I'm just visiting."

"Lots of people come to N'awlins for Carnival. Even from around the world," Mike said. "There was a guy here this morning from China."

"Japan," Mike corrected.

"Whatever!" Max shot his brother a glower.

"Hey, are you a Navy SEAL?" Mike asked.

"Oh, wow!" Max added.

"Huh?" *How would they know that?* he wondered, then saw the direction of their eyes. *Well, duh!* Normally SEALs didn't announce themselves with T-shirt logos and such, but it had been cool this morning and he'd grabbed a windbreaker that said U.S. NAVY SEALS with an official emblem on the front. Actually, most SEALs carried, even when not on duty, and the jacket concealed the pistol tucked into the back of his jeans. "Well, actually... yeah, I am," he admitted, figuring it wouldn't hurt for a couple of kids to know what he did for a living.

"Man, that is so cool!"

"Awesome!"

"Bet you have women crawlin' all over you," Max said wistfully.

"Oh, yeah. Like lice."

"Huh?" Max blinked at him.

"Just teasin'." And actually, the kid was right. Women did want to hook up with SEALs. Like rock stars, SEALs also had their groupies. Even obnoxious guys like their teammate Frank Uxley, appropriately named F.U., had no trouble getting a date.

"I saw *American Sniper* last year with Bradley Cooper. Man, you SEALs can kick ass and take names without blinking," Mike said.

Oh, God! Another movie that was almost a parody of SEALs. Rarely were those flicks vetted by anyone with military creds. Although he had to admit, *American Sniper* was better than most, recounting the life of a true American hero, Chris Kyle.

"Do you know Bradley Cooper?" Max wanted to know, a hopeful expression on his young face.

What? Did he think they were good buds, that the

famous actor was just sitting outside in Cage's car, slumming the Quarter? He laughed. "No."

"Oh, I just thought of something," Mike said, his face bright with whatever new thought had popped into his young head. "Did you kill Osama bin Laden? I mean, were you one of the SEALs that took him out?"

Everyone asked him that.

The boys were gazing at him now as if he was some kind of superhero.

"No. I was in Somalia at the time."

A young couple came in then, and the boys reluctantly moved off to wait on them.

Cage felt like he had dropped down into some rabbit hole, an alternate universe, where he met up with the sons of a woman...okay, a girl...he'd once loved. Sons that could have been his. They even looked a little bit like him.

After meeting with MawMaw's doctor, he wasn't sure how many more shocks he could take today. He should leave. Forget Em and her new life. Let old dogs...rather old loves...die.

The young couple purchased a booklet about Mardi Gras and a poster that could later be framed when they got back to Kentucky. The boys turned back to him.

"You oughta check out those doubloons over there. Some of them are, like, a gazillion years old," Max said, pointing to the glass case on the other side of the room.

Cage walked over and pretended interest, trying to get his emotions under control. Never a problem before, or not for a long time.

"You're limping," Max remarked. "Didja get hit by an AK-47 or somethin'?"

Son, if I got hit by an AK-47, I wouldn't be here. "Naw, just landed the wrong way in a Halo jump."

The slack-jawed boys stared at him as if he'd said he just invented the latest video game or, better yet, told them he knew the model on the cover of the latest *Sports Illustrated* swimsuit issue.

"So you live here in N'awlins?" Cage inquired with seeming casualness. Meanwhile his heart was beating like a drum. *Ka-thump. Ka-thump. Ka-thump.*

"Yep. With our mother. We have a little house on the outskirts of town," Mike said. "Do you wanna see any of those tosses up close?"

"Tosses?"

Mike pointed to some of the items in front of Cage in the glass case. "Things that get tossed during parades. You know, beads, medallions, coins, and stuff," Mike explained.

He used to know what tosses were. He'd forgotten. What else had he forgotten, deliberately or not? "Nah, I'm just looking. A little souvenir for my grandmother," he said but then his tongue developed a mind of its own. "So you mentioned a little house and your mother. How about your father?"

There was a silence behind him and he turned to look at the boys.

"We don't have a father," Max said.

"Of course you have a father," Cage told him. "Everyone does." *Good Lord! I sound like an absolute moron.*

"Not us. At least not one our mother ever admitted to," Mike said sadly.

"But what about Bernie?" *Yep, diarrhea of the tongue.*

"Bernie? Bernie who?" Max's brow was furrowed with puzzlement. Then he laughed. "Do you mean that dweeb Bernie Landry?"

"Max," Mike chided his brother. "Mom doesn't like

us calling him that." Mike turned to Cage then and said, "No, Bernie is not our father."

Dweeb? I like the sound of that. He concentrated on making sure a smile didn't emerge, before remarking, "But your mother married Bernie. I know she did."

"Our mother was never married," both boys said.

Now Cage was the one who was confused. "I don't understand."

"Mom says we are the joyous result of a one-night stand," Max elaborated. "And that's all she'll tell us."

"Impossible! Your mother is not the type to…" His words trailed off as he realized he was saying too much.

Max put his hands on his hips. "Do you know our mother?"

"You could say that." Cage's hesitation was telling.

Mike and Max exchanged a glance, then turned as one to stare at him.

"Are you our father?" Mike demanded.

"Whaat? No. Of course not." *Not unless you two are older than you look.* "How old are you guys?"

"Thirteen," they answered as one.

"Then I am definitely not your father."

"Whoa, are you saying you did the deed with our mother?" Max asked. "Eew! That is gross."

"I think it's cool. A Navy SEAL! Mom usually brings creeps home, like that biker dude last month, remember?" Mike said to his brother.

A biker dude? Em with a biker dude? That's like Mother Teresa with Howard Stern. "This is very con-fusing." Cage sighed and then asked the one thing he shouldn't. "Where's your mother? I need to talk to her."

"Mom won't be here for an hour or so. Do you want to talk to our aunt? She's back in her workshop."

"Aunt?" Cage asked dumbly. Em didn't have any brothers or sisters. So how could the boys have an aunt?

"Honorary aunt, sort of," Mike elaborated.

Then, instead of stepping back to the room, or rooms, behind the shop, Max let out with a holler, "Yo! Aunt Em. Someone wants to talk to you."

Aunt Em?

Slowly, the gears in Cage's brain began to move. Emerging into the doorway was Emelie Gaudet. Or was that Emelie Landry? She looked a little bit older, but just the same. Dark hair pulled back off her face into a high ponytail. A white coverall marked with new and old paint spatters, over a short-sleeved white T-shirt. No makeup.

"Boys? You *called*?" she said, wagging a forefinger at Max and Mike, a gentle reminder that they weren't supposed to shout in the shop. Then she glanced up, and did a double take. Her brown Cajun eyes went wide with shock before she whispered, a hand over her heart, "Justin?"

For seventeen years, Cage had become the comedian of the teams. Always lighthearted. Always the one ready to share a joke or a beer. Always game for a new adventure...or a new woman. It was a ruse, of course, and not all that original. The clown covering his inner tears.

So he tried for a bit of humor now, tipping his head at Em. "Honey, I'm home."

No one laughed. Least of all him.

The years, and other things, melted away...

Emelie stood frozen in the doorway.

Justin LeBlanc was a man now, of course, but still she

would have recognized him anywhere. A bit taller. He had already reached six foot by his seventeenth birthday, but he appeared about six two or three now. The same lean frame, except his shoulders were wider, his waist narrower, and the muscle definition, visible through the T-shirt under his open windbreaker, was more defined. SEAL training, she assumed. One thing remained the same, though. The boy could fill out a pair of jeans nicely. Very nicely. His hair was military short, unlike the long hair he'd worn as a teenager—his rebel statement—but still attractive.

Seventeen years! And Justin stood before her, staring at her in the same old way, his dark Cajun eyes smoldering some hidden message. Hungry eyes, she used to call them. Except in the old days, she'd known exactly what that message meant. Desire for her. Now his eyes seemed to be sparked with anger. At her? What reason did he have to be angry?

"What are you doing here?" she asked, making a pre-emptive strike.

"Hello to you, too, Em. Long time no see, darlin'." He hadn't lost his Southern drawl.

She bristled. How dare he darlin' her? He'd walked out on her seventeen years ago with never a backward glance. And what was with the "Honey, I'm home" crap? Did he imagine he could walk back into her life and she would welcome him with open arms? Like they would be lovers again? Not a chance! Like they remained good buddies? Not a chance! "What are you doing here?" she repeated. The ice in her voice was a clear barometer of her feelings for him. She hoped.

His lips twitched with amusement at her blunt question, but his eyes weren't smiling.

There was a time when that little hint of a grin would

have melted her heart. Now her heart was frozen solid where he was concerned.

"Here in Louisiana or here in your shop?" he asked.

"Both."

"I'm here to visit my MawMaw."

"For how long?"

He shrugged.

Emelie recalled what Bernie had told her, and now she felt guilty for her rudeness. "Sorry. I heard that Miss Mae-Mae's been ill. Hope it's nothing serious."

He didn't answer, and she could tell by the way his jaw went rigid that it was very serious. Just then, she noticed Mike and Max watching the interplay between her and Justin, and without thinking, she said to Justin, "Would you like to come back and have a cup of coffee?"

He hesitated, which should have felt like an insult, but she understood what he clearly did, too: shaky ground. "Sure."

She led him through Belle's workroom and into her studio. He studied the area, both hers and Belle's, with interest.

"How long have you and Belle been in business?"

"Five years," she said, going over to the counter on the side and starting a new pot of coffee. Her hands were shaking. Darn it!

"Didn't your Grandmother Delphine used to live here?"

"I'm surprised you remember that."

"Me, too."

What did that mean? "Yeah, this house belonged to MawMaw Delphine. She left it to me when she died seven years ago. I'd been living with her for a few years before that, working for an artist over on Chartres Street."

She turned, leaning back against the counter. She

could see her answer raised other questions. But instead of asking any more, he walked around the studio, examining her masks, both those already completed, resting in special, pre-formed velvet boxes, and the works in progress. "You're very talented, Em. But then, I always knew that." He picked up the box that had been a gift from him for her sixteenth birthday. The colored pencils were long gone, but she used it now for her assorted paintbrushes.

Their eyes connected for a long moment as they both recalled that long-ago moment when he'd given her the gift. In those days, she'd been the only one to see any good in him, aside from his grandparents. But then, he'd been of an opinion, *If you've got the name, you might as well play the game.* In other words, he acted down to his bad reputation.

"You kept it," he said, fingering the carvings on the box, which wore a patina of aged cypress.

She shrugged. "It's a nice box," she replied, as if that were the only reason she'd kept it. It was, she insisted to herself.

Like it was only yesterday, she recalled the pure joy on his young face when he'd handed her the clumsily wrapped gift. A lump formed in her throat now, as it had then, and she feared she might cry. Why, she wasn't sure. "Have a seat outside by the fountain? I'll bring our coffee out."

His head was tilted in question, as if he wanted to ask her something, but then he nodded, without speaking, and went out the French doors.

With knees almost buckling, Emelie picked up her cell phone and called Belle. "Where are you?" she demanded.

"I'm on my way. Is there is an emergency?"

"Hell, yes!"

"Em? Are you crying?" Belle asked with concern.

"No. Of course not," she replied, swiping at her eyes.

"What's wrong?"

"My past is sitting out in my courtyard, and I'm afraid . . . I'm afraid, that's all. Come quick, and rescue me."

Chapter Six

Some things were just meant to be...

Cage's emotions were banging off the walls of his aching chest like Ping-Pong balls.

What the hell am I doing here? Go home, you idiot. Go back to the bayou and forget you ever saw her again.

Hah! Like I can ever forget Em as she is now.

A woman.

Not the girl I loved.

But better.

Different.

And the same.

Cage inhaled deeply and exhaled to calm himself down. He was sitting on the far side of a wrought iron patio table, a position that gave him a view of all his surroundings, a SEAL reflex built in after years of training. *Secure your perimeter. Never give your enemy a chance to surprise you.*

But Em wasn't his enemy. Just a danger. To his well-being. To his heart.

He could see through the glass door that Em was puttering away, putting cups of coffee and other dishes on a tray. He'd already been through the downstairs retail space and workshops, and wondered what was upstairs. All he could see was a covered gallery, or balcony. Probably an apartment. But who lived there? The boys had mentioned living outside the city; so it must be Em's home. Did someone live here with her? Well, duh! Her husband, of course. Bernie the Wienie—that's what he'd been called when they were kids.

Just then, he noticed a paper lying on the ground under the table. Reaching down, he picked it up and scanned the words on it with increasing incredulity. Under the letterhead, Southern Reproductive Services, a Dr. Charles Benoit was thanking Emelie Gaudet for her interest in artificial insemination.

Cage dropped the paper as if it had burst into flames in his fingers, and it fluttered to almost the same spot where it had lain previously. He tried his best to look nonchalant, knowing without a doubt that Em would consider his reading the letter an invasion of privacy, even if it had been unintentional.

But Holy Hell! Em was considering having a baby with some anonymous guy's swimmers? What about Bernie? Maybe he had problems with the old . . . wiener.

Cage smiled with warped satisfaction. He even hoped Bernie couldn't get it up. That would be justice, wouldn't it?

But then, maybe the problem was with Em. Aaahh, that was too bad. Well, then, he could see why she would seek this alternative.

But wait. That letter had been addressed to Em as Emelie Gaudet, not Landry. What did that mean? Maybe nothing. Lots of women kept their maiden name today or hyphenated the hell out of their surname. One of his team members had a wife who went by the name of Mary Lou O'Brien-Spilhowsky. *Shiiit!* Try saying that real fast.

So many questions.

He heard the French doors opening. Em held the door open with her butt and eased her way through with the laden tray, letting the door slam behind her. Two mugs of coffee and a plate of what appeared to be doughnuts. He stood to help her.

An idea came to him then, out of the blue. Was it inspiration or madness? Probably both.

Cage's MawMaw yearned to hold his baby before she died.

Em wanted a baby.

For some reason, Bernie was not to be the father.

Did he want a kid?

Didn't matter. What mattered was his grandmother.

But he couldn't just pop the question to Em. Like, "Hey, *chère*, wanna shake some sheets and make a rugrat?" Nope, he needed a plan. He was an expert at planning. Well, battle planning, but same thing. Right?

As Em set the tray on the table, he watched her every move. Only when she sat down across from him and he'd taken a sip of his coffee—made just the way he liked it, by the way, with one spoon of sugar and a dash of milk— he smiled and said, "You look really good, Em."

She arched a brow skeptically, as if she knew he'd been thinking something else. "You, too." She stared at him directly and said with the honesty he'd once loved about her, "You've come a long way, Justin. The Navy appears to have been good for you."

So, that was the way it was going to go. Polite conversation. Okay, he could do that. For now. "It was hard at first. The military has a way of breaking a man down, then building him back up into the mold they want. A difficult process when a grunt was there by choice. Much harder when it was a forced decision. Signing up, I mean." Damn! He hadn't meant to mention his involuntary exit out of good ol' Loo-zee-anna and, by implication, her part in the virtual kick in the ass.

She didn't appear offended, though. Maybe his zinger had passed over her. Maybe that was how little she'd care about what happened to him. Maybe he was pathetic.

"You were so wild as a teenager," she was saying. "I can't imagine how they managed to tame you."

"With a lot of pain," he told her. "Then later, when the SEALs approached me, I found a niche I loved."

"A niche?" she commented with a laugh. "That's not even a word you would have known at one time."

"Hey, bite your tongue. I have a college degree now."

"You?" she exclaimed, then quickly added, "Sorry. That was insulting."

He waved a hand dismissively. "No offense taken. The Loser of Bayou Black an academic success? Talk about! Hell, I surprised myself. But I needed a degree in order to gain officer status."

She arched her brows in question.

"Lieutenant, second grade."

He waited for her to comment on him being an officer, but instead she said, "Justin, I never thought of you as a loser."

"Hmpfh! You were the only one."

She stared into her coffee cup for a long moment before raising her eyes. "I didn't know what my father did. Not back then."

That was a surprise, but then not so much of a surprise when you considered what a domineering, single-minded bastard her father had been. "He threatened to have me charged with statutory rape, you know. I would have been classified as a pedophile. Hard time. Of course, as sheriff of Terrebonne Parish, he had Judge Benoit in his pocket. It wasn't an empty threat."

"I know. I found out a year after you were gone."

"Was that before or after you married my cousin?" The question slipped out before Cage had a chance to bite his tongue.

She blinked with surprise at his surly tone of voice. "After. At the time of our divorce actually."

Divorce? Whoa! That raised a boatload of questions. And answers, like, that's why Bernie wasn't going to be planting any seeds. "You weren't married for very long then."

"Six months," she said.

"So is your father still running your life?" That was blunt and insulting, but it was the truth. Her father had ruled her life like a dictator, allowing her little freedom.

"He still tries, but he hasn't had much luck. In fact, I didn't speak to him for years. We only made up about two years ago, and even now we're on tenuous ground."

That shocked him. Despite his overprotection, Em and her father had been very close. "Because of me?" he asked.

"Only partly." Then, steering the conversation away from what was obviously a painful subject for her, she remarked, "You mentioned your grandmother is ill."

He nodded. "Lung cancer. I just came from visiting her oncologist this morning."

She reached across the table and placed a hand over his. "Oh, Justin, I'm so sorry. But you know, there have been great strides in cancer research. With treatment, she could have years to live yet."

He was shocked at how good that mere touch of her hand felt and so it was moments before he slipped his hand away and shook his head, "Too late for MawMaw. The doctor says six months to a year."

She put a palm over her mouth and her eyes brimmed with tears. She had always been sensitive like that. "I should go visit her sometime. I mean, she was always nice to me, except at the last, but then she was only obeying your orders."

The last? What last? He stiffened. "What orders?"

"Not to give me your address or telephone number. I have to admit that I made a nuisance of myself. Begging for information to the point that your grandfather told me that I had to stop asking."

"I have no idea what you're talking about," he said.

But they had no chance for further discussion because Em's partner, Belle Pitot, arrived.

He stood and smiled, having known her since they were kids at Our Lady of the Bayou School. She'd been Em's best friend.

"Well, well, well! Look what the cat dragged in," Belle said, coming up and giving him a warm hug and a kiss on the cheek. A greeting that had been noticeably missing from Em, he realized.

Em used Belle's arrival to leave. "I've got to get back to work. It was great seeing you again, Justin."

Yeah. Right.

Cage and Belle talked for a while, and he happened to mention all the animals that his grandmother had rescued and his dilemma in finding them homes.

"Hey, maybe my boys can come over this weekend and help clean up the yard. They always need spending money, and it would get them out of my hair just before Mardi Gras."

"That would be great," he said.

"By then, I might have ideas for placement of some of the animals," she added. "Do you think I could visit a spell with Miss MaeMae when I drop the boys off? I haven't spoken with her for ages."

"Sure."

"I'll bring a box of chocolate-covered cherries. Those used to be her favorites."

Cage had forgotten how easily Southern folks reached out to help others and how thoughtful they could be. Plus, MawMaw would enjoy the company. Bless Belle for remembering the chocolate-covered cherries.

A short time later, he was driving back to his grand-mother's home on Bayou Black, his mind spinning with everything that had happened this morning, starting with the visit to Dr. Pozniak, ending with Emelie. He felt so hopeless—where his grandmother was concerned, of course, but about Em, too. After all these years, he shouldn't care. He *didn't* care. Still . . .

He stopped at Boudreaux's General Store for the milk his grandmother had asked him to buy on the way home, and decided to pick up some beer. He stood in front of the glass doors of the refrigerated shelves, contemplating whether he should try Abita Turbodog or Tin Roof Voo-doo Bengal Pale Ale—*Only in Loo-zee-anna*, he thought with a rueful shake of the head—and decided to take a six-pack of each.

When he was about to pay for his purchases, who did he run into but Tante Lulu. He hadn't seen her since she'd flown back to Louisiana with him last week. She was wearing her usual outrageous gear . . . a red Annie-style wig, black skinny jeans that molded her nonexistent butt, topped with an orange stretch T-shirt that molded her flat chest with OLD CHICKS ROCK! printed on it in sparkly letters. On her feet were white orthopedic shoes.

The old lady's face lit up on seeing him enter. "I was jist thinkin' 'bout you," she squealed.

Uh-oh!

"Here. I got somethin' fer you." She dug into her purse, which was about the size of Vermont, and pulled out a little plastic statue. Handing it to him, she said, "Thass St. Jude. He's the patron saint of hopeless cases."

Cage tilted his head to the side, at the same time marveling at how warm the statue felt in his hand, almost like it throbbed with heat. "How did you know I was feeling hopeless?"

"Sweetie, we all feel hopeless one time 'r another."

ℒℰ

The heart remembers...

Emilie was a basket case, having trouble concentrating on her work. She couldn't stop thinking about Justin.

Finally, she gave in to an impulse she'd suppressed for seventeen years. She brought out a step stool and accessed the crawl space above her bedroom, pulling out a shoe box.

Going into her bathroom, she dampened a washcloth and wiped off the thick layer of dust, then carried the box out to her second-floor balcony that overlooked the courtyard and set it on a table. Tears burned her eyes before she even lifted the lid.

On top was an old BITE ME BAYOU BAIT COMPANY T-shirt of Justin's. She'd worn it home when the air turned chilly the first night they'd made love on a picnic table at Cypress Park. They would have been more comfortable on the grass, but there was always a fear of snakes. Neither of them had minded the discomfort, though. They'd waited so long and were so hot for each other. She held the shirt up to her face, imagining that she could catch his scent, which was ridiculous, of course.

She smiled at what she saw next. A program for the Christmas Pageant at Our Lady of the Bayou School. She'd been an angel, and Justin had been one of the shepherds placed in the back of the stage, way back, where he couldn't cause any mischief. He'd had a cowlick in those days, and he'd claimed that was why he wasn't chosen to be an angel; the halo wouldn't fit. It never would as he got older, but not because of a cowlick.

There was a junior varsity football letter he'd given her in ninth grade. That was the last year he'd played any sport, probably because about then his father was killed in prison, where he'd been serving yet another sentence, armed robbery that time, she thought. After that, Justin went wild. Went to school only when he felt like it. Got into fights. Had a chip on his shoulder the size of a bayou barge. Her heart ached at how hurt and rebellious he'd been then. It got even worse the next year when his mother committed suicide—or died of an overdose. It was never clear since she'd been living in Miami at the time.

Justin had only been a boy, really, but he'd had to face some serious adult issues. He hadn't been much older than Mike and Max. She could only imagine how they would be under similar conditions.

She had to laugh at what she saw next. A little ziplock baggie of dried shrimp with a cardboard attachment advertising the Grand Isle Shrimp Emporium. She wasn't about to check and see if the shrimp could still be used after almost twenty years. She'd heard the company had lost everything during Hurricane Katrina.

It had been a day out of time, one of those periods in your life that even when it's happening you know it is a magic moment. Her entire eighth grade class had been looking forward to the field trip, not so much for the lesson they would be getting in a historic cultural industry, but to be out of doors on a warm spring day.

The highlight of the day had been "dancing the shrimp," in which the main participant had been none other than the scampy Justin LeBlanc.

Long ago, Filipino and Chinese immigrants came to Southeastern Louisiana, bringing their shrimp harvesting techniques to this new world. One particularly colorful practice had involved the drying of shrimp, keeping in mind that there were no refrigerators at that time for freezing. When the shrimp had been dried on platforms over the marshes in direct sunlight, being turned often until they were the perfect dryness, the men and women and children would dance on the shrimp to separate the hulls and heads. It was a practice that was soon adopted by the Cajun fishermen.

When the owner of the plant had put on some rowdy Cajun music and asked for volunteers from her class to "come dance the shrimp," no one would step forward. At fourteen, the girls were too shy, and the boys worried that dancing would make them look like fools. In the end, Justin raised his hand, to the snickers of his classmates. After having his bare feet wrapped in burlap and his pant legs rolled up, Justin had jumped up on the platform and begun to dance rhythmically in tune to the music, stomping his feet, rolling his hips, spinning. When his eyes caught Emelie's, he beckoned her with wagging fingers to join him. "Come, *chère*, it's fun."

At first, she'd resisted, but then she heard someone

remark behind her, one of the mean, popular girls whose name Emilie couldn't recall now, "*Pfff!* Who would dance with such trash? His father's in Angola, and his mother is a hooker." Raising her chin high, Emilie had stepped forward, shrugged off her sneakers, put on the burlap wraps, and let Justin help her up onto the platform. After that, she'd tuned out the crowd, her focus being on the music, "Big Mamou," blasting from a loudspeaker, her hands held in Justin's, the sun beating down on them, and pure joy. Until the day she died, she would remember the smile on Justin's face. They'd been friends before, but that day they fell in love. The following year his father died in prison and not long after, his mother had died in some Miami brothel.

Tears streamed down her face as she tossed the packet in a nearby trash basket.

She gasped as she saw what lay at the bottom of the box, and her tears turned to sobs. With shaking hands, she lifted the tiny baby sweater of the softest yarn, hardly bigger than her widespread palm, the one and only item she'd bought for her baby…the baby that died before it was born.

Emelie's heart was breaking all over again.

Chapter Seven

The bayou twists and turns were nothing compared to the twists and turns in his sorry life…

Cage arrived back at the cottage by midafternoon to find his grandmother taking a nap. She'd left the old Bakelite Motorola radio on in the living room at low volume. It was playing a soft ballad in French. Only in bayou country would you find radio stations that played the old songs in their original Acadian French dialect.

Of course, once he'd stepped inside, the birds started squawking and talking and setting up a general ruckus. He was teaching one of them to say, "Hoo-yah!" If he had a way to carry it back, he might even keep that one in his Coronado condo. But no, he was away too much to have a pet of any kind. Even a bird.

He set some of the paperwork he'd gotten from the doctor on the 1930s-era enamel kitchen table, which was already set for dinner with woven place mats and the old Fiestaware plates that were part of a set that had been a

wedding gift to MawMaw and PawPaw all those eons
ago. As a boy, he'd loved them because they were such
vivid colors.

On the stove, cooking at a slow simmer, was his favorite dish, red beans and rice. Well, the rice—about a gallon
of it—was already cooked and set aside on the counter
in a covered casserole. In the cast-iron pot were the red
beans that had no doubt been started early this morning,
right after he'd left, with the traditional Holy Trinity of
Cajun cooking—onions, bell peppers, and celery—as
well as andouille sausage, which he hadn't tasted in so
many years, he couldn't recall. And for his benefit, she'd
probably given the dish an extra douse of Tabasco, best
known as Cajun Lightning. His mouth watered at the
tempting aromas. He couldn't help himself. He stirred the
pot with a wooden spoon and took a taste.

In the old days, before automatic washers and dryers,
red beans and rice was the Monday meal in all Cajun
households, according to MawMaw. The meal was easy
to prepare and could cook all day while the housewife did
the family laundry. Today, it was a staple on every Cajun
restaurant's menu.

There was a note taped to the cypress cabinet. *Taking a
nap. Not to worry. I'm feeling fine. Your boss called. Nice
fella, Commander MacLean. Stir the beans.*

He put the milk and beer in the fridge, but left out a bottle for himself. Going out on the porch, he saw about fifty
animals rush to line up on the steps behind the child gate.

When they realized that he wasn't about to give them
midday snacks, they went back to the yard, or settled down
on the steps to rest.

He was going to have to take care of these animals
ASAP. In fact, he pulled a small notebook and pen from his

back pocket and sank down on an Adirondack chair with a groan and carefully propped his feet on the banister. His knee was aching like a bitch. He'd done too much walking.

But what a day!

He sighed and let himself relax, taking in his surroundings.

Many folks said that the bayou was a touchstone for those who had left and ultimately came back. Cage felt it, deep in his soul. Sure as sin, he still had bayou mud in his veins.

Cage had dated a Realtor at one time who claimed, "If you are lucky enough to live on water, you're lucky enough." How true! Even here where the conditions were a far cry from the waterfront estates his Realtor friend had been thinking about. Maybe more so.

The scents, the sounds, the smells were so unique to the bayou, it was hard to describe them to outsiders. Even the colors were magnified by the humidity and tropical sun.

Not that it was hot today or humid, it being February with mild temperatures, but he knew too well what summers were like. Lazy, sweaty days filled with wonder for a young boy, despite the swarms of insects, especially those bothersome no-see-ums that got everywhere, even the mouth if a person wasn't careful. Too hot to do anything but toss a line baited with cow lip to catch the crawfish, best known as mudbugs, that flourished here.

And if you were poor, as they had been, and couldn't afford even cow lips or chicken necks, a leafy branch could be dipped into the slow-moving, coffee-colored waters, and come up with crawfish clustered in its midst. A memory came to him all of a sudden, so powerful he flinched at the pain in his gut.

He must have been five years old, or less. Standing at the edge of the bayou, right down there where a rotting pirogue lay under an aged tupelo, he saw in his mind's eye himself as a young boy standing next to a tall man. Black hair. Handsome, he'd heard some people say. Wearing a white T-shirt and faded jeans. Barefooted. The man was hunkered down, teaching the little boy how to remove the squirming crawfish quickly from the branches before they could get away. The white bucket next to them was half-full. When the little boy had succeeded in plopping a particularly big one into the bucket, he'd looked up to the man for approval. Laughing, the man had picked up the boy and stood, hugging him warmly. "Way to go, *mon petit ange*!" Probably the last time anyone referred to him as an angel. Burrowing his face into the man's neck, the boy smelled cigarettes and Old Spice.

To this day, Cage couldn't stand the scent of that aftershave, and he'd never smoked.

It had been his father, of course. A man Cage never, ever allowed himself to think about. The memories were too painful.

Cage shook his head and built an invisible wall around his thoughts, keeping out certain subjects and certain events. A defense mechanism he'd learned early on. But he realized in that moment before he shut down, as he swiped a tear from his eye, that it wasn't just Emelie that had kept him from returning to the bayou.

Taking a swig from his longneck, Cage tapped his pen on the notepad and thought instead about all that he needed to do. He began writing.

To-Do List:
1. Get rid of animals.
2. Clean yard.
3. Hire housecleaner and yard man.

His grandmother's house—a cottage, really—had only two bedrooms... and would require only a few hours a week to maintain, although a couple good full days at first. The windows hadn't been cleaned in ages. He usually wouldn't have noticed that kind of thing, but when he'd glanced out his bedroom window this morning to check on the weather, he'd thought there was fog, but it was only a film of dirt.

As for the yard, Belle's two boys were supposed to come out here on Saturday, day after tomorrow, and help him clean up all the crap and debris. He was going to borrow a pickup truck from one of Tante Lulu's nephews to haul the junk to the dump. He would have started already, but other jobs seemed to gain more priority, such as repairing the threshold on MawMaw's bedroom door; she'd complained about tripping over it. And the gate on the chicken coop needed to be fixed to keep the squawking critters confined. Then he'd spent hours trying to corral the birds. Boy oh boy! The guys back at the base would have had a laugh if they'd seen him chasing chickens. If he'd had a rifle handy, he would have shot every one of the blasted tail feathers. Only later did his grandmother tell him that, if he'd waited until dark, they would roost, and he could have used a flashlight and quick hands to gather them up.

4. Make a schedule of MawMaw's medical appointments.
5. Find a physical therapist to work on my knee while I'm in Louisiana.
6. See if MawMaw has a will, or any instructions for what happens when... well, eventually.

God, he hated thinking about details like that, but he had no idea if she wanted to be cremated, donate her body to science, or be buried next to PawPaw. One thing was for sure—come hell or high water, he was going to be here.

7. Ask MawMaw if she has a bucket list.

He had to smile at that. MawMaw would probably say she already had a bucket, thank you very much. But really, did she want to see the Grand Canyon? Go to the Grand Ol' Opry? Watch one last Mardi Gras parade? Jump out of an airplane like the older George Bush had?

Hell, who was he kidding? He knew what she wanted. A baby. And probably her only grandson happily married. Not necessarily in that order.

Which caused him to think of Emelie, of course, something he'd been avoiding ever since he left her place hours ago. There was an ache in his heart, like a stone, just picturing her.

Luckily, his cell phone rang just then.

"LeBlanc here."

"Hey, Cage, how you doing?" It was Commander MacLean.

"So-so."

"Your grandmother?"

"Stage four, lung cancer."

"Ah, man! I am so sorry."

"I talked to her oncologist this morning. She's refusing any more treatments. So it could be months, or even a year."

"We need to talk about that."

"Yeah. Listen, Commander, I have to stay with her. If it means giving up the teams to do that, I will."

"Now don't jump the gun. We'll work something out.

First off, you have six weeks' liberty coming to you. Not to mention medical leave."

He hoped that wouldn't be near enough time.

"You wouldn't be able to go active anyhow. You'd just be twiddling your thumbs here in the office or out training BUD/S."

Yeah, that's what I want. Training grunts.

"Maybe when you have things settled with your grandmother, you can go out on some short ops, then return there."

It would have to be in the early days. He assumed he would be needed nonstop toward the end. He hated thinking about practical things like that. Morbid, that was how it felt.

"How's your knee, by the way?"

"Okay. I'm going to line up a physical therapist here. I think there's a rehab center in Houma."

"This is what we're gonna do. You take care of what you have to there. I'll have my assistant or one of the guys from your team give you weekly updates on what's going on here. If there are materials you need to study, we'll send them. Do you have a secure computer there?"

"I have my laptop, but I might need some upgrades..."

"If you need help, I can send Geek." Geek was Darryl Good, a computer genius and one of his best buddies.

"That would be great. I'll let you know if I have a problem. At the least, I'll probably need Geek to walk me through some stuff."

After exchanging some news and laughing at his commander's version of what his wife, Hilda, and his kids had been up to lately, Cage pressed the off button and drank the rest of his beer. He could hear his grandmother moving around.

"Hey, darlin'," he said when he went inside. "How you feelin'?"

"Jist fine. You hungry?"

"As a bear." He noticed that she did look better, and she wasn't using oxygen at the moment. Instead, she was padding around the kitchen with ease in a pair of comfortable house slippers. But she didn't ask about his visit to her doctor; she knew what he'd learned today.

"I made your favorite." His grandmother squeezed his arm and walked over to the stove.

"I noticed."

"Didja call yer boss?"

He nodded. "He called me. I can stay here as long as I want. So you're stuck with me, baby."

Her face brightened before she swatted him with a dish towel. "I'll give ya 'baby'!" But then, she added, "I doan want ya ta think ya gotta babysit me here. You have a job ta do."

He patted his bum knee and said, "I can't go on active duty now anyhow."

She motioned for him to sit at the table and handed him a St. Jude paper napkin. A gift from Tante Lulu, he imagined. Once she'd served them both and sat across from him at the small table, she bowed her head and prayed, "Bless this food, Lord, and my grandson for sharin' it with me. Amen."

He was about to dig in when he heard a car pull onto the clamshell driveway at the side of the house. Before he had a chance to get up, he heard the car door slam, the sound of crunching shells, the animals setting up a ruckus, and a male voice swearing, "Holy shit! It's a damn zoo here." A pounding up the steps and across the porch, then knocking at the screen door and coming in at the same time was none other than his frickin' cousin.

"Bernard!" her grandmother exclaimed, leaning up for the bum-who-married-Cage's-girl to kiss her cheek.

"Aunt MaeMae! I was just drivin' by on my way home and thought I'd stop by to visit." She wasn't really his aunt. More like his grandmother and Cage's grandmother were third cousins.

"Just drivin' by on your way to Lafayette?" Cage asked incredulously. That was where Bernie's family home and business were located.

MawMaw *tsk*ed at Cage for his rude question.

And Bernie just ignored him.

"I heard my favorite aunt was feeling under the weather, and I brought you some flowers. My mother always said you can't go wrong with roses."

His favorite aunt, my ass! After all these years, the bastard shows up here, just when I'm here. Bernie is up to something.

All the time Bernie was speaking, his grandmother was putting the flowers in a mason jar with water, and Cage kept glaring at the bastard, who continued to ignore him. "Is that red beans and rice, Auntie? It smells like heaven. I haven't had good red beans and rice since my dear mother passed, bless her heart."

His *dear* mother had been a world-class bitch. Snooty. Country Club type. Never had anything to do with Cage's family. And now Bernie was showing up, like family? *I don't think so!*

"I declare, a lady cain't never have enough flowers," his grandmother, the traitor, was saying. "Sit yerself down, honey. I'll set you a plate."

Only after Bernie had dug in heartily did he turn to Cage. "I heard you were back in town, Justin. How're things goin'?" Bernie was as Cajun as Cage, but he sounded like a

Yankee academic. Which he very well was. Sort of. Having graduated from Princeton with high honors before taking over his dad's pyrotechnic business.

"Just dandy," Cage replied.

Bernie was no fool. He knew Cage was pissed at him. Still, he persisted, "Actually, I need to talk to you about something, cuz." Bernie's face was red as a beet, and he distractedly pushed his black pop-bottle glasses up farther on his nose.

Cage couldn't imagine what Bernie would have to discuss with him. And where did this chummy cuz crap come from? They were not close and never had been. Before Cage could control his fool tongue, he blurted out, "I hope it's not about your ex-wife."

"What?" Bernie appeared startled at the remark. "Oh. No." But then he paused. "Have you seen Em yet?"

Not that it was any of his business, but Cage admitted, "Yeah, I saw her this morning."

His grandmother gasped and put a hand to her heart. "Ya did?"

Now why would his grandmother have that reaction?

"Her dad's gonna have a shit fit," Bernie commented, then apologized for his language, "Sorry, Auntie."

The odd thing was that Bernie didn't appear surprised by Cage's answer or threatened in any way. Bernie just stared at Cage, and adjusted his slipping glasses again.

But then Cage remembered something. "By the way, MawMaw, Em said the strangest thing today. Did you and PawPaw refuse to give her my Navy address after I enlisted?"

"Um," his grandmother, who was never at a loss for words, said.

He cocked his head to the side, "Did you tell her that I ordered you not to give her my address?"

His grandmother and Bernie exchanged a meaningful glance. Meaningful to them, not him.

"Well, that I *can* answer. We never said *you* gave us orders," she said, and before he could question her further, she stood. "But remember, ya did tell us never ta mention her name again."

"That was after I heard about the wedding." He gave Bernie a disgusted look. "I got the distinct impression from Em that she was referring to some other time, like right after I left."

"Can we talk about this later? I need ta go get my oxygen," his grandmother said. "I'm feelin' kinda wheezy."

"Do you need my help?" Cage stood, too.

"No, no, you sit here and talk with yer cousin. Catch up on old times. I'll be back in a few minutes. Help yerselves to some of the Peachy Praline Cobbler Cake that Tante Lulu sent over."

Now he was confused. Maybe Em had been referring to that time after her wedding. But why would she have been trying to contact him then?

His grandmother didn't come right back and the silence in the room was deafening. He for damn sure wasn't in the mood for any friggin' cake or "catching up" with Bernie.

"What the hell is goin' on?" he asked Bernie, who was still scarfing down red beans and rice like an inmate's last meal on death row. "You weren't married to her for very long."

"Who?"

"Who the hell do you think? Been married that many times, have you?"

"Nope, only once," the idiot replied with a smile. Did he have any idea how close he was to having those glasses smashed into his face with a fist? "Six months. The ink hardly had time to dry on the marriage certificate." Bernie didn't appear at all shattered by his failed marriage.

Odder and odder!

"I never knew you had the hots for Em when we were in school," Cage mused. Bernie had been two years older than Cage and already in college when Cage had been boot-kicked out of Louisiana and into the Navy.

Bernie studied him for a minute, suddenly serious. "Guess I hid it well." Before Cage had a chance to ask Bernie how the marriage had come about, so soon after Cage had left, so soon after Em had claimed to love him, Bernie wiped his mouth with a St. Jude napkin and set it aside, leaning toward him. "Justin, I have a problem at Landry Pyrotechnics."

And I should give a rat's ass...why? "Pffff! The economy's bad all over."

"Not that kind of a problem. There are these guys who work for me on the assembly line. A couple of them are Arab or Iranian or something."

"Whoa! Today judgments about people based on their appearance or ethnicity will get you slapped with a racial discrimination suit quicker than you can say ACLU."

Bernie shook his head. "That's not what I meant. These guys, no matter the color of their skin, are kinda scary. Can you check them out for me?"

"Geez, Bern, I'm not a private investigator. And you don't investigate people just because they're 'scary.'" *Besides, dipshit, why should I do you any favors?*

"You're a Navy SEAL. I thought you SEALs cared about terrorists."

"Terrorists! Slow the train down here, Bern. You better explain that remark."

"This time of the year we hire dozens of part-timers

to prepare for the Mardi Gras Fireworks Extravaganza. At first, Muhammed and Abdul worked out fine on the assembly line. They're very proficient in English." Bernie helped himself to a big slice of cake and took several bites before continuing.

Cage was getting impatient.

"They're really smart guys. College educated, I think. Working at a minimum wage job?"

"Hey, I know lots of college grads who can't get work in their specialties today. They do whatever to earn a living. Think waitressing and Domino's delivery."

"Something is just off about them. The questions they ask. The way they keep to themselves. A few times they were in parts of the factory where they had no business being. I just have a gut feeling they're up to no good."

Alarm bells went off in Cage's head. Sometimes the best intel didn't amount to beans compared to a gut feeling. "Why don't you just fire them?"

"Without cause?"

"Have you thought about going to the police?"

"Are you kidding? *You* have trouble believing me without any evidence. What do you think the cops would say?"

"Look. Send me whatever info you have. Social security numbers. Addresses. Don't companies dealing with explosives have to do security checks?"

"Yeah, but not for line workers."

"Maybe they should."

Bernie shrugged. "I made copies of the employee files on these two," he added, pulling out some sheets that had been folded over and over to fit in his back pocket.

Cage arched his brows. "You were that confident that I would help you?"

"Just hopeful," Bernie said, and looked as if he might hug him.

Not in this lifetime! Cage stepped back and busied himself with putting their plates in the sink.

Once the awkward moment was over...awkward only for him, apparently...Bernie appeared ready to leave. "Should I go in and say good-bye to Aunt MaeMae?"

"No, I'll tell her you had to leave." Cage walked him to his car, to make up for his lack of a hug, he supposed. Bernie's vehicle was a late-model BMW, the kind worth about 75k new. The firecracker business must be good.

"I really do appreciate this," Bernie said.

And Cage ducked another hug. *Jeesh! What was with Bernie and the man hugs? Probably watched too much Dr. Phil, or something.* "Yeah, well, you can do something for me," Cage said with a grin, a sudden inspiration having come to him.

"Anything," Bernie said.

Cage reached down and picked up a kitten. Handing it to a startled Bernie, he said, "You look like a cat man to me."

"Hey, I already have a cat."

"See, I sensed that about you. And did you know, scientists claim all pets should come in pairs?"

"Bullshit!" Bernie tried to hand it back, but Cage folded his arms over his chest. Mumbling some swear words under his breath, Bernie stretched a fleece jacket over the leather backseat and set the mewling kitten on it. Immediately, the cat shifted around to get comfortable and fell asleep.

"A match made in heaven," Cage said.

"Or hell," Bernie grumbled through the open driver's door window. "And by the way, Cage." An evil grin came over Bernie's face now, and Cage was going to be hit with the proverbial "last word," he suspected. "You're wondering why Em and I got married...and divorced. Ask her."

Hah! Like she'd tell me anything. "It has nothing to do with me."

"Buddy, it has everything to do with you." On those mysterious words, Bernie backed up and drove away, leaving a fishtail of crushed shells and a befuddled Cage.

Eventually, Cage turned around, about to go back in the house, when he swore the St. Jude lawn statue winked at him.

&

And the plot thickens...

On Thursday night, Emelie had just showered and shampooed her hair, after a long but productive day and evening in her studio following her breakdown over the memento box. She was determined not to think about Justin anymore. He was a page from her past in a long-closed book, and that was all.

She was surprised to hear her phone ring at 10 p.m. The only one who called that late was Belle, but caller ID showed a number she didn't recognize. With a towel turban about her head, and a ratty old robe quickly wrapped around her body, she picked up the cell phone on her bedroom dresser.

"Hello."

"Em-el-ie?" a female voice with a rich Cajun accent inquired.

"Yes," she said tentatively.

"This is Mary Mae LeBlanc. How are ya, dear?"

At first, Emelie was confused, but then she gasped

softly. *Justin's grandmother? Why would she be calling me?* "Miss MaeMae?" she said. In the South, "Miss" was an appellation often attached to any older woman, a sign of respect.

"Yes."

Emelie wondered if she should mention that she'd heard about MaeMae's illness, but decided that was the kind of thing you only discussed if the other person brought it up first. "How are you, Miss MaeMae? It's been so long since I've seen you."

"I know. Do ya come back to Bayou Black ever?"

"Occasionally. My father still lives outside Houma. In fact, his seventieth birthday is on Saturday, and his friend Francine is planning a little lunch celebration." Emelie was rambling, nervous for some reason. Maybe she was afraid to learn why the old lady was calling.

"Well, that would be jist perfect. Do ya think ya could stop by that mornin' ta talk with me?"

What? No way! was her first reaction, immediately followed by, *She's ill. She has cancer, for heaven's sake. Can't I bend my pride just a little bit?*

Emelie's hesitation spoke volumes apparently, because Miss MaeMae said, "Justin will be gone fer a few hours that mornin'. He's goin' inta the hardware store fer shovels and rakes and bags. Belle Pitot and her boys are comin' over in the afternoon, ya know, ta help clear up the yard. I've let things go a little. Talk about! Anyways, I should be here alone fer a spell; so we kin have some private time." A long sigh followed, and heavy breathing, as if the old lady was having difficulty putting so many words together.

Emelie felt guilty, of course. Still, she persisted, "Are you sure we can't just talk over the phone?"

Miss MaeMae was equally persistent. "Some things are best said in person."

"I'd love to stop by and see you again," she conceded. "Will nine thirty be okay?"

"Wonderful!" As an afterthought, Miss MaeMae added, "Yer ex-husband, Bernard, was here today. Lovely boy!"

Huh? Bernie hardly knew Miss MaeMae. And he lived in Lafayette. What was he doing on Bayou Black and why this particular place to stop? "Why? Why was Bernie there?"

"He was jist passin' by, and I think he had some bizness ta discuss with Justin."

Business? Oh, this does not sound good.

After Emelie said good-bye and set her phone back on the dresser, Emelie put her face in her hands. She had a premonition of bad things to come. Why did it feel as if her life was spinning out of control?

⁂

There are itches, and then there are ITCHES...

"I got an itch," Tante Lulu said out of the blue to her niece, Charmaine, who was helping her prepare some casseroles and breads and desserts to be frozen and taken over to her friend MaeMae in her time of need. There would be enough to last a month.

"Do you want me to get some calamine lotion from your medicine cabinet? Do you have a rash, honey?" Charmaine asked as she leaned over Tante Lulu to check for rashes and practically split the seam in her jeans, which were plastered on her behind tighter'n white on rice. "I swear, Charmaine, those britches 're so tight I can see yer religion."

Charmine just grinned.

You had to admire a woman who was over forty and could still maintain her figure. *Like me*, Tante Lulu thought with a giggle.

"About the itch," Charmaine reminded her.

"Not that kinda itch, silly! An itch to matchmake." Tante Lulu fashioned herself the yenta of the bayou. She had more marriages under her belt than any of them high-falutin' Internet sites, that was for sure.

"Besides, if I had that other kinda itch, I'd know 'zackly what to do fer it, being a traiteur and all." For more years than Tante Lulu could count, she'd been the best folk healer hereabouts. Her pantry off the kitchen overflowed with herbs and ointments and potions that were a testament to that profession.

Charmaine straightened and grinned at her. "Who ya got in yer crosshairs now, Auntie?"

"That grandson of MaeMae's. Justin. I'm thinkin' I oughta be startin' on a hope chest fer him."

It was Tante Lulu's practice to make hope chests for the men in her family, more so than the women. And for male friends, as well. She filled them with crocheted bedspreads and doilies and such. And of course St. Jude items.

Charmaine groaned.

"What? You think he ain't ripe fer pluckin'?"

Grinning at her choice of words, Charmaine said, "And I suppose you have a woman in mind already."

"'Course I do. That gal he was head over hiney in love with back when he was a young'un."

"Emelie Gaudet? Oh, Lordy! Her father will be comin' after you with a shotgun."

"I ain't afraid of that ol' fart."

"Old" being relative, of course. Tante Lulu was considerably older than Claude Gaudet, the bull-headed former sheriff who'd run roughshod over some folks in the parish when he was ridin' his police car 'round like he was lord of the roost.

"Anyways, Auntie, what makes you think there's still a sizzle between those two?"

"Some sizzles never die out."

"Did you read that in a book?" Charmaine grinned at her.

Tante Lulu grinned right back. "Nah. I made it up. By the way, couldja use one of them midget horses back at yer ranch?"

"Huh?"

People were always accusing Tante Lulu of skipping from one subject to another like grease in a hot skillet, but really, to her, it made perfect sense to go from talking about Justin LeBlanc, to thinking about his grandmother, Mae-Mae, then remembering the small horse and all the other animals in the yard. She explained it all to Charmaine.

"Why didn't you say so to begin with?"

"I jist did." Lordy, some folks were thicker 'n roux.

Charmaine blinked her long lashes at her, then smiled. "Where should we start? With the matchmaking, I mean. Not the horse, though I suppose Rusty won't mind, and the kids will love it." She paused, "Oh, please God, you're not planning another Cajun Village People show, are you?"

Tante Lulu was known for persuading—okay, conning—her family members into putting on outrageous, but very entertaining, events, based loosely—very loosely—on the old Village People group. Usually they happened in the middle of one of her matchmaking plans. They all complained about them, but deep down, Tante Lulu suspected that they loved to participate.

"No. No Cajun People act. Leastways not yet." Tante Lulu pondered the possibilities, then said, "I already gave that LeBlanc boy a St. Jude statue. I'm thinkin' Miss Gaudet might be in need of one, too. Mebbe you and me need ta take a ride into N'awleans."

Charmaine shook her head and made some *tsk*ing noises at Tante Lulu, as if she was hopeless. Tante Lulu knew all about hopeless. Nothing was hopeless. She had it on good authority.

Chapter Eight

Oh, the webs we weave when first we practice to deceive...

Emelie arrived at Miss MaeMae's house on Bayou Black about nine thirty. To her relief, she saw no vehicles about. Except...Good Lord! Did they still have Priscilla? Oh, the memories that car evoked!

I will not go there! I will not go there! I will see what Miss MaeMae wants, then get the hell out of Dodge. Dodge being anywhere within fifty miles of Justin Le-Blanc, Emelie told herself and wiped her mind clean. "Clean" being the key word because what she'd done in that old car was far from "clean."

The next thing she noticed—and how could she not notice—was a virtual zoo in and around the old cottage. Belle had mentioned something about Miss MaeMae's rescue efforts having gotten out of hand, but no one could have prepared her for this mess. It was amazing that the animal control people hadn't stepped in, but then none of the animals appeared to be malnourished or abused in any way. God bless people like Miss MaeMae, and her husband before he died, being willing to rescue these abandoned creatures!

Emelie should feel guilty for not offering to help Belle and the boys clear this up today, but she didn't have the time. At least, that was the mental excuse she made. *Dodge*, she reminded herself.

She inched her way carefully up the steep back steps through the maze of barking, meowing, baaing, neighing, oinking cries for attention, and then eased around the child's rail. Just then, she noticed Miss MaeMae standing on the other side of the open wooden screen door.

"Em-el-ie! It does my heart good ta see ya, child!"

It had been almost seventeen years since she'd last seen Justin's grandmother, and the changes were dramatic. Not just aging, as in black hair turned to pure white, or wrinkles on a face that had been unusually smooth even when she'd been in her fifties. No, it was the short cap of curls indicative of a chemo patient, and the frailness of her tall frame. The clincher, of course, was the cannula in her nose and the portable oxygen tank on wheels at her side.

Justin must be dying inside, she thought. *Coming home to these changes, then getting blasted with such bad news from the doctor before arriving at my shop. And I was not sympathetic to him. Not nearly enough.*

The guilt that had been nagging at Emelie amped up tenfold. Yes, Miss MaeMae had turned her away when Justin left town abruptly, even rudely when Emelie had pestered her incessantly for his address. Still, Emelie had known this lady since her grandmother brought her for visits when she was a toddler. As Justin used to tease her, "I've seen you in diapers, babe."

Her MawMaw Gaudet would be so ashamed of her!

Miss MaeMae pulled the cannula from her nose and set it and her oxygen tank aside. Then she opened her arms wide to welcome Emelie into her home. For some reason, Emelie began to weep against the old lady's bony shoulders, which didn't feel bony at all, more like the cushioning comfort of a mothering woman.

Pulling apart finally, they laughed and dabbed at their eyes with napkins imprinted with, of all things, images of St. Jude, thanks to that infamous bayou traiteur Tante Lulu, Miss MaeMae explained with a laugh.

"Come, come, sit yerself down, *chère*," MawMaw encouraged Emelie, leading her to the kitchen. Without asking, she placed a cup of coffee in front of her with a sugar bowl and creamer.

"Don't you need your oxygen?" Emelie asked as she took a sip. It was delicious. Black, strong, and fresh, the way she liked it.

"I already gassed up," Miss MaeMae said with a laugh, referring to her oxygen. "I doan need it all the time. Yet."

"Yet" being such a sad word in this context. "I'm so sorry for your...illness."

"Thass what happens when ya get old. If it's not one thing, it's another." Miss MaeMae shrugged. "But I'm the one who's sorry, and thass why I asked ya ta come see me."

Emelie tilted her head in question.

"All those years ago, when ya asked for Justin's whereabouts...when ya wanted his address or phone number, I kept tellin' ya that we was ordered not to give them to ya."

"Oh, Miss MaeMae! There's no need to rehash all that now. It's long forgotten. I was a foolish girl harassing you folks so. Forgive me for being such a pest."

Miss MaeMae shook her head sadly. "There is every reason, child, and I'm the one needin' forgivin' . . . for lettin' ya think Justin did the orderin'. I know I dint say that precisely, but I knew what ya were thinkin' and I let ya."

Emelie flinched. Of course Justin had done the ordering. He was the one who'd wanted to cut off ties with her. Yes, her father had pushed him to enlist in the Navy, but it was Justin who'd used that as an excuse to break up with her.

Wasn't it?

"All these years, it's been eatin' away at me, knowin' I cain't go to my Maker with that on my conscience. Then, when Justin mentioned the other day that he'd been talkin' to ya, well, I knew the time was now."

"If Justin didn't order . . ." Understanding began to seep into Emelie's brain, along with a pain that was almost unbearable. "What did my father do?"

"The details doan matter. Jist know it weren't Justin."

"I need to know. What did my father do?"

Miss MaeMae inhaled sharply, then exhaled on a sigh of resignation. "Yer father came here with Mr. Thompson from the bank. The loan was overdue on my husband Rufus's shrimp boat, and without the boat, we had no money comin' in. 'Til the day he died, Rufus felt shamed that he'd chosen money over honesty." Miss MaeMae raised her hands helplessly.

Again! Another of my father's betrayals! How many more are there that I don't know about? I forgave him for threatening Justin with statutory rape, but this . . . to do that to innocent folks?

Miss MaeMae reached across the table and took one of Emelie's cold hands in hers. "Can ya forgive me?"

"Of course," Emelie said without hesitation. "You did what anyone would. You were given no choice."

"We had a choice," Miss MaeMae insisted.

"A Solomon's choice," Emelie insisted.

"Do you still love my grandson?" Miss MaeMae asked of a sudden.

"What? Of course not. But that's beside the point."

"Ya gotta forgive yer father then."

What her not loving Justin and forgiving her father had to do with each other was beyond Emelie's understanding. "I don't think I can." Something occurred to her then. "Does Justin know about this?"

Miss MaeMae shook her head. "Not yet."

"No, no! You can't tell him. Justin doesn't care about me after all this time," *if he ever did*, "but it would crush him to find out how you'd been threatened. He's under a lot of stress right now. Please don't add to it to ease your conscience." She took Miss MaeMae's thin hands into hers. "Most important, don't think for one minute that Justin won't go after my father with fists or a gun. You don't need to have Justin arrested at this stage."

"Oh, dear one, how can I not tell him?"

"For him. You have to spare him."

"You're right. I'm being selfish, placing the burden of this secret on you, and him, to ease my conscience."

Emelie squeezed the old lady's bony hands gently. "No. You did the right thing in telling me. But not Justin."

"Ya do care fer him," Miss MaeMae concluded, not with happiness, but sadness, because she had to know as well as Emelie that things were even more hopeless than before.

Emelie stood suddenly and started for the door. "I'm sorry but I can't stay. I'll come back another day."

"But ya haven't finished yer coffee. Besides, there's somethin' else."

Oh, God! How much more can I take? Emelie turned

and saw the old lady walking slowly toward one of the bedrooms. "I'll be right back." When she returned, she handed Emelie a pile of letters tied together with butcher's string. Emelie knew before she studied them what they were. All the letters she'd written to Justin during those first months after he'd left, letters she'd given to his grandparents, begging them to forward them to Justin. And she'd assumed he'd chosen not to respond.

"Now do ya see why I feel so bad? I doan wanna go to my Maker with my only grandson hatin' me." Tears filled Miss MaeMae's rheumy eyes.

"Oh, sweetie, Justin could never hate you. Never! But you are not to worry. I'll burn these when I get home. He'll never know."

She and Miss MaeMae exchanged sad looks. There was nothing more to be said.

Emelie staggered outside and down the steps. When she got to the driveway, she leaned against her van and bawled.

So many lies. So many misunderstandings. Choices made and paths taken that could never be reversed.

It took me years to recover from the pain seventeen years ago. How will I ever survive now?

One thing was for sure. She was not going to be singing "Happy Birthday" to her father today.

⚘

The best-laid plans of mice and tempting women . . .

Cage arrived back to the cottage earlier than expected, having avoided a trip to the hardware store, for the time being anyway.

When he'd gotten to Remy LeDeux's house to borrow his pickup truck, Remy had also lent him a wheel-barrow, rakes, shovels, a lawn mower, a weed whacker, and a leaf blower. He'd even given him some heavy-duty landscaping bags he'd bought at a surplus store and never used.

Cage was surprised to see a van parked in the drive-way. A van with the E & B Designs logo on it. Belle and her sons must have come earlier than they'd planned.

But then he saw a woman leaning against the van on the other side. A woman who was crying as if her heart were breaking. Emelie? What was she doing here? And why so upset?

His adrenaline kicked in. There could be only one reason why Em would be outside his grandmother's house, crying hysterically. Something must have happened to MawMaw. *Oh, God, please don't let her be dead.*

"Em? What's wrong? Is it MawMaw?"

She shook her head, staring up at him with wet, leak-ing eyes; a red, dripping nose; and parted lips. Clutched to her chest was a packet of letters.

But he couldn't question her about the letters...yet. She was in too fragile a state, sobbing once again, gut-tural words that made no sense between moans of dismay. "Again. He did it again. I didn't know. Oh, God, I didn't know! But I should have known."

"Who? Who did it?" Not that he knew what "it" was, but if it made Em cry, he was going to knock out *his* lights.

"Nobody," she cried.

Yeah, right. Nobody made her leak like a sieve. He acted instinctively and yanked her into his arms. At first she resisted, but then she spooned into his body and bur-ied her face in his neck. For a moment, he felt light-headed with the pure joy of holding Em again. Didn't matter if she came into his arms for comfort, or something else. It felt so damn good.

He rubbed his hands over her shoulders and back, relearning her shape, crooning soft words to her. "Shh. It's okay. Just let it out, and then we'll talk about it later. Okay, darlin'?"

She nodded into his neck and soon her sobs turned into whimpers.

Leaning back against the van and spreading his legs so she could fit into the cradle of his hips, Cage realized something in that moment. He had never stopped loving Emelie. He kissed the top of her head...she still used that lemon-scented shampoo...then he kissed her chin and the knuckles that continued to hold the packet of letters in a death grip. Pulling a handkerchief out of his back pocket, he used it to wipe the tears off her face and made her blow her nose hard.

Then he framed her head with trembling fingers that combed into both sides of her hair, and he really kissed her. With all the love and yearning he'd built up over the years. Suppressed emotions exploded in him, emotions he hadn't even known he'd been suppressing, not this late in the game anyhow. He was out of control.

Then, *Thank you God*, she was out of control, too. Somewhere along the way she'd dropped the letters to the ground and wrapped her arms around his neck, kissing him back with equal fervor.

There was a roaring in his ears, and his mind went blank. His body zapped into sensory overload with each of her soft caresses to his neck and shoulders, with the arching of her body against his, with the opening of her mouth to his deep kisses.

At one point his palms had landed on her butt and he raised her against his erection. Sweet! Sweet agony!

Women had two surefire weapons when it came to men. Sex and tears. Cage was being assaulted by both of them, and he welcomed the attack, even if he would be bullet-ridden in the end.

At this moment, as he feasted on the woman in his arms, there were no jagged splinters of past betrayals, no dark shadows of regret, no questions of what might have been, or could be. No anger. Not even a Toby Keith cynical message of "How Do You Like Me Now?" which he had to admit he'd harbored on occasion in the past. Just the now. And now was glorious.

MawMaw was probably watching them through the kitchen window, but he didn't care. This was the girl he loved and she was back in his arms. Nothing was going to stop him now.

Except something did.

The slamming of car doors.

"Yoo-hoo!" someone yelled, and it wasn't Belle and her boys. It was that Cajun wackjob Tante Lulu, with pink hair that matched a pink T-shirt proclaiming I MAY BE OLD, BUT THERE ARE PARTS OF ME THAT STILL ZING. With her grinning niece Charmaine in a hoochie-mama, leopard print catsuit. Noticing the direction of his stare, Tante Lulu remarked, "I know. I tol' her ta be careful. That getup's so tight, folks will see the dimples in her butt."

"I do not have dimples in my butt," Charmaine insisted with a laugh.

Cage pressed his forehead against Em's, praying that his hard-on wouldn't be evident. Em moaned; she had a few things to hide, too, like her nipples under the thin silk shirt she wore, tucked into a pair of denims.

"We came to help," Charmaine said, smacking him on

the butt as she passed by, carrying a box overflowing with plastic containers of food.

"Jist in time, by the looks of things," Tante Lulu remarked. She was also carrying food. Looked like one of those lidded cake carriers. "Best I hurry up with your hope chest, boy. Guar-an-teed!"

Tante Lulu had mentioned a hope chest to him back in Coronado. He hadn't understood then any more than he did now, and he wasn't sure he wanted to.

Charmaine's husband, Rusty, pulled up then with a small horse trailer. Apparently, he was going to take the midget horse off their hands.

"Are you sure you can't use a pig, a sheep, and a few chickens?" Cage asked him.

"Don't push your luck, boy," Rusty replied, a scowl on his face.

Apparently, a midget horse for the ranch hadn't been his idea.

Two of Remy's teenagers, a boy and a girl, were carrying a long folding table, along with a CD player.

With perfect timing, Belle and her boys arrived. The boys were carrying a huge cooler between them. For drinks? He hoped there was beer. Or whiskey. Belle grinned knowingly at them and said, "I thought you were going to Francine's for your father's birthday."

"I changed my mind," Em answered with more vehemence than the question warranted.

Belle just arched her brows. "Maybe you can make some sweet tea then. Yours is so much better than mine." With those words, Belle was gone, and they were alone again.

Tante Lulu ambled by again, giving him a wink, and came back with another armload of food. This time a basket of breads and rolls. "We's gonna have us a *fais do do*."

"A party? A party down the bayou?" he translated incredulously.

"I thought Belle and the boys were going to help Justin clean the yard today," Emelie remarked.

"The more the merrier! Yep. A work party." Tante Lulu beamed at them and waddled to the back of the house.

A stunned Emelie looked up at him. Cage was surprised she hadn't attempted to bolt. Or smacked him silly. He imagined she soon would if he didn't take matters into his own hands. But actually, once company started to arrive, he'd taken one of Em's hands in his, the one not clutching the letters again, and he held on tightly. She wasn't going anywhere until he was ready.

"Em, please stay. We need to talk."

At the same time, she said, "This was a mistake. My fault. I was feeling weepy, and... well, I wasn't myself."

He thought she was very much herself, unlike the cool woman he'd met in her shop days ago. "It was not a mistake. It was the first right thing that has happened in days. Why were you crying?"

She shook her head and tried to disentangle her hand, but he was having none of that. "I'm just stressed out over all the work I have to do for Mardi Gras, and then seeing Miss MaeMae like this, well... I imploded."

Buuuullllll shit! He cocked his head to the side. "Why are you here?"

"Miss MaeMae asked me to... I mean, I was passing by and thought I'd stop by to visit."

"Lots of passing by going on here lately," he observed, thinking of Bernie. "Em, you always were a lousy liar. Your nose turns red."

"That's because I was crying, you fool."

He leaned down to give her a quick kiss on the nose

to show he didn't care. She was here; that was all that mattered.

But then, even more visitors arrived. The most suprising visitors of all—Geek and JAM, two of his SEAL teammates—and they were driving Cage's red Jeep Cherokee, which they honked repeatedly to announce their arrival.

"What the hell?" he said when they walked up with wide grins on their suntanned faces. Geek was sporting whitewalls—a high and tight—but JAM's long hair was tied back at the neck with a leather thong. They both wore sunglasses, white T-shirts, cargo shorts, and flip-flops. They probably thought going to the bayou was like going to the beach.

The two men explained that they had a few days of liberty coming and decided to bring him his vehicle. Plus, Geek had an already secure computer for him.

Cage's heart swelled with pride and a deep thankfulness for the friendship that would bring them all this way. And he knew what had prompted the trip. Forget cars and computers. They were here to offer support for him and his dying grandmother.

"F.U. wanted to come, too, but we figured the South wasn't ready for such a shock," JAM said with a grin, showing pure white teeth against his dark skin. Frank Uxley was the type of soldier you wanted at your back in combat, and really, he was a primo demolition/explosives expert, but he was the most obnoxious man Cage had ever met, and that was saying a lot in the military.

"Thanks for coming, guys," he said in an emotion-husky voice. Then he belatedly introduced Em to the two men, who were eyeing her with way too much interest. "Guys, this is an Emelie Gaudet, an old...friend of mine. And, Em, this is Jacob Alvarez Mendozo, or JAM.

And this other goofball is Darryl Good, better known as Geek."

"JAM? Geek?"

"All the SEALs are given nicknames. Mine is Cage . . . for Cajun," he explained.

Em was gawking at his friends like they were eye candy. SEALs had that effect on some women.

"So she's the one, huh?" JAM said, looking pointedly at his hand, which was still entwined with Em's.

"The one what?" He actually felt himself blush.

"True love, dumbbell," Geek said. "The one that got away. The Cajun sweetheart. Soul mate. The bitch that ripped your heart out. Yada, yada, yada."

"I never mentioned any woman," he protested.

"You didn't have to. We knew," JAM replied and winked at Em. Cage did not like that wink. At all.

The two idiots waggled their eyebrows at him, then had the good sense to walk toward the backyard, where music was already playing, "Knock, Knock, Knock," a rowdy Cajun song about a man being in the doghouse again. And much laughter could be heard, along with the sound of a machine being powered up. Probably the weed whacker.

"I've got to go," Em insisted, finally pulling her hand free.

But then she soon found out that she had to stay after all. Her van was blocked in by five other vehicles.

"Did you plan this?" she asked, hands on hips, eyeing Cage suspiciously.

"Of course not." He glanced around and came up with the best answer he could under short notice. "St. Jude planned it all."

That might even be true. Tante Lulu was "in the house," after all.

Cajuns will use any excuse to have a party...

Despite herself, Emelie was having a good time. The best time she'd had in ages.

New Orleans was only sixty miles from bayou country, but it felt like six hundred sometimes. Emelie tended to forget her Cajun roots when living in the upscale Creole city. It was hard to forget them here today.

The camaraderie that filled the clearing behind the stilted cottage was pure Cajun. Friendly, teasing, open-hearted, close-knit, fun-loving. Even the visiting Navy SEALs were made to feel welcome...honorary Cajuns, according to Tante Lulu, who had her eye on the one called JAM for one of her hope chest enterprises. He clearly had his eyes on Belle, who had her eye on him for an entirely different kind of enterprise. Of course, Justin was first in line for a hope chest, Tante Lulu was quick to assure him, much to his dismay.

Miss MaeMae was sitting on the back porch in a cushioned chair, enjoying the whole spectacle, clapping to the music, answering questions about where she wanted this or that placed. She'd only had to go inside once to take a short nap.

Emelie went up to sit with her for a while, as had just about everyone at one time or another during that day.

"Are you all right, sweetheart?" Miss MaeMae asked her, knowing the condition she'd been in when she fled earlier.

"Honestly, I don't think I'll ever be all right. Well, that's too dramatic. This, too, will pass, as they say, but it's going to take a while for me to understand and forgive my father. It was evil, what he did to you."

"I forgave him long ago, child."

Emelie didn't want to ruin the old lady's day with all this gloom and doom. So she scanned the yard, where everyone was working industriously. Already there was a huge difference from what she'd seen on arriving here hours ago. "Aren't people wonderful?" she remarked.

"Yes. I have so much to be thankful for. Especially..." She choked up looking toward Justin, who was standing with his two SEAL buddies, talking and laughing, occasionally jabbing each other in the arm.

Tante Lulu joined them then, huffing and puffing up the steps. "Lawd a mercy! You should get one of them elevator thingees, MaeMae. The kind where you sit down and it scoots you up the steps, faster 'n spit."

"I'll think about it," Miss MaeMae said, but they all knew she wouldn't. It wouldn't make sense with the time she had left.

"Get me a sweet tea with ice, will you, hon?" Tante Lulu said to Emelie, easing her little butt down into an Adirondack chair.

Inside the cozy cottage, Emelie was greeted by the singing of canaries and the squawking of exotic birds. When she peered closer at one brilliantly colored one, it said, clear as day, "Hoo-yah!" And the voice was identical to Justin's. She had to smile. At least he wasn't teaching it obscene words. Yet.

Emelie had spent so much time in this cottage over the years, until Justin left. Whereas her father would have had a hissy fit if Justin had even dared step over their threshold, she'd been welcome here. And it didn't seem to have changed at all.

Thinking about her father made her realize they would be celebrating his birthday about now. She didn't feel guilty at all about her absence. As soon as she'd decided to stay—or had been forced to stay—she'd called Francine's number and left a brief voice mail. "Can't come today. Sorry. Will talk later." Then she'd turned her cell phone off and left it in the van.

She delivered the iced sweet teas to Tante Lulu and Miss MaeMae. The two women were totally engrossed in some reminiscence about Tante Lulu's fiancé, who had apparently been Miss MaeMae's brother. He'd died during World War II. Then Emelie went back to the yard, where JAM motioned her over to help unwind a tangled mess of hoses under the porch. Tante Lulu had told her that he'd studied for the priesthood at one time, something she'd learned after a spirited discussion about St. Jude.

"Have you known Justin long?" Emelie asked.

"We were in BUD/S together. Geek was in the same class."

At her raised brows, he explained, "Basic Underwater Demoliton/SEALs. The training program for SEALs."

"It's hard to picture Justin as a special forces guy. I mean, it must take all kinds of discipline."

"A wild one, was he?"

"The wildest."

"He's a great soldier. The best. I would trust him with my life. I don't suppose he's told you how many medals of valor he has?"

"He hasn't told me anything." She thought for a minute. "Is that why he's limping? Did he get injured in some battle?"

JAM laughed. "Nah. He just landed the wrong way on a high-altitude jump."

She put a hand over her heart. "He jumps out of airplanes?"

"Sweetheart, that's the least dangerous thing he does."

At the concern on her face, he asked, "Why'd you let him get away?"

"I didn't leave him. He left me."

"Are you sure about that?"

"Absolutely."

"Hmmm." They worked in silence for a few minutes before JAM asked, "By the way, where's Cage's brother, Phillipe?"

"Huh? Justin doesn't have any brothers. He had an uncle Phillipe who died during World War II. Phillipe Prudhomme was engaged to Tante Lulu before his death."

"Yeah, we know who Phillipe Prudhomme was. One of the early Navy SEALs."

"What? I didn't know SEALs were around back then."

"Well, the precursors of SEALs. Frogmen, they were called." They both paused again, taking in all this new information. Then JAM continued, "I could swear Cage told us about his brother who hated catfish and his MawMaw—that's what he calls his grandmother—giving him this hokey proverb-type advice that ended up with him loving catfish, but all the catfish were gone."

She shook her head, equally baffled. "Why would Justin tell you he had a brother?"

JAM laughed. "*Pfff!* Cage is always making up these crazy-ass stories about his grandmother and life on the bayou. The ultimate joker! We don't believe half of his wild tales."

"Are we talking about the same person?" Maybe Justin had changed over the years. Hah! Who was she kidding? He'd definitely changed.

They finished rolling up three hoses and tossing two in the trash.

Back in the yard, the men and teenagers were just about done bagging up all the animal poop. So she joined Charmaine and Belle in setting out massive amounts of food and drinks on several folding tables around the hard-packed dirt clearing. The animals had done a job, literally, on what had been a lawn at one time leading down to the bayou, but Justin would have to wait until springtime to have the area roto-tilled and seeded. Would he still be here by then? God, she hoped so, for Miss MaeMae's sake, because that would mean she was still alive.

Additional pens were built for some of the animals—a potbellied pig, a sheep, a goat, and a dog. During the following week, they all agreed to try to find homes for these abandoned animals. And no, Emelie had insisted, she was not interested in a potbellied pig. Nor the monster dog, which kept sidling up and staring with different-colored doleful eyes at her. A cat, maybe. That dog, no. Not even if it did have silky fur once Max and Mike had shampooed it under a hose and brushed its tangled hair. Not even if everyone said it would make a good burglar deterrent for a single woman living alone. Still, she was the one to give the dog a name. Thaddeus.

Tante Lulu let out a whoop of pleasure when she heard. "Didja know thass St. Jude's second name? St. Jude of Thaddeus. It's an omen, I declare."

An omen of what? Emelie wondered but wasn't about to say aloud. Tante Lulu had been making too many hints about her and Justin. Speaking of whom, she and the scoundrel, who'd somehow managed to get her to stay here, were acutely aware of each other the whole day. Even when he wasn't touching her shoulder in passing, or brushing a strand of hair out of her eyes when she was mixing another pitcher of sweet tea, he was always watching her, his heavy-lidded eyes following her every movement. And she watched him, too, which sometimes caused the edge of his mouth to quirk into the lopsided grin she had once loved.

"Haul your sweet self over here, hon," Justin said at one point near the end of the afternoon and led her to a two-seater wooden swing that hung from the limb of an oak tree down by the water. Mike and Max had painted it red that afternoon, half of the fast-drying paint going on their T-shirts and jeans. The boys were having a good time, competing with each other for the attention of Remy's daughter, who was a mere two years older than them.

"You're being awful bossy with me," Emelie complained, but allowed herself to be pushed down into the swing. She hadn't realized how tired she was and leaned back, closing her eyes for a moment. As Justin lifted one arm over the back of the swing, she smelled the deodorant or soap he'd used that morning. Something piney, like Irish Spring. And either the swing was smaller than she'd thought or else Justin was taking up more room than needed because his thigh and hip and chest were aligned tightly against her.

"Thanks for stayin', Em," he said. "I appreciate it, and I know my grandmother does, too."

"She looked good today, didn't she?"

He nodded. "She's happy. It's my goal to bring her as many of those happy moments as I can." His voice cracked on the end, and she squeezed his thigh to show she understood.

"You could do that up higher if you want," he said, his wicked Cajun eyes dancing with mischief.

She jerked her hand away. "What kind of things will you do to make her happy?"

"Hah! The only thing she wants is... well, never mind." He grimaced, then said, "She's a simple woman. She really doesn't want much. Nothing that money can buy anyhow."

"You," Emelie guessed. "You being here is probably what makes her happiest."

He nodded and twirled a strand of her hair around one finger of the hand lying over her shoulder. Disconcerted, she ignored his finger and asked, "How long will you be able to stay?"

"As long as it takes."

She arched her brows. "Can you stay as long as... well, indefinitely?"

"I will, even if I have to quit the teams, but it probably won't come to that. I've got liberty and medical leave coming. After that, I can probably go out on short missions if there were someone to stay with my grandmother until I return."

"I would do that."

He tilted his head in surprise. She thought he would ask her why she would volunteer, considering their history, but she beat him to the punch. "My grandmother was a friend of Miss MaeMae, as you know. And don't bring up that 'I've seen you in diapers, babe' nonsense."

He raised both hands in surrender as if the thought had never occurred to him. But he grinned companionably and returned his arm to her shoulders.

"Anyhow, my grandmother would be the first one here."

"So you would do it for your grandmother?"

She shook her head. "I'm not saying it right. I was thinking a little while ago about how easily I've forgotten my Cajun roots. Being here today reminded me how wonderfully giving the Cajun culture is. Everyone is family. You help those in need, without being asked."

Justin nodded. "Same thing for me. The guys all call me Cage back in Coronado, short for Cajun, but it's only back here on the bayou that I'm reminded of exactly what it means to be Cajun. Wanna dance?"

"Huh?" She looked up to see several couples dancing a lively Cajun two-step to "Diggy Diggy Lou." Max and Remy's daughter. Charmaine and Rusty, who was one absolutely gorgeous man, cover model material, with his cowboy shirt and hat. He was a rancher, after all. Rusty did not look too happy to be dancing, unlike most Cajun men, who had a dance gene in their makeup. JAM was with Belle, who beamed her way and mouthed, "Wow!" Even Tante Lulu was dancing with Mike, who had to bend over to meet her diminutive height.

"Do you remember the time you danced the shrimp?" she asked Justin suddenly as he pulled her up from the swing.

"I remember the time *we* danced the shrimp," he said, tugging her close into a tight embrace. He whispered against her ear, and his breath caused tingles to ripple to all the erotic spots in her body. "I remember a lot of things." Then he twirled her under his arm.

Justin liked to dance, obviously, as evidenced by his skill as well as his intermittent smiles and sometimes bursts of laughter. He danced around her. He came up behind her and brushed her behind in a suggestive way. When she turned to reprimand him, he swung her into a dizzying spin that forced her to hold on to his shoulders tightly. She laughed then.

Emelie liked to dance, too, but she couldn't remember the last time she'd let loose so freely. Music was in her soul, of course, and many a time when she sang at the club, she watched couples dancing and envied them. Unfortunately, there had been no man in her life for a long time. And Bernie, when they'd been together, had exhibited the smoothness of a moose on the dance floor.

The next song on the CD player was slower. "Louisiana Man." Most of the other couples had exerted themselves on the fast dances so much that they gave up now and went over to the refreshment table for drinks. Beer or the sweet tea, which Emelie had, in fact, made several times so far.

Not Justin, though. He seemed to be on an adrenaline high as he tugged her close with both arms around her waist and lifted her arms to wrap around his shoulders. "At last," he said, smiling down at her.

Oooh, she was in dangerous territory. Justin's smiles were deadly. He turned serious then. As they swayed from side to side, he stared down at her. The expression on his face could only be described as hungry.

"Don't look at me like that, Justin."

"How?"

"Like we're going to start something up again. We're not."

He didn't say anything, just smoldered down at her... and maybe tugged her a little bit closer. Or maybe she'd moved closer on her own.

"I mean it, Justin. Stop smoldering at me."

He laughed then. "I do not smolder."

"Oh, you smolder all right," she said teasingly.

"So maybe my smolder should ignite your spark."

"Oh, please! Light my fire? That's a little dated, don't you think?"

"Are you trying to say I'm not smooth? I'll have

you know, I'm known as the king of smooth back at Coronado."

"I don't doubt that for a minute. And that's my point, by the way. I'm here. You're in California. The twain are not going to meet, buddy."

"Twain? I can think of another word for it." He laughed.

"Seriously, do you plan on staying here in Louisiana? For good?"

"Hell, no! I have a job."

"Exactly. Don't think for one minute that I'm going to have a one-night stand, or two, with you, then stand by when you dump me again."

"I never *dumped* you."

She waved a hand dismissively. "That's all water under the bridge. We're not going to rehash old history. *And*"— she glared at him—"we are not going to repeat old history either. As in, no sex."

He grinned. "That was blunt."

"Are we on the same page here, Justin?"

"Not even close," he said, and yanked her forward so far a gnat couldn't fit between them. His teeth nipped at the curve of her neck before he repeated, "Not even close."

Just then Belle rushed up to them. "Em, it's Francine. When she wasn't able to get you on your cell, she called me."

Emelie could guess why she was calling. Daddy Dearest was missing her at his birthday bash. Big frickin' deal! "Tell her I'm busy."

"It's an emergency, Em," Belle insisted.

She and Justin stopped dancing and Belle handed her the phone.

"Hello."

"Thank God, Emelie! Listen, your father had a heart attack. We're on the way to the hospital."

Emelie slapped a hand over her own suddenly racing heart. "Is it bad?"

"We won't know until we get there. He's awake, though, and asking for you."

Despite her hard feelings for her father, she said, "I'll be there within a half hour."

"Say a prayer, honey," Francine concluded.

Emelie told Justin and Belle what she'd been told. She was already rushing toward the house to say her good-bye to Miss MaeMae and grab her handbag.

"I'll go with you," Justin offered.

"Are you crazy? One look at you, and my father will have another heart attack."

Justin shrugged, an admission that she was right. Justin LeBlanc was the last person her father would want at his bedside.

"I'm okay going myself. The hospital is in Houma."

Thus it was that her day, which had started with a shock on visiting with Miss MaeMae, was ending with a shock. She shuddered to think what would come next.

When she was about to back the van out of the driveway after several people moved their vehicles, Justin said to her through the open window, "We're not done yet, *chère.*"

She knew better.

Chapter Nine

There are benefits to some friendships...

Emelie was nuts if she thought he'd let her go to the hospital alone to face God only knew what. So he jumped in his Jeep and followed her.

She was already in the emergency room of Terrebonne General Medical Center, asking a nurse for information about her father. Her voice was shaky and her skin was pale as a ghost when the nurse told her that her father was in surgery, an urgent bypass, but she could wait in the intensive care lounge for news. It would probably be at least three hours before he was in recovery.

"Em?" Cage said when he came up behind her and put a hand on her shoulder.

She jerked with surprise, gave him a glower, but then squeezed his hand. "Thanks for coming, but I really don't think—"

"I'll stay out of the way," he interrupted. "Your father will never know I'm in the building. I'm here for you, babe."

"Are you family?" the stern-faced nurse asked Cage.

"Yes," he answered quickly.

"No," Em said at the same time.

The nurse folded her arms over her chest.

"We're engaged," Cage lied. Where that one had come from, he had no idea, but Em was not amused. "Practically family," he told the nurse with a grin. Before the nurse could ask any further questions, he took Em by the hand and led her away.

"You're outrageous," she said.

"I know."

But then tears filled her eyes. "My father's never had any heart issues before. He always claimed to be healthy as a horse. What if he dies?"

"He's not gonna die, Em," *though he probably deserves to, the old bastard*, "Your dad's a tough old bird." *A buzzard, if you ask me.*

"I'm so angry with him over . . . well, things he's done. How can I still love him and worry over him when I don't like him?"

"That's life, sweetheart. What's he done now?"

"I can't talk about it."

It was no skin off his nose, but the old fart must have really screwed up this time. "No problem. It has nothing to do with me."

"Actually . . ." she began, looking as if she might argue the point, but then nodded.

There was a story here, but she was in too fragile a condition to be pressed.

He tucked her into his side, and they walked toward the elevators. When they got to the visitors' lounge, an attractive older woman was there. He soon realized that it was Francine Lagasse, whom Emelie introduced as her father's longtime friend. Francine appeared to have been crying and still held a wad of wet tissues in her hand.

"What happened?" Em wanted to know.

"We were having lunch…the birthday lunch. When you didn't come and you didn't come, and the praline ice cream cake I made with his favorite frosting began to melt, your father got more and more agitated. He guessed that you might be with 'that LeBlanc loser.' Sorry." She gave Cage an apologetic shrug.

He shrugged back. He knew how the old man felt about him seventeen years ago. No big surprise that he wasn't forming a fan club for him now.

"Then when I got your text message that you wouldn't be coming," Francine continued, "your father went into a rage. Before I knew what was happening, he was bent over, complaining of chest pains."

Oddly, Em didn't appear guilty over her failure to attend her father's birthday lunch. She was concerned, though. "Have you spoken with the doctors?"

Francine nodded. "We got here in the ambulance about three hours ago. I kept trying your cell phone but got no answer. After an examination in the emergency room, a heart specialist was called in. It wasn't a major heart attack, but your father has a blockage that could prove fatal in the future if not corrected. So they decided to operate right away."

"Why don't I go down to the coffee shop?" Cage suggested. "Give you two a chance to talk."

Em nodded her thanks to him.

When he was about to purchase three coffees, he noticed the woman standing in line before him. "Adele?" he asked.

"Justin!"

He hadn't seen Adele Hebert since high school, but she hadn't changed all that much with her flaming red hair and six-foot-tall frame. They hugged, though they hadn't been close friends back then.

He noticed she was wearing a white medical-type jacket with a name label: DR. ADELE HEBERT.

"Whoa! Look at you," he said. "A doctor?"

She nodded. "Physical therapist."

"Now that's synchronicity." He grinned and told her how he was in need of a good physical therapy program.

Then she smacked him on the shoulder playfully. "And how 'bout you, *cher*? I hear you're a Navy SEAL now. Talk about!"

Guys in the teams didn't advertise their jobs. In fact, they kept a pretty low profile. But there were no secrets on the bayou grapevine.

"Yep. Lieutenant, second grade. A lifer."

"Well, you always were wild. Guess special forces kind of work can be wild sometimes, too."

"Sometimes," he agreed. "Other times it's as boring as any other job."

"And you live in California?"

He nodded. "Coronado."

"What are you doing back in Louisiana?"

He explained about his grandmother's cancer.

"I'm so sorry. Is she here at the hospital?"

"No. I came in with Emelie Gaudet. Her father had a heart attack."

"Ah," she said. "You two are a couple again."

He hesitated. "Nah. Just friends."

She glanced at his ringless finger. "You're not married?"

"Nope. Never have been." He pointed to her badge. "Hebert. So you never married either?"

"Actually I did, but it didn't work out. Luckily I kept my maiden name."

"Listen, give me your card and I'll set up an appointment for therapy. I've got to get back into a regular routine."

"I don't have any cards with me. They're in my office. I'll bring one up to the lounge in a bit. And maybe I can get some inside info on Claude Gaudet for you."

"Thanks a lot."

Adele squeezed his arm. "It was good meeting you again, Justin."

"Likewise," he said, and knew instinctively that he could hook up with her if he was so inclined. She was a very attractive woman. A few years under the belt, just like him, but sexy as hell. Unfortunately, he was not inclined. Maybe JAM or Geek would be interested.

When he got back to the lounge with a cardboard container of three coffees, Emelie was alone, Francine having gone off to the ladies' room.

"Have you heard anything?" he asked her.

"Not a thing." She took one of the coffees and sipped at it with a sigh of appreciation.

He drank from his cup, too, and it wasn't all that bad, for hospital coffee. "So is Francine the same woman your dad was dating way back when? A schoolteacher, I think."

She nodded. "She retired a few years ago, as did my dad."

So he'd still been the sheriff for most of those seventeen years. "And he hasn't made an honest woman of her yet."

"Francine is divorced. A marriage when she was very young. You know my dad, Catholic to the core." She shrugged.

"I didn't think they were still so strict about those things today."

"Some are. And yes, I know what you're thinking. A warped set of morals that has my father refusing to marry a divorced woman, but doing the kind of things he's done to . . . you, among others."

What others? he wanted to ask, but Francine had returned and was grateful for coffee and the caffeine she claimed to need. Soon after that, Adele came in and he introduced her to Em and Francine.

Em looked from him to Adele and back again before saying, "Nice to see you again. I was sorry to hear that your mother died last year."

"Thanks. It was a shock. A car accident."

And Francine said, "I taught you in first grade, didn't I?"

Adele laughed. "Yes. I can't believe you remember that."

"Hard to forget your pretty red hair. You wore it in pig-tails, though, as I recall."

Adele told them that her father was in recovery, and that the physician would be here soon to talk with them. Just before leaving, Adele handed him her card and said, "Call me."

A silence followed. When he glanced up, he saw Em staring at him with arched brows.

"What?"

"You and Adele Hebert?"

"She's going to hook me up with physical therapy for my knee," he said.

"Hooking up is about right."

He loved the fact that Em was jealous. That *was* jealousy sparking in her eyes, wasn't it?

The doctor came in then, wearing green surgical pants and shirt and cap, booties still on his shoes. He scarcely looked old enough to drive a car, let alone perform a heart operation. How was it doctors were getting younger and younger? Maybe Cage was just getting older.

Dr. Dumaine, who turned out to be thirty-five years old, told them that the operation was a success. If Claude exercised and changed his diet and avoided stress, he could live a long, normal life.

"Stress?" Em said weakly.

"Well, at least during the beginning stages of recovery. He'll be in the hospital for observation and therapy, but if he progresses as we expect, he could go home in a week."

"Can we see him?" Francine asked.

"In about an hour. Once he wakes, they'll bring him up to the intensive care ward."

"Thank you so much," Emelie and Francine both said, each shaking the doctor's hand.

The doctor leaned over and shook Cage's hand, too. "A Navy SEAL, huh? Adele told me about you."

Small world!

Emelie was back to glowering at the mention of Adele. A good sign, in Cage's opinion.

"I appreciate you being here, Justin. More than you can know. But I think you should go now."

He agreed. What Claude Gaudet didn't need was the bane of his life standing at the foot of his hospital bed, shocking him into another heart attack.

Em walked him to the elevator and said, choosing her words carefully, "It was nice of you to be here today for me, as a friend, but that's all you and I can ever be. Don't be offended."

"Offended? Who's offended?" He yanked her into his

arms and kissed her like a bloody maniac with open lips
and teeth and tongue until she moaned. Only then did he
lean back and say, "See ya, *friend*."

A young orderly, who came up and pressed one of the
elevator buttons, grinned and winked at Em. "Can I be
your friend, too?"

"Over my dead body," Cage muttered and entered the
elevator after the chuckling young man.

Em was still there staring at him, dazed, as the doors
closed.

Hoo-yah! Cage thought and gave the orderly a high five.

&

Home is where the heart is, for sure...

Mary Mae LeBlanc sat at her kitchen table early that evening, a small computer, of all things, sitting before her.
Alone, except for Justin's computer genius friend over
there sleeping on the couch in front of the television—
Who was babysitting who? she wondered with a smile—
just waiting for her grandson to return from the hospital.

What a day it had been! Like old times on the bayou...
when everyone pitched in to help.

She should have been exhausted, dead on her feet.
Inwardly she laughed at her choice of words. She'd be
just that soon enough. Death didn't scare her. In fact, she
welcomed it. She could hardly wait to meet her Maker.
Just not yet. Too much unfinished business. Still, she wondered, was her husband, Rufus, up there preparing a place
for her already? She liked to think so. And her boy, Beau,
Justin's daddy? *Please, God, let Beau be up there.* He'd
been a good boy at heart.

She couldn't think about Beau now, or the tragic turn his life had taken after meeting Marie, Justin's mother, and her addiction. Not that they'd called it that then. Could she and Rufus have done a better job guiding Beau? Maybe. It broke her heart to think they were at fault for all that happened.

Her heart ached and her breath turned wheezy when she thought of the suffering in Beau's short life, mostly due to that lost wife of his. And lost she had been, whether in the bottle at a young age or later in a needle. Mary Mae didn't like to remember the last time she'd seen the once pretty Marie. Pitiful! Pretty no more by the time she died.

Mary Mae's mind seemed to be racing tonight. So many images.

Even after taking a nap this afternoon, she'd needed to take a pain pill. And she'd been sucking up oxygen like it was manna from heaven. Maybe it was. The blasted disease was growing throughout her body; she could practically feel it. Her clock was ticking away. So far she'd been able to hide its progress from Justin, but she knew there would come a time when he would see with his own eyes how bad off she was becoming. She would spare him that if she could.

She ought to make a list. "Things to Do Before I Die." Oh, not a bucket list like folks on the television talked about. She had no wish to go jumping out of an airplane like an idiot or climbing some high mountain, just to get to the top, or dancing a jig, though she wouldn't mind one more Cajun two-step. No, hers would be a "taking care of business" list. And no, she wouldn't be making her list on this machine in front of her that Justin's friend Darryl—she refused to call any man Geek—had set up for her. She could write faster with a pad and pencil. She could make a mental list for now.

—Give Justin my will and explain my wishes.

A copy of the will was in the office of Tante Lulu's nephew Lucien LeDeux, a Houma lawyer, along with some important papers, such as insurance, bankbooks, burial plots.

—Make arrangements with Father Matthew at Our Lady of the Bayou Church about last rites.

None of this waiting until the last minute for her, when she would be tied up to machines or unconscious with drugs. She wanted a priest to pray over her when she was still aware of what he was saying. Would they do that? She wasn't sure. Betcha Tante Lulu would know.

—Ask Tante Lulu about the Church's stand on extreme unction for the living.

—Don't sell the house.

She shouldn't put that kind of pressure on her grandson, but deep down, she sensed that Justin would need this place someday. A place to come back to. In fact, deep down, she wished he would stay now, but that was unrealistic, him having a job in California and all.

With all her heart, she wished she could see Justin here, with a family. A woman to love, who loved him, and children. Oh, how she would have loved to hold Justin's baby! But that was not to be. Like so many things. "If wishes were kisses..." like Rufus used to tell her before giving her a bunch of little kisses to make up for some hurt or other.

—Care for the animals.

Well, that job was mostly done today, with the good folks spending the day building pens and runs, and a few of them even taking some of the animals home as pets. Remy's teen-aged children had taken a cat and a potbellied pig. The pig caused an argument with their father, but their father lost.

Charmaine's husband, Rusty Lanier—*Lordy, was there ever a handsomer man in all the world!*—carried off the midget horse, and Charmaine knew a neighbor up in Northern Louisiana who raised sheep; so that annoying baaing beast was gone. For some reason, Mary Mae never could cozy up to a sheep.

Belle Pitot had a friend who might take the chickens, but Mary Mae didn't want to give them all up...yet. There was nothing like fresh eggs, whether for breakfast or in a cake. A far cry, for sure, from those ones in the supermarket that were weeks away from having been anywhere near a laying hen's butt.

There were two small dogs, one of which Belle's sons begged her to adopt. She was thinking on it. And everyone kept saying that the big dog, Thaddeus, had taken a special liking to Emelie, though Emelie was resisting. Time would tell.

And speaking of liking...that Navy buddy of Justin's—the dark one from Mexico or Spain or something—sure did like Belle. She'd heard him making a date with her. And that was another odd thing in her life that was becoming odder by the minute. He had studied to be a priest at one time, a Jesuit. Maybe he was the one she should be asking about last rites for the living. JAM, his nickname was, which struck Mary Mae as silly. Good thing he didn't become a priest. Imagine his congregation calling him Father Jam? She giggled at the image, and realized that she hadn't giggled for ages. Weren't giggles wonderful little gifts from God?

Back to the animals.

Justin and his friends had taken a liking to the squawky birds here inside the house. Even if they didn't take them across the country to their homes, apparently these noisy feathered friends wouldn't be hard to unload, them being expensive pets. A thousand dollars for a bird? She couldn't imagine. Their departure wouldn't be too soon for Mary Mae, especially since Justin, and now his friends, were teaching them naughty words.

—Finally, she needed to have a sit-down, serious talk with Justin about his daddy. There was so much her grandson didn't know, had refused to know, but it was important before she passed that Mary Mae give him all the missing pieces, even the ones he might not like to hear.

She heard a car pull into the driveway. The slamming of a car door. The crunching of boots on crushed shells. A few animal sounds, mostly the three dogs. Then a stomping over the porch and through the screen door. It must be Justin.

Tears welled in her eyes, and her heart swelled with sheer joy.

Even before he announced, "I'm home," she thought, *He's home.*

✍

Some gifts cost no money...

It was good to be home.

Not just good to be back in Louisiana after all these years, but good to come back to the welcoming atmosphere of his grandmother's house after hours spent in that dismal hospital waiting room.

But then he took in the setting. His grandmother was sitting at the kitchen table, puffing away on her oxygen with a small notebook computer in front of her. MawMaw wouldn't know a cursor from a curser. At least she never had before.

Then there was Geek, popping his head up, like a gopher in that old movie classic *Caddyshack*, from where he'd been lying on the sofa, in front of the television. He'd been having a little catnap, so to speak, if the cat sprawled out over his chest was any indication. Carefully Geek lifted the cat off him so its claws wouldn't do bodily injury and stood, stretching with a wide-open yawn.

"Where is everyone?" Justin asked, coming up to give his grandmother a kiss on the cheek.

"All gone home, 'ceptin fer Darryl here, who was baby-sittin' me."

Justin glanced meaningfully at the couch; Geek just grinned. But then SEALs were trained to sleep on a dime and wake on a rustle as soft as a feather. If his grandmother had hiccoughed, he would have shot off that couch like a bullet.

"And what's with the computer? You gonna turn inta some kinda Bill Gates or somethin'?"

"Yer friend was kind enuf ta teach me ta play Internet poker," she explained.

Justin laughed and gave Geek a pretend scowl. "Turnin' my sweet grandmother into a gambler?"

"Hey, she was the one who hustled me into a card game, but then she couldn't find any cards."

"A likely story!"

"I'm only playin' fer nickels."

"You really are gamblin'? Holy shit! I mean, holy crawfish!"

The two men exchanged grins at his cleaning up his language for her.

"How is Emelie's father?" MawMaw asked.

"He'll survive. The bad ones always do."

"Tsk-tsk-tsk!" she clucked her tongue. " You shouldn't talk lak that."

"Sorry," he said, but he didn't look one bit sorry. He knew for damn sure the old man would be bleeding his condition for all it was worth, making Em kowtow to his every wish. Just like old times. "He had a mild heart attack, but on examination they discovered a blockage that could prove fatal. So they went in and did an emergency bypass. He's in recovery now."

"All that in one afternoon?" she asked.

"My grandfather had a bypass and was playing golf the following week. Heart surgery isn't the big deal it used to be," Geek told them before walking off to the bathroom.

"But Emelie stayed at the hospital with her father?" MawMaw wondered. "I mean, she dint seem ta want to be with her father t'day, even on his birthday."

Yeah, and that was another puzzle in a myriad of puzzles that Cage needed to solve before he left the bayou. "She stayed, along with Francine Lagasse, Claude's girlfriend. Em isn't too happy with her dad for some reason—hell, Claude always gives a person reason to hate his guts—but when somethin' like this happens, I guess past grievances prove unimportant."

"If you only knew . . ." he thought he heard his grandmother murmur.

"What?"

She waved a hand dismissively. "So ya think all will be forgiven?"

"I have no idea." Justin stared, suddenly suspicious of her interest in a man no one particularly loved, except maybe Em and Francine.

"Are ya hungry?" she asked. "We got lots of leftovers."

"Any of that red beans and rice you made on Monday?"

"Plenty," she said with a smile. "There ain't nothin' does a grandmother's heart more proud than havin' her family like her cookin'."

"You should be real proud, then."

"I am," she said, standing and patting him on the shoulder. "I am so proud of you."

And that meant everything in the world to him. A gift, really. Too bad it had taken seventeen years of absence and his grandmother's illness to bring him to that realization.

Chapter Ten

Baby, please stay...

Y ou look like ten miles of bad bayou road, girl," Belle said when she came into the shop, carrying a completed ball gown in a clear plastic E & B garment carrier. "I swear, your bags have got bags."

"Thanks for sharing that," Emelie said from behind the counter, where she was boxing up two new masks to be picked up by customers that morning.

She wasn't at all offended by Belle's comment. She knew how bad she looked. When she'd brushed her teeth this morning, she'd noticed the dark circles under her eyes and tried her best to cover them with makeup. To no avail, apparently.

It was ten days since her father's heart attack and three weeks until Mardi Gras. The weather had turned chilly... well, chilly for Louisiana, the mid-fifties and wet. A perfect backdrop to her dreary mood.

She *had* to work every day, but she went back to the

bayou every evening, at first to the hospital in Houma and then to her father's house on the outskirts, once he'd been discharged. If prizes were given for impossible patients, her father would be covered with blue ribbons. He didn't want to stay in the hospital. He didn't like being in the first-floor bedroom at home. The food was too hot, or too cold. No, he didn't bloody damn need help going to the bathroom. *Where's the newspaper? The pills are too big, or too small, or bitter. What would it hurt to have one cigar and one little glass of bourbon?* And forget about special diets.

She had to sing at Ella's tonight, and boy, did her dad raise a stink about that. "I never shoulda let you take those music lessons."

"You made me stop when I was fourteen."

"Shoulda never started. A low-down dive is no place for a girl like you," he'd complained.

"Ella's is not a dive. It's a very nice supper club."

"I never did care for that Ella Pisano. My mother spent way too much time with her when I was growin' up."

Blah, blah, blah! She'd heard it all before. Frankly, her grandfather had been a grouch, and Emelie could understand why MawMaw Gaudet would have preferred the company of her friend Ella, who led a more independent, happy life. At some point her father was going to have to accept that Emelie wasn't a girl anymore.

Further complicating her present stress levels was the fact that her father refused at-home nursing and he needed to start physical therapy. Francine was running herself ragged trying to please him, and Emelie was burning the candle at both ends...soon to be burned out. Top that all off with the tension of having to suppress an over-whelming urge to confront her father with the news she'd heard on his birthday of how he'd threatened Justin's grandparents.

And then there was Justin himself. She was still attracted, maybe even still in love with him, God forbid! And she knew why he was calling. Pretty it up any way he would, the bottom line was that he wanted to get laid, and she had to nip that temptation in the bud. At some point, whether it was a month from now or twelve months from now, he would be leaving. Again. She didn't think she could survive the pain. Again.

"Justin called me last night," Belle said as if reading her mind. "Says he's sick of your answering machine messages. If you won't talk to him, he's going to come over here and carry you out over his shoulder to a quiet place where you can...talk." Belle grinned on relaying the message.

"So how's your jelly buddy...JAM?" Emelie had become adept at changing the subject.

"You know what they say about Navy SEALs?"

"I have no idea what they say about Navy SEALs."

"Great endurance."

What did that mean? She wasn't going to ask. No way!

Of course, Belle told her anyway. "Staying power, baby."

Emelie rolled her eyes at her friend, knowing she was just trying to lift her mood, but instead she would be having Emelie wondering if Justin had "staying power," too. But then Belle asked, "How's your dad doing?"

"Medically he seems okay. But Francine needs help in caring for him, and he needs to start physical therapy, but he doesn't want to leave the house. Same old, same old."

"Maybe you need to do what's best for him, regardless of what he wants."

"That's what Francine and I decided last night after he had a hissy fit over us wanting him to come to the kitchen to eat, instead of having a tray in his bedroom. I wonder if we couldn't get a therapist to come to the house at first."

"Surely there must be folks who do that," Belle said. "After all, some people can't get up and travel to outside facilities."

After Belle went through to her work area, Emelie tried to decide whom to call about arranging therapy. His heart specialist? The physical therapy centers mentioned on the brochure that Francine had in a packet from the hospital? She didn't want to burden Francine with one more thing. Wait. How about Adele Hebert? She was a physical therapist.

Before giving herself a chance to second-guess herself, Emelie called information for the hospital and put in a call. "Could I please be connected with Adele Hebert?" she asked.

"Dr. Hebert is over at the therapy center this morning," the receptionist said.

Doctor, huh? Emelie was about to give her name and number and ask for a call back, but the woman continued, "I'll transfer your call."

Within seconds, she heard, "Adele Hebert here."

"Adele...I mean, Dr. Hebert...this is Emelie Gaudet. We talked at the hospital a week or so ago when my father had a heart attack."

"Oh, yes, I remember. What a coincidence! Justin is here right now."

Oh, that is just great. I'm calling Justin's new girl-friend. How awkward is that?

"How's your father doing?" Adele asked.

"Not so good. That's why I'm calling. I mean, he seems

to have come through the operation fine, but he's resisting any exercise, at all. Walking to the bathroom is the most we can get him to do."

"That's not unusual. Heart patients fear a recurring attack, and therefore avoid the least amount of activity, thinking it will trigger more trauma. In fact, exercise is what they need—with proper diet, of course."

"Well, what I was wondering, and really, I shouldn't have bothered you, is—"

"Please don't apologize. I'm glad to help. And really, any friend of Justin's is a friend of mine."

I don't think so! "Do you know of any therapists who could come to the house initially?"

"Of course. Give me the address and telephone number, and I'll send someone over tomorrow."

Emelie gave her Francine's name and number as a contact person and thanked her profusely for her help.

"My pleasure. I hear you are quite the artist, designing beautiful masks."

Where did you hear that? Could it have been Justin? She felt an inordinate pleasure at that thought. Which was pathetic, considering that Adele had no doubt heard about her work from someone in Houma. "Yes, I've been designing masks for some time, and then five years ago, Belle Pitot and I opened a shop together here in the Quarter. Do you know Belle?"

"Yes, she dated my older brother at one time."

Among many others, Emelie thought, but not in a mean way. Belle had been very popular in high school.

"I'd love to stop by sometime," Adele said.

"I'd love to have you, but not right now. This is my busiest season, at a time when my father needs me, too."

"Don't let him manipulate you. Some patients do that

to family members, and before you know it, they're in the hospital themselves."

"Bingo!"

Adele laughed and said, "Do you want to talk with Justin before we hang up?"

Oh, my God, no! "Uh, not right now. Gotta go. Someone just came into the shop. Thanks again, Dr. Hebert. You're a lifesaver."

"Adele," Dr. Hebert said.

"Bye-bye, Adele." She clicked off.

Emelie let out a long breath she hadn't realized she was holding. That was just great. Now she would be picturing Justin with Adele. And imagining his staying power *with her.*

❧

He wasn't the only one singing the blues...

On Saturday morning, a half-dozen members of Our Lady of the Bayou Church Rosary Society arrived to pray with his grandmother. Cage considered that his cue to leave.

It wasn't a death vigil or anything morbid like that. Apparently, until her illness, MawMaw had belonged to the society and met with the group once a week at the church to say the rosary together for special intentions and then socialize afterward. The women had brought enough food to socialize for a week.

"Are you sure you'll be okay, MawMaw?" he asked.

"Go," she said, practically pushing him out the door. "Yer makin' me nervous, hoverin' all the time." She eyed him with a mischievous grin. "Unless ya want ta stay an' pray with us."

He left. And now he was driving his Jeep onto the crushed shell driveway of Tante Lulu's little cottage, where JAM and Geek had been staying for the past ten days. His buddies would have been long gone by now, except that Bernie's suspicions about a few of his employees had proven well founded. In fact, several more team members might very well be needed before this operation was completed.

Right off, he saw Tante Lulu on her back porch tossing little bits of orange snack food to a monster gator named Useless.

"I really don't think you should be standin' so close to that animal," he said, not for the first time.

"Oh, he's harmless as a peckerless man in a brothel, as long as a body is feedin' him Cheez Doodles."

Did she really say that word? Is it even a word? "Peckerless"? "And when the Cheez Doodles run out?"

"Run like crazy, I s'pose." She grinned at him. Not one bit frightened, even when Useless let out a loud bellow of impatience that pretty much translated to, *Hurry up or I'll bite your fool head off.*

He reached into the bag of Cheez Doodles and grabbed a huge handful, pitching them farther into the yard, past the St. Jude birdbath. Once the animal turned and began to lumber away toward the treats, he headed toward the door, almost knocking his head on the St. Jude wind chimes. The porch rockers were covered with cushions imprinted with images of…what else? St. Jude. And there was a St. Jude doormat, too. As if a visitor didn't get the message that the saint of hopeless cases ruled here!

Tante Lulu was dressed fairly normal today, probably because of the cool weather, in blue jeans, which had probably been purchased in the children's department of Walmart, a Ragin' Cajun sweatshirt, also child size, and white sneakers. Of course, she wore a blond Farrah Fawcett–style wig and enough makeup to plaster a wall.

"I really appreciate your puttin' up the guys for so long," he said. "I still say that they can stay in a motel somewhere nearby if you're being inconvenienced."

"There ain't no motels nearby what serve good food. Besides, I enjoy havin' company."

"Where are they now?"

"In the kitchen. Computin'. Never saw so much computin' or talkin' on cell phones in all mah life."

Welcome to the twenty-first century, honey. Have you been to the mall lately? Every other person has a phone glued to his or her ear. Silence is no longer golden. Gotta talk 24/7.

"'Course, Jacob goes off ta N'awleans on occasion ta court Belle..."

I hardly think "court" is the right word to use.

"But Darryl jist keeps on computin'. I'm beginnin' ta wonder if he ain't visitin' some of them porno places."

"Why don't you ask him?"

"I did, and he tol' me that you know all the best ones."

Well, I guess I deserved that.

"I wouldn't mind checkin' one out, if they had a man what looked like Richard Simmons. Ooh, boy, he could shake his bootie at me anytime. A bootie is a hiney, in case you didn't know."

"I know what a bootie is."

"Some folks still think a bootie is a knitted baby shoe; so it wouldn't be awful if you dint know."

She really thought he didn't know what a bootie was. *I would go nuts if I had to live with this dingbat.*

"By the by..." They'd just stepped into the kitchen

when Tante Lulu finished her babbling by asking Cage, "How's your lovemakin' comin' along?"

His mouth dropped open, but JAM and Geek both grinned, already used to the old lady's popcorn brain and blunt questions.

"Uh, well," he stammered, "I haven't had much time for sex lately."

"What?" she practically squawked. "I dint mean sex, you idjet. I meant the thunderbolt of love and your path ta wedded bliss. You cain't jist sit on your tushie and wait fer love ta come, y'know."

Whoa! "Honestly, there's been a lot of rain lately, but not a single thunderbolt that I could hear."

"Then you ain't listenin'. Mebbe you need another St. Jude statue."

"Maybe," he said, just to halt the conversation.

But that didn't stop the old broad. "You 'spectin' Emelie ta wait fer you forever?"

"Seems ta me, Em never did much waitin' for me. She got married, you know."

"Pfff!" She waved a hand airily. "You mus' be thicker 'n a bayou stump."

What was that supposed to mean? He was tired of people hinting at mysteries that he should understand, but didn't.

"Besides, you cain't 'spect Emelie to be jist sittin' with open arms while you're already tomcattin' after other wimmen."

"I beg your pardon."

JAM and Geek were rolling their eyes, barely suppressing chuckles, and generally enjoying his discomfort.

"Adele Hebert ring any of yer dumb bells?"

"What does Adele Hebert have ta do with anything?"

He couldn't believe he was actually arguing with this bayou dingbat. "She's my physical therapist."

"Does Emelie know that?"

"How would Emelie even hear about me and Adele Hebert, not that there's anything to hear?"

"Aintcha ever heard of the bayou grapevine? Better 'n any cell phone fer communicatin'." She gave Geek a pointed look as he stared at his computer screen...and snickered.

Cage sank down into a kitchen chair and put his face in his hands.

Luckily, the old lady was already off on another tangent. "Charmaine's comin' ta take me grocery shoppin'. There's plenty a food ta hold you over 'til I get back." She placed a St. Jude mug of black coffee in front of him. A printer sat on an appliance stand and a fax machine whirred beside the microwave, but between the two laptops on the table were platters of boudin sausages, scrambled eggs, fried green tomatoes, homemade jellies, buttered toast, and fresh-baked biscuits. On the stove, shrimp gumbo simmered away in a huge cast-iron pot. Wide-eyed with wonder, he turned to JAM and Geek.

"I've gained five pounds this week," JAM said proudly.

"We ran six miles this morning, instead of our usual five," Geek told him.

Cage was eating well himself with MawMaw's fine cooking, although they still had a lot of food left over from the cleanup party.

"How's MaeMae doin'?" Tante Lulu asked with that uncanny ability to sense what a person was thinking.

"Good and bad days. Sometimes she needs the oxygen continuously just to breathe. Other times she can go without it for short periods." He'd even caught her smoking out on the porch a few times, but it was hard to cut her off completely when smoking was one of the few pleasures she still had. As long as she didn't do it near her oxygen tank. "Today the church ladies have come ta pray the rosary together."

"Thass the best thing. Prayer." She turned to JAM then. "You should start a prayer group here, jist fer family and friends."

Cage wondered what her family would think of that idea.

"I keep telling her that I'm not a priest," JAM said to Cage.

"Same as. Almost," Tante Lulu concluded. "Lessen you be doin' somethin' unpriestly with Belle."

JAM's face turned red.

Geek let out a whoop of laughter.

"Doan you be settin' yerself up as a saint, boy. I heard 'bout that invention of yours." Tante Lulu wagged a forefinger at Geek. "Charmaine tol' me it's jist like that warm wax hand massager in her spa, 'ceptin' it's used on men down below."

Now, it was Geek's turn to blush. Geek was making tons of money as an inventor, selling goods from his website, www.penileglove.com. Enough said!

And speaking of Charmaine. In walked the self-proclaimed bimbo with class, Charmaine LeDeux-Lanier. In keeping with her image, she wore an outfit that matched Tante Lulu's...their going-to-Piggly-Wiggly-Supermarket attire, he supposed. Except that Charmaine's jeans were painted on, her Ragin' Cajun T-shirt was two sizes too small, and instead of sneakers she wore high-heeled red shoes. Her black hair was teased to high heaven, her eyelashes could fan a little wind of their own, and her lips were shiny with sexy red gloss. Lordy, Lordy!

He and JAM and Geek exchanged looks...and grinned. Really, a guy couldn't help but look when a woman like Charmaine walked in the room.

She winked, knowing exactly what effect she had on men. "You ready, hon?" she asked her aunt.

"Yep. You boys gonna be all right while I'm gone?"

They all nodded, still transfixed by the bayou sexpot.

"While I'm gone, you kin do all yer secret SEAL bizness with the house empty. No need ta be whisperin' lak I'm some All Cado spy or sumpin'."

"She means al-Qaeda," Charmaine translated.

"Thass what I said." Tante Lulu slapped her niece with a St. Jude towel, then folded it to hang from the oven handle. "If the phone rings, doan answer. It's prob'ly someone needin' my folk healin' services. They kin jist leave a message. Or else it's that Jeremy Chevaux wantin' a date. The ol' fart's lookin' fer a love connection ever since he discovered Vi-ag-ra."

On those words, Charmaine steered her aunt toward the door, making sure the old lady took her purse with her. Think fake leather, purple saddlebag the size of... let's say...a Buick.

Navy SEALs had pretty much seen and heard it all, but Cage and JAM and Geek were shocked by Tante Lulu's insinuation that she might be getting it on with some old coot. The picture would be imprinted on his brain forever.

"Do you think she's serious?" Cage asked when he managed to click his jaw shut.

"Probably. You won't believe some of the stuff she comes out with," JAM said. "And she seems to think I've got some connections with St. Jude, like a personal pipeline up to heaven."

"She's got a heart as big as the heavens, though," Geek

pointed out. "I never met anyone so generous, and I've gotta tell you, she is an accomplished folk healer. I've been helping her collate all her recipes and potions into a computer file. She could write a book, especially with the stories she has to tell about the different herbs she uses and the folks she's used them on. Apparently several people have tried to help her organize them in the past, but something more important always comes up. She claims that she's been approached by publishers, and I believe her."

"I'm not surprised," Cage said. "Tante Lulu has been a legend on the bayou for as long as I can remember." He helped himself to a platter of sausage, eggs, and toast, even though he'd already had breakfast, before saying, "Okay. Down to business. What's new with the pyrotechnics plant?"

"Well, Geek and I are going to start work there tomorrow. I'll be on the assembly line, and Geek'll be the new accountant."

"It's not just the two fellows Bernie suspected at first," Geek elaborated, tapping away at his laptop. "There are at least five inside the plant, including a truck driver." Geek turned his laptop so that Cage could see photos of the five men in question.

"There's a woman in Lafayette who rented them a three-bedroom apartment six months ago. They're all living there."

"Al-Qaeda?"

"We think so," Geek said. "Or least some al-Qaeda cell."

"I think they're planning something around Mardi Gras," JAM said.

"It makes sense, you know," Cage said as he wolfed

down the food, which was incredibly good. "Explosives, fireworks. Real bombs, cherry bombs. Things that go boom, and things that make a lesser boom."

"I'm going to rent an apartment in the same building today. In fact, two of them," Geek informed Cage. "That way there'll be room for K-4, Magnusson, and Slick when they get here, and we'll be better able to set up our satellite equipment in a secure location. Bernie said we could use his house, but it's best we're not linked to the boss."

Cage nodded. "Any decision on informing local police or FBI?" Cage asked.

"That's up to CentCom. Should know more this afternoon," JAM said.

"Tante Lulu has a nephew in the Lafayette Police Department. He used to work in Fontaine, but he transferred to Lafayette last year," Cage told them. "Maybe we could start with him without attracting any special attention."

"Good idea. I'll mention it to the commander when I talk to him."

"What do you want me to do? I can come to Lafayette as needed, but I don't want to leave my grandmother for any long periods."

"We understand that. The main thing we need from you is a calming hand with your cousin Bernie. He's a basket case, and we're afraid he's going to blow our cover if he doesn't calm down."

"First off, Bernie isn't really my cousin. Our grandmothers were like second or third cousins or something. Second, I don't like the bastard. Third, I'll do whatever I can. He's comin' here today, isn't he?"

"Yep. Should be here any minute," Geek said. "On another subject..." Geek pulled out a folded newspaper from under a pile of documents and pointed to a large ad. The newspaper was a New Orleans weekly, and the page in question was from the entertainment section. The ad was for Ella's supper club in the French Quarter, featuring Italian-Cajun food, whatever that was, and jazz/blues music. "I didn't know your girlfriend was a singer."

"Huh?" Peering closer, Cage saw the itinerary for the week, various singing acts and bands. The Saturday night headliner was blues singer Emelie Gaudet. He guessed that made sense. Emelie always did have musical talent, as well as artistic talent, as evidenced by her Mardi Gras masks. She'd even taken voice lessons at one time. *Well, well, well*, he thought. *She might be able to ignore my phone calls, but she for damn sure won't ignore me when I'm sitting front row center.*

"I assume by the shit-eating grin on your face that you're going clubbing tonight," JAM remarked.

"You bet your ass I am. *If* I can find a babysitter for my grandmother." He looked at Geek.

"Only if I can raise the ante on our poker games to a quarter," Geek said with a grin.

"Buddy, you can raise it to a dollar if you make it a sleepover."

Geek and JAM both said, "Hoo-yah!"

Chapter Eleven

Stormy weather on the horizon…

Emelie was about to begin her first set at Ella's.

She adjusted the spaghetti straps of her black silk sheath dress to cover some of her overexposed cleavage and tugged the hem over her ample hips, down to mid-thigh. The dress accentuated her small waist, her best asset, in her own opinion, though men's eyes homed in on those other, more obvious parts. Her glittery silver stiletto heels matched the dangly silver earrings and the glittery combs that held her hair, a mass of curls tonight, off her face, which was heavily made up to cover the shadows under her eyes.

Normally she looked forward to performing, but tonight she had butterflies. She was off her game; she could just feel it.

The three-piece house band—piano, guitar, and trumpet players—had been on for the past half hour. Now Ella stepped out onto the little stage, more like a raised dais in the corner, and said, "Ladies and gentlemen, please give a N'awleans welcome our very own Emelie Gaudet."

There was a full house tonight, which meant twenty tables of up to eighty people total, and they welcomed Emelie with resounding applause. She was a favorite of some of them. In fact, the nightspot was popular because it served meals during the entertainment in the old style, which some people still appreciated.

She walked over to the mic and said, "Hello, everyone. Welcome to the Crescent City and to Ella's. I think my first song is appropriate, considering all the rain we've had lately." Then she eased with a low alto range, accompanied only by the piano, into that old Lena Horne song "Stormy Weather." Funny thing, Emelie didn't have a husky voice in normal conversation, but when she sang, it came out that way.

Once she began to sing, Emelie relaxed. All her troubles disappeared. Stress melted away. There was only her and the music. She was taken back to her MawMaw Gaudet's parlor in her little house next door to theirs outside Houma. Clear as day, she recalled her grandmother singing along with all the old blues singers playing on the record player. Etta James, Bessie Smith, Nina Simone, Billie Holiday, Lena Horne, Ella Fitzgerald. She especially remembered Billie Holiday wailing out, "God Bless the Child."

Some people likened the clear tones of Emelie's voice to a combination of Norah Jones and Alicia Keys. Quite a compliment! Obviously, she was not as good, not even close, and never would have been even if she'd continued voice lessons, but that was all right. She'd never aspired to fame as a singer. Besides, her grandmother had died soon after Emelie's fourteenth birthday, and no one had ever encouraged her on a musical path after that. In fact, her father had banned "that sinful trash" from the house. If it hadn't been for her hiding the precious records in the attic, he would have destroyed them all.

After that first song, she morphed from one blues favorite to another, sometimes with the piano as the only musical background, but other times also joined in by the lonesome wail of the trumpet, or the syncopated rhythm of the guitar. She sang all her favorites, which luckily appealed to the crowd, as evidenced by their applause and the fact that some of them stopped eating to listen more attentively. "Nobody Knows You When You're Down and Out." "Ain't Nobody's Business If I Do." "Lover Man." "Give It Up or Let Me Go."

Near the end of her first set, she looked out at the audience and noticed the tall man leaning against the bar at the back of the room. He wore jeans, a white T-shirt, and a dark sport coat. His hair was short and his eyes were piercing in intensity as he concentrated on her.

Justin.

Her heart skipped a beat and she missed a few words of the next stanza, then she looked away and forced herself to concentrate on her singing. But it was hard, and she couldn't help herself from glancing his way from time to time. Especially when, launching into the last song of her set, the poignant Etta James classic "At Last," she noticed Justin moving slowly along the side of the room until he was only several feet away, staring at her with such surprise on his face. And joy. When she ended the song, he applauded loudest. She told the crowd she would be back in fifteen minutes, and if they had any requests, she would be glad to sing them if she could.

No sooner had she stepped off the stage than Justin

took her by the upper arm and guided her to the side into an employee's corridor.

"Oh, babe!" was all he said.

"Did you like my singing?"

"Would you be offended if I said your voice turns me on?"

She smiled, the wicked kind of smile women had perfected over the ages to torture men. She hoped Justin felt a little bit tortured. "Well, I wouldn't want to have that effect on everyone."

"Just me," he insisted with a growl, then pulled her into his arms and kissed her with both hunger and tenderness.

This was not the time or the place, and they both recognized that fact.

Pulling back, she asked, "Does that mean you liked my singing?"

He twisted one of her spiral curls around a forefinger and tugged her closer. "Sweetheart, I love all of it. I love your singing. I love your body in that sexy dress. I love your bed-mussed hair and hot red lipstick. I love your passion... for everything you do. I love your talent."

What he didn't say was that he loved her, but that was okay. She hadn't expected that. Not really. Okay, a little. But it would have felt phony to her.

"What I don't love is that I had to find out about your singing in a newspaper. Why didn't you tell me?"

Men! Honestly! "You didn't ask. Besides, you haven't been around for, oh, seventeen years."

He winced.

"I had no reason to think you'd be interested."

"If you know nothing else, know that I've always been interested."

What was that supposed to mean?

"Why aren't you recording your music? Why aren't you singing on some TV program? *American Idol* or *The Voice*, if nothing else?"

"I'm not that good." He was about to protest, but she put up a halting hand. "Really. I have a passable voice, good enough for a local gig, but not for the big time. Besides, I've always concentrated more on visual arts than music. Any fame I garner will have to be for my masks."

He nodded and then smiled at her.

"What?"

"I'm happy that you continued with your music."

Despite your having dumped me? she wanted to say, but didn't want to bring up the subject. "I didn't for a long time," was all she was willing to admit.

He cocked his head to the side in question.

Ella popped her head around the corner. "Are you all right, Emelie?"

"Yes." She introduced Justin as an old friend to Ella, who nodded, but didn't smile, as if she sensed Justin was bad news for her. Which, of course, he was.

"Are you ready to come back for your second set soon?"

"I'll be there in a minute." She liked to circulate through the crowd first to get any special requests.

"I'll wait for you," Justin said when she was about to go.

"You don't have to wait."

"Oh, yes, I do. I really do." On those words, he pressed her up against the wall and kissed her with a raw sound deep in his throat. His hands rubbed the silk fabric of her dress against her butt. His tongue explored her mouth. His erection pressed against her belly. If he was trying to give her a message, it couldn't have been clearer than a blinking neon sign: I WANT YOU, I WANT YOU, I WANT YOU!

She was the one who made a raw sound deep in her throat then.

He drew away from her reluctantly and said in a hoarse whisper, "I'll wait."

⌒

As a wise old philosopher, Toby Keith, once said, "I'm not talkin' 'bout forever, I'm just talkin' 'bout tonight . . ."

Cage walked hand in hand with Em down the late-night streets of the French Quarter. Despite it being off-season and rather chilly for the South, there were still people going in and out of restaurants or bars or seedier establishments. The Quarter never slept.

He had never loved Em more than he did at this moment, and he was scared. Scared at the intensity of his feelings. Scared of where this reignited love would take him, or not take him. Scared because this love was not going to end in happily ever after. More like happily until dawn. With a little closure, or if he was lucky, a lot of closure, he could return to Coronado and no longer be haunted by dreams of what might have been.

As if sensing his intentions before he'd left tonight, MawMaw had said to him, "Doan play with that girl, Justin, lessen yer serious."

Serious? No way. Just a little fun between friends who happen to love each other. "We're just friends."

"*Pfff!* Some folks drink from the fountain of knowledge; others jist gargle. I never took ya fer a gargler. Doan be a fool, boy. Ya could hurt that girl bad."

"What about me?" he'd asked, a little offended.

"Yer both playin' with fire." She'd patted him on the hand. "I doan want you hurt either."

"I thought you liked Em at one time."

"I did. I do." She'd paused as if wondering whether to say something. Then she did, and he wished she hadn't. "If ya ever decide ta stay here in the bayou, I want it should be because thass what ya want more than anythin'. Doan be like yer daddy. He shoulda gone ta Nashville lak he allus planned, but he stayed fer yer mama, and lived ta regret it."

He wasn't at all like his father, who'd played a mean guitar at one time and had dreams of the Grand Ol' Opry. Instead, he'd landed in the Grand Ol' Prison. Cage played the guitar himself on occasion. Poorly. But some women liked to hear him play.

His father was a subject he refused to discuss, ever. Without responding, he'd kissed his grandmother on her old lady, parchment-like skin and left.

Now that he had Em at his side, letting him hold her one hand while she held an Ella's take-out bag in the other, he wasn't about to let her go 'til they were both satisfied. He was going to be in her bed within the hour, or die trying.

"Why are you grinning?" she asked.

"You don't want to know," he said and tugged her into his side, putting an arm around her shoulder. With her high heels, they fit together just right. Maybe he'd make love to her with those heels on and nothing else.

Or maybe he'd have her sing to him, some sexy blues song, while leaning against the open French doors of her bedroom leading out onto the balcony, assuming she had French doors in her bedroom. She would be naked, except for those high heels, while she sang, her eyes being held by his as he lay on her bed, also naked, of course, with his hands folded behind his head. The anticipation would be excruciating. Foreplay without even touching.

"I know what you're thinking."

What? No way!

"And it's not going to happen."

"It?"

"Sex?"

"Define sex."

"I mean it, Justin. This was nice. Your coming to hear me sing. Walking me home. But that's the end of it."

"That kiss didn't feel like an ending."

"That kiss was a mistake. Consider it a good-bye kiss."

Not. A. Friggin'. Chance!

"I'm sure we'll run into each other now and then while you're still in Loo-zee-anna, and I'd like to visit Miss Mae-Mae occasionally before she . . . well, while she can still have visitors. Friends . . . can't we just be friends now?"

"Friends with benefits?"

"Have you heard a word I've said?"

"I've heard everything."

"No sex."

"Uh-huh," he agreed. *Unless you beg me, and baby, you are gonna beg. Guar-an-teed!*

She decided to change the subject then, which was probably a good idea, considering the state of the hard-on he'd been sporting since he first saw her on the stage in that skimpy dress, which was fortunately covered now, on top at least, with a short, fleecy, jacket-shawl thingee, or he would probably be taking her in a wall-banger along some alley before they ever got home.

"How come your friends are still here and staying with Tante Lulu?"

"They have some liberty and have taken a liking to the bayou," he lied. "Sort of a vacation."

"But staying with Tante Lulu? I would think their 'liberty' would be kind of restricted there."

"What? No place for orgies?"

She gave him a sideways, teasing glance. "Well, I've heard stories about Navy SEALs. Not necessarily orgies, but..."

"Oh, really? Exactly what have you heard?"

"Belle said... well, never mind about *that*."

She seemed to be blushing. Cage reminded himself to ask JAM what Belle might have told Em.

"SEALs are supposed to be kind of wild."

He acknowledged that might be true with a shrug.

"Another thing. I understand that Bernie has been going to Tante Lulu's cottage. All chummy, chummy with your pals."

"Where did you hear that?" he asked, suddenly alert.

"My father. Bernie and my father keep in touch."

"That figures. How is the old geezer anyhow?"

"Getting better. Especially since your girlfriend has been helping him."

"My girlfriend?"

"Adele Hebert. *Dr.* Adele Hebert. Who else? Do you have girlfriends lined up and down the bayou already?"

Em had put special emphasis on Adele being a doctor, as if that was a surprise. Maybe she thought he'd only be able to attract barmaids and brainless bimbos. Nah, that wasn't it. She was jealous. Cage took that for a good sign and gave himself a mental high five. "Adele is just a friend. She's been helping with therapy for my knee. Actually, she and Geek have a lot more in common. Turns out Adele is a computer geek, too."

Em seemed skeptical of his explanation, but conceded, "I've noticed that you're limping less. Does that mean you'll be going back to California soon to work?"

He shook his head. "I'm here for MawMaw as long as I'm needed. I might have to go out on short missions, but as long as she's here, this will be my base."

They'd arrived at Emelie's building, but instead of going into the shop and up the interior stairs to her apartment, she headed under the porte cochere, where the E & B van and a VW bug were parked. When they got to the back, exterior stairway, she halted and turned. "Well, it's been nice." She leaned up to kiss him on the cheek, as if to dismiss him.

I don't think so!

"I'll walk you to your door, *chère*," he said.

She made a *tsk*ing sound but allowed him to follow her up the staircase, which gave him the opportunity to take note of her nice, heart-shaped ass as her dress ruched up with each lift of her legs.

She glanced back at him over her shoulder, saw the direction of his stare, and *tsk*ed some more.

If she only knew how sexy that *tsk* sounded, a librarianish contrast to her hot mama outfit.

And yes, thank you, God, there were French doors leading to her bedroom. In these old shotgun-type houses, the upper floors would be one bedroom leading into another into another. This was the back one.

"You know, Em, this isn't really a very secure setup for a single woman."

"We have a security system around the entire first floor, and cameras inside the shop and showrooms."

"A burglar or rapist could access your upper floor with ease, bypassing the security system. Those French doors—much as I like them—they're practically an invitation to an intruder. You should let me bring Geek over here one day to check it out."

"I don't need you—your friends—coming here to check my building. If I want more security, I'll hire someone myself."

He wasn't about to be deterred by her slip. What she'd really meant was she didn't want *him* coming around. He had a lot of work to do in a short time. But first. "Darlin', what you really need is a dog."

She laughed. "You're not still trying to schluff that mongrel on me, are you?"

Cage pretended affront. "Thad misses you. Honestly." *Like I do.* "The big lug jist lies on the porch whinin' all the time." *Well, I don't whine, but I do pine.* "Every time a car pulls up, he gallops out to the driveway, hopin' it's you." *I don't gallop with this bum knee, but I would if I could.* "But then he comes back with his tail draggin' between his legs." *Something else is draggin on me in the same general region.* "Like he lost his best friend." *Precisely.*

"You're making that up."

"No, I'm not. You should come see him." *Or check out my tail.*

She just smiled. Inserting the key in the lock, she turned to him and said, "Well, good night."

No, no, no! Not going to happen. Time to make a move.

Moving forward, he backed her up against the door. Bracing both arms on either side of her head, he took a deep breath and began, "I want you, Em. More than anything in the world."

"No offense, Justin, but men say that all the time."

"Not me." At least he didn't think he'd said those words. If he had, he didn't mean them. He meant them now. "My bones turn to butter when I look at you, babe. My heart swells when you smile. I can scarcely breathe when you turn your head a certain way. I ache for you."

"Well, you've certainly developed a new repertoire of seduction lines."

"Such a cynic!" He shook his head at her. "Hear me out, Em. I'm not promising you forever. I can't, and I'm not sure you'd want me to. We're both too raw, even after all these years."

Her big eyes blinked at him. Bingo! He'd hit a sore spot. Raw...she was still raw.

He licked his lips and continued. "What I can promise you is pleasure. And maybe closure. Doesn't it feel to you as if we never really ended things?"

She nodded. He was definitely making inroads.

"I still dream about you."

She nodded again. Definite inroads.

"You ruined me for any other woman." He could tell she was going to argue that point, but he rushed on before she could interrupt his spiel. "I need you, Em. Please end this nightmare of longing. Please. Let me love you again." He blinked back tears. *Tears! Damn, I'm falling apart here.*

Her eyes were misty, too. She seemed to gulp several times.

"You'll hurt me. Again."

"Not if we both go into this knowing it's short-term," he argued. "Two friends enjoying each other. When it's convenient for both of us. Knowing I can't always get away, because of MawMaw, and other things. You're busy, too. Then finally closing a door forever. We start this affair as friends and end it as friends." *I've just sung a pile of crap or the best romantic overture of my life.*

"Do you really think that's possible?"

"I do." Lifting one hand off the door frame, he used a forefinger to trace the line of her jaw from ear to ear, setting the sparkly chandelier earrings to jangling. He smiled as they shimmered in the moonlight.

"An affair, Justin. That's all it would be," she said softly.

His heart began to race. Was she actually agreeing? *Oh, man!*

"No talk of love, ever," she demanded.

He started to ask her how he was going to stop himself from saying the words that were on the tip of his tongue all the time when he was around her.

But she put a hand over his mouth to halt the words.

He kissed her palm.

Casting him a chastising glare, she drew her hand away and went on with her demands. "No discussing the past or the future."

"I can live with that, although there are a few questions—"

"I would insist that you be monogamous during the time our affair lasts, and I would be, too, but only because I'd be uncomfortable sharing. STDs and all that."

"I'm clean, Em. I get tested all the time."

As if he hadn't even spoken, she went on, "Friends, nothing more, nothing less. That's all we will ever be now. Those are my conditions. Can you live with them?"

A male fantasy, for sure, sex with no commitments, but somehow it felt wrong to Cage. Too sterile. Too business-like. Plus, he was pretty sure Em had managed to turn the tables on him. Had she played him at his own game? Did it matter?

Hesitantly, he nodded, but he'd be damned if he sealed

the deal with a handshake. Instead, he picked her up in his arms and licked the inner whorls of her ear before promising in a husky whisper, "I am going to lay you down, sweet Em, and show you what a good *friend* I can be."

⚜

Yep, it was true what they said about SEALs...

This was probably a mistake. No, it was definitely a mistake, Emelie decided, but she'd already crossed the line, and mistakes be damned, she was looking forward to a night of lovemaking with the only man who'd ever made her enjoy the sex act, the only man she'd ever loved.

She'd never envisioned surrendering to Justin's charms this night. She wasn't even sure when her resolutions to resist him had melted away, but somewhere between the kiss in Ella's restaurant corridor and the walk to her home, she had decided to grab for the brass ring. Oh, not the kind of ring that meant happily ever after, but happily for a while.

While Justin went into the bathroom, she removed her pashmina, lit several scented candles, and turned down the comforter on the double brass bed, an antique handed down to her from her grandmother. She straightened when she heard the bathroom door shut.

He was wearing nothing but a pair of black boxer briefs, and oh, my goodness, had his body changed from the lean boy she'd once known! His shoulders were wider and muscular, as were his biceps and the sculpted planes of his abdomen, leading to a narrow waist and hips. Even his thighs and calves showed muscle definition. In his hand he carried a strip of foil-wrapped circles, which he tossed onto the bed.

"Self-confident, were you?"

"Just hopeful," he said. "Don't take those off."

She was about to remove her high heels, but stopped, staring up at him.

"I have a fantasy about those shoes."

Oh. My. God. What have I opened myself to?

"Don't look so afraid. We won't do anything kinky... unless you want to." He waggled his eyebrows at her. "I'm not the clumsy kid I was before, Em. I've been to a few rodeos. I know what I'm doing now."

She arched her brows. "Rodeos?"

"Uh-huh."

"I never thought you were clumsy." She paused for a moment as he approached her. "Have you had a lot of sexual partners?"

He nodded.

"I haven't." Actually, only two, but he would think she was pitiful if she told him that.

"It doesn't matter. Only now. Remember, that's what you said. No past. No future."

I have a feeling my words are going to come back and bite me on the butt.

He tugged on the spaghetti strap of her dress, drawing her closer so he could kiss her. With her high heels on, they were almost the same height, which was kind of nice. She went to put her arms around his shoulders, but he held them firmly at her sides. "Not yet," he murmured against her mouth and wet her lips with his tongue, then moved his lips back and forth across hers as if seeking just the right fit before kissing her harder and deeper. When his tongue slipped into her mouth, she tasted bourbon and coffee, both of which he'd had at the supper club.

His kisses were wet and openmouthed and hungry, and

she already felt a thrumming ache between her legs. She arched her breasts out to rub the hardened nipples against his chest hairs.

He must have liked that because he groaned and caressed her bare shoulders before sliding the straps midway down her arms and then lower, causing the top of her dress to fall and then catch on her ample breasts, which were encased in a strapless black lace bra.

"Oh, Em," he said, staring at her.

Emelie was tall, but she had breasts, no question about that, 34Ds. Her hips and butt were ample, too, but set off by her small waist. It was a voluptuous figure she always complained about, but men seemed to like it. Marilyn Monroe-ish. Pamela Anderson without the artificial enhancements.

Before she could blink, he had her bra undone from the back—*Where did he learn to do that with such ease?*—and was lifting her breasts from underneath, strumming the nipples with his thumbs.

Her knees almost buckled, causing him to grab her by the waist and chuckle. "Still so sensitive."

"How about you, sweetheart? You still sensitive?" she said peevishly, brushing her palm against his erection, which was—*whoo-boy!*—very impressive.

His knees did buckle and he fell backward onto the bed, bringing her with him on top. "Witch!" He laughed and nipped at her shoulder, then soothed the bite mark with the laving of his tongue.

He undid the zipper on the back of her dress—*with the ease of experience*—toed off her shoes with his own toes—*another learned talent*—and rolled over so she was on the bottom. Straddling her hips, he looked down at her with a grin of triumph, as if he'd won some prize, then made quick work of the dress, tossing it over his shoulder. "Nice," he murmured then, staring down at the black lace bikini briefs she wore, a match to the bra she no longer wore.

Then, as if an idea had suddenly occurred to him, he slid off the bed and onto his knees, yanking her forward so that her heels were on the edge of the bed but spread wide. She tried to sit up, but he wouldn't let her. She tried to close her legs, but he wouldn't let her. Only then did he kiss her, *there*, through the lace of her panties, but she felt it as if she was bared to him. Oh, how she felt it! He nuzzled her with his nose, then raised his head to stare at her as he used only the palm of his hand to press and release, press and release, press and release, against just the right place, until the ache became a pulse, and the pulse became a rhythm, and the rhythm increased faster and faster until there was an explosion of pleasure so intense she began to cry.

"Shh, shh, shh!" he said, lifting her up and onto the pillow and arranging himself on his side, looking down at her with a smile. "That was just to take the edge off."

"For me! What about you?"

"My turn is coming," he said, winking at his clever play on words.

"I never did that before," she confessed.

His raised his eyebrows in surprise. "Not even with Bernie?"

"Definitely not with Bernie." And that was all she was going to say on that subject.

When he realized that she wasn't going to disclose anything else, he began to play with her breasts. Palming them. Tweaking the nipples, then strumming them with fluttering fingers. "I love your breasts," he said.

When he lowered his head and began to suckle her, she let out a long, keening wail, arched her hips up off the mattress, and climaxed again.

She turned her head away. "I am so embarrassed."

He gripped her chin and forced her to look at him. "Never be embarrassed about something so beautiful. Your coming almost made me come."

That made her feel a little better, but only a little. All thought left her head then as he stood and shimmied out of his shorts. His penis was large and engorged, the veins standing out as if oversensitized, the mushroom head ruddy with arousal.

"Are you like that all the time?" she asked before checking her hasty tongue. "I mean when you're having sex, not when you're just walking around." *Jeesh! I sound like a blushing virgin.*

He chuckled and shook his head. "Only for you. I've been wanting you for a long time, baby." He knelt on the mattress at the end of the bed, tugged off her panties, then crawled up and over her. "Talk about embarrassing, I don't think I can wait much longer." He rolled a condom on one-handed... *another talent bespeaking his experience.* Then, without asking if she was ready again—*he must know*—he nudged her knees apart with his own, then slowly, excruciatingly slowly, he eased his penis inside her body, which welcomed him with grasping clasps of her inner muscles as they adjusted to his size. She was too far gone in excitement to be embarrassed anymore.

Buried inside her fully, he closed his eyes and seemed to be counting when what she wanted was for him to begin moving. In fact, she urged on a soft moan, "Move, dammit."

He tried to laugh but it came out as a choked sound. "Wait, or this will be the fastest fuck in history."

"Nice language."

"Sorry," he said, but he didn't look one bit sorry. In fact, he appeared to be in pain. Beads of perspiration broke out on his forehead. The muscles in his shoulders appeared tense. And he was panting.

So she decided to jump-start things herself. While she couldn't lift his big body off her by raising her hips, she could move from side to side, and that was almost as good. Bliss!

And it must have felt blissful to him, too, because he lifted himself up on extended arms until he was almost out of her body, then slowly, slowly, slowly down. Over and over he performed this maneuver until the sweat was dripping off his body, and every nerve ending in her body was quivering with tension.

"Harder," she pleaded.

"Like this?" he asked, slamming into her, hitting her clitoris dead on. But he only did it once.

Darn him!

When he raised himself up the next time, she reached between his legs and tickled the underside of his balls at just that place which he'd once told her was his happy spot. With an expletive bursting from his gritted teeth, he pushed her knees to her chest and looked at her directly. "Game on, *chère*?"

"Game on, *cher*," she countered.

Justin made love to her then with all the expertise he'd garnered over the years. Alternating between long and short strokes. Embedding himself in her and, at the same time, kissing her until she was a whimpering mess. Then plunging into her depths again. Occasionally, he murmured words to her in a foreign language, which she hoped were endearments, but were probably coarse sex words.

He told her things he liked her to do. "Touch my shoulders, baby." "Put your hands on my butt. Yes, like that." "French-kiss me, sweetheart. Suck on my tongue."

And she found herself telling him the same. "My breasts. Touch them some more. Not so hard. Yes. Gentle." "I like when you caress the back of my knees." "Oh, no, stop! I'm ticklish *there*."

It must be true what they said about Navy SEALs and their staying power because Justin stayed hard for what seemed an exceedingly long time. By the time he finally reared back and thrust himself deeper than ever inside her, roaring out his ejaculation, she might have climaxed two or more times. Amazing!

As he lay over her, still inside her, his face buried in her neck, she wished that he might say the words that hummed in her own brain, *I love you.* But of course, he didn't because she'd told him not to. It was for the best, really.

When he finally raised his head and looked down at her, he said with a wicked grin, "You are the best friend I've ever had."

Chapter Twelve

I'll tell you my fantasy if you'll tell me yours...

Cage was serious. He'd never had sex so good, and to his shame, that was saying a lot, considering the number of notches on his belt. Literally.

When he'd left Louisiana the first time, he remained celibate...for a while. Saving himself for Emelie. Despite the way he'd been railroaded out of town and despite his lack of success in contacting her by phone or mail, he'd never doubted that she still loved him. Until he'd come home after boot camp and discovered that she was married.

He didn't like to think about that time in his life. Although the military hadn't been his choice initially, he'd actually liked basic training. It was something he could do and do well. He fit in for the first time in his life. He'd been so full of himself on that first liberty, coming home to see his girl, perhaps take her back with him. There was married housing on the base; he'd checked into it.

He'd gone crazy then. So many women, he'd lost count. And then, when he became a SEAL, there was a whole new pool of women. Honest-to-God SEAL groupies. Aside from them, willing females abounded in every port, on every mission.

And now he'd come full circle to find that the best sex was still with the woman he'd loved from the beginning. How pathetic was that? Or soul-searingly wonderful?

"Wait here," he said, giving Em a quick kiss and going into the bathroom to make quick work of the used condom, then washing his hands. Looking into the mirror over the sink, he couldn't help but notice the loopy grin on his face. He was a goner. Turning on the faucets in the shower stall, he opened the door and beckoned Em with a crooked finger. "Come here, you."

She was sitting up in the bed, propped against the pillow, a sheet drawn up and over her breasts, which incidentally he really, really liked. Really! Her bed-mussed curls looked really bed-mussed now, and her lips were rosy and swollen from his kisses. Fifty shades of sexy, and she knew it. All she did was arch her eyebrows mischievously at his invitation.

"You forgot to turn off the water," she told him.

"I didn't forget. Haul ass, babe." He motioned her again. "Time's a-wastin', and I have plans."

"Well, why didn't you say so?" She slid off the bed and walked toward him, a vision of pure, naked, Southern belle sexiness. When she passed him in the doorway, she wiggled her butt saucily, and glanced back at him over her shoulder through half-slitted eyes.

"Tease me, will you?"

He picked her up by the waist and walked them both into the shower, closing the door to create the perfect steamy cocoon. The warm spray soon covered them both and her wet hair was plastered against her head. He combed his fingers into her hair, pushing it behind her ears.

She cradled his face with her hands, as though he were precious to her, and kissed him. A short kiss, but intense with unspoken words.

"Time to teach you some of the lessons I've learned in the SEALs."

With water running down her upraised face, she asked, "What? Chinese water torture?"

He laughed. "No. Another type of torture." He took a washcloth and folded it over into a triangle, then folded that several times until he had a narrow band. "I want to blindfold you. Will you trust me?"

She hesitated but only for a second before nodding.

Once he'd tied the washcloth over her eyes, he lifted her arms so that she could hold on to the showerhead above her, which caused her breasts to arch up and out.

"Don't move," he ordered, then groaned.

"What?" she asked.

"Have I told you how much I like your breasts?"

"Only about a thousand times."

Her breasts were large, like halved navel oranges, with pretty pert nipples that were slightly uptilted, but they were especially attractive because her rib cage was narrow and her waist small. And then, as if to counterbalance the weight on top, her hips swirled outward.

Her belly was flat, leading down to the wet, black curls that formed a nest between her thighs. No Brazilian wax for her. Which was kind of nice. Old-fashioned. He'd seen all kinds of pussies. Bare, bare except for a narrow landing strip of hair, short cut, trimmed into a heart shape or a diamond, adorned with jewelry, tattooed, pierced, and even braided, of all things. He was probably biased, but he liked Em's best. Not that he would be telling her that.

"You're so quiet. What are you doing?"

"Just looking."

"Is that part of the torture?"

"Do you feel tortured?"

"A little bit."

"Good," he said, and picked up the bottle of shampoo sitting on the ledge. Pouring a huge dollop into his hand, he smiled. Lemons.

He shampooed her, and then he soaped her arms and underarms, her breasts and belly and butt, her legs, from her ankles, up one thigh and down the other. Then her cleft.

"This really is torture," she said, squirming.

"Good."

She sniffed the air then. "Are you shampooing my entire body?"

"Yep."

"Why? There's soap there."

He was rinsing off all the lather now, including between her legs, which caused her to squirm some more. "Yeah, but I wanted the lemon flavor."

She hesitated before asking, "Why?"

"The better to eat you, my dear," he growled and went down on both knees before her. He realized his mistake immediately as his bad knees protested in pain. Thinking quickly, he said, "Hold on tight, darlin'. This is gonna be a rough ride." On those words of warning, he edged his shoulders between her legs and stood all in one motion.

"Yikes!" she yelped and held the showerhead tighter. "Are you crazy?"

With a little adjustment of her knees over his shoulders, he looked at the palate before him. And grinned. *Man, I am good!*

"Let me down, Justin. I don't like this. I have no way of bracing myself."

"You mean, you're too open, too vulnerable?"

"Exactly," she said with relief, fully expecting him to let her down. *Foolish girl!* That was just how he wanted her.

His hands were on her butt, holding her up, but his long fingers were able to come at her from between her thighs, spreading her folds. "You are so pretty here, Em. All pink and slick." He licked her up one inner fold and down the other.

She moaned.

"Was that a good moan or a bad moan, honey?"

"Bite me!" she snarled.

"Okay," he said and nipped at her inner thigh.

"I didn't mean that literally."

"I know."

"I swear, I am going to kill you."

For that he flicked her Bic with a wide swath of his tongue.

She went stiff and silent.

"You liked that, didn't you, Em? No answer? That's okay. I can take it from here." And he did.

Using a forearm to brace Em's rump, he used the other hand to enter her with a long middle finger until he found her G-Spot. Only then, when he was palpating that knotted muscle, did he take her clit in his mouth and begin to suck softly.

She screamed as her orgasm began. He could feel the spasm around his finger. Then she wailed one continuous

"Ohohohohohoh!" When the oh's ended and the inner spasms stopped and he could swear she ejaculated around his finger, he kissed her clit, then eased her back down to her feet.

Immediately she sank to her knees and ripped the blindfold off her eyes. "You!" she said, handing him the folded washcloth. "Your turn."

She could scarcely speak for the anger or deep satisfaction she was feeling. He wasn't about to ask which.

"You heard me. Blindfold yourself and," she repeated his words back at him, "hold on tight, darlin'. This is gonna be a rough ride." She was still on her knees and she was staring at his cock, which was erect and ready to boogie. It took him only a moment to understand. Then he smiled. If what she planned was intended as a punishment, let the pain begin.

He blindfolded himself and held on to the showerhead, which was eye level to him.

"Stop smiling."

He could tell she was standing now. Damn! Then he heard a squirting sound. The shampoo. Okay.

She started with his head and shoulders and chest. Good thing she didn't start at the bottom coming up or this show would be over real quick. He'd already held off too long, and he didn't have any condoms in the bathroom. The shower had been running for so long that the water was turning tepid, but that was good because he was so hot.

She remarked on certain body parts as she went along, which distracted him somewhat from what he really wanted to concentrate on. Blowing his wad.

"Your body is different than it used to be."

"I'm seventeen years older. Of course it's different." But then he thought. "Don't you like it now?"

"I like it, but..."

But? She has a but? "I was a skinny kid when I left here," he said in a disgruntled voice.

She laughed softly. "Yeah, but I lo...liked that skinny kid. And you have scars now, like this one on your belly. Looks like it was stitched."

"I got knifed in Kabul."

She gasped. "And that knotted scar on your thigh." She seemed to be kissing a place high on his leg, way too close to sex central, and he moaned. "Does it hurt?"

"No," he gritted out. "That was a bullet wound from a Pakistan mission two years ago."

"Are all your missions dangerous?" She was still kneeling. He felt her breath on his belly.

"No," he gasped.

"Are you ever afraid?"

Talk, talk, talk. A little less words, and a little more action, he thought. But he knew when to keep his cool. So instead, he answered her, "Yeah, fear is your best friend. That's a SEAL motto." *But, honey, I'm more afraid that your mouth is so close to my cock, and it's not going to do anything.*

She touched him then. Just a fingertip tracing some design, but man, it felt like heaven.

"You have veins bulging out again. Is that a good thing?"

At first, he couldn't speak as she continued to trace said veins, and he had to huff a few breaths to keep from ejaculating. "A very good thing," he said finally. "Em, do you remember how I taught you to hold me back then?"

"Like this?" she asked and took his cock in both her hands, one above the other, and began to pump.

He jerked back, hitting his head on the tile, which

caused the blindfold to slip down his face to land around his neck. Glancing down, he saw her concentrating as she worked his cock up and down. "Not so hard," he gurgled out.

"Oh. Like this?"

He nodded, but then realized that she hadn't yet noticed that he could see her. "Yes."

And then she licked the bead off the tip and put the head in her mouth. He almost fainted with the sheer, incredibly intense pleasure. "More," he encouraged her.

And she did, little by little, until he was in all the way, before glancing up at him. And winking. The little minx knew all along that he could see her.

She worked him then, in and out of her mouth. Not with any great expertise. But that didn't matter. This was sex at its best, from a male point of view.

When he was unable to handle any more, he lifted her up and kissed her deeply, tasting himself on her tongue, as he came all over her belly. He held her for a long time afterward, just held her.

Then they had to shower again, and it was cold. Neither of them minded, they were laughing so much, on a high of joy as potent as any whiskey buzz.

After that, at 2 a.m., they were both hungry, and they went into the small kitchen, where they warmed up Ella's supposedly famous crawfish gnocchi, which they ate with a Caesar salad, warmed-up Italian bread, and a bottle of red wine.

They talked while they ate.

"How are you occupying yourself while you're staying with your grandmother? I mean, you must be busy all the time when you're working."

"I've had plenty to keep me busy so far. The house, the

yard, and the animals have been a job in itself, and the work's still not done. Have I mentioned a lovesick dog?" He batted his eyelashes at her.

"Give it up, buddy. I am not adopting that huge dog. Can you imagine the damage it would do down in the shops?"

"He can be trained. Until then, you could keep him in your apartment or down in the courtyard."

"No."

"We'll see." He grinned suddenly. "Maybe Thad and I will come for a sleepover one night."

"No."

"No to me, or no to Thad."

She just shook her head at him as though he were hopeless. He was when it came to her. Which was probably the reason why he blurted out, "Why did you never answer my letters?"

"What letters?"

They came to the same realization at the same time.

"Your father."

"My father."

He tilted his head to the side as an impossible idea nagged at him. In his mind, an image flashed and was gone, but he'd caught the gist. Emelie standing in the driveway of his grandmother's house, crying as she clutched a packet of letters. "No," he said. "No, don't tell me. You wrote me letters but they never made it past my grandparents' home. Please tell me that isn't true."

She said nothing.

"Answer me," he yelled, then immediately regretted his anger and took her hand in his, kissing the knuckles. "I'm sorry. It's just kind of shocking."

"You can't ask your grandmother about this. Please. Promise me you won't. She already feels so guilty."

Cage was an intelligent man, smarter than many people gave him credit for, largely because of the joking, never very serious attitude he'd adopted over the years. But his mind was working overtime now. Her father. His birthday. Her crying over letters that might have been addressed to Cage. The decision not to attend her father's birthday celebration. Her father's heart attack. Bernie's sudden appearance on the bayou. Hell, Emelie's marriage to Bernie itself.

So many questions.

"But why? Why would my grandmother do that?" He frowned, trying to get the time frame in order. "Or was it my grandparents?"

"I can't talk about this. Not now. And your grandmother is in no condition to have a breakdown in the midst of her medical crisis. Just let it go, sweetheart."

Breakdown? This must be really serious. There was no friggin' way that he would "let it go," but arguing with Em about it now would solve nothing. He inhaled and exhaled to tamp down his impatient temper. "Okay. Back to what I'm doing to keep myself busy. When I'm at Coronado, even when I'm not on an active mission, I have to work out every day, run five miles, sometimes ten, hours of PT, physical training, breaking down and keeping safe my weapons, meetings with the teams and staff to update us on new warfare methods and devices. My days are full."

"Wow!" she said.

"I didn't say that to impress you, just to show that while I'm really busy there, I'm busy here in a different way. There's so much I have to do. Boxes and boxes of paperwork that my grandparents have saved need to be gone through. Hell, my dad's belongings are still there. I need to meet with Lucien LeDeux, MawMaw's lawyer. Most important, I need to sit down and talk to MawMaw about her last wishes. Believe me, I'm not looking forward to that."

She took one of his hands in both of hers and squeezed. "Believe me, I understand. I need to have a serious talk with my father and not just about... well, his heart attack has put a hold on that talk, but it's going to happen eventually. And I'm not sure if we'll have any relationship at all after that."

Well, that was certainly mysterious.

"Time for a change of subject. You have a nice home here, Em."

"I do. I feel blessed. Because MawMaw Gaudet left me this house. Because of my business. I have a good life."

He glanced around. It was clearly a woman's home, not a man's. The kitchen table was small and the spindly chairs more suited to a woman's weight than a big-sized man's. Even the plates were kind of smallish. He knew SEALs who filled plates twice this size at a meal, and went back for seconds. All that exercise burned up calories. And yeah, he thought, they'd already burned up some calories tonight. He couldn't wait to see what they did next.

After two glasses of wine, Em was starting to get a buzz. He was barely fazed. He looked forward to what Em might do while under the influence, which gave him ideas. Wicked ideas. But no, he didn't want to scare her with too much, too soon. There would be other nights. He hoped.

"C'mon, darlin', let's go back to your bedroom." He stood and began to lead her out of the kitchen.

"Wait. I should clean up first."

He shook his head. "Later. I have some ideas that demand immediate attention."

She laughed and let him tuck her into his side, walking side by side. "Seems to me you have way too many ideas."

"A man can never have too many ideas when it comes to sex."

"That sounds like a *Playboy* motto."

"I'm wounded," he said with a smile, putting a hand over his heart. "But no kidding, Em, when I was watching you sing tonight at the club, I had the best idea... okay, the best fantasy."

She stopped in the middle of the bedroom. She was wearing a silky kimono-style robe and nothing more. He shimmied out of his briefs and walked over to the bed, laying himself down with his hands folded behind his head.

She gave him a head-to-toe survey, unable to ignore the pole standing up in his middle. But she wasn't budging a bit. With hands on her hips, she said, "Well? What is this big fantasy, big boy?" She put special emphasis on "big boy" and Big Boy sort of flexed in a bow.

"I was imagining you standing against those open French doors over there, naked except for those killer high heels you were wearing. And you were singing the blues, a sexy ballad just for me."

She blinked and a blush rose on her cheeks. "Oh, good Lord," she said. Then, "Wanna hear my fantasy?"

Is she kidding? "Maybe."

"I'm picturing you standing in the same doorway wearing a cowboy hat and cowboy boots and nothing more. Except for the guitar you're playing for me. While I lie in my bed, naked, waiting for you. How do you like my fantasy, big boy?"

He didn't have to speak. Big Boy did the talking for him. But then he said, "I actually wear a cowboy hat and boots sometimes back in California when I go out to the local bar, Wet and Wild. The women love it."

"I'll bet they do."

He wagged a forefinger in warning to her. "I even play the guitar on occasion. Not very well. But honestly, Em, I don't have any of those things here in Loo-zee-anna."

"Get them."

Okaaay.

She nodded slowly and leaned down to put on first one high heel, then the other. Then she went over to lean against the doorjamb, staring at him.

"Lose the robe, sugar." His voice was so husky with passion, it came out as little more than a whisper.

She shook her head, but she did let the robe slide down until her shoulders were exposed along with the top of one tempting breast. Nobody would ever believe him—especially not his team members—but she looked sexier than if she was totally naked.

At first, her voice was soft, almost a whisper, but then he realized that she was singing that old Etta James song "If I Can't Have You." Was the choice deliberate? Was there a message in the song lyrics in which the woman was telling some man that if she can't have him, she doesn't want anyone? She sings of the way he hugs her, the way he squeezes her, the way he kisses her. Em's voice was clear and husky, huskier than her regular speaking voice, and Cage was touched deep to his soul. What had started out as a lighthearted teasing challenge turned on him. Big-time.

"Ah, Em!" He slid off the bed and went over, tilting her chin up to see the tears welling in her eyes. "Ah, Em!"

Picking her up, he carried her back to the bed and lay her down like the precious object she was. Wiping her tears with the edge of the sheet. Brushing loose strands of hair, still damp from their shower, off her face. Kissing her softly on the lips.

When he made love to her then, that was what it was. Making love. She'd told him there were to be no words of love. So be it. But he would show her with every bit of his being how much he loved her.

For the next hour, Cage dedicated himself to a slow, gentle loving of Emelie. Murmuring soft words of compliments or encouragement. Butterfly kisses. Whispery soft caresses. He used every talent he'd perfected over the years to give Emelie the most pleasure. When they both came to a climax, it wasn't with a bang or an explosion, but rather a slowly rising crescendo and then a release of such incredible satisfaction, the only thing Cage could liken it to was warm honey flowing through their veins.

Em fell asleep instantly in his arms. He would have stayed with her the entire night but he heard the slight buzz of his secure cell phone sitting on the bedside table. Taking the phone with him into the bathroom, he saw the text message, *Stop at Tante Lulu's on way home. News on Operation Boom.*

He dressed quickly, and dawn was already lightening the sky when he went over to the bed and sat down. Nudging Em, he said, "Honey, I have to leave. Something has come up."

Her eyes shot open and she started to rise. "Is it your grandmother?"

"No. Something else. Go back to sleep. It's only five thirty. I'll call you later."

She sank back down and snuggled into the pillow.

He waited until he was certain she was asleep again before kissing her cheek and whispering, "I love you, Em."

What he didn't see when he turned his back and went out the door was the small smile on her face.

Chapter Thirteen

Her future was looking rosy…

Emelie was up soon after dawn and remarkably ener-
gized, despite her small amount of sleep. In fact, to her
surprise, she noticed that the bags under her eyes were
gone and there was a healthy glow on her cheeks. A sex
glow, she thought with a giggle.

She sang softly as she dressed for the day, made herself
a toasted bagel with peanut butter and honey, and took it
downstairs to eat with the pot of coffee already started by
the timer on her coffeemaker. By the time Belle arrived
at eight, Emelie was well into her mask making, having
accomplished more in the past few hours than she had in
days.

Belle took one look at her and burst out laughing.

"What?"

"Someone's been doing the dirty. *Woot-woot!*"

"I don't know what you mean," Emelie said, fighting
a grin.

"Honey, it's obvious what you've been doing. Your life is suddenly coming up rainbows."

"I don't know what you mean," she repeated and pretended to be having trouble picking from a selection of colored feathers for a particular mask.

Belle put her hands on her hips and tapped one foot. "No fair, girl. Dish! I already told you what I heard about SEALs and staying power."

To her chagrin, Emelie felt her face heat.

Belle let out a hoot of laughter, then gave her a warm hug. "Whatever happened, I'm glad to see you looking so...um..."

Emelie arched a brow in question.

"Satisfied." Belle left to open the shop. An hour later, Belle called her to the front, saying, "You know that thing you've been doing but don't know what I'm talking about..." Belle stepped aside to show her a flower arrangement that had just been delivered for Emelie Gaudet. Two-dozen long-stemmed pink roses in a crystal vase. There was no card, but Emelie didn't need one. She took the vase back to her work area, and she smiled every time the scent of roses wafted her way.

Her good mood lasted all morning and was topped off by the most amazing proposition. No, it wasn't a marriage proposal, not that she was expecting one, but the offer of a job that was beyond her wildest dreams. Harry Duval, the well-known Creole chairman of the Mardi Gras Museum of New Orleans, whom she'd met at various charity events over the years, came in around noon and asked to speak to Emelie. She brought him back to her workshop and offered him a cup of coffee. While she was puttering with the coffee-maker to brew a fresh pot, Harry walked around, examining her work. His oohs and aahs were compliments enough.

Harry was a spiffy dresser, and today was no exception. He wore a burgundy sport coat with a multicolored silk scarf tucked in behind the open top button of a pristine white shirt, like a nineteen forties film star. His pants were a darker shade of burgundy, almost black, and his dress shoes were white. Yes, white shoes in the winter. On a man.

"You're probably wondering why I asked to see you," he said after taking several sips of coffee with more oohing and aahing. Emelie had learned long ago that Cajuns and Creoles loved their coffee strong enough that it gelled when cool.

She nodded.

"The museum has received a half-million-dollar federal grant for the arts, and we're using it to build a new wing. Among other things we'd like to have masks made replicating all the important masks that have been worn in Mardi Gras parades over the years. As you know, some of the early ones have disintegrated through lack of care, and others we never had, but we do have photographs. We would like you to do the work."

She was stunned. "How many pieces?"

He shrugged. "We're not sure. Possibly fifty, initially. But there's a deadline. We want to open the new wing the week of Mardi Gras next year."

"Oh, my goodness. That would be a tight schedule. One a week, practically. It wouldn't leave much room for my regular business."

"Ah, I understand, but you are so suited for this opportunity. Please, don't tell me that you are declining."

"No, no, I'm just thinking out loud." There would actually be other things to consider, as well. She'd planned to start a baby this year, if she could. And now that Justin had reentered her life... well, she didn't want to get her hopes up, but he *had* said he loved her, even if he hadn't meant for her to hear.

Harry told her the amount she would be paid and the amount set aside for materials, which was more than satisfactory. Not to mention the publicity she would get for her work.

"I'm very flattered by your offer. Can you give me some time to consider whether I would be able to handle it?"

She could tell that Harry was a bit disappointed that she hadn't jumped at the chance. "Yes, dear, but not too much time. You are the only artist we considered, but if we need to find someone else, time is of the essence."

"I understand. Would one week be too long?"

"That would be fine. Shall we meet again next week, same time and place?"

They shook hands, and he left.

Belle came back right away, anxious to know what Harry Duval had wanted. When Emelie explained, she said, "Wow! Kudos to you, honey." Noticing the expression on her face, Belle added, "Or not. What's the problem?"

"Well, no problem exactly. But you do know that I was considering artificial insemination, and I wouldn't want to go into that being overworked and stressed out. A child should... *would* be my number one priority."

"I would help as much as I could," Belle offered.

"I know you would, sweetie." She squeezed Belle's hand.

"One thing, have you considered getting a baby the fun way with Justin? You know, better the devil you know than the one you don't?"

"I don't want an absentee father in my baby's life, but

at least with artificial insemination the child can't be hurt by his absence."

"That is the most convoluted bit of illogic I have ever heard," Belle said. Then with a shake of her head, she added, "Please don't let worry over the shop enter into your consideration of the museum's offer. I can handle things here, or get some part-time help if need be."

Emelie nodded.

"What about your singing at Ella's?"

Emelie waved a hand dismissively. "I could drop that in a heartbeat for a job like this."

"So?"

"I have a week to decide." She looked at Belle then and said, "I meant to ask, how are things going with JAM?"

"Eh! So-so! Haven't seen him for a couple of days."

"Not 'the one,' huh?"

"Probably not." She paused. "Something's fishy with those SEALs being here, if you ask me."

Emelie grinned. "Something fishy with seals?"

"Yeah, and more SEALs are supposed to be arriving soon."

"Really?"

"Maybe I'm imagining things. The whispering that stops when I walk in the room. Bernie being chummy with a bunch of macho guys."

Emelie frowned, recalling that she'd had an uneasy feeling as well. Bernie had never been cool. Why was he suddenly hanging out with the cool guys? And why were the "cool guys" suddenly interested in Bernie? "I don't know about the other SEALs, but I'm sure that the reason Justin is here is because of his grandmother's illness."

"Yeah, and I could see two of his buddies coming for support. For a day or two. But it's been over a week now.

And staying with that dingbat Tante Lulu for a vacation? Doesn't fit."

They looked at each other and shrugged.

Her cell phone rang then. Looking at the caller ID, she said with a sigh of resignation, "My father."

"Good luck!" Belle said and went back to her workroom.

"Dad," she said into the phone.

"Emelie, darlin'," he said way too sweetly.

Uh-oh. That tone of voice meant he wanted something. "What is it?"

"Are ya comin' down to the bayou t'day?"

"No, Dad, I can't. I'm too busy with work. Are you sick?"

"'Course I'm sick. Ah had a heart attack."

She rolled her eyes. "Are you doing your exercises?"

He ignored her question, which was telling. "When are ya comin' ta see me?"

"Can I talk to Francine?"

"Why? Ain't I good enuf fer mah baby girl?"

"Dad, put Francine on the phone, or I'm hanging up."

He banged the phone down, and there was a rustling sound, and a pause before Francine arrived and picked up the phone. "Hello, Emelie," Francine said in a tired voice.

"Francine, here's the deal. If it's an emergency, I'll come. If it's not, I'm just too busy."

"There's no emergency. Your father's just scared."

"Of another heart attack?"

"No. Something else."

Ah. Now she understood. Her father suspected that she knew about more of his machinations, which she did. Unless there were more. On top of his threatening Justin's grandparents, she'd learned last night that he'd apparently hidden or destroyed letters that Justin had sent her. When would it ever end?

"Francine, we both need to take a stand. If we don't, he's going to make us both sick. I've got work to do here. I'll come when I can. And you, Francine, bless your heart, you need a break, too. Why don't you come into town and stay with me for a few days?"

"I can't do that, but I am going to insist that he do more for himself. A home helper is coming today, and he has a physical therapy session this afternoon. If he refuses to cooperate, I'm going to take a more drastic step. My sister still lives in Baton Rouge. I can go there." She could tell that Francine was weeping. "Maybe I should have never given up my own home."

This was bad. Very bad.

"Listen, Francine, let's play it by ear today. I'll talk to you tonight. If there's no change today, I'll come tomorrow, and we'll make all the changes that are needed. If nothing else, we can put Dad in an assisted living facility."

"Oh, he would hate that!"

"Yeah, well, you and I hate the way he's being at home. Sounds like a standoff to me."

"Okay," Francine finally agreed and hung up.

Talk about a buzzkill for a good mood. No rainbows now.

Emelie resumed painting a porcelain mask then after inserting a Nina Simone disc in the CD player. Music... even the blues...always uplifted her.

The phone rang. Her dad's number again. But it was Francine who whispered, "Em, it's working. I read your dad the riot act, and I told him that if he didn't straighten himself out, he was going to lose both of us. He's taking a walk in the garden right now. Said he has some things to think about."

"Justin LeBlanc?"

"What?"

"That's what he has to think about. Francine, he's done some awful things. Some, you may already know about. But more things keep coming to light. He's been living under the fear for years, but especially since Justin is back in town, that we will discover the extent of what he's done."

"Whatever he's done, it's for your own good, Emelie."

"Bullshit! Sorry, Francine, but he's justified his actions with that excuse for too many years. Until he realizes that Justin isn't a bad man and that he owes him a huge apology, I don't think my father will ever change."

"Does it matter so much . . . how your father feels about Justin? Unless he's right that you might connect with the boy again and might go off to California with him."

"First off, Justin is a man, not a boy. Second, I am not leaving Loo-zee-anna, even if Justin asked me to, which he hasn't. Third, it does matter. Tremendously."

"I can hear in your voice how important it is to you."

"No, see, that's what I need you and my father to understand. It's important *to my father* that he stop fixating on Justin LeBlanc. My father has a cancer worse than the one killing Justin's grandmother, and it's been eating away at his insides for more than seventeen years."

Emelie's hard words rang in the silence.

"He must have done something really bad to Justin," Francine said finally.

"Yes, he did, and not any one thing. A number of things. And to me, and other people, too. It's time for it to end."

"Let me get your father straightened out with the home helper and the physical therapy. Then when we're sure that he's physically able to handle the stress, you need to discuss all this with him, one on one."

Surprisingly, Emelie felt better once she'd hung up. As she sat there for a moment, she realized why. It was the scent of pink roses, yes, but more than that, it was the scent of promise.

க

When someone hands you lemons...

It took Cage an hour to drive from New Orleans to Bayou Black, and he spent that time just thinking, thinking, thinking. About Em, of course.

It was like he'd done a cut and paste on his life, wiping out the past seventeen years. He loved Em same as he had when he was seventeen. All those in-between years didn't exist.

Nothing had changed.

And everything had changed.

Her father was still here and as big, or bigger, of an obstacle. He'd probably have another heart attack if he found out Cage had nailed his daughter last night. More than once.

There were a lot of misunderstandings and mistakes, almost none of which had been resolved. And mysteries, dammit. He sensed that people were hiding things from him.

Even if he wanted a future with Em, and he wasn't sure either of them did want that, he lived in California and she lived in Louisiana. He had no intention of leaving the military, and there wasn't any big market for Mardi Gras masks in the Golden State.

He was jumping ahead of himself; he knew he was.

But his body and his mind and his emotions were overflowing with joy at having been with the woman he loved, even for only a few hours. He wanted more. He yearned for more. He had to have more.

The question was: What would that "more" entail? Seeing her and making love when they could grab some spare time between them? Would that be enough? He feared that wouldn't be nearly enough. But it was what he'd signed up for with Em last night. Her conditions.

Cage stopped at Tante Lulu's cottage on his way home. Luckily, Useless was nowhere to be seen, probably off cruising the bayou for a female Useless, or looking for Cheez Doodles from some other brain-dead softie. Without knocking, not wanting to awaken anyone if they were still asleep, he opened the unlocked door and went inside.

It was only 7 a.m., but JAM was already up, tapping with one hand at a laptop on the kitchen table and cradling a cup of coffee in the other. He glanced up at Cage, then did a double take. "Someone's been laying pipe."

Cage actually felt a blush heat his face, and he never blushed. "Why do you say that?"

"*Pfff!* You look like every cell in your body is relaxed, for one thing. Besides, you smell like lemons. Not sure what that means, but since you didn't smell like fruit yesterday, I figure it must have something to do with sex. The boy's been fruited!"

"That's some leap of logic. And there's no such word."

"Did someone say somethin' 'bout lemonade?" Tante Lulu asked. She came into the kitchen wearing pink foam rollers in her gray hair, a housecoat with purple and orange flowers, and fluffy slippers. A St. Jude medal the size of a hubcap hung around her neck. "I ain't got no lemons ta make lemonade."

"That's okay," JAM said. "We can just dip Cage upside down in a water barrel."

Tante Lulu sniffed the air. "You do smell lak lemons, boy. Whadja do, take a bath in lemonade?"

"No," he said, but that was an idea he might consider later.

Tante Lulu began to putter around the kitchen, so he and JAM went out on the back porch with coffees and sat down in the rockers. It was chilly, but not uncomfortable.

"So what's the plan?" Cage asked.

"I'm gonna pick up Slick, Magnusson, and K-4 at the airport in Baton Rouge this afternoon," JAM said. "After you go home, Geek will go into Lafayette to open the two apartments. The feds are sending in special agents, as well. They're setting up a command center as we speak, as well as the two apartments for temporary quarters. Geek and I are going to continue to come back here every night as much as possible so we won't raise any suspicions about why we've been staying here so far."

"Right. If you cut off your visit with Tante Lulu abruptly, it will just reinforce those suspicions about why you were staying here to begin with."

"How about you talk to John LeDeux, the Lafayette cop? The commander gave permission for that."

Cage agreed. Once he made sure his grandmother was all right, he'd give the cop a call.

Unfortunately, other matters took precedence.

When Cage got to his grandmother's house, he found her up in the attic with Geek, bringing down thirty- to forty-year-old-mementos. Of his father. Including his old guitar.

Cage's heart, which had been aching for Em, now began to ache for an entirely different reason.

❧

A mother's work…rather, a grandmother's work…is never done…

Mary Mae LeBlanc was no fool. Yes, she had lung cancer. Yes, she was dying. But her brain was still fine, and she knew that Justin needed to confront the past, the past being his father. Since he wasn't doing it himself, she was going to have to jump-start his motor.

She was already up in the attic, which was accessed by a drop-down ladder in the ceiling of the hallway outside her bedroom, by the time Justin's friend Darryl woke up. She had to giggle at the expression on the boy's face when he'd found her peering down at him. Nigh had a heart attack, he did. Or a hissy fit.

"Are you crazy?" Geek had yelled at her. "Cage is gonna kill me if he finds out I let you go up in an attic by yourself. It can't be good for your breathing with all that dust up there. You could have fallen and broke your fool neck."

"Then no one would hafta wait fer the cancer ta take me," she'd replied, not at all apologetic.

So he'd climbed up there with her and begun to carry down boxes at her direction. Some she indicated could go to Goodwill. Some to the trash. And some to Justin's bedroom, where she could sort the contents with him.

"Don't you need your oxygen?"

"I'll let ya know when I need my oxygen."

"How about breakfast? Let's go have breakfast."

"I've already had toast and coffee. Oh, ya mus' think I'm a terrible hostess. I shoulda made ya some sausages and eggs and such. Let's go down right now. Lordy, Lordy, what was ah thinkin'?"

"I don't need breakfast yet," he'd grumbled. "Let's finish while we're up here. Who does that guitar belong to?"

"Beau. Justin's daddy. Be careful. It's sort of an heirloom."

They were still up in the attic when Justin arrived. She assumed it was him by the sounds of the animals getting riled up. The dog and cats, and the birds, each of which was squawking, "Hoo-yah! Hoo-yah! Hoo-yah!" and "Hubba Hubba Ding Ding" and "Cage is a hottie," and most recent, "Seal the deal, baby! Seal the deal!"

She heard him calling out for her, "MawMaw? Where are you?" Then, "Geek? Hey, buddy, what's goin' on?"

When he came into the hallway, she and Geek both peered down through the opening.

Justin's eyes went wide, his mouth gaped open, and then he said a bad word before snarling, "Get down here. Right this minute."

She stiffened. "Yer not my momma. Ya doan give me orders. And 'specially ya doan yell at me."

"Sorry for yellin', but son of a brick, MawMaw, you 'bout made me pee my pants I was so scared."

"No need ta be swearin'!"

She thought she heard him mutter, "Ya ain't heard nuthin' yet."

Darryl went down the steps before her and he talked in a low voice to Justin.

"Doan ya be blamin' yer friend fer nuthin'," she hollered down through the opening. "I got an itch ta take care of bizniz up here t'day, and no one was gonna stop me. Not even you."

"Okay, okay," Justin said, raising his hands in surrender. He helped her come down the steps, then told her, "Go put on your oxygen and start breakfast, if you're up for it. Geek and I will bring everything else down. Is there anything that you want to keep in the attic?"

"I won't know 'til I look it over," she sniped, but she *was* feeling short of breath.

Darryl commented to Justin, "Call me crazy, Cage, but you smell like a lemon."

It was true, Justin did smell lemony.

"It's shampoo, if you must know," Justin told Darryl.

"We ain't got no lemony shampoo here," she said. "Why was you washin' yer hair someplace else? Ya ain't got much hair ta wash anyhow."

Justin gulped several times like he wasn't sure what to say, but Darryl came to his rescue. "Must be that lemon air freshener I put in your Jeep. The car smelled like dirty socks before."

Mary Mae nodded, although she suspected Justin had been up to no good. He'd been out all night, after all. "Mebbe I will go lie down for a bit with mah oxygen tank."

Justin and Darryl exchanged glances.

"You want me ta help?" Justin asked.

"No! I doan need no help walkin' ten feet."

By the time Justin came in to check on her...it might have been five minutes or an hour later...she was half asleep. Time was she coulda worked from dawn to dusk and had energy left over for other things. Now the least thing tuckered her out.

"MawMaw, are you all right?" Justin asked, leaning over the bed.

"Jist fine. Lemme take a little nap. Then I'll come out and make some breakfast fer you and yer friend."

"That's okay. Geek already left, and I had something to eat at Tante Lulu's house."

"Good. Musta been lemon meringue pie, by the smell of ya. Which wouldn't surprise me, with Tante Lulu," she murmured when his head almost touched hers as he studied her, *probably to see if I'm dead or somethin'. Not yet!* She adjusted her cannula as she burrowed into her pillow. "One thing, Justin. Promise me you'll look through the boxes I put in yer bedroom."

The boy had to know that the boxes contained papers and photographs and items that had belonged to his father. For too many years, Justin had avoided the painful subject.

There was a long pause, then, "I promise."

When she fell into a deep sleep now, she was at peace. Rufus was there in her dreams, smiling at her. More and more, her beloved husband was in her thoughts and in her dreams. It was a sign, she believed, that her time was winding down.

But first, she had to get Justin settled.

Chapter Fourteen

Fishing works better than any psychiatrist's couch...

First, Cage tackled the oldest boxes, figuring they would be safest for his well-being. These were picture albums of Mary Mae and Rufus as they were courting, then marrying, and the early years of their only child, Beau LeBlanc, Justin's father.

Rufus had been a soldier in World War II when he married Mary Mae Prudhomme. The sepia-toned photograph showed his grandfather wearing a jaunty cap on his head and a dress uniform, standing next to his grandmother in a floaty white dress. They looked so young and so happy as they stared at each other, and actually, they had always looked at each other like that. Yes, there had been hard times and soul-deep grief, like the day they buried their only son, but mainly he remembered the joy of life...*joie de vivre*...that was a part of their everyday lives.

How had they done that?

The one big grief of his life—the loss of Em—had

pretty much destroyed him. And he had to admit, he'd handled it poorly. On the outside, he'd pretended a happy attitude, but inside, he had been bitter, and his resentment had eaten away at him, as poisonous as the cancer that was destroying his grandmother. He was a living, walking cliché. The crying clown.

But no, who was he kidding? It was his father to blame for the self-destructive path his life had taken. A common criminal who died in prison. What kid wanted a father like that? What father wanted his daughter to marry into that family? No wonder Claude Gaudet had been so against Cage as a partner for his only daughter!

Oddly, Cage had never pointed an accusing finger at his mother. She'd never been around after he was born, except for sporadic drug-induced phone calls, her addictions going back even before Cage's birth. The only clean period had been during her pregnancy and then only because of the close supervision of Beau and the grandparents. Maybe that was it. He'd never had her; so it was hard to blame her for doing nothing. But his dad had seemed to try. There had been the promise of a good father-son relationship. Beau LeBlanc had let his son down in the most primal way.

His grandmother walked in now slowly, her hair standing up in sleep-mussed disarray from her one-hour nap. Sinking painfully down onto the opposite twin bed, she adjusted her cannula and portable oxygen tank, before staring at him dolefully.

She looked like hell, and Cage felt fear grip his heart like a claw. *Not so soon. Please, God, not so soon.*

"Hand me that one over there, hon," she said, pointing to the shoe box labeled with a black marker, BEAU'S LAST LETTERS.

"MawMaw, please, it makes no sense to stir up old miseries."

"It does when those miseries have never had a chance to be put away proper. Jist 'cause a chicken has wings doan mean it kin fly."

"What the hell—I mean, heck—does that mean?"

"Appearances doan mean diddly. Fer all yer life, ya been judging yer daddy by appearances," MawMaw declared.

"Huh?"

"Justin, yer daddy loved ya more than anythin' in the world."

"Bullshit!" he said, even though he knew his grand-mother hated bad language. "If he loved me, even a little, as a father should, he wouldn't have been robbin' gas stations, or gettin' into bar brawls, or gettin' himself killed in prison."

MawMaw shook her head sadly. "Yer daddy was a good-hearted man. When yer Momma got pregnant, he gave up all his dreams of Nashville and stood by her. He knew we would take care of ya, me and Rufus, but Marie dint have no one ta catch her when she fell. And she fell lots."

"Are you sayin' my father picked his wife over his child?"

"He saved the one that needed savin' most. You."

"As far as I kin tell, he didn't succeed."

"I'm shamed ta hear ya talk lak that. He did his best, and he loved ya, doan ever doubt that." She opened the box and handed him the letter on top. It was addressed to Rufus and Mary Mae LeBlanc, and it had the Angola Prison stamp across the front, warning the receiver that this was mail from an inmate, in the event they didn't know that already. "Read it ta me," she ordered.

"MawMaw," he protested.

"Read it," she insisted. "I doan ask fer much."

She didn't. That was true.

He glanced at the date on the envelope. December 1993. One month before Beau LeBlanc was killed, when Cage was fourteen years old. He hadn't seen his father for four years before that. With a sigh, Cage opened the envelope and began to read:

Dear Mama and Papa:

Thanks for telling me about the royalties I got for my latest song. Put it in the account for Justin, like the others. Make sure Marie doesn't get her hands on any of it.

He glanced over at his grandmother with question. "This is the first I've heard about my father gettin' royalties and that there was any account fer me."

"I told ya that yer father had talent as a musician. He sang an' he played the guitar, but he also wrote songs, and some of 'em got sung by some important people."

"Like?" Cage asked skeptically.

"That George person. Smith, or some such common name."

"Do you mean George Jones?"

"Yeah, thass the one."

"Holy shit!" he muttered.

His grandmother gave him a dirty look.

"A bank account?"

"All gone now. Well, 'ceptin' fer some what come in recently. I ain't checked the past year or so. How do ya think me and Rufus was able to support ya durin' the lean years when the shrimp weren't comin' in?"

Truth to tell, he'd never wondered. Shame on him!

"The papers on Beau's songs are in a safe at Lucien LeDeux's office. I tol' ya that ya need ta go in one day and look things over."

He put a hand to his forehead. "I could swear that the only thing you mentioned was a will and *your* bank account info."

"Papers is papers," his grandmother said, as if he was thickheaded for not having understood that.

"Luc has been real helpful, y'know. He made sure the songs got copyrighted or whatever they call it when no one kin use yer songs without payin' fer the privilege. Yer papa had an agent who usta call here sometimes. Luc will have his name and number and all."

An agent? My father had an agent? Holy shit!

He'd once dated a well-known romance writer. She'd told him it was harder to get an agent than it was to get a publisher. "You never mentioned songs at the lawyer's office. I thought you meant wills and stuff like that. Just out of curiosity, would I recognize any of the songs my father wrote?"

"Mebbe." His grandmother tapped her chin thoughtfully. "How 'bout 'Prison Is a State of Mind'?"

Cage's jaw dropped. "Are you kiddin'? I know that song. It was one of the last ones recorded by Johnny Cash. And it was just included in an album by Jason Aldean. I heard about it on some country music radio station."

His grandmother shrugged. "That box over there has lots of songs he wrote while in prison. He never got a chance ta do anythin' with them."

Un-be-fucking-liev-able!

It struck Cage then that his grandmother and grandfather must have been suffering intensely having a son in prison and then later a son dying in prison. And all that time, he'd been more concerned with his own hurts and had been running wild, causing his grandparents even more grief.

"Keep on readin'." His grandmother had rearranged some pillows and she propped herself up against the headboard to be more comfortable.

I'm keeping my nose clean, like I promised, and if things go my way, I should be out of here in a year. After that, I'll be taking Justin with me to Nashville, and I will never screw up again. Believe me, Marie will never get another chance to foul up my life again.

Cage glanced at his grandmother. "What does he mean about Marie fouling up his life?"

"He was sent to Angola for armed robbery, but the gun wasn't his. It was Marie's. She talked him inta burglarizing some lady's apartment in the French Quarter fer some expensive jewelry. Oh, doan get me wrong. Beau made mistakes, but so many of 'em stemmed from tryin' ta help Marie."

"Did he love her that much?"

"I'm not sure he ever loved her. When she got pregnant, he married her, and after that, he felt responsible fer her. As he should have."

"That's just great! Now *I'm* the cause for daddy's downfall. If not for me, none of the rest would've happened. Talk about!"

"Doan be an ass," his grandmother said. "You were the best thing that ever happened ta yer daddy, and he said so many a time."

Cage felt like he was being bombarded with conflicting emotions. His father had clearly been a criminal. He had not been there for Cage on numerous occasions when he was growing up. Never having a steady job, he hadn't supported his family. A loser, that was what Cage had always thought.

But maybe his father hadn't been a loser. He'd clearly had talent, and he had been trying to rise above his mistakes. Kids couldn't see beyond their own wants and needs, but Cage was an adult now—he should be able to understand that people were human, and they didn't always do the right thing.

"You have ta understand, MawMaw, that I grew up believin' I was from bad seed, and that I would never amount to anythin'."

She gasped. "Who tol' ya such a thing?"

Claude Guadet, for one. "Lots of folks. Sometimes ta mah face, but mostly behind mah back, loud enough fer me ta hear."

"Ignorant folks! Good Lord, boy, surely ya dint believe them."

He nodded his head. Yeah, he did.

"If you was bad seed, what did that make me, or your grandfather? Do ya really think I'm a bad apple?"

"Of course not."

"I'm glad ta hear that 'cause I'm gonna be meetin' mah Maker soon, and I wouldn't want ta be showing up as a bad apple."

It was a lousy joke, but Cage attempted to smile anyhow.

"Justin, honey, we were all created by God. No one is born bad. Thass not the way the Lord works." She shimmied herself off the bed and came over to the other bed, where he sat. Leaning down, she gave him a hug. "I need ya to make peace with yer daddy afore I kin go. Mebbe ya cain't ever fergit the pain, but ya kin forgive. I hope so."

He read the rest of the letter before she left.

I don't want you and Papa to come visit me here anymore. I know you'll argue with me about this, but it upsets you too much to see me here, and it upsets me, too. The best thing you can do for me is pray and be there for me when I come home.

I like picturing you in the kitchen making my favorite red beans and rice and Papa out by the bayou catching us a mess of catfish for supper. And my little boy, Justin, standing on the back porch, waving at me with a big ol' smile on his face. 'Course he'll be fifteen by then, but he'll always be my little boy. My heart and soul. I have so much to make up to him.

It ain't the big things I dream of anymore. Yeah, I'd like to make it in Nashville, but only for the things I can give my family, you, and Papa, and Justin. No, what I yearn for is to sit on the back porch some dusky evening, after a trip down to the Dairy Queen in Priscilla. The sound of whippoorwills and mourning doves in the air, the scent in the air of your Virgina Slims cigs and Papa's pipe, Elvis playing on the stereo from inside, and Justin sitting next to me on the top step, real close.

By the way, thank Tante Lulu for sending that packet of St. Jude stuff. They wouldn't let me keep the medal or the plastic statue, but I have the laminated prayer, and I've been saying it at night when I'm feeling a little hopeless.

Love you always.
Your son, Beau

As he finished reading aloud, his grandmother began to weep and walked slowly from the room, saying nothing. What could she say? Cage felt crushed, and he wasn't sure why. Secrets and misunderstandings, that was what killed families.

Now that he was alone, he stared around him with dismay at all the boxes to go through. He had to smile on seeing his father's guitar case and in two other boxes an old cowboy hat and well-worn boots, which were incidentally his precise size twelve, because, of course, he was remembering Em's fantasy. Did he dare? Hah! Did he dare not?

There were boxes of clothing, which he put on a Goodwill pile, along with a collection of early *Playboy* magazines, which he figured Geek might be able to sell on eBay. Little boys throughout time had learned where to look for their first forays into the forbidden world of sex. His father's hiding place had been under the floorboard beneath the bathroom sink. The skin mags brought a smile, too.

Any paperwork, whether letters, or legal documents, or handwritten song lyrics, were set aside for later study. There was only so much of an emotional kick in the gut he could take in one day.

By noon he had his Jeep packed to the roof with Goodwill items, some boxes put back in the attic, and only a few boxes left for him to handle. "I think I'm gonna go out and try my hand with Daddy's ol' rod and reel," he told his grandmother, who was sitting on the couch reading the daily newspaper with Elvis crooning a soft ballad in the background and the scent of fresh-baked bread wafting from the kitchen. It was like time standing still. Could have been 1954 or 2014. What would happen to this house once his grandmother was gone? Oh, he knew that all her worldy goods, including the house, would go to him, but would he keep it or sell it? Hard decisions. He used to have a handle on his life. Now the handle was broken, and so was he. He felt lost and confused. Clearing his throat, he said, "I'll see if I can catch us somethin' good fer dinner."

"It's kinda chilly. Better put on a jacket."

He grabbed a hoodie hanging on a peg near the door and went down under the house to the storage area where he'd seen his father's old fishing supplies the day they'd cleaned the yard. He grabbed the rod and reel, along with a bait bucket. Soon he had minnows captured and one of them hooked on his line. Thad was sitting beside him on the bank, looking forlorn. "I'm workin' on her fer ya, buddy," he promised, and the dog actually appeared to nod its big head in thanks.

Before he made his first cast, he could swear he heard his father say, "*Look before ya cast, son. Keep yer eye on the target. No herky-jerky. Smooth and easy.*" And then when he felt a nibble on his line, his father saying, "Jerk ta set the hook. Doan let that ol' fishie get away. Thass the way, thass the way."

Fishing was a calming experience. He'd always known that, but the longer he fished, the more he remembered.

"Life is lak fishin', son. A season fer everythin'. Even the bad times. But storms are okay. Fish lak a little rain.

"Be patient. Small acts kin have big consequences. Small ripples can produce big fish.

"Plain poles catch jist as many fish as fancy ones.

"Jist let it go, boy. Sometimes, thass all ya kin do. If ya catch a small fish, let it go. If someone hurts ya, jist let it go."

Mon Dieu! he thought, swiping at the tears that filled his eyes like a regular girly-girl. *My father was a frickin' phi-*

losopher. He'd bet his Budweiser, nickname for the precious SEAL pins, that when he finally got around to looking over all his father's unpublished songs, he would find more of the same. A poor man's philosophy of life. Well, that was what country music was all about anyhow, wasn't it?

Then, too, there were the times when his father played the guitar for him and MawMaw and PawPaw. Even there, his soul had spoken its own homespun message. "Sometimes the notes you don't play, Son, are more important than the ones you do."

Tears continued to stream down his face now as he cast his line over and over, a repetitive, soothing exercise. He didn't even try to stem the flow. By the time his line went tight for the first time, and he jerked back against the drag, he was already at peace with his father.

He and MawMaw had a mess of catfish for dinner. Symbolic? Maybe.

❧

It wasn't phone sex, but it came close...

Emelie's phone rang about 11 p.m. She'd already relaxed in a bubble bath and was lying in her bed with a glass of white wine and a paperback novel, planning an early night of sleeping. She knew without checking the caller ID who it would be.

"Hi, Justin."

"Hey, sugar, sorry to call so late. It's been one hellacious day."

"Same here. Thanks for the flowers. They're beautiful."

"I wasn't sure what color to order. Red seemed too harsh a color for you. And yellow too much like a friend, and yes, before you remind me, I know that I agreed to our being friends." He paused. "Are you laughin' at me?"

"A little. Pink was perfect. I love them."

"Tell me about your day. What was so hellacious?"

"Well, not hellacious, but very busy and interesting." She told him about the offer from the Mardi Gras museum.

"Em! That's wonderful. Congratulations."

"Thank you, but—"

"But what?"

"I'm not sure if it's what I want to do at this time."

"Why not?"

"Well, time is the most important consideration. It would be a full-time job, and then some. I'm not sure I could handle it with the shop and all that entails. Plus other things might be taking up my time this year."

There was a pause, as if he hesitated to ask her what those things might be. But then he remarked, "Like your father?"

And having a baby? And you? "Yes, there is that."

"Do you want my opinion?"

"Of course. I wouldn't have told you if I didn't want your thoughts."

"Well, first of all, I think you're right to take a few days to think things over. Don't make a rash decision. Second, I'll tell you what always works for me. Take two pieces of paper. On one of them, make a list of the reasons pro, and on the other, all the reasons con. For some reason, it always makes my reasoning more clear when I write things out longhand, rather than typing. Tape those two pages on a wallboard, or a cabinet, or whatever. For a few days, every time you pass, you'll pause and read the lists over, probably make additions or deletions. And at the end of a week, voilà! A decision will be made."

"Does that always work for you?"

"Not always, but a lot of the time."

She wanted to ask him if he'd made those lists on occasion when considering whether to return to Louisiana, or not, and the "not" had always won out? She wanted to ask what the "con" reasons might have been. But they were supposed to be just friends now, and that meant boundaries. So all she said was, "Thanks. I'll try that."

"What else happened today?"

Without giving him too many details, like the things her father had done relating to him and his family, Emelie told him about her conversations with Francine.

"Sounds to me like a little tough love is in order."

"Exactly. And so far so good. Francine says he seems to have gotten the message. My father has done some awful things, but he's still my dad, and I've got to find some way to forgive him. Like you, in some ways." Well, not at all like Justin and his father. In many ways, what her father had done, despite being a sheriff, or perhaps because he'd been in law enforcement, was so much worse.

"I don't want to talk about your dad. I'm in a forgiving mood tonight, and I'm not ready to forgive your father for his interference in my life."

And you don't have a notion of even half of what he's done. "So who did you forgive today?"

"I figured you must have guessed since you mentioned your father. My dad, that's who I forgave today. Do you ever listen to country music, Em?"

That question came to her out of the blue, unrelated to the question of fathers and forgiveness. Confused, she answered slowly, "Sometimes. A lot of country today is a blend with other types of music, like blues or rock."

"Have you ever heard of the song 'Prison Is a State of Mind'?"

"The Johnny Cash song?"

"Yeah. It was also redone recently by Jason Aldean."

"And?"

"My father wrote that song."

There was such pride in Justin's voice that Emelie's heart swelled in empathy for him. "Justin! That's amazing. How did you find out?"

He told her all about his father's last letter and what his grandmother had told him about his professional songwriting.

She was so happy for him. "I would love to look at some of the sheet music you mentioned."

"Come over one day, and we'll go through the box together. It would probably mean more to you than me anyhow, with your musical background."

"That's a deal."

"Besides, MawMaw would like to see you again. She mentioned today that there are some photographs of your mother in one of her old albums."

"Oh, my goodness! I would love to see those. My dad took so few, especially after her being sick for so long." She paused, took a sip of wine, and said, "So news about your dad's song...is that where your forgiveness for the day came in?"

"Well, not exactly." He elaborated about the letters, and royalties, and fishing.

Even though it all came out jumbled, she understood. Having been with Justin at the height of all his pain over his father, she more than anyone understood how what he'd learned today could help him heal.

"So I guess I'm not such a bad seed, after all."

"Oh, Justin! If you were here, I'd smack you silly for making such a statement."

"If I were there, you wouldn't be smackin' me."

"Oh, really?" she teased. "What would I be doing?"

He chuckled. That was enough. But then he mentioned several things that were clearly meant to scandalize her.

"Bad boy!" she said, but then she whispered what she'd rather be doing, and it was even more scandalous.

"Bad girl!" he said, but she could tell that he loved it. "Hey, Em," he added, and his voice was lower and huskier now, "remember those fantasies we were talking about?"

Like she could ever forget! Justin had never made such sweet love to her as he had after she'd acted out his fantasy of singing the blues to him in the nude. Well, not totally in the nude, but close enough. "Yes," she said hesitantly. "You haven't come up with another one, have you?"

"Oh, baby, I have lots of fantasies about you. Have I told you how much I appreciated the one you already fulfilled?"

"You might have mentioned it a time or two."

"What I was referrin' to was *your* fantasy."

Oh, boy, he was going to remind her about that. Her face got hot just thinking about what she'd had the nerve to tell him.

"In case you've forgotten, you mentioned me playing the guitar wearing nothing but a cowboy hat and boots." With a ta-da pause, he said, "Guess what I found in the attic today?"

She laughed. "Could it be a guitar, cowboy hat, and boots?"

"Bingo!"

"Sounds like we have a date."

"Count on it, baby."

"I should go. I have a long day tomorrow," she said then.

"Same here."

"Call me tomorrow night?"

"For sure." There was a short silence before he began, "Em, I love..."

Her heart seemed to stop.

"...having you for a friend," followed by a dial tone.

She shouldn't be disappointed, but she was.

Chapter Fifteen

Beware of old ladies with plans...

Company arrived early the next morning.

Mary Mae heard the soft knock on the door from her bedroom and came rushing out, or at least walking fast, but Cage, who wore only a pair of sleep pants, was already rising from his seat at the kitchen table, where he'd been sipping a cup of coffee and reading last night's sport page.

"Yoo-hoo!" someone said, opening the door a crack.

He glanced at his wristwatch, and Mary Mae heard him mutter, "It's only seven frickin' a.m."

"Tante Lulu!" Mary Mae said. "Come in, you. I'm not ready yet."

"Ready? Ready for what?" Her grandson looked at Mary Mae and seemed to notice for the first time that she had dressed with special care today. She wore black slacks and low-heeled shoes with a two-piece, rose-colored sweater set. The curls of her newly shampooed hair looked soft and fluffy, and her face glowed with a small amount of makeup and lip gloss.

Tante Lulu was dressed for the day, too. Her soft curls were gray, as well, but that was where the similarities ended. Her friend's small body was encased in a long-sleeved, knee-length, zebra print, wraparound dress with a big red vinyl belt and matching red plastic, wedge-heeled shoes. The round circles of rouge on her cheeks and the pouty-outlined lips matched the red belt, too. Lordy, Lordy!

"Um, you goin' somewhere, MawMaw?" Justin asked.

"Dint ya tell him we's havin' a Ladies' Day t'day?" Tante Lulu asked her.

"No chance yet," she said, giving Cage a small smile of apology. "Tante Lulu and me and some of the girls are gonna have a day out."

"What girls?"

Mary Mae didn't like her grandson's tone. Not one bit. She didn't have to account for her every minute to the boy. Did she ask where he'd been all night Saturday?

Recognizing that he might have overstepped himself, Justin said, "I mean, it's nice that you're goin' out with 'the girls.' I actually have to meet with the guys today."

Mary Mae accepted his unspoken apology. "Me and Tante Lulu are gonna join up with Charmaine in her beauty shop in Houma. Some of Tante Lulu's nephews' wives might come with us on a shoppin' trip ta N'awleans, where we's gonna have lunch at Antoine's."

"Are you sure you can handle that much walking?"

"I know enough to sit down and rest if I get overtired."

"Don't you have a doctor's appointment this afternoon?"

She'd moved her medical records from the cancer center in New Orleans to one in Houma to make it easier for her to get to appointments as her disease progressed. "I do, hon, but I canceled and rescheduled fer Friday. I was hopin' ya could come with me, and we could stop by the lawyer's office and the bank on the same day."

He nodded. "Sounds like you've been busy, MawMaw."

Was he upset that she'd done some things on her own initiative?

"I ain't dead yet, boy. If I cain't take care of bizness on mah own, I might as well kick the bucket. And I doan mean one of those silly bucket lists. Ha, ha, ha!"

"Have I fallen down the garden hole?" Justin asked.

"Huh?" she said.

"He means lak *Alice in Wonderland*," Tante Lulu explained. "Folks are allus sayin' that around me."

Just then a male voice on the porch called out, "Can someone hold the door open?"

It was Justin's friend Darryl, and he was carrying a large cypress box inside. It had hand carving on it and painted bayou birds.

"I had a present made fer you." Tante Lulu beamed at Justin.

"You made me a coffin?" Justin stood and backed up against the countertop, horrified.

"A coffin? Fer a midget, mebbe," Tante Lulu scoffed. Then she turned to Mary Mae and said, "Is he allus so thickheaded?"

"He's smarter than a hooty owl and stubborn as a cross-eyed mule," Mary Mae said teasingly.

"It's your hope chest, buddy," Darryl told Justin with a grin.

Justin tilted his head at Tante Lulu. "Men don't have hope chests."

"The men in my family do." Tante Lulu narrowed her eyes at Justin, daring him to make a disparaging remark about the men in her family. He didn't, luckily.

"And I made somethin' fer you, too," Mary Mae told her grandson and picked up the wrapped bundle she'd laid out on a side table the night before. "It's a hand crocheted bedspread fer you and yer bride when ya get married."

Darryl let out a hoot of laughter, which halted immediately when Tante Lulu elbowed him. Justin's mouth gaped open and then he exclaimed, "MawMaw. I'm not gettin' married."

"Ya will someday, and looks lak I won't be around ta dance at yer weddin'. So..." She waved a hand at the hope chest.

He stared at the chest kinda googly-eyed for a minute, then he turned to her and said, "Thank you, MawMaw. And thank you, too, Tante Lulu. It was a super gesture."

Mary Mae suspected Justin was being sarcastic, but luckily Tante Lulu didn't take offense.

"Listen, buddy," Darryl told Justin, "I gotta head off to work. JAM already left. Once the ladies are on their way, you might want to call Slick's cell phone. K-4 and F.U. are here, too. Magnusson stayed behind so that F.U. could come with K-4 because of F.U.'s, you know, expertise."

Mary Mae had no idea who or what Darryl was talking about. Nor did she understand why Darryl and Jacob—that was JAM's real name—would be getting jobs here when they were in the Navy. It was all so confusing.

Tante Lulu pulled a big plastic container out of her suitcase-size purse and put it on the table, motioning for Justin to sit back down. It was beignets. "Ta go with yer coffee," she explained to both Mary Mae and a still-stunned Justin.

"Thass good," Mary Mae said. "I dint have time ta start breakfast."

"Is that yer daddy's guitar I see propped over there?" Tante Lulu asked Justin.

At first, Mary Mae was fearful that Justin might snarl out some rude remark to Tante Lulu. For more years than she could remember, he'd refused to talk about his father. Until yesterday. But, thank the Lord, all he said was, "Yes. MawMaw had it in the attic."

"He usta sing at the Swamp Tavern a long time ago. Didja know that?"

The Swamp Tavern, or Swampy's, was a popular juke joint down on the bayou, though they didn't call them juke joints today. Tavern sounded classier, Mary Mae supposed.

"Actually, I didn't know that," Justin said politely, bless his heart.

"I remember. It was when the tavern first opened, and Beau was so excited ta be paid fer what he loved," Mary Mae mused. "Dint pay worth beans, but Beau got a chance ta sing his songs."

"Ya oughta go over ta Swampy's and look around sometime," Tante Lulu advised. "As I recall, there's some old black-and-white picture of the early days, hanging in the office. Remember that fringed cowboy shirt he usta wear, MaeMae?"

"I do." Mary Mae's eyes welled with tears just thinking about that shirt that he had saved for weeks to buy from the Sears Catalog. She used to wash it by hand and starch it good before hanging it on the line, then ironing it. Those were the days before spray cans of starch. It hadn't been an easy chore, but a labor of love she'd performed with pleasure every Friday until…until…

As if sensing her dismay, Justin changed the subject. "You two aren't plannin' on drivin' yourselves, are you? In Priscilla?"

"Good heavens, no!" Mary Mae told him. "Once yer dressed, ya kin drive us ta Charmaine's shop in Houma. Then either you kin pick us up later this afternoon, or Charmaine will drive us home."

Tante Lulu was at the sink, washing up their breakfast cups even before they'd finished drinking.

"I have a bad feelin' about this, MawMaw."

"Ya gotta trust mah judgment, Justin. I know enough ta stop and rest if I have trouble breathin'. And I won't be doin' much walkin' anyways. Charmaine will drive us wherever we wanna go."

"And you'll call me if there's any problem at all."

"Of course."

"But all the way to N'awleans. I might be an hour away."

"Then I'll just hafta lie down fer a bit when we git where we're goin'."

He put a hand on each hip and narrowed his eyes at her. "And where would that be?"

"Emelie's," Tante Lulu answered for her. "I made a hope chest fer her, too."

Emelie's. Oh, good Lord!

"Ain't that jist great?" Mary Mae said to her grandson.

"Just super!"

Once again, she wasn't sure if he was being sarcastic or serious. Didn't matter. The wheels of her plan were in motion. Now if only St. Jude was listening!

✍

It was a day for visitors, some stranger than others...

Belle was telling Emelie about some new SEALs who had just arrived in Louisiana. "When JAM stopped by with these guys, I about fell over with shock. I haven't seen so many hunks in one place in all my life."

"Hunks, huh?"

"Drop-dead gorgeous. Butts of steel. Packages you'd love to have under your Christmas tree. Well, two of the three were hunks, Slick and K-4, but the third guy, appropriately nicknamed F.U., by the way, he was not so much of a hunk."

"A dog?"

"More his personality than his appearance. Do you know what he said after we were introduced? 'The best thing about Southern belles is they like to have their bells tolled regularly.' Talk about!"

They were both laughing when the shop bell rang and in walked Mary Mae LeBlanc, Tante Lulu, Charmaine LeDeux-Lanier, and two other ladies struggling to carry a large chest between them.

Emelie wasn't dressed for company, having planned to work in the back all day. Quickly, she combed her fingers through her hair. There was nothing she could do about the fleece top and sweatpants she wore for comfort.

"We brought ya a hope chest," Miss MaeMae announced right off. "Tante Lulu had it made special fer you."

Belle choked back a laugh.

"But I'm not getting married. I mean, I was married before, but I have no plans to remarry." She was thoroughly confused. Was Justin behind this? No! He would never send his grandmother here, and he certainly wouldn't be wanting to raise her hopes for marriage. Not that marriage would ever be one of her hopes again either. *I'm losing my mind here.*

"Ya kin allus hope," Tante Lulu said. "I decorated yers with angels and Justin's with birds, but if ya prefer birds, ya kin exchange with him."

"You gave a hope chest to Justin?" *This is not good. Not good at all.*

"She gives them to all the men in her family. Hi, I'm Sylvie LeDeux, Lucien's wife," a pretty, dark-haired, forty-something woman said, extending a hand in greeting.

"And I'm Rachel LeDeux, Remy's wife," another dark-haired woman, late thirties or early forties, offered. "I'm a feng shui decorator. I've been dying to see your shop for ages. Do you mind our dropping by? This is probably a busy time for you."

"It is busy, but we can always take time for a break. Belle, why don't you show the ladies around and I'll take Miss MaeMae back to the courtyard for a cool drink?" The weather was a bit warmer today, especially in the direct sunlight, and Justin's grandmother looked tired.

"That sounds wonderful," Miss MaeMae said, and Emelie adjusted her stride to accommodate the old lady's sickly slow walk. What was she doing, out and about like this?

After Emelie put together a pitcher of sweet tea and glasses out on the white iron table in the courtyard, she sat down next to Miss MaeMae, whose wheezing breaths had thankfully calmed down.

"Dontcha jist love this bluebird weather?" Miss Mae-Mae said, turning her face up to the sun.

"My thoughts exactly." Bluebird weather referred to oddly warm days during winter.

"I'm glad we have a chance to talk in private fer a bit.

I hope ya doan mind us bringin' the hope chest. It was Tante Lulu's idea."

"No, it was a kind thought. Rather misdirected, but appreciated just the same."

"Ya never know. What I wanted ta tell ya, though, is I stopped by yer papa's house today."

Emelie straightened suddenly, almost knocking over her glass of iced tea.

Miss MaeMae patted her hand. "Doan be frettin' none. I jist wanted ta tell yer father that I forgive him."

"Oh, good Lord! What did he say to that?"

"That he couldn't imagine why."

Good ol' dad! "I'm not surprised a bit. He's been living in a state of denial for years."

"Well, he knows now. I reminded him of what he done, and he hemmed and hawed about how I should understand his point of view at the time. Dint matter, though. I made mah peace."

"You are a good woman, Miss MaeMae." Emelie had tears in her eyes as she leaned over and gave the old lady a quick kiss on the cheek. "A better woman than I am, I must say."

"Forgiveness will come in time. Even fer you. Unfortunately, I ain't got that much time left, so I kinda have ta rush things. No, doan go gettin' in a dither. It's a fact of life. All of us gotta face death sometime."

"Not me. Ahm gonna live forever," Tante Lulu said, coming out onto the patio with a jaunty skip. If she wasn't careful, she was going to slip and break a hip in those wedgie shoes. With a sigh of relief, Tante Lulu sank down into the chair opposite Emelie and said, "Yum," when she took her first sip of the tea. "So how's yer love life?"

Emelie choked on her own tea. "Uh." Did she really

ask that in front of Miss MaeMae? The woman was outrageous.

"I dint mean lovemakin', honey. Golly gee, yer gonna sunburn from that blush. No, I meant *love* love," Tante Lulu elaborated.

Oh, well, that was different. Not! "I'm not sure I ever experienced *love* love." Yes, she'd been in love with Justin when they were teenagers, but in retrospect that was probably just puppy love. Infatuation. If they'd stayed together, it would have faded away long ago. Maybe. Probably.

"Remember when I was in love with Phillipe," Tante Lulu said to Miss MaeMae. Then she explained to Emelie, "I was engaged ta marry Mary Mae's brother Phillipe Prudhomme before he went off ta war. Now, that was *love* love." She sighed deeply. "I thought about him day and night. And tingles, ah, that boy could make me get the tingles jist by lookin' at me. If he winked at me, and whoo-boy, Phillipe had a good wink, or if he touched mah shoulder in passin', or if he kissed me kinda deep and hard, or if he pinched mah butt...I was tinglin' all over 'til I was practically screamin' with passion. Tingles, that's one of the big signs of *love* love."

Emelie and Miss MaeMae were both staring at Tante Lulu, slack-jawed.

"No tingles in my life at the moment, I'm afraid," Emelie choked out.

"Well, not to worry, hon," Tante Lulu said, patting Emelie on the hand. "Jist so ya doan go tryin' ta get yer tingles from one of them vibrator thingees. Charmaine says all the ladies use 'em t'day, that they doan need no man, but seems ta me yer va-jay-jay would get all tingled out in the wrong way. Dontcha think?"

"Uh. Yes. Sure."

"Tingles come when ya least expect them, girl."

I can't wait.

"Yer tingles are sure ta come soon. By the way, I brought ya another little present."

Oh, God! Please don't let it be a vibrator. "Really, you've given me too much already."

But Tante Lulu was already standing, watching expectantly for something. The old lady jumped from one subject to another so quickly that Emelie's brain raced, trying to keep up. A hope chest, *love* love, tingles, vibrators, and now *another* gift?

"Rachel and Sylvie and Charmaine are bringing it in from the car. There they are now."

Carrying a big marble statue around the side through the porte cochere, the three women set it down next to her fountain, and let out a communal whoosh of relief at its weight.

"Ain't he cute?" Tante Lulu asked Emelie.

"Uh," she said.

"Ya cain't live within a hundred miles of Tante Lulu and not have at least one St. Jude statue," Charmaine explained with a wink.

Oh, so that was what it was. There was a big smudge mark over one side of the face that had distorted the image. It might have been bird poop.

"St. Jude is the patron saint of hopeless cases," Tante Lulu said.

As if Emelie didn't already know that, having been raised a Catholic! But she wasn't about to offend the old lady. Instead, she said, "Thank you so much. How did you know I was feeling hopeless?"

"We's all hopeless one time or another."

Her visitors stayed for only an hour, having a

reservation for 1 p.m. at Antoine's. Emelie declined to join them, as did Belle, since they both had too much work to do. Plus, Belle had several in-home costume fittings later that afternoon.

After they left, Emelie said to Belle, "That was unexpected, but kind of nice."

"I agree. That Tante Lulu is a piece of work, though, isn't she?'

"Oh my God! Those zebra stripes and red wedgies!" Emelie laughed. "I can only imagine what a character she would have been when she was young."

"Wild, for sure," Belle agreed.

"Miss MaeMae didn't look good at all, did she?"

Belle shook her head sadly. "I see a difference just since the cleanup party last week."

"Maybe it's not the cancer. Maybe she was just overtired today."

"Maybe," Belle said, but there was doubt in her voice.

Late in the afternoon, Belle had gone out and Emelie was working on final touches to several masks when she heard the shop bell ring. Before she had a chance to get up and go wait on a customer, Justin walked back.

"Hey, babe!" he said and gave her a smile that was as warm as a kiss. Maybe not. Because he leaned down and gave her a quick kiss on the lips, and it was hot. No warm about it.

"I'm a mess," she said. "I wasn't expecting anyone today."

"You look fine to me."

Yeah, right. If I was modeling workout apparel. Even then…

"The fleece top would be better if you turned it inside out, assuming you're not wearing a bra. And then the least little movement would brush over...well, you get the idea."

She must have been gaping because he winked at her.

"Remember the time I put that ridged condom on inside out? We were so dumb, we thought that was the way it was supposed to be. But whoo-boy, what a ride that was!"

Having succeeded in planting that image in her mind, he leaned back against the wide, built-in shelf that lined one wall, midway up, like a counter, ankles crossed, arms folded over his chest. He wore a Saints baseball cap, a long-sleeved black T-shirt, jeans, and athletic shoes. A designer stubble gave his face a rakish look. Even with the cap, she could see that the stubble on his head was growing in from its military cut, and it, too, was also a bit rakish.

"What are you doing here?" she asked.

"I missed you." There was a world of promise in those simple words. "Thought you might be lonely."

"Hard to be lonely with all the traffic through here today." She glanced pointedly at the hope chest off to one side adorned with angels gamboling along a bayou stream. It was really rather pretty.

He laughed. "Tell me about it. I got hit with mine at seven a.m."

"Tante Lulu told me yours has birds. Wanna exchange birds for cupids?"

"Nah. I'm fine. I've already got a crocheted bedspread in mine. How about yours?"

"Doilies."

He shook his head at the uselessness of such a gift. "That Tante Lulu is a pure one hundred proof dingbat."

"She really does mean well, though."

"I s'pose so," he conceded. "How was my grand-mother?"

She didn't want to alarm him. "Okay. A little tired, I think, but she seemed to be enjoying herself."

"I should probably be offerin' ta take her more places."

He probably should, while she was still able, Emelie thought, but she didn't say that. "Would you like a cup of coffee?"

"Nope."

"A cold drink?"

He shook his head and continued to stare at her.

"What?"

"Wanna fool around?"

She laughed. "You don't beat around the bush, do you?"

"Darlin', do you really want me ta say what I'm thinkin'?"

She frowned. When she realized that he was referring to a play on the word "bush," she blushed. "You're certainly in a good mood."

"Uh-huh," he said and beckoned with both hands for her to come over to him. The intent in his mischievous eyes was clear.

"You can't be serious. It's daytime."

"So? A little afternoon delight."

"Someone could walk in the shop."

"I locked the door and hung the CLOSED sign."

"You didn't!"

"Yeah, I did."

"That was kind of confident of you, wasn't it?"

"Wanna come over here and punish me fer bein' so... confident?" He waggled his eyebrows at her.

Jeesh! I hate when he does that eyebrow thing. It makes me all melty inside. Or am I tingling? No, defi-

nitely no tingling. "Punish? Are you into those kinds of games?"

"I can be if you want me to."

That sounded kind of alarming. And no, she was not tingling. Yet. "I'd rather play the cowboy/guitar game."

"We'll have ta save that for another time, sweetie. I didn't bring the gear today."

She propped an elbow on the table in front of her, and braced her chin on a cupped hand. "What do you want, Justin?"

"You. Any way I can have you," he said. "Just you."

Tingle, tingle, tingle! "Oh, man! You do know how to rock a girl's heart!" *And tingle her.*

"I aim ta please." He smiled, slow and lazy at first, as she stood tentatively. Then when she walked into his embrace, he let out a whoop of joy. Lifting her off her feet with his arms around her waist, he swung around several times for the sheer pleasure of holding her.

And she held on tight, her face buried in the curve of his neck, gritting her teeth to prevent herself from blurting out something foolish, like, "I love you." Or, "Are you tingling, too?"

"Baby, I wanna pick you up, carry you upstairs, and make sweet love to you, but I don't think my knee could take it." He still held her with her feet off the ground so that she was looking down at him.

His demeanor was so doleful at his physical weakness that she felt sorry for him and suggested, "We could always walk together upstairs."

Even more doleful, he said, "I don't think I can wait that long."

"Is that a fact?" She wriggled herself against him so

that her thigh rubbed against a strategic spot on his body. To set it tingling, she hoped.

"Irrefutable," he gasped out. "I'm in pain, sweetheart."

Pain, tingles, same thing.

"Only you have the cure."

She laughed. "That sounds like something you would have said in the backseat of Priscilla. Are you playing me?"

"A little bit," he admitted with the sideways grin she'd once loved so well. "Oops."

Somehow he'd walked them across the room and he'd just banged her against the wall. Before she could blink, he had his hands inside the back of her sweatpants and both her panties and sweats down at her ankles. He was unzipping his jeans, under which he was commando, surprise, surprise, and putting on a condom so quick she had to say, "You've got that down to an art form."

"Honey, if I can break down, clean, and put back together an AK-47 in three minutes flat, getting prepped for sex is a piece of cake. This is gonna be tricky, though." He yanked off one of her sneakers and pulled off one leg of the sweatpants and half her panties to dangle from the other leg. Raising the one bare leg by the knee and off to the side, he was in her, to the hilt. The whole thing had happened in less than a minute.

She blinked at him in shock.

"Sorry," he said. "I told ya I couldn't wait."

"I thought you meant that you couldn't wait for a half hour, or until we got upstairs."

"Oh, damn! You're not ready." He started to pull out. "I'm sorry."

She grabbed him by the butt and yanked him back. "Don't you dare stop."

He was the one blinking in shock now.

What followed next wasn't short and sweet. It was short and hot, hot, hot. No gentle wooing words. No soft caresses. No buildup of passion.

It was bang, bang, bang, her bottom hitting against the wall, his pubic bone hitting her clitoris, his erection hitting a spot it had never hit before. They both exploded in a bone-melting orgasm that had him sinking to the floor afterward, sitting on his bare ass, her half on and half off his lap.

They burst out laughing then as they tried to disentangle themselves.

"I couldn't replicate that if I tried," he said.

All she could say was, "Wow!"

They were both sitting on the floor, bare-assed.

It was only then that she heard, "Woof!"

"Did you just say 'woof'?"

"Huh?"

Another "Woof!" It was coming from outside.

"Oh, crap! I totally forgot." Justin jumped to his feet, made quick work of disposing the condom, then shuffled from foot to foot as he tried to pull up his jeans.

"What? What's going on?"

He gave her a sheepish look then. "I brought you a present, and I forgot to bring it in."

"More presents? First roses, then a hope chest, then a St. Jude statue. This better be good."

"Oh, it is. It definitely is." He went out to the back courtyard.

She had pulled on her panties and sweatpants and was bent over tying her sneakers when she heard a "Woof!" again, just before being knocked over onto her back and a big beast of a dog was licking every surface it could reach with a goofy look of ecstasy on its face. His mismatched blue and brown eyes were practically crossed at each other in delight.

She glanced up to see Justin peering down at them.

"You didn't!"

"I did. See how much Thad missed you. And he was very well behaved all this time out in your courtyard. He didn't even pee on that statue with the bird shit birthmark on its face, until you started screamin' your orgasm. Good dog! He thought you needed help." Justin batted his eyelashes at her. Thad did, too.

"I did not scream."

"Okay. Groaned real loud."

"Maybe that was you."

"Probably."

"You're being way too agreeable."

"Hey, I just got laid. Of course I'm being agreeable."

"I'm not keeping him."

He helped her to her feet and kissed her softly.

"I'm not keeping him."

Justin found a bowl to fill with water for the dog. As she gazed down at the dog, who kept giving her soulful, pleading looks between slurps, she said, "I'm not keeping him."

Then, having worn himself out woofing and drinking three bowls of water, the dog that could be a horse splatted himself out, paws spread to four corners like a giant rug, and fell asleep.

"I'm not keeping him," she said, but with less conviction.

"I have an idea," Justin said then. "Wanna fool around?"

"I thought we already did that."

"Just an appetizer, *cherè*. Just an appetizer."

"I can't imagine what...hey, what are you doing with those feathers? Be careful. They're for my masks."

He twirled one long-plumed feather in his hand and blew on it. The silky threads fluttered like the tendrils of moss on a live oak tree during a bayou wind. "You don't have to imagine, sweetheart. I've got imagination enough for both of us."

And he did!

And yes, dammit, she was tingling.

Chapter Sixteen

There's always room for humor, even in the direst circumstances...

Y̶ou do realize that you're walking around with the loopiest grin on your face all the time, don't you?" Slick said to him. Slick, or Lieutenant Commander Luke Avenil, one of the senior members of SEAL Team Thirteen, had been around since before Cage first entered BUD/S.

"You're just jealous."

"Whatever."

They were sitting at a conference table in a presumably abandoned warehouse halfway between Houma and Lafayette, waiting for the Fibbies and local and state law enforcement agents to show up.

"He's grinning because he's in *luuuuuv*," said JAM, who sat on Cage's other side.

"I think it's because he found someone to suck his sorry-ass dick." This from F.U., who sat across the table.

Otherwise, Cage would have clocked him a good one. What an asshole! Too bad his demolition/explosives expertise was so critical to this mission.

K-4, or Kevin Fortunato, who'd lost his wife to cancer a few years back, smacked F.U. for Cage and said, "If it's love, go for it, Cage my friend."

"Well, be careful. Before you know it, you'll be paying alimony out the eyeballs. You never really know a woman until you meet her divorce lawyer," Slick remarked as he idly checked text messages on his cell phone. Slick's ex-wife had been taking him back to court every other year to bleed him for more cash, mainly because he'd inherited some posh home in Malibu that she hadn't been able to tap into yet. As long as he resided in the domicile and didn't cash in, she was SOL, which gave Slick immense pleasure. In fact, he'd been known to take pictures of himself reclining on a deck chair in sunglasses with a hot babe and sending them to her. Immature, yeah, but totally understandable from the male POV.

"Uh, I think there has to be a marriage and a divorce before there's alimony," Cage made the mistake of pointing out.

"Not necessarily," Geek said from behind them. He was checking out the array of high-tech computer and camera equipment lined up on tables along both walls. Equipment so complex only Bill Gates or geniuses with Mensa credentials would be able to operate. Geek was rambling on about partner privilege and common law marriage and other legal mumbo jumbo that had nothing to do with Cage or Cage's grinning.

Cage was happy. Enough said! And really, he didn't want to discuss this with the guys. The feelings he had for Em were too precious, and fragile, to share. He had

no idea where they were going, or if they were going anywhere, but he sure as hell was enjoying the moment.

John LeDeux came in with a contingent of local and
state police. Best known in the bayou as Tee-John, or
Small John, for reasons unknown since he was over six
feet tall, LeDeux had already met with Cage. He came
over and Cage introduced him to his SEAL buddies.

"How's yer grandmother doin'?" John asked him.

"Good days and bad days. Tante Lulu and the rosary
ladies are with her today, putting together a quilt, I think."

"For yer hope chest?"

"Oh, God! I hope not."

All of his SEAL buddies' ears perked up at the mention of "hope chest." No way was he getting into that
discussion, or he would never hear the end of it when he
got back to Coronado. SEALs loved to gossip about one
another and loved nothing more than to rattle one another's chains, taking razzing to a new level. There were no
secrets when you knew your fellow operatives so well
you could recognize their individual body odor at twenty
paces. "Can you show me that map of the Mardi Gras
parade route again?" he asked John.

Bernie came in then and joined them.

"Bernie, you look like death warmed over," Cage said.

"I've lost ten pounds. My hair is falling out. And I can't
sleep," Bernie told them. Under his breath, he added to
Cage, "And I'm suffering from ED."

It took a moment for Cage to realize that Bernie
referred to erectile dysfunction. He shifted away from the
man. Way too much information!

"Ya gotta get yer act t'gether, Bern," John said in his
heavy Cajun accent.

Cage had an accent, too, even after all these years, and

it was getting stronger by the moment. More fodder for the razz mill! F.U. would be making more jokes about Southern men sounding like pussies.

"If yer not careful, yer gonna blow this whole setup," John told Bernie.

"I got a prescription for sleeping pills. Maybe I'll try those." Bernie looked at Cage. "Maybe I could come stay at your house with you and Aunt MaeMae until after Mardi Gras."

"Are you crazy? You're not living with me. You married my girlfriend." When would Bernie get it through his thick skull that they were not friends? Not even close. No matter their blood connection, distant as it was.

"She wasn't your girlfriend anymore. I told you, you need to ask Emelie about that."

"Forget about it. You're not becoming my sleep buddy."

"Cool yer jets, Bern," John said with a laugh. "We have a female detective who's gonna move in with you today. A live-in lover." He motioned with his head toward a woman whose statuesque build couldn't be hidden by her jeans and blazer.

"Really?" Bernie immediately brightened up.

"It's just a pretense," John told him.

"Oh, right." Bernie licked his two forefingers and tried to flatten down his unruly eyebrows.

Cage and John rolled their eyes at each other.

The Fibbies strolled in then, fortunate timing since F.U. had just gotten a gander at the female detective, and Lord only knew what vulgarity would come out of his mouth. John Elliott introduced himself as leader of Project Boom. "Since the SEALs were first on the scene here, and because there is clearly a terrorist threat, I will turn the meeting over to Lieutenant Commander Luke Avenil."

Luke, who was in civvies, as were the other team members, not wanting to announce their military backgrounds to the tangos, got up and stood at the head of the table.

"We have a full-fledged terrorist threat here in Louisiana. Our intel shows that the al-Qaeda cell headed by Abdul Hassid is the one directly involved; he's the same tango who claimed responsibility for the bombings in Paris last month. Open your folders, and check out page three. Study them well while you're here, but do not take them with you. I repeat, the folders stay here."

There were plain black folders in front of each of them, except for Bernie. Opening them, Cage saw page after page of intel. Diagrams, news clips, and everything relevant to this mission. He'd have to be a genius to memorize it all in an hour or so. He and the other SEALs would do their best, then rely on Geek to regurgitate it all back to them.

"Project Boom is expected to happen on Fat Tuesday, during the major Mardi Gras parade through New Orleans," Slick continued. "We know the grade of explosives that will be used, the amount that was shipped into this area, and the types of pyrotechnic rockets they will be hidden in. What we don't know is where those hot fireworks are at the moment or where they are scheduled to go off. We do not believe they are intended for the official fireworks arena."

John LeDeux stood up and gave a short brief on Mardi Gras celebrations. "Carnival begins in Loo-zee-anna at the beginning of January and parades are held throughout that season all over the state, leadin' up to the big ones on Fat Tuesday, the day before Ash Wednesday when Lent begins. We'll concentrate on the parades and outdoor events in N'awleans on that last day, the King Rex parade and others through the Quarter. You have to realize there are hundreds of thousands of tourists in the state for Carnival. When it comes to terrorist attacks, the crowd on Fat Tuesday on Bourbon Street alone would rival the numbers that went down in the Twin Towers."

Silence met John's ominous words.

"Can't we just go in and take the perps into custody?" one of the cops asked.

"Not yet. The worst-case scenario is that we arrest the tangos and they refuse to disclose where and when the explosives are to go off. We'd end up having to evacuate the whole city. As you all know, some of these fanatics will consider it a holy jihad to go up in flames before giving up any secrets."

"Plus, we can't torture information out of terrorists anymore. Too politically incorrect!" one of the Fibbies complained. When his superior glared at him, he slunk down into his seat, grumbling. They might all agree that it was a ridiculous policy, but they weren't supposed to express that opinion in public.

Different members around the table stood up then. Outlining the main parade route. Detailing where Landry Pyrotechnics were to be set off in safe public demonstrations. Showing trucks to be used for deliveries. Listing all the employees involved in the various jobs, from the business side down to the assembly line. Explaining the surveillance of the tangos in question. Showing how GPS chips had been slipped into every single pallet or skid, which carried dozens of boxes of pyrotechnics leaving the factory, from high-powered rockets right down to seemingly harmless sparklers. Then outlining a day-by-day schedule of what would happen between today and Fat Tuesday, which was fifteen days away. Each of the twenty-one people in the room knew by the end of the afternoon exactly what their role would be to bring about a successful mission. In the best of circumstances, no one would be killed on either side, and the bad guys would end up in custody.

After the meeting, Cage and his SEAL team members decided to stop at the Swamp Tavern for a drink. Cage, JAM, and Geek were headed in that direction, and Cage had his own reasons for that particular choice of beer joint; so the other guys decided to follow them.

Cage got there first and introduced himself to Gator, longtime waiter/bouncer/co-owner of the tavern. He explained his special request to the bald-headed waiter, with his trademark gold loop earring in one ear only. Gator led him back to the office, and left him alone. "Hope you find what you're lookin' for, buddy. And by the way, I appreciate your service to our country."

Lots of folks said that to him when they learned he was in the military. You'd never know there was that kind of grassroots support by watching the national news networks. Cage wondered idly how Gator knew he was military, but then the bayou grapevine was a remarkable communicator.

At first, Cage just stood in the office. He was already feeling like a fool. But then he took a deep breath and began to examine the photographs displayed around the small room. It took him only a second the find the black-and-white one with his father in it. Standing with several members of a band, The Country Swingers, he wore a fringed cowboy shirt and a white, wide-brimmed cowboy hat. About twenty-five, Cage figured, and yeah, he was a good-looking dude. The smile on his face was so innocently open and friendly. It broke Cage's heart to think of all that happened to him between the night this photo was taken and the night he was stabbed in Angola Prison.

Geek peeked in just then and said, "We're ordering a pitcher. Did you want . . . hey, something wrong, bud?"

Cage shook his head. "Nah, I'm just checkin' out the old photographs here. That's my dad there." Cage had every intention of borrowing the picture at some point and having it duplicated. He was fairly certain it was the only copy.

"Whoa, he looks just like you."

"He does?"

"Yeah. Same grin," Geek said.

At one time, Cage would have denied any resemblance, but he didn't now. How odd! Even odder, as they walked out of the office, Cage said, "Did I tell you my father wrote the song 'Prison Is a State of Mind'?"

"No shit! I saw a special on Johnny Cash one time where he sang that song. I'm pretty sure he said that he'd met the songwriter."

After that, Cage was much more relaxed as the group sat around a table in the dark bar, which was mostly empty in this late-afternoon lull before the dinner and evening crowds. They all had beers in front of them, and a heaping pile of crawfish, or mudbugs as they were known in the South, sitting on the newspaper-covered table.

Cage flexed his hands and told the guys, "Watch an expert, boys. This is how it's done." He then demonstrated the proper procedure for breaking off the head and sucking the juices from it, then cracking open the tail horizontally along its back, pulling out the succulent meat to pop into his mouth.

"I used to have a T-shirt about this very thing," F.U. said. "SHUCK ME, SUCK ME, EAT ME RAW."

"That refers to oysters, dickhead," Cage told him.

"Same thing," F.U. insisted.

"Not even a little."

It took them a while to get the knack but they eventually agreed with Cage when he declared, "Crawfish is food of the gods, next to hot wings."

They talked as they ate, and soon Cage was caught up on all the news back at the base, who was doing whom, who got done wrong, the usual.

"It's amazing that you just fell on this case," Slick commented to Cage as he wiped his hands and mouth on a paper towel. "This whole thing could have developed into a major SNAFU, without anyone ever knowing about it."

"Forget SNAFU. It could have been a monumental catastrophe," said K-4 as he wiped some foam off his mouth with the back of his hand.

New Orleans was a big city, but it turned Cage's stomach to think that Emelie might have been in danger from what these fanatics were planning. Still might be. Somehow he would make sure before that time that she was nowhere in the vicinity of the parade route on that day.

"Well, there have been rumblings for a long time about another 'event' coming down involving Hassid but no details. We probably wouldn't have got the details in time," Geek said after taking a long draw on his brew.

"Sometimes that's the way the best operations go down. Chance can never be minimized." Cage shrugged his opinion. Often the least likely sources proved most helpful, and missions deemed sure things were total FUBARs.

"Well, good for you for recognizing the possibility of a threat from the beginning," Slick said, raising his beer in a toast to him. The others joined in, "Hear, hear!"

Cage shrugged. It was what they were trained to do.

In fact, it was hard to believe, as they sat here talking and drinking casually, that they were involved in an urgent mission that might have the potential for disaster. But SEALs were trained professionals, working with other trained professionals. Teamwork. And you took your breaks when you could, always alert to danger and a call to action. Each of them had secure phones attached to their belts.

"Things are really heating up in Iran again," K-4 remarked. "I expect we'll be deployed there next. When do you think you might be back, Cage?"

"I really don't know. My knee is almost a hundred percent, and I could go off on short missions, but I doubt if Iran will be on my radar anytime soon."

"You are coming back, aren't you?" Slick asked.

"Of course. Why would you ask that?"

Slick exchanged glances with JAM and Geek, and he knew his buddies had been talking about him. What else was new? "Well?"

"You wouldn't be the first guy to give up the teams for a woman," Slick said.

"I never, ever said I was thinkin' about giving up SEALs. Well, the only time I ever mentioned the possibility was when I first told Commander MacLean about my grandmother. I said that, if I couldn't have an extended liberty, I would quit. It's that important that I stay with MawMaw until the end."

"Don't get your tail in a twist," JAM told him. "No one's accusing you of anything. And by the way, how come you told us you had a brother Phillipe?"

"Did I say that?" Cage continued to eat.

"Damn straight you did."

"I also told you I had a sister Doris who was a nymphomaniac, as I recall. Then there was my cousin Brutus who whistled 'Dixie' every time he whacked off. And a great-uncle Larry Jo, who was descended from Robert E. Lee." At the look of consternation on their faces, he added, "*Pfff!* You guys are a bunch of gossips. You're worse than—"

"Tante Lulu?" JAM and Geek said at the same time, grinning at him like idiots.

He couldn't stay mad at guys like that.

"We wondered if you made up all those stories. We even wondered if you had a MawMaw," Geek said.

"The best liars are ones who mix truth with fiction," K-4 told them.

"What, you're suddenly a bullshit philosopher?" F.U. remarked to K-4.

"Kiss my ass," K-4 retorted to F.U.

"No thanks," F.U. said, pleased with himself that he'd been able to goad K-4.

"Hey, you guys should come back with us to Tante Lulu's for dinner," Geek said to Slick, K-4, and F.U. "You have never met a woman like Louise Rivard in all your life."

"Is she hot?" F.U. wanted to know. He'd already got shot down after hitting on one of the waitresses. "Louise the Tease?"

"Yeah, she's hot. Just your style," JAM said, with a straight face even.

"Hoo-yah!" F.U. exclaimed with his version of a lascivious grin.

Cage was still laughing as he drove back to his grandmother's cottage. Tante Lulu might be the woman to finally straighten out F.U.

He wasn't laughing when he traveled down the last stretch of the single-lane highway toward his grandmother's cottage ... and he passed an ambulance coming in the opposite direction.

❧

Secrets always come back to haunt us ...

Two days later, Emelie walked down the corridor toward Miss MaeMae's room in the Houma hospital. She was carrying a potted pink rosebush, which she intended to replant for Justin's grandmother once she got home. So many times, the abundance of cut flowers in a hospital room made it feel more like a funeral parlor. At least a potted plant gave the promise of going home.

It was a good thing Miss MaeMae had a private room because Emelie saw immediately that it was overflowing with visitors, and they were all talking at once, including a few ladies from Our Lady of the Bayou Rosary Society, who were murmuring over their beads in the corner. They finished up, but the others in the room didn't even notice when they waved and blew kisses as they left the room.

"This is my nephew Daniel LeDeux. He's an on-colliejest. He and his twin brother, Aaron, moved here from Alaska," Tante Lulu told Miss MaeMae from one side of the bed, where a tall handsome man in a dark suit was examining her medical charts. He was thirty-something and drop-dead gorgeous, like all the LeDeux men. "Daniel's gonna tell us what's what."

Daniel rolled his eyes and told Miss MaeMae and Justin, whose back was to Emelie, "I was a pediatric oncologist. I'm no longer practicing, but I can tell you that your doctor is doing everything possible. With proper bed rest—"

"See, that's what I've been tryin' ta say. You need ta stay here in the hospital and rest," Justin interjected. Emelie could tell by his wrinkled clothes that he hadn't slept in days.

"That's not really what—" Daniel tried to say. To no avail.

Miss MaeMae was on a rant, insisting, "I doan care what ya say, Justin Joseph LeBlanc. I'm goin' home. I aim ta die in mah own bed in mah own time with fresh gumbo on the stove and Elvis playin' on the stereo, not some dumb piped-in Yankee music."

What "Summer in the City" had to do with Yankees, Emelie wasn't sure.

But Justin was equally insistent. "That's fine, but I've hired a nurse to stay with you when I can't be there. It's bad enough that you fired the home care worker after I got here, *without telling me, by the way.* We're not gonna have another episode where you pass out for lack of sufficient oxygen."

"Doan take life so serious, boy. None of us gets out alive," Miss MaeMae joked.

Justin was not amused.

"*Pfff!* I passed out 'cause I was laughin' so hard at Tante Lulu tellin' us 'bout her trip to a Bourbon Street adult store named Mother Hubbard's Adult Cupboard."

"Actually, it was when I was tellin' ya 'bout the rabbit that vibrated its little wee-wee that ya almos' bust a gut," Tante Lulu corrected the lady in the bed.

Miss MaeMae was fighting a grin.

"I don't care if you laugh your ass off," Justin asserted. "Unless you're willin' ta have a nurse at least part of the time, I'm not signin' you out of here."

"And who says yer my boss fer any kinda signin' out?"

The grandmother and grandson glared at each other, with Miss MaeMae saying finally, "Yer as nervous as a hooker at a Holy Roller convention. Lighten up, boy."

"Nervous? Nervous? How about ready to pull my hair out frustrated?" Justin practically shouted.

"It ain't fitten fer you ta talk ta your grandma that-away," Tante Lulu tried to interject.

This fussing couldn't be doing Miss MaeMae any good.

"Excuse me," Emelie said loudly, stepping into the room.

Everyone turned to look at her.

"Hi, Miss MaeMae," she said, walking over to the bed next to Justin and kissing the old lady on the cheek. "Now you don't look so bad. Here I was expecting to see you all weak and frail. You didn't sound frail to me when I stepped in."

Justin, who hadn't shaved in two days and looked as disreputable as he was, pinched her on the butt, but she ignored him and continued, "I brought you some pink roses. When you get home, I was thinking I could plant them against the chicken pen. Don't you think they would look good there? You could watch them grow from your rocker on the back porch."

"That is so nice of you, dear. Put them over there on the windowsill where I can see them, next to the St. Jude statue Tante Lulu brought," Miss MaeMae said.

"Pink roses, huh?" Justin murmured. "Where'd you get that idea, *chère*?"

"Shhh. Behave yourself."

"Emelie, this is my nephew Daniel. He's a special doctor," Tante Lulu said.

They all understood that Tante Lulu meant specialist. Was that a bad sign that they were coming to understand her particular lingo?

Daniel rolled his eyes again and said, "Pleased to meet you."

"Likewise," she said.

Justin growled behind her. He actually growled.

"Thank ya fer comin' all this way ta see me," Miss MaeMae said. "That was a long drive fer so late in the day."

"I had some other errands to do down the bayou," *one of which should be showing up soon*, "and besides, I wanted to invite Justin here to one of the Mardi Gras balls being held this Friday in N'awleans."

"You mean, one of those black tie, pike-up-the-ass, formal affairs?" Justin asked with distaste.

"Yes, but very nice, and for a good cause."

"Unfortunately, I can't go because my grandmother is insistin' on comin' home tomorrow and I need to stay with her." He put on a fake face of regret.

"Who sez ya cain't go?" Miss MaeMae said. "I 'spect I kin abide a nurse once in a while."

They all laughed then, including Justin, who had been finagled into attending the type of formal event he hated. Too bad!

"Besides that, I don't have my dress whites with me. Oh, well, maybe some other time."

"You can rent a tux at the Speedy Tux Shop in Houma," Emelie said.

"Damn!"

"An' they have every color in the world. Black, white, green, lavender, even pink. Oooh, oooh, oooh, I even saw one in cammy-flahg."

"That is just super," Justin said and gave Emelie a cross-eyed look of annoyance.

Daniel LeDeux made his excuses and left, winking at Emelie as he passed, just to annoy Justin, she assumed. Tante Lulu was fidgeting around the room, tidying up, waiting for Charmaine to come pick her up, although Justin offered to drive her home. A nurse was checking Miss MaeMae's vitals.

"Ya oughta go to Charmaine's shop before yer ball," Tante Lulu told Emelie. "She'd give yer hair a good Texas mousse. Ya know what they say, 'The higher the hair, the closer ta God.' Plus, she knows this place where ya kin buy these nipple rings what pinch yer nipples soz they stick out nice and proud in yer ball gown, jist lak cherries ripe fer pluckin'. I tried 'em myself but I couldn't find them suckers nohow."

Miss MaeMae giggled in the bed. The nurse almost dropped her thermometer. And Justin was bent over at the waist trying not to laugh out loud while murmuring, "Please, God, let there be cherry pluckin'."

"'Course you got a pretty good bosom; so mebbe you doan need any help in that regard. Me, mah biggest failin' is no tushie. Somehow I lost my hiney about twenty years ago and cain't get it back even with those panties with the built-in butt cheeks." When she realized everyone was staring at her, she said, "What? A gal's gotta do what a gal's gotta do ta succeed in this world. Doan men wear tight pants ta show off their packages?" She was staring pointedly at the crotch of Justin's jeans.

Fortunately, or unfortunately, the nurse left, but there were new arrivals. Claude Gaudet and Francine Lagasse. Emelie had stopped at her father's house on the way there and given him orders. Apologize or he wouldn't see her again.

"Miss MaeMae," Claude said, stepping up to her bedside.

"Wait a damn minute," Justin said and started toward her father.

Emelie tugged on his arm and led him over to the window. "Now you listen here, Justin. My father has some things to say to your grandmother, and to you, and you're going to let him say his piece. You're not going to like some things you learn, but you're going to keep your mouth shut, and think before you act. You're going to do this for your grandmother, y'hear?"

He hesitated, then gave her a little salute. "Yes, ma'am."

They both stood at the end of the bed. Tante Lulu wouldn't leave now if St. Jude was standing in the hall. Or Richard Simmons. Well, maybe then, but it would take a miracle of that magnitude to uproot her from this juicy event.

Francine backed into the corridor, within view if her father needed her help, but wanting no part in this particular travesty.

"Miss MaeMae, when ya came ta my house offerin' fergivness, I treated ya poorly."

"When? When did she go to the bastard's house?" Justin wanted to know.

"Shhh. Last week," Emelie said. "Be quiet and let him talk."

Justin arched a brow at her bossiness.

"I'm the one that shoulda come ta you beggin' fergiveness, instead of ya havin' ta take the first step. I'm not proud of what I done. I shoulda never made those threats ta you and Rufus all those years ago. I used my influence with the bank ta get poor folks ta do my will, and it was wrong. I am deeply sorry."

Miss MaeMae patted his hand where it rested on her blanket. "I already tol' ya that ya have mah fergiveness. From others?" She glanced at Justin. "Ahm not so sure."

With a sigh of resignation, her father turned to Justin, who stood shoulders back with all his military bearing, staring down at the older man. When had her father shrunk in size, or was it just that Justin had grown? The disparity was alarming.

"What. Did. You. Do?" Justin gritted out.

"Ya already know what I did with Judge Benoit ta get you out of Loo-zee-anna. Ya weren't the man for mah Emelie then, and ya probably still aren't, but thass not fer me ta say anymore. I regret mah methods, and I might even have been wrong about the bad seed/bad blood business. You've certainly proven that a man can rise above his roots."

"If that's an apology, then shove it," Justin snarled. "I'm proud of my roots."

"I'm sayin' this all wrong. I'm tryin' ta say I shouldn't have judged ya by yer family but by yer deeds, which were mighty bad, as I recall."

Justin tilted his head, conceding that point.

"No question, I handled things ass backwards and too many folks suffered as a result. It wasn't enough fer me ta get ya away from mah little girl, I wanted ta make sure that ya never came back, or that she never went with you. So I took a banker with me ta visit yer grandparents. Yer PawPaw was sufferin' some financial straits with his shrimp boat at the time. I knew that, and I had the bank threaten ta call in the loan if they let any letters or phone calls pass between you and Emelie." He sighed deeply, as if he'd gotten a huge weight off his chest. "Thass what I done, and I'm not proud of myself either."

"Those letters you were clutching that day at my grandmother's, were they my letters to you, or yours to me?" Justin asked Emelie.

"Mine to you. Your grandmother saved them."

"And the ones I wrote to you?" When she didn't answer, he turned to her father. "Did you intercept them?"

"I did."

"And?"

"Burned them, every single one."

Emelie could see the rage boil up in Justin. His face was flushed and his hands were fisting and unfisting at his sides. She feared more than anything that he would hit her father, and with him being so much bigger and stronger, it wouldn't be a fair fight.

There was a long silence before Justin spoke. "Let me get this straight. You manipulated the legal system to get me booted out of the state. Then you manipulated the financial system to keep me and Em further apart. Then you cut off any means of communication I might have had by letters. What else?"

"Well, I talked Emelie into marryin' that wuss Bernie. Thought it would be better 'n you, but look how that turned out." The look of disgust on his face was priceless.

Justin let out a hoot of laughter at that, and the rest of them began to laugh, too. In relief.

"You are one pathetic son of a bitch," Justin told her father.

"I was," her father admitted. "I'm reformed." He glanced at Emelie for confirmation. "I promised my daughter."

"What do you want from me?" Justin asked her father. "Forgiveness? A pat on the back for finally admitting your sins? A pass through the Pearly Gates when you finally get there, if you do? That we become good buddies and share a beer on occasion?"

"*Mon Dieu!* None of those. I mean, yeah, forgiveness would be nice, but I did this fer Emelie, and fer myself, as much as anything. Besides that, I'm not allowed ta have beer on my heart diet."

Justin eyed him suspiciously. "I'm escortin' Emelie ta some charity ball on Friday night. How do you feel 'bout that?"

Claude gritted his teeth at Justin's surly attitude. "Hope ya look like a fool in one of them monkey suits."

They all relaxed then, and Francine came in to join Claude in talking to Tante Lulu and Miss MaeMae. While they were busy, Emelie took Justin by the hand and coaxed him outside.

"Thank you," she said, squeezing his hand.

"For what?" he grumbled.

"Not taking a potshot at my dad."

"I was tempted."

"I could tell." She took a tissue from her pocket and swiped at her eyes.

"You *should* be thankin' me," he said then. There was a mischievous sparkle in his eyes, which had been so angry only moments ago.

"For what?"

"For not cleaning your dad's clock."

"I already thanked you for that."

"*Pfff!* You call that thanks." On those words, he opened a door marked HOSPITAL LINENS, and shoved her inside.

"What?"

"On *Grey's Anatomy* and all those hospital shows, there's always a place in these rooms fer a quickie. A perfect place fer showin' gratitude."

In the gray light coming through a single window, she saw shelf after shelf of bed linens and towels. And at the far end... a cot.

They saw the cot at the same time and made a dive for it, almost causing it to collapse to the floor. They ended up with him on the bottom and her straddling him. Her hair had come undone from its ponytail and hung down like a screen as she bent over him.

"How do I thank you?" she purred. "Let me count the ways."

And she did. There were twelve.

When they were both sated a short time later, she lay in his arms and asked, "Do you ever tingle?"

"Is that a trick question? Yeah, I 'tinkle' about a half-dozen times a day. More when I've been drinking."

She smacked him on the arm. "Tingle, not tinkle. Tante Lulu has this theory about tingling."

"Please, don't tell me. I haven't recovered from the nipple pinching yet."

"She is outrageous, isn't she?"

"And good as gold. Honestly, she would do anything for anyone. Before you came, she asked me if MawMaw had enough medical insurance. She said she has fifty thousand in her checking account—her *checking* account!—if we needed it. Thankfully, my grandmother's covered, but that's some generosity."

"I know. You weren't in the South after Hurricane Katrina. She single-handedly formed some charity to help families in need. Raised millions, I heard."

He kissed her softly and started to rise. "We better get

going before the old lady comes looking for us. Or your father, God forbid. Just one more thing. Can we agree, no more secrets between us?"

"Sure," she said. Except for one, which she prayed God he never uncovered.

Chapter Seventeen

Old loves never die...

Cage was proud to attend the Angel Krewe Ball with Em, even if he was wearing an uncomfortable tuxedo. And knowing how much Em enjoyed every aspect of Mardi Gras, from the vivid colors to the elaborate costumes to the music and rowdy good fun, Cage found pleasure in doing something for her.

If only the band wasn't playing such dorky music!

Cage loved to dance...fast, slow, dirty, sweet, plain, fancy...but this band knew only one type of music. Glenn Miller. Cage was doing his best, and really, moving from side to side with his arms around Em's waist and her arms around his shoulders, well, that was good, too.

He was still "on call" for active duty regarding Project Boom, but his team members were watching his back tonight, and unless something exploded, speaking figuratively, he could relax and enjoy himself. And man, did he have some "enjoyment" on his mind.

"You look beautiful," he told Emelie as they danced. *How soon can we make love?*

She wore a strapless red ball gown that was tight down to her hips but then flowed out into a full, ankle-length skirt that almost but not quite brushed the floor and out of which peeked red strappy stilettos. The fabric of the gown was sprinkled with crystals that sparkled like diamonds under the hotel chandeliers. On her face was a half-mask of the same red fabric as the dress with upswept feathers of cream and pink on either side like angel's wings. The only jewelry she wore was a thin chain with a red ruby pendant and small diamond stud earrings. She'd sprinkled some kind of cream on her shoulders and arms that contained glitter. When she turned a certain way... well, let's just say, ten kinds of sexy would be an understatement. Her hair was curled into some kind of up-do with little tendrils deliberately hanging about her graceful neck, and there was glitter in her hair, too.

By the end of this night, Cage expected to have glitter on him, too. And not from a jar. He sure hoped it was edible.

"You look good, too, Justin."

He made a little bow. *How soon can we make love?*

"Thank you for coming. I know formal attire wouldn't be your first choice."

He wore a black half-mask to match his tuxedo. One of Em's designs, it was contrasted with red feathers. Maybe he would wear it later...hmm. *How soon can we make love?* "I was just ragging you about wearing a tux. We SEALs—any single officers on the Naval base, for that matter—are always bein' asked to wear our dress uniforms at formal affairs. Visiting dignitaries and their families. Politicians. Stuff like that. Usually at the Hotel del Coronado. The Del is a famous place where movie stars and famous people stay all the time."

"And are you expected to dance at these events?"

"Sometimes." *Or run an extra five miles in the morning.*

"I bet you look really hot in uniform."

He grinned. "Sizzlin'." *How soon can we make love?* He twirled her around then till she got dizzy and had to clutch his shoulders to stay upright. He kissed her shoulder and murmured against her skin, "I'll show you someday."

They circulated among the crowd, too, and picked at some of the buffet offerings. Em introduced him to lots of folks...some of them artists like herself, others, community bigshots giving huge donations to the cause, a shelter for homeless single women. She never mentioned his SEAL background, on his advice, but just said that he was an old friend who was visiting Louisiana. That last *hadn't* been his idea. *Old friend, my ass! How soon can we make love?*

After that, a new band took over for the second set, a local Zydeco group that livened up the joint immediately. Now this was Cage's kind of music. He and Em danced and danced and danced. He showed off his moves. She showed off hers. They were really good together. They even participated in a sort of Cajun line dance that had everyone in the room howling with laughter. A good time. And they hadn't even had that much to drink. Two glasses of wine, max.

By the time the old fogies were back on the stage playing big band songs, they were glad to see them. Slow and easy was the way they wanted to end. Barely moving, just holding each other. Cage couldn't hold himself back any longer. Against her ear, he whispered, "I love you, Em."

And yes, he thought, *How soon can we make love?* But not in a crude way. Well, maybe a little crude.

Instead of protesting with that "just friends" crap, she whispered against his ear, "I love you, too."

He pulled back to stare at her. "Let's get out of here."

It seemed like everyone in the world wanted to talk to them from the dance floor to the coatroom to the car park. The fifteen minutes seemed like fifteen hours before they were ensconced in his Jeep. He turned on the ignition but then turned to her. "Come here, you."

She slid over as far as she could with the bucket seats and her voluminous gown. He leaned as far as he could and kissed her. Soft, her lips were so soft. And pliant. Open for whatever he wanted or offered. And he wanted so much and would offer her anything. Everything.

Reluctantly, they drew apart and they drove in silence to her home about ten blocks from the hotel where the charity ball was held. He didn't ask if he could spend the night. He just pulled into her driveway, all the way into the back courtyard, went around the vehicle to help her get out with her gown intact, then put an arm around her shoulder, tucking her against him as they walked side by side up the back stairs.

A mounting tension rose between them, but it wasn't an urgent, gottahaveyougottahaveyou need. More like a dreamy intimacy of slow, slow, slow arousal, rising a beat higher with every look they exchanged, every accidental brush of skin against skin, every sigh or breathy exhale. All of his senses seemed enhanced. The smell of the flowers in her garden and the light, flowery perfume she wore. How her silk gown felt when he rubbed a section between his fingers. The flavor of her lip gloss, which he could still taste on his tongue from their brief kiss in the car. And sounds . . . well, who could hear anything with Thad barking up a storm inside her French doors?

"At least you know that he'll be a good warning against burglars," Cage said.

"Hah!" Emelie laughed. "He'd probably lick them to death."

Thad and me, both. Well, me licking you, not burglars.

His phone binged then, his regular line, not the secure one. It was from JAM. Cage quickly read the text. *All clear on Boom front. Make your own fireworks tonight, good buddy.*

"Everything okay?" Em asked.

"Perfect," he replied and gave her a quick kiss.

Once the door was unlocked, Thad barreled out and galloped down the stairs, two steps at a time, and was about to raise his leg.

"No, Thad, no! Not St. Jude," Em shouted.

The dog gave her an apologetic look—Cage swore he did—and moved his raised leg over to a bonsai kind of tree. Still not good, but at least not a sacrilege.

"Have you come to appreciate my gift yet?"

"He's growing on me," she admitted.

"I knew it, I knew it, a match made in doggie heaven."

"Don't push it," she said, tapping him playfully on the arm with her hand-painted Mardi Gras fan, a favor from the ball.

Now that he'd done his business, Thad galloped back up the steps, gave Em a few doggie kisses, which left glitter on his fool tongue, then sprawled out on the balcony, about to settle into his guard duties. Or else sleep, if that wide yawn was any indication.

Cage and Em looked at each other and smiled, closing the doors behind them as they entered the bedroom. Cage was not sharing his bed with a dog tonight. He locked the door, and Em turned on a soft bedside lamp. Cage set his backpack on the floor by the door and removed the pistol, which he placed on the nightstand. Em watched him setting up his emergency gear, but didn't ask anything. Thank God! He wasn't in the mood for discussions on SEAL protocol at the moment.

As if they had all the time in the world, they took turns undressing each other. His jacket, her gown. Her high heels, his dress shoes. Her thigh-high hose, his socks. Her red, almost-nothing panties—which he had plans for later—and his red—yes, he'd worn red for the occasion—boxer briefs. In between, they murmured soft compliments, chatted, even smiled and laughed.

"Do you ever wear thongs?" he asked.

"No. Do you?"

"*What?* I'd be drummed out of the teams."

"Do you have to work out a lot to have muscles like that?"

"Every day." He struck a pose for her that had them both falling over onto the bed with laughter. Suddenly serious, he looked down at her and said, "I can't hold it in anymore, Em. I love you. I never stopped lovin' you." *Please don't say we're just friends. Please don't buzzkill this high I'm on. Please...just please.*

She reached up a hand to tenderly cup the side of his face. "I love you, too, Justin."

He turned his mouth into her hand and kissed the soft skin of her palm, then her wrist. "I don't know where we go from here, but—"

She put a forefinger to his lips. "No promises."

"All I know is that I can't go on pretendin' that I don't think about you night and day. I fantasize about all the ways I want to make love to you. I imagine the look on your face when I take you to all the places around the globe where I've been. The Middle East. Europe. South America. Even parts of the good ol' U.S. of A. that you might not be aware of. And I want to show you off to all my friends and brag that you're mine." He saw that she was listening intently to everything he said. He summed it up with a shrug. "You're my world, babe."

She smiled. "How about rocking *my* world then, *babe*?"

He wanted more than those teasing words. A confession of how he consumed her life, too. How she dreamed about him and yearned for him and all that stuff that should be hokey but wasn't. It would come later, he promised himself. For now, he growled at her and said, "That sounds like a challenge to me, and I should forewarn you, there's nothin' a SEAL likes better than a challenge."

She giggled, but not for long.

After he'd kissed her for a long time, about three minutes, and caressed her breasts and belly and lower, way more than three minutes, he asked in a sex-husky voice, "Do you ever fantasize about me, Em?"

"No. Never."

"Them are fightin' words," he told her and used his fingers, which could be tools of sweet torture, if he did say so himself, to tease her secret places to the point where she finally screamed and said, "Stop! Yes, I do fantasize about you sometimes." And she whispered something particularly wicked in his ear, something that surprised even him.

Without skipping a beat, he said, "I could do that. But later."

For now, he settled in what he'd wanted to do all night. Make love to his girl. That's how he would always think about Em. His girl. Even when she was eighty and he was eighty-one, she would be his girl.

By the time he'd settled into the deep hard strokes of making love with Em, he'd already told her over and over how much he loved her. She held his eyes with hers as her climax approached, the whole time repeating his words back at him, "I love you, I love you, I love you."

Later, much later, he felt himself falling asleep, despite his best efforts to stay awake. After all the stress with his grandmother's illness and Project Boom and his worry over how he was going to convince Em that he still loved her, and the fact that it was already 2 a.m., his body shut down for needed rest.

"I'm sorry," he kept saying on yawn after yawn.

"It's okay. Go to sleep."

"Don't go away. Don't leave." He was afraid to fall asleep and find this was all a dream. Or that she would have second thoughts. But he was so tired.

"Where would I go? You're in my bed," she said, laughing.

"Right." *Jeesh! I must be whacked out if I forgot that.*

Still, he pulled her over, half on top of him with her face resting on his chest, his arms firmly holding her in his embrace, just in case. Now that he had her back, he wasn't letting her go.

"I love you," he said one last time.

⚘

The road to love is filled with potholes...

Emelie was too hyped up to sleep. She lay propped on one elbow for a long time and watched Justin sleep. Just watched.

He loved her, he'd said so. And she loved him. They'd brought it out in the open. But now what would they do?

Emelie tried to imagine all the scenarios, how they might make this new love work. Logistics, that was their problem. He lived in California, and she lived in Louisiana, and she didn't see any way the twain could reasonably meet. Would they get together whenever they could for hot weekends? Here? There? In-between? Would that be enough? It would have to be. And really, maybe they would last longer than most couples who lived together. Absence making the heart grow fonder and all that.

By 4 a.m. Emelie couldn't hold out any longer, and she fell asleep, with questions still swimming in her head. It seemed like only minutes, but must have been an hour when she was awakened by Justin, who was wide awake and raring to go. Dawn light was rising in the sky beyond her courtyard.

She squirmed under him and said, "What is it about you and making love in the daylight? I must look a wreck."

"You look sexy as hell and hot as heaven," he said. "Besides, haven't you heard the best thing about sex in the morning?"

"No," she said hesitantly.

"It's like you have a secret the rest of the day. An image you carry in your head, but can pull out whenever you want and get turned on all over again." He waggled his eyebrows at her.

"You're impossible," she said. "But I love you."

"Ditto, darlin'. I can't wait to make plans with you for our future. We'll get married, won't we, Em?"

"Uh. Was that a proposal?"

He tilted his head to the side. "I thought that was

understood. Love, marriage, the whole works. Oh, damn! I should get down on one knee, shouldn't I?"

She grabbed his shoulders when he started to move off her. "No, I don't need a formal proposal." Besides, he'd asked her once when she was sixteen, and for her that was the one she wanted to remember forever, now that the heartache that followed was over.

"But you will marry me?"

"I don't know. Yes. Probably. I mean, there's so much else we need to talk about first."

"No, you're wrong. As long as we love each other, we'll find a way to work out the details. They're incidental. Do you believe me?"

She nodded, although the logical side of her brain told her that life wasn't so simple. On the other hand, maybe they would come up with a solution that worked for them. Possibly not a traditional one, but one suited to their particular situation.

He kissed her and caressed her idly as he talked with so much enthusiasm that she didn't have the heart to disagree with any of his plans. "I have at least three more years before I can retire after twenty years in the Navy. I always thought I'd be a lifer, but now..." He shrugged.

"I thought you loved being a SEAL."

"I do, but we all burn out sooner rather than later. Most SEALs don't last as long as I have."

"Why?" She was tracing his jawline, making little circles on his chest hairs, occasionally leaning down to kiss his shoulder.

"We see and do some awful things, Em. After a while, it eats away at the soul. Oh, I'm not apologetic about the fact that SEALs get real good at killing because, frankly, the terrorists we go after deserve to die. Still, a man can do that only so long before he goes over the edge, or backs off."

"Oh, sweetheart," she said and hugged him.

He hugged her back and ran the palms of his hands over her shoulders and back and rump.

"What would you do if you left the military?"

"I'm not sure. My options are wide open really. Private security. Police work. Even teaching. Heck, maybe I'll buy a shrimp boat and take up my PawPaw's old business."

She smiled at that possibility. "You would want to move back to Louisiana?"

"Yeah, I think so. You know what they say about bayou mud being in a man's veins?"

"And Cajun music in his heart," she completed for him.

He squeezed her shoulder. "That's right."

"But in the meantime...three years is a long time."

"Maybe you could take on that museum job you were offered. I have a two-bedroom condo in Coronado. We could turn one of them into a studio. You could work on the masks there some of the time. Then when I'm out on active ops, you can travel back here to work in your shop, or complete the mask work here. I don't know, it's not ideal, but maybe we could figure out some kind of schedule. It would only be temporary, until I retire."

"You've thought about this a lot, haven't you?"

"All the time." He kissed her long and deep and he played with her breasts until she was arching up and pulling his head down to suckle her. "So what do you think?" he asked when he'd ministered to one breast and was about to take care of the other.

"About what?"

"Our future together."

She grabbed his head and yanked him down. "The only future I care about is now and how you're about to make me come just by doing my breasts."

He laughed against her breast and he did, in fact, bring her to climax just by suckling her, with a few nips and licks tossed in.

When he raised her knees then and spread her wide, his eyes were half-slitted with arousal and his mouth parted. "Look at you, darlin'." He stared down at that most intimate part of her. "Can I say one more thing, Em?"

She rolled her eyes. "If you must."

"Let's make a baby."

She blinked. This was not what she'd expected, with herself widespread and aroused to the pitch of madness, and him with a hard-on that was poised to drill. "*What?* Are you crazy? Later—we can talk about this later."

"No, listen, honey. You want a child, and it would be the greatest gift I could give my grandmother before she goes. Let's skip the condom. Okay?"

He had the foil packet in his hand and was about to toss it when she grabbed his wrist.

"How do you know I want a child?"

"That artificial insemination nonsense, you know, but we can discuss it later." He held the condom in front of her. "Yes or no, sweetheart?"

"Neither," she said, and shoved him off her.

"What the hell?" He actually looked confused as he righted himself.

She sat up and pulled the sheet up and over her breasts. "Your grandmother wants you to have a baby?"

"Yeah. It's the one thing she told me would make her life complete. She told me that the first day I came home.

It was only wishful thinking, of course. I told you about that."

"No, I'm pretty sure you never told me that your grandmother wanted you to have a baby." Any arousal Emelie had been experiencing was fading fast. Justin looked crushed, and still aroused. Too bad. "How did you know about the artificial insemination?" She was going to kill Belle if she'd blabbed to him. Belle was the only one who knew.

"That day I stumbled onto your shop. When I was waitin' for you out in the courtyard, I saw a paper under the table. From the sperm doctor. I just put two and two together." He stared at her as if it were no big deal.

It was a very big deal. The dummy! "And you just figured, why not have a baby with Emelie? Em and my grandmother want one, so no big deal!"

"That's not exactly how it was."

"I think that's exactly how it was. You had a goal even before you set out to seduce me."

"Me? Me seduce you?" Justin stood angrily and began to pull on his tuxedo pants, obviously no longer aroused. "You're the one who sucked me right back in, even when you knew all the things your father had done to me and my family. Was this some kind of revenge thing?"

Huh?

Justin bundled up all his clothes and shoes and was about to storm out the door. He stopped midway and shook his head at her. "I still love you, Em. All I wanted to do was give you a baby. Is that so wrong? My baby in your body."

"You could have told me," she argued.

"Is it my baby specifically that revolts you? Some anonymous donor will do, but not the bad seed of the bayou?"

"Don't you dare turn this around on me," she cried.

"This is a monumental stab in the back! I can't believe that you, of all people, would be so deceptive. Admit it. *My* baby, that's the problem."

She was weeping and angry at the same time now. Somehow he had managed to make her the bad guy here. That was the only excuse she had for blurting out, "Been there. Done that. Had the T-shirt."

He turned slowly, inch by inch, and stared at her incredulously. A roaring grew and grew in his ears. "That's it. The missing piece of the puzzle. You were pregnant with my baby. That's it, isn't it?"

She nodded, horrified that her secret would come out this way.

"You were pregnant with my child when I left," he accused her.

She nodded again, unable to speak over the lump in her throat.

"What happened? Did you give it away? Bad seed and all that?"

She picked up the fan she'd got as a favor at the museum ball and threw it at him. "No! Don't you ever say anything like that. I miscarried at five months."

To her chagrin, he caught the fan and said, "I was hit by bomb schrapel in the back in Kabul a few years back. I thought that was the greatest pain I'd ever experience. Not even close!"

That was a low blow, but she couldn't back down now. "You're not the only one hurting here, bud."

He stared at her for a long moment. "Ah. The reason why you married Bernie, to give *my* child *his* name. Seriously?" He frowned with confusion.

"Don't be so damn judgmental. I was confused at the

time, and my dad was pressuring me, and I was so young." Her excuses sounded lame, even to her.

"Excuses!" he spat out. "Why didn't you let me know?"

"I tried," she cried out. "The letters."

"And since I've been back? What's your excuse for not tellin' me these past few weeks?"

"Come on, Justin! It was seventeen years ago. I never heard from you either. Not once in all those years. What was I supposed to think?" When he didn't answer, she continued, "I thought you didn't care. I thought you'd moved on."

"I wish I had."

She gasped.

He stared at her for several long moments, with disgust or pity, she wasn't sure, but then he turned and left. He just left.

"Don't come back," she yelled after him, tears streaming down her face. "If you leave now, don't come back."

But he was already gone.

Thad came in and put his chin on the bed next to her, as if he sensed her pain. And pain there was. Excruciating, through the heart, agony.

Heartbreak, all over again.

Chapter Eighteen

Dumb men do dumb things...

Cage called Em later that morning and got her answering machine. He left a message, "Em, we need to talk. Call me."

An hour later, while he was in the shower, a message had been left on his answering machine by Em. Short and sweet. "Justin, we do *not* need to talk. Do *not* call me. If you ever cared for me at all, leave me alone."

Yeah, right. As if! Now that he'd calmed down, he realized that fault could be spread just about everywhere, and he was ready to forgive. But what was with that "if you ever cared for me at all" bullshit? Women!

So that afternoon after working out with the physical therapist on his knee and meeting with his team members to get an update on Project Boom, he tried Em again, figuring she'd had time to calm down, too. And got her answering machine again, surprise, surprise. He tamped down his annoyance and tried for a lighter tone. "Em, remember how good we were together. Maybe I should just come over and lay you down to work out our differences in the way we communicate best. Call me."

She didn't respond immediately. It was after a dead zone on his way back to Bayou Black that he got her message. "No, I don't recall how good we were together. It's a blip on the screen of what's important to me. As for communication, don't bother calling."

He immediately responded, to her answering machine, which she must have on permanently now, "Fuck that!" Pulling over to the side of the road, where he knew he had a good number of bars on his cell phone, he waited, not wanting her to get his voice mail again.

But somehow Em outwitted him, and he was unloading groceries and fumbling for his phone when she sent him a blunt reply, "Been there, done that, not gonna do it again."

We'll see about that!

Now the calm was gone, and he was even angrier, having been betrayed, lied to, insulted, and generally made to feel like a fool. Besides that, he'd had a baby that had died and he'd never been given a chance to mourn. Had it been a boy or a girl? Did Em even know? Had MawMaw known about the pregnancy? How many people had been in the know while he'd been kept in ignorance?

Watching his frustration as he played phone tag with Em and kept mumbling his opinion of stubborn women, his grandmother pulled out one of her cornball proverbs. "There are three kinds of men who doan understand a lick 'bout women. Old ones, young ones, and middle-aged ones."

"That's a lotta help," he grumbled.

"Ya know what the worst thing is 'bout anger betwixt a man and woman?"

He refused to rise to her bait.

"The juice ain't worth the squeeze, and it can be bitter as green persimmons."

"Now that definitely makes no sense."

"It does if ya realize that anger only makes ya more bitter." His grandmother just grinned then.

Maybe it was a conspiracy of women.

Once dinner was over and he was sitting on the couch with his grandmother watching *Wheel of Fortune*, he got up the nerve to ask her, "MawMaw, did you know that Em was pregnant when I left Loo-zee-anna?"

She went immediately alert and turned to stare at him directly. "What?"

Well, that answers that question. MawMaw hadn't known. "Em was apparently pregnant when I left seventeen years ago. That's why she married Bernie."

"You have a baby?" The light of joy in his grandmother's eyes was precious and pitiful.

"No, no, MawMaw. The baby died at five months, before it was born, about seventeen years ago."

Before he had a chance to console her, his grandmother reached out and took one of his hands in both of hers. "Oh, sweetheart, I am so sorry. Was it a boy or a girl?"

He shook his head slowly, unable to speak at first over the lump in his throat. "I don't know," he rasped out.

For the next half hour, he explained everything that he knew, and he surprised himself by weeping with his grandmother over his unborn child. Cage had never been big on having kids, not after he left Emelie leastways, and he never would have suspected that he could care so much now.

"Did they bury the child? I'd like ta visit the grave," his grandmother floored him by saying.

"MawMaw, the fetus was only five months along."

"Sometimes they give them a regular burial in the Catholic Church, I think. Even unborn babies."

"They do?" More questions for which he had no answers.

His message to Em that night was short and not-so-sweet. "Call or suffer the consequences."

Her response was equally short and not-so-sweet, "Don't call. Suffer away. How're the blue balls?"

It was in a foul mood the next morning when he pounded on the door of Bernie's house in Lafayette. A very nice, ranch-style home on about two acres in an upscale neighborhood. Not for the first time, Cage mused that Bernie must be riding high cotton in the firecracker business.

Bernie opened the door a crack and said to someone behind him, "It's just my crabby cousin, Justin LeBlanc."

You don't know crabby yet, dipwad! Cage shoved the door open and faced a woman in a low crouch with two hands holding a pistol, aimed at him. "Whoa!" he said, putting his hands in the air.

"It's okay," Bernie told the undercover cop Cage had seen at the warehouse meeting. Bernie shut and locked the door behind him. Then he had the nerve to say, "What do you want?"

"Hey, great welcome, cuz. Especially after bargin' into my grandmother's house a few weeks ago, invitin' yourself to dinner, and generally makin' a nuisance of yourself ever since."

Bernie flushed and continued dressing. He knotted the tie on his dress shirt and put on his suit jacket.

"Goin' somewhere?" Cage asked.

"Yeah, some of us have to work," Bernie answered snidely. He was clearly acting biggity to impress the lady.

"Hi, I'm Justin LeBlanc." Cage extended a hand. "We met briefly at the Project Boom meeting."

"Simone LeDeux." She took his hand and shook it firmly. Simone was tall, slim, dark-haired, with dancing brown Cajun eyes. A babe! If Bernie the Wuss was making any hay with her, Cage would eat his dirty sweat socks.

"LeDeux? Any kin to Tante Lulu?"

"Not that I know of, but who knows, maybe some distant connection that I'm unaware of."

"That crazy woman!" Bernie commented. "Tante Lulu suggested I visit her niece Charmaine's beauty spa for a makeover. Me? A man? Claims she has a male section."

And you think that's crazy? More like on the mark. Turning back to Simone, he said, "Be careful. If Tante Lulu gets a whiff of another LeDeux here in the South, you'll have a hope chest in your backyard before you can say 'Dixie.'"

"Huh?"

He just smiled. "Would you mind lettin' me have a minute alone with Bernie?"

"Sure. I'll go into the kitchen and make some coffee."

The minute she left the room, Cage clipped Bernie a good one in the chin, knocking him backward. Bernie barely caught himself by clinging to the door frame.

Rubbing his chin, Bernie whined, "What was that for?"

"For not tellin' me that Em was pregnant."

He kept rubbing his chin and said, "Ouch," a time or two.

"Don't be a wuss. I just gave you a little tap."

"Why blame me? I told you to ask Em."

"Well, now I'm askin' you." He flexed his fists in

warning; not that he intended to hit Bernie again. That particular rage was over.

"Em was really distraught after you left...I know, I know...her father finagled your leaving so suddenly, but Emelie didn't know that at the time. I was working a Fourth of July Fireworks Extravaganza in Houma that year, and her father was the sheriff. I never knew Emelie very well in school; she was two years younger than me, and we didn't travel in the same crowds."

"Who are you kiddin', Bern? You didn't travel in *any* crowds."

Bernie shrugged as if it didn't matter, which it didn't.

"Her dad took a liking to me, said I was 'enterprising,' and started inviting me over to their house for supper and stuff. At first, to try to get her interested in some other guy besides you."

I'd like to bust his enterprising nose. Cage made a growling noise, which Bernie noticed but wisely passed over.

"Later, when he found out that Emelie was pregnant—with your child, which he likened pretty much to demon seed—he talked me into proposing to Emelie. He honestly thought he was doing the best thing for his child."

"Bullshit!"

"Keep in mind, Justin, we didn't know then what her father had done. None of it. And marrying to give a child a name might seem old-fashioned to you, but I was willing."

"And Em? Was she willing?'

"Not at first. All she talked about was contacting you somehow. She wrote. She made phone calls. She badgered your grandparents. It was pitiful to see her come home disappointed every time. Then when she discovered she was pregnant, she became even more frantic, unable to believe that you wouldn't want to know about your own baby. I remember the day she finally gave up. Somehow she'd gotten an idea in her head that if she went to the Navy recruitment center in N'awleans and explained her predicament, they would just hand over your address and phone number. Instead, the guy laughed and asked Emelie if she'd never heard about sailors having a girl in every port. 'Go find yourself a nice dependable plumber,' he advised her. Instead, she accepted me."

Didn't help matters that when Cage had come home immediately following basic training, Em was married to another man. "What a travesty!" Cage muttered. "All due to a failure to communicate."

Just then, he noticed two cats walking by, strolling the way cats do, as if they owned the world. One was the one he'd sort of pushed on Bernie those weeks back. Behind scrambled a litter of kittens.

He arched his brows in question.

"You didn't tell me the cat was pregnant," Bernie complained.

"I thought it was a kitten."

"Even small cats can get pregnant," Bernie informed him, as if he didn't know that.

"Oh, Bernie, you just made my day." In the end, turning serious, Cage had to ask, "Was it…the baby… buried?"

Bernie seemed to understand immediately and nodded. "Em insisted."

Cage felt as if a vise was squeezing his heart as he waited for the final shoe to drop. "Mary Delphine LeBlanc, September 20, 1997, Our Lady of the Bayou Cemetery." *Named after our two grandmothers! And me!*

Even when she'd been married to Bernie. How many hits can I take today?

Cage left soon after that. As he drove away, he began to calm down, for about the fiftieth time in this roller-coaster of emotions that had become his life. He was beginning to understand the reasons for all the "sins" against him, which weren't really sins, of course. Fear, it was all about fear. Even that asshole Claude had acted out of fear. And Em…sweet Em…she'd only been sixteen at the time. She must have been terrified.

Okay, he was glossing over the fact that no one had bothered to tell him the truth since he'd come home. And that included his grandmother about some things.

Feeling a bit shattered, he called Emelie, about to make some major amends. Of course, he got her frickin' answering machine. Gritting his teeth—he hated leaving this particular message on voice mail—he said, "Hey, honey. I just learned more about Mary Delphine Le-Blanc." He paused to get his voice under control. "I am so sorry."

She never responded to that message.

Luckily, during that week and a half, he was kept busy with Project Boom. The private practice nurse he'd hired, thanks to help from Adele, had proven invaluable, especially because her hours were flexible; Mrs. Ryan, a middle-aged widow, came from Houma whenever she was needed, which was a godsend when he was called on suddenly to be in Lafayette for a meeting.

In the end, it was almost anticlimactic the way Project Boom worked out. Because of the expertise of all the professionals involved working together, they were able to locate all the explosives, where they were currently stored, and where they had been set to go off at four spots along the parade route. After that, it was only a question of bringing in all the tangos to be interrogated and imprisoned...ten in all.

The outcome could have been monumentally disastrous. Any one of those explosives had the power to devastate up to a two-block perimeter, and with the crowds expected on Fat Tuesday in the Crescent City, well, suffice it to say, tragedy was averted. The mayor of New Orleans was particularly thankful that word of this terrorist plot hadn't leaked out; otherwise, tourism—the lifeblood of the city—would have been severely curtailed.

His SEAL buddies hadn't returned to California yet because they wanted to see the Mardi Gras parade in two days, especially F.U., who'd apparently been amassing a large supply of beads to be thrown to women at the parade, a practice that usually resulted in the baring of female breasts. John LeDeux had pulled a few strings to get them a prime viewing spot for the parade on the second-floor balcony of a Bourbon Street hotel.

But suddenly, there was a lull in his frenzied activity, and he had to face the mess he'd made of things with Em. Unfortunately, while he was ready to kiss and make up, she still wanted nothing to do with him. He called repeatedly and always got her blasted answering machine message.

"Thass the trouble with young folks t'day," his grandmother said when he confided in her. "Ya think everythin' kin be handled with a phone or a text message or an e-mail. I thought ya were smarter than that."

"Em was in the wrong, too," he insisted. "She's the one who should be makin' the first step."

"First step. Last step. No steps. Who cares? If ya really love that gal, you'll crawl if that's what it takes."

Well, that was a lot of help.

But he did suck it up and drive to her shop in hopes he'd have more luck in person. Thad greeted him with loud, unfriendly barking, as if they hadn't been best pals just a few weeks ago. The dog sensed that Cage was in the doghouse more than he was.

When he walked into Em's workroom without knocking, she glanced up at him. No warm welcome. In fact, there was hostility in her dark eyes, and she told him in no uncertain terms that she wanted nothing to do with him.

"I came because you haven't been answerin' my phone calls."

"Didn't that tell you something?"

"Not even fond regards for my blue balls," he joked.

She didn't crack even a hint of a smile.

"You look good."

"I look like hell. I'm working twenty hours a day, and I haven't washed my hair in two days."

Her hair was pulled back into a high ponytail, and she wore no makeup. A gray sweatshirt, gray sweatpants, and sneakers were her plain attire. Honestly, she looked good to him, but he wasn't about to tell her that. She would assume it was just a line.

"Your busy time should be over soon, with Mardi Gras."

"I'm thinking about taking on the museum project, not that it's any of your business."

"Oh, it's my business all right. Everything you do is my business."

She rolled her eyes. "Not anymore."

"You said you loved me, Em."

"Loved. Past tense."

"You can't get over love that quick."

"You did."

"I did not! I never stopped loving you."

"You have a funny way of showing it." She yanked a calendar off the wall and pointed to one day after another, eleven days since they'd made love after the Mardi Gras ball.

"I called."

"*Pffff!* You said some pretty damn nasty things last time you were here."

"I was shocked and hurt. You can't toss a grenade like you did and expect a guy to just pass it off as no big deal."

"How about the eleven days since then?"

"I've been busy." He couldn't tell her about Project Boom. Or about his intermittent pride and anger. Not now. Maybe later. "Trust me. I had good reasons for stayin' away. Some important things came up."

She flinched and put a hand over her heart. "Miss MaeMae?"

"No, she's fine, or not too bad anyway."

She arched her brows, waiting for a further explanation. When he had none to give, she said, "Go away, Justin. I have work to do, and you're bothering me."

"We have to talk sometime."

"No, that's where you're wrong. The time for talk is long gone. I don't want you anymore."

"That's what you think, babe."

"Puhleeze with the babe nonsense. Did you ever see that Johnny Cash movie *Walk the Line*, where Reese Witherspoon says to Joaquin Phoenix, 'Baaby, baaby, baaby!' That's you all over, Justin. Well, not me."

He had no idea what she was talking about, but he sure as hell would watch the flick when he got home. "I went to see Bernie," he told her.

"And I should care...why?" He could tell she was interested, despite her words.

"I punched him in his weak chin, for one thing."

"Why? What's he ever done to you?"

"Married the girl I love. Didn't tell me you were pregnant."

"I did the same thing. Are you going to punch me?"

"Nah. I'd rather do other things to you." When she didn't respond to that, he said in a choked voice, "You named our baby girl after my MawMaw and your Maw-Maw, and you gave her my surname. Thank you." Her eyes went wide with shock, whether at the news that he knew or that he'd had the nerve to bring it up, he wasn't sure. Well, he might as well go for broke. "I'd like to see Mary's grave. Will you take me sometime, Em?"

She gasped and bent over at the waist, as if in pain.

He tried to put a comforting arm around her shoulders, but she shoved him away. Too much, too soon, he realized belatedly.

"I'm sorry if I hurt you by bringing this up, but it had to come out in the open sometime. I'll retreat for now, but we *are* going to talk about this, and we are going to be together." *For the time being anyhow.* "You are mine. Get that through your stubborn head. You. Are. Mine."

Big mistake! Em looked at him as if he'd lost his mind. She stood and braced her hands on the table. "Get. Out!"

"I love you, Em," he said as he began to walk away.

She threw a softball-size skein of yarn at him, hitting him squarely in the back of the head. He just laid it carefully on the table and winked at her.

Which infuriated her, of course, if the scowl on her face was any indication. Thad scowled at him, too, as if even a dog could do a better job than he had.

Then, still dumb as dirt, seeking answers in typical male deficit misunderstanding of the female sex, he decided to go around to the front of the building and enter the shop. There he point-blank asked Belle to intercede on his behalf.

Belle told him point-blank that he'd lost his chance. "She didn't want to get involved with you again, Justin. You hurt her so bad before. Now you've done it again."

"Hey, I got hurt, too." He hadn't meant to say that and knew even before the words were out how whiny-assed he sounded.

"Pull up your big boy pants and get over it."

"My undies are just fine. And I want her."

Belle shrugged. "We don't always get what we want, do we?"

On the way home, he stopped at Tante Lulu's to see if JAM and Geek were up for a few beers and a game of poker that night. The guys had gone to the Carnival Crawfish Boil over in Lafayette with the other SEALs and their new best buddy, Bernie.

"C'mon in and sit yerself down," Tante Lulu told him. "You look lak you been run over by a thousand-pound gator on roller skates."

He sat at her kitchen table, where she'd apparently been putting together some of her folk remedies for Geek to put into a word processing program. Handing him a glass of sweet tea, she sat down across from him.

"Well, spill, boy. What did you do ta screw things up?"

Me? Why not Em? "Why do you assume I'm at fault?"

"Doan go gettin' cross-legged. It's a known fact that men are clueless 'bout love. Ninety-nine an' a half percent of the time they say or do somethin' ta muck up the thunderbolt's path. They cain't help themselves. They's clueless."

She was probably right about the clueless part. "Do you really believe all that thunderbolt of love crap?"

"I surely do. God throws the bolt, but then we humans gotta follow through. He cain't do all the work fer you. Remember what the Good Book says. Ask an' you shall receive."

"I asked and I didn't get shit . . . I mean, nothing."

"Well, you came to the best person fer love advice."

Is that what I'm doing? Oh, my God, I'm discussing my love life with a woman who was old when the Dead Sea was still alive. How pathetic is that?

"Tell me what happened."

And he did. All of it.

Tante Lulu clucked at some points, *tsk*ed at others, and shook her head in dismay at his dumb mistakes. "Are yer man parts still in workin' order?"

"What? Yes. Of course. That's not the issue." *What left field did that one come from? Am I actually blushing?*

"You never know. I vow, some men are jist dummies and doan know that a woman needs good lovin' once in a while."

"Are you actually suggesting sex to solve problems?"

"You are an idjet. Lovin' and boinkin' 're two different things. Do I hafta explain the difference?"

"No, no!" *Please, no!*

"Of course, ya prob'ly figgered that once ya got the deal signed, sealed, and delivered, yer job was done. Ha, ha, ha, didja get that about sealed? Anyways, once we get her in a lovin' mood, I kin give ya advice on how ta keep yer lady satisfied."

"I honestly don't need that kind of advice, but I do

need help getting Em to the point where she'll even talk to me about some important issues, let alone forgive me fer being such a clumsy idiot."

"Well, ya came ta the right place fer help."

"I did?"

"I do mah best work with clumsy idiots. Ask mah nephews. I'm thinkin' it's time ta pull in the LeDeux troops."

Uh-oh! He didn't like the sound of that. "Can't you just give me some advice?"

"Nah, you've let it go too far fer that. Mebbe we could hold our Cajun Village People act at Swampy's. We ain't done one of those in a while."

Cage had heard about those events. The men made total asses of themselves in public in an effort to woo a woman.

"Mebbe some of them Navy SEAL buddies of yers could help. A whole line of hunky men in military uniforms dancin' and shakin' their hineys ta Cajun music. I sure do wish someone could convince mah Richard— thass Richard Simmons, the hottie—ta put on a uniform and join the group. You could be the leader."

Cage's eyes were about bugged out. "No way! Not gonna happen!"

"You're awful picky fer someone in desperate straits."

"It's not that I'm afraid to play the fool for Em..."

My SEAL buddies would die laughing at this idea, and even worse, they might do it.

"But honestly I don't think that kind of thing would work for her."

Surely a bunch of SEALs taking it all off wouldn't break down her barriers. Would it? She'd probably laugh, but then laughter might be a good starting point. No, that's crazy.

"She's a private person and..."

His words trailed off as he thought of something. "I wonder..."

"What?"

"There is this one thing Em mentioned that she would like." He told her in non-X-rated terms about Em's fantasy of him wearing a cowboy hat and boots and playing the guitar for her.

"Hmmm." She tapped her little fingers on the table. "It might work. We could book a time at Swampy's. René's band would work with us. And I doan care what ya say, we could still do a little of the Cajun Village People stuff, and then...oh, I'm jist not sure 'bout this. It's kinda short notice."

"Actually, now that I think about it, Em would be appalled. No, I'll have to think of something else. I've already given her flowers and a dog. Maybe I could buy her a piece of jewelry, or a kitten," *or nipple rings. No, no, no, I didn't just think that.*

"Put this love sit-ye-a-shun from your mind, boy. I'll come up with somethin', dontcha worry. Then, I'll get back to you. In the meantime," she told him as they walked to the door, "ya could allus ask the big guy fer help."

"What big guy?"

Tante Lulu motioned with her head toward a picture on the wall. St. Jude.

He could swear he heard a voice in his head say, "It's about time."

⚓

Memories never die...

Emelie did not regret cutting off things with Justin, but she did miss him. And the loneliness on this last night of Carnival weighed particularly heavy on her heart.

From the time she was eight years old until he left when she was sixteen, they'd spent Mardi Gras together in one way or another. Amazing, the details that remained imbedded in her mind. Like the floats one year when "Livin' La Vida Loca" was popular, or the foods they ate only on that date, like his grandmother's king cake, or the beautiful costumes that instilled the seeds of her later artistic leanings. She remembered how Justin had looked the first time he'd seen a woman bare her breasts for beads. And she remembered how he'd looked the first time she'd bared her breasts for him, which couldn't have been all that exciting since she'd been ten and flat as a board.

Yes, Emelie had made a clean break with Justin last week when he'd barged in here. It had to be done. She never should have opened herself up to the hurt again. And she didn't blame him. Not totally. She just wished that he would leave the state and she could begin the process of healing again.

But of course, that was selfish of her because he wouldn't leave until Miss MaeMae was gone, and Emelie couldn't wish for the quick passing of the dear old woman.

She and Belle closed the shop at noon since the parade route passed less than one block from their street and the revelers could get rowdy, sometimes even destructive, when under the influence. Besides, Belle and her sons were joining Justin and all his SEAL buddies over on the balcony of the Pelican Hotel. Belle had asked her to come, and Justin had, too, via one of his incessant voice mails, but Emelie had declined all offers. Even in a crowd, she wouldn't be able to handle being near Justin.

"Isn't it odd that those SEALs have stuck around in Loo-zee-anna for so long?" Emelie mentioned to Belle as they were pulling the barred screen over the windows and drawing shades. "And their friendship with Bernie is just weird."

"I thought so, too, but JAM told me there was some mission that came up in this area that required them all to be here. Whatever it was is over now. They'll be leaving on Thursday."

Emelie tilted her head to the side. "I thought SEALs dealt with terrorists."

Belle shivered. "Terrorists in Loo-zee-anna?"

Emelie shivered for another reason. "Bernie involved in some special forces operation?"

They both laughed at that and decided there must have been some other reason. Maybe just what Justin had claimed, that SEALs were tight, and supported each other in times of trouble, like his grandmother's cancer.

Once Emelie was alone, she went up to her apartment, gave Thad a bowl of dog food (he ate like a horse), and took out a frozen dinner from Ella's that she planned to have later. Pouring herself a glass of chilled white wine, she sat down to watch the local TV network's coverage of Mardi Gras.

And she tried not to remember the last year she and Justin had watched the event on the small TV in his grandparents' cottage, where they'd been left alone for an hour. It was amazing what two horny kids could do in an hour. She didn't even want to consider what two horny adults could do in an hour.

Maybe watching the Mardi Gras events on TV wasn't such a good idea.

⌒

And then the other shoe (bomb) dropped...

Everywhere around him, people were having a great time.

The music, the drinks, especially the Hurricane drinks, the parade, the bawdy behavior of the men and women on the floats, as well as the streets and balconies. Mardi Gras was nothing new to him, but all his memories of the Carnival events were somehow tied in with Emelie, whom he refused to think about tonight and ruin the good time his friends were having. She'd declined all invitations to watch the parade with them, but he would get to her later, once his friends left town, guar-an-teed. He felt the need to be a host of sorts, one last time.

Truly, the Mardi Gras parade—all the Mardi Gras events—had to be seen to be believed. Yeah, Carnival was celebrated in other parts of the world, but nothing like this. One float boasted that its artist creator had used a couple million recycled beads for its decorative mosaics. Each krewe vied to outdo the other in their eye-catching parade floats. Gorgeous costumes and masks, some of which might have been designed by Em and Belle. Jazz could be heard everywhere, and laughter. Good times.

F.U. was going practically ballistic with the ogling of women's breasts and had to be warned more than once to tone down his language in front of Belle and her sons. Jugs, and hooters, and headlights were not the way men referred to those female parts in mixed company, F.U. had been told, and the idiot had actually wondered what he should call them then.

JAM was getting along well with Belle, although there didn't seem to be any serious, long-lasting connection. Geek had brought Adele, Cage's physical therapist, and they, too, seemed to get along well, but more like friends. Friends with benefits maybe, but no more than that. The other guys were striking up conversations with folks who stepped in and out of the hotel onto the balcony. Bernie's police officer "friend," whom he'd become chummy with since their forced living together situation, was here, but Bernie had yet to arrive. In all, for everyone, it was a nice day of camaraderie.

Even Slick seemed to be more relaxed than usual as they watched the passing parade. "You Cajuns do know how to have a good time," he conceded.

"Well, not just Cajuns. Creoles. Native Americans. Whatever," Cage replied. "We're a real melting pot here in Loo-zee-anna, more so than other parts of the country, I think."

"How much longer do you think you'll be here, buddy?"

"Impossible to say. MawMaw's deteriorating, there's no question of that, but her doctor tells me that folks have been known to hold on for a really long time when the will is there."

"And is the will there for your grandmother to hang on?"

"Not so much as before. We've settled a lot between us, and she feels better that I now know certain things about my dad. To tell you the truth, Slick, and I hate sayin' this, I hope she dies sooner than later. I just can't stand the thought of her sufferin'."

Slick put a hand on his forearm and squeezed. "I understand completely. No way to live in the latter stages. My aunt...the one who left me my house in Malibu... lingered on for years. It was painful to watch."

"She would hate to be tied up to machines in a hospital, and I promised her she would die at home, if possible." He blinked back the tears in his eyes.

Suddenly, Slick straightened and put his hand to the phone attached to his side. Cage hadn't heard anything, but it must have been vibrating. Slick clicked a button, read some text message, then glanced up at the rest of them with horror. "Gentlemen, we have a situation here."

Almost immediately, the secure phones of every other SEAL on that balcony went on red alert. *Mayday, Mayday!* the message said.

"Situation" didn't begin to describe this new development. More like a goat fuck of monumental proportions, Cage soon concluded. They'd been blindsided by the tangos.

Taking them all to the edge of the balcony that curved around the other side, away from the parade street, Slick said quickly, "One of the tangos spilled. There was a fifth box of explosives. In one of the Landry trucks. Parked somewhere here in the French Quarter."

"But we examined every one of those vehicles," JAM said. "And double-checked."

"One of the boxes contained false fuses, meant as a decoy," Slick explained.

Geek was already clicking away on his iPhone. "It just can't be. Every single one of the trucks that went in and out of that factory lot has been accounted for. Unless..." Geek looked up with horror. "I think the explosives might be in Bernie's van." Then he yelled, "Where's Bernie?"

Simone LeDeux, Bernie's police officer friend, said, "Bernie is parking his van."

"Where?" Slick demanded.

"In his ex-wife's driveway. About two blocks from here."

Ex-wife? Emelie? Cage was already running, practically flying down the stairs. All of the SEALs here were carrying weapons of one type or another. Standard procedure. And pray God that F.U. had his compact bomb deactivation kit in his back pocket. "Are you with me, F.U.?" he shouted without turning around.

"I'm on your tail, buddy."

It was hard wending his way through the crowd until he turned off a side street. Then he ran full-out. He hoped his knee didn't fail him now. *Oh, my God! I'll never make it.* He was on his cell phone to Em at the same time, and of course got the usual frickin' voice mail. Punching in Bernie's number, he got nothing, just "Call failed." Not a good sign.

He and F.U. kept yelling as they tried to make good time. "Sorry, ma'am!" "Out of the way, out of the way!" "Fuck you, too, buddy!" "Yes, we're police officers!" Not far behind he could hear some of his other teammates bringing up the rear.

Em's place was two blocks away but it felt like two miles. *Oh, God! I'll never make it.*

What was it they'd been told about the capabilities of these bombs? A block or two? The tangos probably figured they could still take out hundreds of folks even from the distance of Em's street. *Oh, my God! Oh, my God! Oh, my God!*

If anyone could dismantle a bomb, it was F.U., but would there be time? Cage could hear everyone on their cells phones as they followed after them, including the police officer. "Secure the perimeter, secure the perimeter!" Slick was shouting.

Cage's lungs were burning, and his knee was probably back to injury status by the time he rounded the corner to Em's shop and apartment. Everything appeared peaceful, and yes, the van was parked under Em's porte cochere. Bernie was slumped over the wheel, and there was a large box in the rear, visible through a side window.

"Don't touch the damn bomb," F.U. warned. "I'll take care of the explosives, you take care of the guy."

A quick check with a thumb to a pulse point in his neck showed Bernie was alive with a huge lump on the back of his head. Probably coldcocked from behind. JAM arrived and helped to pull him out and carry him away. F.U. went to work on the bomb while K-4 held a huge flashlight that he'd probably knocked off from some shop along the way.

Cage raced up the back stairs, into Em's bedroom, through the kitchen, and then the living room, where she was sitting calmly watching the Mardi Gras events on TV with her guard dog, who hadn't even raised his fool head. "Thank God you're all right! Come on, hurry." He yanked on her hand, knocking over a glass of wine, and pulled her toward the front stairway. "Hurry! We've gotta get out of here."

"Justin! Are you crazy? Let go of me."

They were halfway down the stairs. "Bomb! No time!" he huffed out and struggled with the lock on the front door. Once open, he kissed her quickly, said, "I love you, baby," then shoved her out. His knee gave out, and he went down hard, but only for a moment. "Run. Run as far away as you can, sweetheart."

Cops were already setting up roadblocks, and sirens could be heard in the distance. Geek was on his iPhone trying to locate a spot where the van could be driven if the effort to deactivate the bomb failed. In fact, that was exactly what they did moments later. Cage drove with wailing police cars providing point guard in front of him. Geek was in the passenger seat, and F.U. and K-4 were in the back.

Em watched with horror as the van flew by. She was still running, with Thad at her side, panting for breath... both of them. She didn't know exactly what was going on, but it seemed as if someone, maybe terrorists, had planted a bomb in Bernie's van. Oh, no! Had Bernie been killed? But no, she saw him on his back in a small grassy parklet up ahead, being administered to by a man. Bernie was half sitting up, but groggy. Belle came up to Em then and gave her a hug. "Oh, my God! Oh, my God!" they both kept muttering.

"Is he okay, Slick?" Belle asked the guy leaning over Bernie.

"Yeah. His head will hurt like hell, but he'll be okay."

Emelie had an aha moment then as she began to put the pieces of the puzzle together. This was why all of Justin's SEAL friends were hanging around Louisiana. They'd known all along that there was a terrorist threat.

Just then, in the distance, a huge explosion went off. They, along with any folks still on the street, stared at the huge cloud that rose into the sky.

The van. The explosives. Justin.

Emelie and Belle began to weep.

But Slick held a hand up as he listened to someone on his cell phone. "All parties safe," he told them.

"Justin is alive?" Emelie asked.

"Alive and swearing up a storm." Slick laughed.

How could he laugh in the midst of such a barely missed travesty? But then she guessed he...and all SEALs, like Justin...were used to this kind of danger.

Shivering, Emelie sank to her knees with relief, her brain slowly registering that she'd almost lost Justin. How she could feel like this when she'd actually lost him long ago, she didn't know. But she was shaken at the prospect of a world without Justin in it.

What did that mean?

"That was one son-of-a-bitch close call," Slick was telling someone on his cell phone. "That building would have been dust and people within five hundred yards, pink mist." Slick shrugged sheepishly as he realized Em and Belle were listening and the building in question was Emelie's home. "Sorry."

Going back later, Emelie saw that her building was yellow-taped. An officer explained that it was only for the time being. Belle helped Emelie pack a suitcase and went home herself. Both of them were probably in shock. Emelie, with Thad riding shotgun, made her way slowly to her father's place in Houma.

Emelie had a lot to think about.

◈

It would be all in fun, or so they claimed...

Emelie hadn't seen Justin since Fat Tuesday, a week ago. She was still avoiding him, although she had spoken to him the day after the averted disaster. She'd told him that she needed time, and he'd agreed reluctantly to wait for her move.

She'd been so scared, for herself, for the people scurrying away from the potential bomb scene, but mostly for Justin, who'd ridden off in a bomb-laden van. She'd known he had a dangerous job, but to experience it first-hand was another thing altogether.

And yes, she was proud of him, too. The way he and his teammates had worked together to handle a disaster had been beyond impressive. Although they hadn't used names or photographs, the local and national news media had given much attention to the bravery and expertise of the SEALs, who just happened to be in the city visiting a friend. Yeah, right.

Emelie had gotten the scoop from Bernie on the Project Boom mission that had drawn and kept the SEALs in Louisiana for so long. Apparently Justin wasn't permitted to disclose any of this. She didn't blame him.

Emelie was being bombarded with conflicting emotions all the time, and she was considering taking a short vacation. Maybe a cruise.

She hadn't given the museum an answer yet, and they'd been very patient and accommodating, believing that she was overstressed by the near explosion on her premises. She also hadn't made a firm decision on the artificial insemination, although she was leaning in the direction of scrapping it.

It was in this mood that Emelie agreed to go to a girls' night out one Friday with Belle and some of her friends. Only after she was in the car and on the way with the laughing women did she find out that their destination was Swampy's Tavern and a performance by the Cajun Village People, a Tante Lulu extravaganza.

"Lighten up, Em. It'll be fun," Belle promised.

Emelie had a bad feeling.

Chapter Nineteen

If all else fails, just dance...

Cage was desperate, and desperate men did desperate things. At least, that was what he told himself.

His buddies had long since gone back to Coronado, taking the birds with them. His grandmother had been playing Elvis's "I'm So Lonesome I Could Die" so much that he felt like he could do just that. Tante Lulu was egging him on to do something or stop complaining. So he'd agreed to the dingbat's crazy-ass, last-ditch effort to solve his love problems.

Yeah, he could have gone back to Em's place. He could have begged. He could have forced her to listen. But somehow he agreed with Tante Lulu that he needed a grand gesture to convince Em that their love was worth fighting for.

So here he was standing in the back office of Swampy's tavern, wearing jeans, cowboy boots, a cowboy shirt that had once belonged to his dad, and a cowboy hat. Em might have asked for nude, but this was as far as he was willing to go in public. He felt like an absolute fool and was nervous as hell, but not as bad as he would feel if he were the other guys, standing around out in the hall waiting to go on the stage where René LeDeux's band was already playing. There were the LeDeux men...Luc, the lawyer, wearing a business suit with no shirt; John, the cop, with no shirt but a police cap and twirling a baton; Remy, the pilot, whose handsome face had been burned on only one side in an Iraqi battle, wearing an Air Force uniform, unbuttoned; a frowning Rusty Lanier, Charmaine's husband, in cowboy gear; and a friend of the family, Angel Sabato, as a hunky biker dude.

And the women in the act were no better, wearing tight spandex dresses of different, vivid colors, even Tante Lulu, who kept telling Cage to have another shot of bourbon to calm his nerves. Any more bourbon and he'd be joining the Cajun Chippenduds or falling over unconscious.

"She's here," Tante Lulu said, peeking into the office. "It'll all be over soon."

"Are you sure this is gonna work?"

"Sure," she said, then handed him a little statue of St. Jude, "but mebbe you should say a little prayer jist in case."

"Oh, hell!" *She thinks I'm hopeless.*

⌘

And the star of the show was...oh, no!...

Emelie was glad she'd come.

The ladies were all nice, and the music was lively, and

the dancing was fun to watch. René LeDeux, a teacher and former environmental activist, was entertaining the crowd with his band, The Swamp Rats.

Part of the reason for her good mood might be the oyster shooters that everyone kept pushing on her. She was feeling a little woozy.

There had been a hefty door charge when they entered to benefit a charity of Tante Lulu's. Apparently, every so often she and her family put on this outrageous show for a good cause, and folks didn't mind paying for the experience.

Just then René LeDeux put up both hands to silence the crowd. "Folks, we have a special treat for you tonight, as you know. The Cajun Village People."

Much applause and wolf whistles and hooting greeted his words.

Starting with "Macho Man," the band played, except they substituted "Cajun" for "Macho" and the crowd sang along with them, especially when each of the hunky LeDeux men and their friends put on a sexy performance. Not quite the Chippendales, as in stripteases, although John LeDeux had a good time showing everyone how he could dance and twirl a baton at the same time in a most suggestive way.

When the ladies came shimmying out to "I'm Sexy and I Know It," René introduced each of them by saying, "This is Sylvie LeDeux, a shy chemist married to my brother Luc." Sylvie glared at René, then rolled her hips into the rump of her husband, who grinned wickedly at her. "And Rachel LeDeux, a decorator who has feng shuied my brother Remy into about a dozen kids. I've lost count." Rachel did a little shimmy, too, which seemed to embarrass her husband, who had an ugly burn mark on one side of his face only. The other side was gorgeous. "Then there is Celine LeDeux, who usta be a reporter but now has a full-time job tryin' ta keep my brother John in line." John didn't give Celine a chance to blush or shimmy or anything; he just tugged her into a front-to-back embrace and dirty danced her across the stage. She kept slapping at him but the crowd loved it. Next came Grace Sabato, a friend of the family, a former nun, and a professional poker player, of all things. She was now married to Angel, the biker dude, who pretended to roar a motorcycle right up to her. Charmaine had to coax her glaring husband, Rusty, a rancher, out on the stage by shimmying up and down his backside. Finally he grabbed her by the arm and they both walked out. "And of course there is my wife, Valerie, a lawyer, who has threatened to sue the pants off me more times than I can count, but I always tell her, 'Honey, all ya gotta do is ask.'" Shaking her head at his foolishness, Valerie came out and let René swing her around several times under his arm before pulling her close.

The band segued into a loud rendition of "YMCA" as the couples snake danced around the little stage. When they were done, they all stepped back and Tante Lulu wobbled out onto the stage. She wore shocking pink, high-heeled pumps that matched a shocking pink spandex dress, and yes, a shocking pink wig. The woman was outrageous.

Beaming from ear to ear, she said, "We have a special attraction fer you folks tonight. As ya know, I'm a traiteur, a folk healer, but I've been known ta matchmake on occasion, 'specially during our Cajun Village People acts. I hope y'all will give a special welcome ta our next act. He's a Southern boy, born and bred, though he's been away from home fer a spell, and he's mighty shy about singin' in public."

The old lady stepped back to stand with her family and a stool was placed in front of the microphone. The lights dimmed, except for a single spotlight, and a cowboy stepped onto the stage, carrying a guitar. He sat on the stool, head bent over, as he tightened the strings on the guitar in a nervous manner.

A stone silence permeated the room as he strummed softly, then sang, almost in a whisper at first, the lyrics to that old Elvis song, "Love Me Tender." Only then did he look up, directly at Emelie, and she saw that it was Justin.

Not nude as she'd once jokingly requested, but wearing an open cowboy shirt over jeans tucked into well-worn cowboy boots. On his head was a white Stetson, and he was playing what must have been his father's guitar.

"Oh, my God!" She slapped a hand over her mouth, and darted a glance right and left to see that everyone at her table had left her alone, even Belle, who stood a short distance away, giving her a little hands folded in prayer gesture of encouragement.

This was so humiliating, Emelie thought, but then immediately realized that it must be way more humiliating for Justin, who was not a professional singer, by any means. Not even that good of a guitarist. But he was doing this . . . why?

When he finished the first song, Justin kept strumming and spoke as he played soft chords, "Y'know, us men are clueless when it comes ta women."

Laughter rippled among the crowd, and one woman yelled, "Tell us about it, cowboy!"

He sang a few stanzas of "Are You Lonesome Tonight?" and then said, "Are you ever lonesome, Em? I sure as hell am."

People were craning their necks to see who he was talking to.

"A wise person told me that men need to make a grand gesture if they want to win a woman's love."

Tante Lulu waved from behind them to let everyone know that she was the wise person in question.

"I thought about hirin' a band ta serenade her beneath her window, but that seemed too corny." Under his breath, he muttered, "Like this isn't corny!"

"Aaah," the women in the audience said, and the men agreed, "Corny!"

"I could hire an airplane to fly overhead with a banner reading, FORGIVE ME, *CHÈRE*, but waitin' fer you ta make the first move just isn't workin'."

"Why dint ya jist knock down her door and carry her off?" a drunk called out.

Cage tilted his head to the side. Why hadn't he thought of that? He laid down the guitar, kicked the stool aside, and jumped off the stage. Before she could blink, and to the howls of the crowd, he picked Em up off her chair and carried her across the dance floor toward a hallway.

"Are you crazy? Stop it! Put me down. Good Lord, we're not kids anymore, Justin."

"No, we're not, baby," he said. "The things I want to do to you are definitely not for kids."

She was swatting at him and squirming to beat the band, speaking of which, was now playing a rowdy Cajun country classic, "Knock, Knock, Knock," with the crowd joining in with howls and stomping feet every time the band hit the stanza "Knock, Knock, Knock."

Gator was coming out of the office, took one look at Cage and opened the door wide for him to enter, then closed it after them.

He kind of lost it then as he set Em on her feet. He was kissing her and murmuring love words against her open mouth and unbuttoning her blouse all at the same time, afraid to stop or pause to be zapped with one curt "No!"

But there was no protest. In fact, Em was yanking his open cowboy shirt out of his jeans and kissing his chest.

He pulled back and looked at her. Her blouse was half off one shoulder, dangling outside the waistband of her jeans. How had he managed that? Exposed was a red lace bra. "Oh, man, I love red, and lace, and you," he said.

She smiled.

Thank you, God!

She was rolling his shirt off his shoulders and undoing his buckle. When she said, "Keep on the cowboy hat," he knew he was home free.

"Whatever you say, babe." He was no fool.

"You were almost killed," she murmured, kissing the scar on his belly.

Oh, damn! She was kneeling before him. When had that happened? No way could he handle *that* right now.

He drew her up and set her rump on the desk, which was fortunately cleared. " 'Almost' is the key word, honey. 'Almost' doesn't count in baseball or life."

She arched her brows. "You saved Bernie's life."

"Hah! And now he trails me like a caboose everywhere I go. I keep tellin' him this is what we do."

"SEALs?"

"Uh-huh."

"I'm proud of you, Justin."

He grinned. "How proud?"

It might have been the shortest fuck in history, but it was mighty satisfying, for both of them. By the time they finally crawled off the desk and set it to rights, and tried to straighten out each other's clothes and hair, they were laughing. It was only then that they realized that the band was still playing "Knock, Knock, Knock" over and over.

"They're waiting for us to come back," Em said, horrified. "They all must know what we were doing."

"Yeah," he replied with a wink.

She smacked his shoulder.

"Before we go back, Em, you need ta be forewarned," Cage said, "I wanted ta do somethin' real sentimental fer you, and that's why everyone is waitin' fer us."

"Uh-oh!" She narrowed her eyes at him.

As they stepped out of the corridor onto the dance floor, Cage had his arm around Em's waist. The band stopped playing, and there was a sudden silence. Just then, thanks to Tante Lulu's pull with some engineering people, a shower of white confetti fell from the ceiling, covering them, like snowflakes.

He went down on one knee before her and said, "I always said I wouldn't come back to Loo-zee-anna 'til snow fell on the bayou. Honey, here I am. For you."

She tried to pull him up as she blushed with embarrassment. "Stop it. I don't need this," she whispered.

"I do," he said. "Em, I love you. I want to spend the rest of my life with you. Will you marry me?"

The crowd began to pound its feet, and the band began to play "Love Me Tender" again, waiting for her response.

"I thought you'd never ask . . . again."

Huh? Would he ever figure out women?

Loud applause greeted her announcement, and he began to twirl her around, doing what Cajun men did best. Dance. Well, the second best thing.

Epilogue

And the beat goes on…

Justin LeBlanc and Emelie Gaudet were married on June 15 at Our Lady of the Bayou Church in Houma, Louisiana.

Justin's grandmother, Mary Mae LeBlanc, was not there, having passed a month before, but she did get to share in the happiness of their engagement for several months. During the last few weeks, Emelie had moved into the Bayou Black cottage with Justin, and with the help of hospice, they were able to provide the comfortable setting Miss MaeMae wanted for her last days on this earth. At her funeral, Elvis sang "Amazing Grace," a song Miss MaeMae had said that Rufus insisted he wanted singing her home. When Rufus had told her that, no one was sure, since she'd been having numerous conversations with him in her dreams near the end.

After the wedding ceremony, Justin in his dress whites led his new bride through an archway of swords provided by Justin's SEAL buddies—JAM, Geek, Slick, K-4, F.U., Magnusson, Omar, and Pretty Boy, all of whom wore dress whites, too. All of the guys wanted to come because no one had believed that Cage would ever settle down, and they had to meet the woman who could clip his tail feathers. Marie Delacroix, a close friend of Justin's and a member of the elite Navy WEALS, was also in the sword brigade.

Women were said to be crashing the wedding reception at the convention hall right and left, just to be able to get a look at all the handsome men. One woman was heard to remark, "And I thought the LeDeux men were sexy!" One man said, "I should have stayed home." Two hundred people attended the reception; and both Justin and Emelie kept exclaiming that they didn't know they had that many friends.

Belle, who'd designed Emelie's ivory wedding gown and veil, was the maid of honor. Francine, Charmaine, and Tante Lulu were her attendants. Belle, Francine, and Charmaine looked classy and sensational, everyone said so, in identical ankle-length sheath dresses in pastel shades of blue, lavender, and green. Tante Lulu also wore an identical sheath, but hers was hot pink. Think Pepto Popsicle. Enough said!

There was no flower girl or ring bearer. The hit of the show was Thad, who marched perfectly down the aisle, without a single woof, on a leash held by Belle, the big red bow around his neck holding the ring.

Emelie's father, who'd married Francine the previous month, walked Emelie down the aisle, and everyone held their breath until he handed her over to Justin. Some said the old man had a shot of bourbon before the "ordeal," despite his heart condition, just to give him the courage to let her go to his least favorite person. Justin was heard whispering to Claude at the altar, "I'll grow on you."

Beer and beer and more beer flowed to wet parched throats at the reception, along with sweet tea, of course. Every possible type of Cajun food was laid out on groaning tables, thanks to the supervision of Tante Lulu, who claimed to be taking over for Miss MaeMae and for Emelie's mother, both deceased but watching closely from *up there*. The wedding cake was a humongous Peachy Praline Cobbler Cake extravaganza. The napkins at each place setting were St. Jude ones, of course.

Justin and Emelie danced first to his daddy's song "Prison Is a State of Mind." In the past month, Justin had learned that his father's song was earning impressive residuals, and a prominent agent was interested in Beau's entire collection of unpublished songs.

After that it was a wild Cajun/Navy SEAL affair with drinking and dancing and laughing until the wee hours. Tante Lulu was standing, watching the shenanigans, and remarked to her twin nephews, Daniel and Aaron LeDeux, who were standing on either side of her, "St. Jude allus comes through." But then she looked at one of them, then the other. "I wonder who's next?"

"Have you met Simone LeDeux? She's a cop," Aaron interjected quickly.

"What? Where? A LeDeux, you say?" Tante Lulu could barely contain her excitement.

For some reason, Daniel, Aaron, and Simone all departed early.

Justin and Emelie were leaving in the morning for a honeymoon to California and a stay in the famous Hotel del Coronado. They planned to divide their time between the West Coast and Louisiana for the next three years, after which they would live in Justin's homestead, which was already in the process of what would be a slow renovation.

They weren't able to give Miss MaeMae the gift of a LeBlanc baby, or even news of an upcoming one, before her death. But as always, when men and women think they are the rulers of their own destinies, God, or St. Jude, sticks out His big toe and trips them. Emelie was one month pregnant when she walked down the aisle. If it was a girl, Emelie threatened to call her Snowflake. Justin was horrified. "Kids will give her Flake for a nickname." They decided to hold off on names until the big event, not wanting to risk any more celestial "big toes" if they set their preferences for girl or boy. After all, the powers-that-be could give them twins.

Later on their wedding night, as the newly married couple lay in their bedroom, he said to her, "Wanna fool around again?"

"Forever and ever."

Snowflakes were probably falling somewhere.

A Letter from the Author

Dear Readers:

Many of you have been begging for a new Tante Lulu story. How did you like this one?

When I first started writing my Cajun contemporary books back in 2003, I never expected Tante Lulu would touch so many people's hearts and funny bones. Over the years, readers have fallen in love with the wacky old lady (I like to say, Grandma Moses with cleavage). So many of you have said you have a family member just like her; still more have said they wish they did.

Family...that's what my Cajun/Tante Lulu books are all about. And community...the generosity and unconditional love of friends and neighbors. In these turbulent times, isn't that just what we all want?

You should know that *Snow on the Bayou* is the ninth book in my Cajun series, which includes: *The Love Potion*; *Tall, Dark, and Cajun*; *The Cajun Cowboy*; *The Red Hot Cajun*; *Pink Jinx*; *Pearl Jinx*; *Wild Jinx*; and *So Into You*. And there are still more

Cajun tales to come, I think. Daniel and Aaron LeDeux, and the newly introduced Simone LeDeux. What do you think?

For more information on these and others of my books, visit my website at www.sandrahill.net or my Facebook page at Sandra Hill Author.

As always, I wish you smiles in your reading.

Sandra Hill

Miss Mae Mae's Red Beans and Rice

1 pound dried red kidney beans
½ pound bacon
1½ cups diced onions
1 large bell pepper, chopped
1 cup chopped celery
2 cloves garlic, minced
2 tablespoons butter
1 pound boudin sausage (smoked sausage can be substituted or ham hocks)
2 quarts water (more if needed)
1 teaspoon cayenne pepper (to start, add more if you want)
Tabasco sauce, to taste
Salt and pepper, to taste
4 cups cooked white rice
Thinly sliced scallion for garnish

Soak the beans overnight in a covered pot or bowl of water. In the morning drain and set in a cast-iron pot or a slow cooker.

In a frying pan, sauté the bacon until it is done but not crispy. Add the Holy Trinity of Cajun cooking (onions, bell pepper, and celery) and the garlic. Sauté until the vegetables are soft and add to the beans. Put the butter in the same frying pan, and add the sausage, which has been cut into chunks. Brown the sausage and add that to the bean pot.

Add at least 2 quarts of water so that the bean mixture is covered. Simmer for 2 hours, uncovered. You will probably need to add more water.

Add as much cayenne as you want, and leave Tabasco on the table for those who dare. Salt and pepper to taste, as well.

Serve over white rice. Garnish with the thinly sliced scallions. Six to eight hearty appetites will be satisfied with this dish.

Glossary

al-Qaeda—militant Islamic organization
Bluebird weather—warm temps in autumn or winter
Blue devils—depression
Budweiser—nickname for the garish Navy SEAL pin
Café au lait—hot coffee with an equal amount of hot scalded milk, light brown in color
Carnival—the season immediately preceding Lent, starting in January, often filled with merrymaking activities
Cher, chère—"friend" or "dear" when addressing a male, "dear or darling" when addressing a female
Fais do do—party down on the bayou
Fibbies—FBI
FUBAR—Fucked up beyond all recognition
High and tight—military haircut
Joie de vivre—joy of life
Krewes—private social clubs that sponsor balls, parades, and other events as part of Mardi Gras
Lagniappe—a little something extra
Mardi Gras—Pre-Lenten festivities that end on Ash Wednesday, the day before Lent begins
Mon Dieu!—My God!
Mon petit ange—my little angel

Pink mist—what happens to a body during a bomb explosion

Pirogue—Cajun canoe

Porte cochere—the covered carriage entrance leading into a courtyard

Shotgun house—a narrow, rectangular house with one room behind the other

SNAFU—situation normal all fucked up

SOL—shit out of luck

Tangos—terrorists or bad guys

Traiteur—folk healer

Zydeco—blues-influenced Cajun dance music

Enjoy another spicy, funny love story
from Sandra Hill!

Please see the next page for
an excerpt of

Tall, Dark, and Cajun.

Chapter 1

When the thunderbolt hits, duck, baby, duck

Happy birthday to you..."

Remy LeDeux's head shot up from the mug of "burnt roast," the thick Cajun coffee he'd been nursing at his galley table. Who came out to Bayou Black to visit him on his houseboat?

"Happy birthday to you..."

Oh, no! Oh, no, no, no! Please, God, not today!

Steps were approaching his door.

It better not be Luc and René. I am not in the mood for their games. Unbidden, a memory flashed through his mind of a birthday twelve years ago when his brothers Lucien and René had shown up at the VA burn hospital following one of his numerous operations. They had brought with them Ronald McDonald, but what a Ronald McDonald! Underneath the clown outfit had been a half-naked, six-foot-tall, Bourbon Street female impersonator with a body that could rival Marilyn Monroe's, appropriately singing, "Happy, Happy Birthday, Baby!" There had been a lot of military vet patients cheered up that day when she…he…whatever…had passed out Happy Meal cartons as favors, all containing talking condoms, red vibrator lips, and edible thongs.

"Happy birthday, dear Remy…"

Remy peered through the dust-moted dimness toward his open door. It was definitely not Ronald McDonald, or a sexy stripper, not even his teasing brothers. Much worse. It was his seventy-nine-year-old great-aunt Lulu, who was all of five feet tall, and she was carrying a cake the size of a bayou barge with a pigload of candles on top.

"Happy birthday to you," she concluded and used her nonexistent butt to ease the wooden screen door open and sidle inside. Today his aunt wore a Madonna T-shirt with cone cups painted in the vicinity of her nonexistent breasts, and a flame red spandex miniskirt. Who knew they made them in midget sizes? On her feet were what could only be described as white hooker boots. Her hair today was short and curly and pink—no doubt due to the efforts of his half-sister Charmaine who ran a hoity-toity beauty spa over in Houma, Looks to Kill, as well as a regular hair salon, Kuts & Kurls, in Lafayette. Uncertain whether the pink color was in honor of his birthday or an accident, he decided not to ask.

Despite her age and always outrageous appearance, his aunt's services as a noted *traiteur* or healer were still needed up and down the swamp lands. Unfortunately, of late she believed that he was the one most in need of her care.

If he could have, he would have fled, but where could a six-foot-two ex–Air Force officer hide in a houseboat? Besides, he couldn't ever be rude to his aunt, who was dear to him.

"Tante Lulu! Welcome, *chère*, welcome."

He stood and emptied his mug into the sink, then took the cake from her, placing it on the table. On its white iced top, mixed in with the thirty-three candles, was the message, "Happy Birthday, Remy," in bright blue letters. Typical sentiment. But in the corners stood four tiny plastic statues of St. Jude, the patron saint of hopeless cases. St. Jude was a favorite of Tante Lulu. He almost asked her what his birthday and hopeless cases had in common, but he caught himself just in time.

She kissed him on the cheek then, which involved her standing on tiptoes and his leaning down. And wasn't it just like his aunt to kiss his bad cheek, the one so disfigured by that 'copter crash in Desert Storm twelve years ago? Most people would at least flinch. She didn't even blink.

"Didja think I'd let you stay here alone like a hermit on your special day? Bad bizness, that—being alone so much. Lost your *joie de vivre*, you have. Never fear, I have a feelin' this is gonna be your year for love. Whass that smell? *Poo-ey!* Stinks like burnt okra."

He plopped back down to the bench seat and watched his aunt sniff the coffee in his pot, wrinkle her nose, then dump the contents down his sink. Within seconds, a fresh pot perked on the stove.

"Tante Lulu, this is not my year for love. Don't you be starting on me. I am not interested in love."

"Hanky-panky, thass all you menfolks are interested in. I may be seventy, but I ain't blind."

"More like eighty, sweet pea," he reminded her. "And don't for one minute think I'm gonna discuss *hanky-panky* with you."

"Not to worry, though, sweetie," his aunt rambled on.

"I got time to concentrate on you now. I'm gonna find you a wife. Guar-an-teed! Love doan ask you if you're ready; it jist comes like a thunderbolt."

Over my dead body, he vowed silently. "That's nice." He decided to change the subject. "How did you get here?"

"Tee-John drove me in his daddy's pickup truck." His aunt was bent over now—and, yes, he'd been right about her having no behind anymore. She was trying to shove off to the side the saddle he'd left in the middle of the room—a reminder of his ranching days.

But then his aunt's words hit him belatedly, like a sledgehammer. "Tee-John? *Mon Dieu*, Tante Lulu! He's only fourteen years old. He doesn't have a license." Tee-John was his half brother, the youngest of many children, legitimate and otherwise, born to Valcour LeDeux, their common father.

His aunt shrugged. "My T-bird's in the shop. This place, she needs some light. Mebbe you oughta install a skylight. It's so dark and dreary. No wonder you're always so grumpy."

A skylight in a houseboat that's as old as I am? "About your car?" he asked grumpily.

Now she was checking out the mail on his desk. "Someone stole the spark plugs. Can you imagine that?"

Yeah, he could imagine that. It was probably one of his brothers, trying to keep their aunt off the highways.

"Where *is* the brat?"

"Outside playin' with that pet alligator of yours, I reckon. You oughta get yerself a wife. A man your age should be pettin' his woman, not some slimy bayou animal. If I dint know you better, I'd think you were into those pee-verse-uns I read about in one of Charmaine's *Cosmo* magazines. You got any heavy cream for *café au lait*?"

He decided to ignore the wife remark, and the perversion remark, and, no, he didn't keep heavy cream in the house. "Useless? I do not pet Useless." He'd named the old alligator who lived in his bayou neighborhood Useless because he was, well, useless. "I toss him scraps occasionally. Tee-John better not be feedin' him Moon Pies and RC Cola again. Last time he did that, Useless was so jazzed up he practically swam a marathon up and down the bayou. A sugar high, no doubt."

Tante Lulu was nosing around in his cupboards now. Most likely, searching for evidence of perversions.

"Dad's gonna be furious at Tee-John for driving without a license—and taking his vehicle."

"It doan take much to make that Valcour red in the face... which he use'ly is from booze anyways," Tante Lulu said icily. His great-aunt hated their father with a passion, with good reason. "He's already spittin' mad at Tee-John. The boy is grounded for two weeks."

Remy was about to point out that driving her to his remote bayou home didn't count as grounded, but figured logic was not a part of any conversation with his aunt. "Why is he grounded?"

"Went to an underwear option party up in Natchitoches. That boy, he is some kind of wild." She shook her pink spirals from side to side and clucked her tongue to show her disgust.

"Huh?" *A lingerie party? A teenage boy at a lingerie party? That doesn't sound right.* Then, understanding dawned. "Oh. Do you mean underwear *optional*?"

"Thass what I said, dint I? There was a hundred boys and girls running around with bare butts wavin' in the wind when the police got there. Lordy, Lordy!"

He started to grin.

But not for long.

She was standing before his open freezer, empty except for two ice-cube trays. The way she was gawking you would have thought he had a dead body in there—a very small dead body, considering the minuscule size of the compartment. "You ain't got nothin' in your freeze box," she announced, as if he didn't already know that. "Where's the ice cream? We sure-God gotta have ice cream with a birthday cake."

"Tante Lulu, I don't need ice cream." Really, the old lady only meant good. At least, that's what he told himself.

"The youngens do."

His neck prickled with apprehension. "What youngens?"

"Luc and Sylvie's chillen, thass who. You dint think we'd have a party for you without the rest of the fam'ly, didja?"

Of course not. What was I thinking? He would have put his head on the table if the cake didn't take up all the space.

"René couldn't come 'cause he's in Washington on that fish lobby bizness, but he said to wish you 'Happy, Happy Birthday' and to expect a Happy Meal in the mail. Do you know what he's talkin' 'bout?"

"Don't have a clue," he lied.

In walked Tee-John. What a misnomer! Tee-John was definitely no Little-John. At almost fifteen, he was not done growing, not by a Louisiana long shot, but already he was close to six feet tall. And full of himself, as only a born-to-be-bad, good-looking, bayou rascal could be. He was soaked from the neckline of his black "Ragin' Cajun" T-shirt to the bottoms of his baggy cargo shorts. He grinned from ear to ear.

"Hey, Remy."

"Hey, Tee-John."

"Happy birthday, bro."

"Thanks, *bro*."

"Can I go check out your 'copter up there on the hill?"

Nice try, kiddo. "NO!" The boy would probably decide to take the half-million-dollar piece of equipment for a spin. Never mind that it was the backbone of Remy's employment or that he was in hock to the bank up to his eyeballs. Never mind that Tee-John didn't know a propeller from a weed whacker.

Tee-John waggled his eyebrows at him, as if to say he had just been razzing and Remy had risen to the bait.

"You jump in that pickup, boy, and go buy us some ice cream at Boudreaux's General Store," Tante Lulu ordered Tee-John. "How come you wearin' those baggy ol' shorts? Yer daddy lose all his money and can't afford to buy you new pants?"

"That's the style, auntie." He chucked her playfully under the chin.

"What style? Thass no style, a'tall." She swatted his teasing fingers away. "And don't you be flirtin' with that Boudreaux girl, neither. Her daddy said he's gonna shoot yer backside with buckshot next time you come sniffin' around."

"Me?" Tee-John said, putting a hand over his heart with wounded innocence.

Outside, a car door slammed, followed by the pounding of little feet on the wooden wharf. The shrieking of three little girls could only be three-year-old Blanche Marie, two-year-old Camille, and one-year-old Jeanette. The admonition of Luc and Sylvie echoed: "Do not dare to touch that alligator."

Remy heard a loud roar of animal outrage, which pretty

much translated to, "Enough is enough!" Then a loud splashing noise. Useless was no fool; he was out of here.

Tee-John headed out the door to buy ice cream, or to escape the inevitable chaos that accompanied Luc's family. "Guess what Luc is considerin'?" He threw over his shoulder.

"Putting you in a dimwit protection program till you're, oh, let's say twenty-one?" he offered. Luc was a lawyer, and a good one, too. If anyone could tame Tee-John down, it was Luc. Look what he'd accomplished with him and René.

Tee-John ignored Remy's sarcasm. "Luc is thinkin' about gettin' neutered."

"The hell you say!" was Remy's immediate reaction.

"Well, kiss my grits and call me brunch," Tante Lulu said. "Where did you hear such a thing?"

"Sylvie told her friend Blanche who told Charmaine who told everyone in Houma that Luc went to see a doctor about one of those vas-ec-to-mies. Luc and Sylvie got a scare last month when Sylvie thought she might be knocked up again. She wasn't but, whoo-boy, they were sweatin' it. Guess those little squigglies of his are too potent." He grinned as he relayed the gossip.

Really, keeping a secret in the bayou was like trying to hold "no-see-ems" in a fishnet. The little gnats were impossible to contain.

On second thought, Remy could see Luc taking such drastic action. After having "Irish triplets"—a baby born every nine months—he and Sylvie were both ready to shut down the baby assembly line. But a vasectomy? He cringed at the thought. And wasn't it ironic that Luc was determined to stop having kids when Remy would never have any of his own?

Just before Tee-John went out the door, his aunt added, "Tee-John, when you come back, remember to bring in Remy's birthday present from the truck." She smiled broadly at Remy. "Your very own hope chest."

"A hope chest? A hope chest for a man?" Remy winced. "No friggin' way!" he exclaimed, then immediately chastised himself. He didn't speak that way in front of women, especially Tante Lulu. "Sorry, ma'am."

"You'll be feeling lots better, once I get your hope chest filled, and we find you a good Cajun wife. I made a list." She waved a piece of paper that had at least twenty names on it.

Remy groaned.

"Plus, I'm gonna say a novena to St. Jude to jump-start the bride search."

Remy groaned again.

"I'm thinkin' we should launch this all off with a big *fais do do*, a party down on the bayou."

"Launch what?" Remy choked out.

"Your bride search. Ain't you listenin', boy? With all the women there, you would have a chance to cull down the list."

"Bad idea, auntie."

"Mebbe we could have it at Luc and Sylvie's place. They have a big yard where we can set up tents for food and a wooden platform for the musicians and dancing. René might even come play with his old band."

She talked over him as if he wasn't even there.

He shouldn't be surprised. It was *se fini pas*, a thing without end, the way his family interfered in each other's lives.

Forget about the government contract he was about to undertake. If he had any sense, Remy would run off to some faraway country, like California, where no one could find him, especially his interfering family. But first, he'd set fire to everything here: the houseboat, the 'copter, all his belongings, the hope chest.

He was only half kidding while playing out this tempting fantasy in his head.

It would be the biggest bonfire in bayou history, though.

Then, he would be free.

Yeah, right, some inner voice said.

It was probably St. Jude.

THE DISH

Where Authors Give You the Inside Scoop

From the desk of Marilyn Pappano

Dear Reader,

The first time Jessy Lawrence, the heroine of my newest novel, A LOVE TO CALL HER OWN, opened her mouth, I knew she was going to be one of my favorite Tallgrass characters. She's mouthy, brassy, and bold, but underneath the sass, she's keeping a secret or two that threatens her tenuous hold on herself. She loves her friends fiercely with the kind of loyalty I value. Oh, and she's a redhead, too. I can always relate to another "ginger," lol.

I love characters with faults—like me. Characters who do stupid things, good things, bad things, unforgivable things. Characters whose lives haven't been the easiest, but they still show up; they still do their best. They know too well it might not be good enough, but they try, and that's what matters, right?

Jessy is one of those characters in spades—estranged from her family, alone in the world except for the margarita girls, dealing with widowhood, guilt, low self-esteem, and addiction—but she meets her match in Dalton Smith.

I was plotting the first book in the series, *A Hero to Come Home To*, when it occurred to me that there's a lot of talk about the men who die in war and the wives they leave behind, but people seem not to notice that some of our casualties are women, who also leave behind spouses, fiancés, family whose lives are drastically altered. Seconds behind that thought, an image popped into my head of the margarita club gathered around their table at The Three Amigos, talking their girl talk, when a broad-shouldered, six-foot-plus, smokin' handsome cowboy walked up, Stetson in hand, and quietly announced that his wife had died in the war.

Now, when I started writing the first scene from Dalton's point of view, I knew immediately that scene was never going to happen. Dalton has more grief than just the loss of a wife. He's angry, bitter, has isolated himself, and damn sure isn't going to ask anyone for help. He's not just wounded but broken—my favorite kind of hero.

It's easy to write love stories for perfect characters, or for one who's tortured when the other's not. I tend to gravitate to the challenge of finding the happily-ever-after for two seriously broken people. They deserve love and happiness, but they have to work so hard for it. There are no simple solutions for these people. Jessy finds it hard to get out of bed in the morning; Dalton has reached rock bottom with no one in his life but his horses and cattle. It says a lot about them that they're willing to work, to risk their hearts, to take those scary steps out of their grief and sorrow and guilt and back into their lives.

Oh yeah, and I can't forget to mention my other two favorite characters in A LOVE TO CALL HER OWN: Oz, the handsome Australian shepherd on the cover; and Oliver, a mistreated, distrusting dog of unknown breed.

I love my puppers, both real and fictional, and hope you like them, too.

Happy reading!

Marilyn Pappano

MarilynPappano.net
Twitter @MarilynPappano
Facebook.com/MarilynPappanoFanPage

From the desk of Kristen Ashley

Dear Reader,

In starting to write *Lady Luck*, the book where Chace Keaton was introduced, I was certain Chace was a bad guy. A dirty cop who was complicit in sending a man to jail for a crime he didn't commit.

Color me stunned when Chace showed up at Ty and Lexie's in *Lady Luck* and a totally different character introduced himself to me.

Now, I am often not the white hat–wearing guy type of girl. My boys have to have at least a bit of an edge (and usually way more than a bit).

That's not to say that I don't get drawn in by the boy next door (quite literally, for instance, with Mitch Lawson of *Law Man*). It just always surprises me when I do.

Therefore, it surprised me when Chace drew me in while he was in Lexie and Ty's closet in *Lady Luck*. I knew in that instant that he had to have his own happily-ever-after. And when Faye Goodknight was introduced later in that book, I knew the path to that was going to be a doozy!

Mentally rubbing my hands together with excitement, when I got down to writing BREATHE, I was certain that it was Chace who would sweep me away.

And he did.

But I *adored* writing Faye.

I love writing about complex, flawed characters, watching them build strength from adversity. Or lean on the strength from adversity they've already built in their lives so they can get through dealing with falling in love with a badass, bossy alpha. The exploration of that is always a thing of beauty for me to be involved in.

Faye, however, knew who she was and what she wanted from life. She had a good family. She lived where she wanted to be. She was shy, but that was her nature. She was no pushover. She had a backbone. But that didn't mean she wasn't thoughtful, sensitive, and loving. She had no issues, no hang-ups, or at least nothing major.

And she was a geek girl.

The inspiration for her came from my nieces, both incredibly intelligent, funny, caring and, beautiful—and both total geek girls. I loved the idea of diving into that (being a bit of a geek girl myself), this concept that is considered stereotypically "on the fringe" but is actually an enormous sect of society that is quite proud of their geekdom. And when I published BREATHE, the geek girls came out of the woodwork, loving seeing one of their own land her hot guy.

But also, it was a pleasure seeing Chace, the one who had major issues and hang-ups, find himself sorted out by his geek girl. I loved watching Faye surprise him, hold up the mirror so he could truly see himself, and take the lead into guiding them both into the happily-ever-after they deserved.

This was one of those books of mine where I could have kept writing forever. Just the antics of the kitties Chace gives to his Faye would be worth a chapter!

But alas, I had to let them go.

Luckily, I get to revisit them whenever I want and let fly the warm thoughts I have of the simple, yet extraordinary lives led by a small-town cop and the librarian wife he adores.

♥ ♥ ♥ ♥ ♥ ♥ ♥ ♥ ♥ ♥ ♥ ♥ ♥ ♥ ♥ ♥

From the desk of Sandra Hill

Dear Reader,

Many of you have been begging for a new Tante Lulu story.

When I first started writing my Cajun contemporary books back in 2003, I never expected Tante Lulu would touch so many people's hearts and funny bones. Over the years, readers have fallen in love with the wacky old lady (I like to say, Grandma Moses with cleavage). So many of you have said you have a family member just like her; still more have said they wish they did.

Family…that's what my Cajun/Tante Lulu books are all about. And community…the generosity and unconditional love of friends and neighbors. In these turbulent times, isn't that just what we all want?

You should know that SNOW ON THE BAYOU is the ninth book in my Cajun series, which includes: *The Love Potion*; *Tall, Dark, and Cajun*; *The Cajun Cowboy*; *The Red Hot Cajun*; *Pink Jinx*; *Pearl Jinx*; *Wild Jinx*; and *So Into You*. And there are still more Cajun tales to come, I think. Daniel and Aaron LeDeux, and the newly introduced Simone LeDeux. What do you think?

For more information on these and others of my books, visit my website at www.sandrahill.net or my Facebook page at Sandra Hill Author.

As always, I wish you smiles in your reading.

Sandra Hill

♥ ♥ ♥ ♥ ♥ ♥ ♥ ♥ ♥ ♥ ♥ ♥ ♥ ♥ ♥

From the desk of Mimi Jean Pamfiloff

Dearest Humans,

It's the end of the world. You're an invisible, seventy-thousand-year-old virgin. The Universe wants to snub out the one person you'd like to hook up with. Discuss.

And while you do so, I'd like to take a moment to thank each of you for taking this Accidental journey with me and my insane deities. We've been to Mayan cenotes, pirate ships, jungle battles, cursed pyramids, vampire showdowns, a snappy leather-daddy bar in San Antonio, New York City, Santa Cruz, Giza, Sedona, and we've even been to a beautiful Spanish vineyard with an incubus. Ah. So many fun places with so many fascinating, misunderstood, wacky gods and other immortals. And let's not forget Minky the unicorn, too!

It has truly been a pleasure putting you through the twisty curves, and I hope you enjoy this final piece of the puzzle as Máax, our invisible, bad-boy deity extraordinaire, is taught one final lesson by one very resilient woman who refuses to allow the Universe to dictate her fate.

Because ultimately we make our own way in this world, Hungry Hungry Hippos playoffs included.

Happy reading!

Mimi

P.S.: Hope you like the surprise ending.

♥ ♥ ♥ ♥ ♥ ♥ ♥ ♥ ♥ ♥ ♥ ♥ ♥ ♥ ♥ ♥

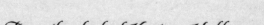

From the desk of Karina Halle

Dear Reader,

Morally ambiguous. Duplicitous. Dangerous.

Those words describe not only the cast of characters in my romantic suspense novel SINS & NEEDLES, book one in the Artists Trilogy, but especially the heroine, Ms. Ellie Watt. Though sinfully sexy and utterly suspenseful, it is Ellie's devious nature and con artist profession that makes SINS & NEEDLES one unique and wild ride.

When I first came up with the idea for SINS & NEE-DLES, I wanted to write a book that not only touched on some personal issues of mine (physical scarring, bullying, justification), but dealt with a character little seen in modern literature—the antiheroine. Everywhere you look in books these days you see the bad boy, the criminal, the tattooed heartbreaker and ruthless killer. There are always men in these arguably more interesting roles. Where were all the bad girls? Sure, you could read about women in dubious professions, femme fatales, and cold-hearted killers. But when were they ever the main character? When were they ever a heroine you could also sympathize with?

Ellie Watt is definitely one of the most complex and interesting characters I have ever written, particularly as a heroine. On one hand she has all these terrible qualities; on the other she's just a vulnerable, damaged person trying to survive the only way she knows how. You despise Ellie and yet you can't help but root for her at the same time.

Her love interest, hot tattoo artist and ex-friend Camden McQueen, says it perfectly when he tells her this: "That is what I thought of you, Ellie. Heartless, reckless, selfish, and cruel ... Beautiful, sad, wounded, and lost. A freak, a work of art, a liar, and a lover."

Ellie is all those things, making her a walking contradiction but oh, so human. I think Ellie's humanity is what makes her relatable and brings a sense of realism to a novel that's got plenty of hot sex, car chases, gunplay, murder, and cons. No matter what's going on in the story, through all the many twists and turns, you understand her motives and her actions, no matter how skewed they may be.

Of course, it wouldn't be a romance novel without a love interest. What makes SINS & NEEDLES different is that the love interest isn't her foil—Camden McQueen isn't necessarily a "good" man making a clean living. In fact, he may be as damaged as she is—but he does believe that Ellie can change, let go of her past, and find redemption.

That's easier said than done, of course, for a criminal who has never known any better. And it's hard to escape your past when it's literally chasing you, as is the case with Javier Bernal, Ellie's ex-lover whom she conned six years prior. Now a dangerous drug lord, Javier has been hunting Ellie down, wanting to exact revenge for her misdoings. But sometimes revenge comes in a vice and Javier's appearance in the novel reminds Ellie that she can never escape who she really is, that she may not be redeemable.

For a book that's set in the dry, brown desert of southern California, SINS & NEEDLES is painted in shades of gray. There is no real right and wrong in the novel, and the characters, including Ellie, aren't just good or bad. They're just human, just real, just trying to come to terms with their true selves while living in a world that just wants to screw them over.

I hope you enjoy the ride!

♥ ♥ ♥ ♥ ♥ ♥ ♥ ♥ ♥ ♥ ♥ ♥ ♥ ♥ ♥

From the desk of Kristen Callihan

Dear Reader,

The first novels I read belonged to my parents. I was a latchkey kid, so while they were at work, I'd poach their paperbacks. Robert Ludlum, Danielle Steel, Jean M. Auel. I read these authors because my parents did. And it was quite the varied education. I developed a taste for action, adventure, sexy love stories, and historical settings.

But it wasn't until I spent a summer at the beach during high school that I began to pick out books for myself. Of course, being completely ignorant of what I might actually want to read on my own, I helped myself to the beach house's library. The first two books I chose were Mario Puzo's *The Godfather* (yes, I actually read the book before seeing the movie) and Anne Rice's *Interview with the Vampire*.

Those two books taught me about the antihero, that a character could do bad things, make the wrong decisions, and still be compelling. We might still want them to succeed. But why? Maybe because we share in their pain. Or maybe it's because they care, passionately, whether it's the desire for discovering the deeper meaning of life or saving the family business.

In EVERNIGHT, Will Thorne is a bit of an antihero. We meet him attempting to murder the heroine. And he makes no apologies for it, at least not at first. He is also a blood drinker, sensual, wicked, and in love with life and beauty.

Thinking on it now, I realize that the books I've read have, in some shape or form, made me into the author

I am today. So perhaps, instead of the old adage "You are what you eat," it really ought to be: "You are what you read."

♥ ♥ ♥ ♥ ♥ ♥ ♥ ♥ ♥ ♥ ♥ ♥ ♥ ♥ ♥

From the desk of Laura Drake

Dear Reader,

Hard to believe that SWEET ON YOU is the third book in my Sweet on a Cowboy series set in the world of professional bull riding. The first two, *The Sweet Spot* and *Nothing Sweeter*, involved the life and loves of stock contractors—the ranchers who supply bucking bulls to the circuit. But I couldn't go without writing the story of a bull rider, one of the crazy men who pit themselves against an animal many times stronger and with a much worse attitude.

To introduce you to Katya Smith, the heroine of SWEET ON YOU, I thought I'd share with you her list of life lessons:

1. Remember what your Gypsy grandmother said: Gifts sometimes come in strange wrappings.
2. The good-looking ones aren't *always* assholes.
3. Cowboys aren't the only ones who need a massage. Sometimes bulls do, too.

4. Don't ever forget: You're a soldier. And no one messes with the U.S. military.

5. A goat rodeo has nothing to do with men riding goats.

6. "Courage is being scared to death—and saddling up anyway." —John Wayne

7. Cowgirl hats fit more than just cowgirls.

8. The decision of living in the present or going back to the past is easy once you decide which one you're willing to die for.

I hope you enjoy Katya and Cam's story as much as I enjoyed writing it. And watch for the cameos by JB Denny and Bree and Max Jameson from the first two books!

♥ ♥ ♥ ♥ ♥ ♥ ♥ ♥ ♥ ♥ ♥ ♥ ♥ ♥ ♥

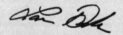

From the desk of Anna Campbell

Dear Reader,

I love books about Mr. Cool, Calm, and Collected finding himself all at sea once he falls in love. Which means I've been champing at the bit to write Camden Rothermere's story in WHAT A DUKE DARES.

The Duke of Sedgemoor is a man who is always in control. He never lets messy emotion get in the way of a rational decision. He's the voice of wisdom. He's the one who sorts things out. He's the one with his finger on the pulse.

And that's just the way he likes it.

Sadly for Cam, once his own pulse starts racing under wayward Penelope Thorne's influence, all traces of composure and detachment evaporate under a blast of sensual heat. Which *isn't* just the way he likes it!

Pen Thorne was such fun to write, too. She's loved Cam since she was a girl, but she's smart enough to know it's hopeless. So what happens when scandal forces them to marry? It's the classic immovable object and irresistible force scenario. Pen is such a vibrant, passionate, headstrong presence that Cam hasn't got a chance. Although he puts up a pretty good fight!

Another part of WHAT A DUKE DARES that I really enjoyed writing was the secondary romance involving Pen's rakish brother Harry and innocent Sophie Fairbrother. There's a real touch of Romeo and Juliet about this couple. I hadn't written two love stories in one book before and the contrasting trajectories throw each relationship into high relief. As a reader, I always like to get two romances for the price of one.

If you'd like to know more about WHAT A DUKE DARES and the other books in the Sons of Sin series— *Seven Nights in a Rogue's Bed, Days of Rakes and Roses,* and *A Rake's Midnight Kiss*—please check out my website: http://annacampbell.info/books.html.

Happy reading—and may all your dukes be daring!

Best wishes,

Anna Campbell

Find out more about Forever Romance!

Visit us at
www.hachettebookgroup.com/publishing_forever.aspx

Find us on Facebook
http://www.facebook.com/ForeverRomance

Follow us on Twitter
http://twitter.com/ForeverRomance

NEW AND UPCOMING TITLES

Each month we feature our new titles
and reader favorites.

CONTESTS AND GIVEAWAYS

We give away galleys, autographed copies,
and all kinds of exclusive items.

AUTHOR INFO

You'll find bios, articles, and links to personal websites
for all your favorite authors—and so much more.

GET SOCIAL

Connect with your favorite authors, editors, and
other Forever fans, and share what's important to you.

THE BUZZ

Sign up for our monthly romance newsletter,
and be the first to read all about it.